FATHOM

FATHOM

A Donaldson-Gilks Mystery

JACQUI BLACK

First published 2022 by Mystery Publications Ltd.

ISBN – 978-1-7398953-0-3 – eBook

ISBN – 978-1-7398953-1-0 – paperback

Cover image © Design for Writers

For Bob, who passed away peacefully during the writing of this novel.
A good dog, and a most faithful and loving companion.
2008–2018

CHAPTER 1:
A MYSTERIOUS
TELEGRAM

Thursday, June 5th 1919
Apartment 4, Belgravia Mansions, London, SW1

LANCELOT DONALDSON-GILKS, AFFECTIONATELY KNOWN as Lance to his friends and family, leaned back in his dining chair, neatly folded his napkin and stared gloomily at a breakfast plate that seemed to reflect everything his life had become – empty. Letting out a long dejected sigh, he looked down fondly at his newly acquired black Labrador who lay stretched out at his feet.

'What shall we do today, Bob, eh?' Lance asked.

On hearing his name, the dog sat up, stretched his neck and peered longingly over the tabletop, his intense gaze willing a few uneaten scraps to come his way. Lance looked about his apartment, absentmindedly stroking Bob's velvet-soft ears as the dog cast increasingly sorrowful glances at his master.

Grabbing his cane, he rose unsteadily from the table and made his way towards his favourite tan leather wingback chair, where he sank down heavily into the well-worn seat and let out another jaded sigh. Bob padded over to his master and settled once again at his feet.

It was an inescapable truth that since being unceremoniously invalided out of the Royal Navy the previous year, following a torpedo attack in which he had been seriously injured and his best friend killed, Lance had been feeling inadequate, useless and without direction. He had been one of the navy's youngest and most capable sea captains, and to go from that to virtual retirement was a bitter pill to swallow. It was made worse by having to deal constantly with the pain of his debilitating injury, and he had slowly been losing interest in other people and the world around him.

The quiet swish of the kitchen door announced the appearance of his otherwise silent, ever-efficient valet, Bentley.

'May I clear away breakfast, sir?' he asked.

'Yes, please go ahead ... but before you do, pour me a large malt whiskey, there's a good chap.'

Bentley went to a desk in the corner of the room where a Tantalus containing three cut-glass decanters glinted in the early morning sunlight streaming in through the large sash window. Exuding an almost undetectable note of disapproval, the valet placed a glass containing a finger of whisky on the occasional table next to the wingback chair.

'Has the newspaper arrived yet?' Lance asked, peering gloomily into the glass.

'Indeed, sir. I also have the post.' Bentley produced a silver salver on which lay that day's edition of *The Times*, two letters and a brown foolscap envelope.

'Thank you,' Lance said, flicking through the post. 'They all appear to be bills. Please deal with them in the usual way.'

'Very good, sir,' Bentley said, removing the breakfast debris before gliding out through the kitchen door.

Lance took a sip of whisky and felt the warmth of it at the back of his throat. He sat for a while, waiting for it to begin the daily process of blotting out his thoughts, then he opened the paper with a loud rustle.

'Well, Bob, let's see what news there is this morning.' Without raising his head, the dog opened one eye. 'Don't worry, I won't forget our morning walk,' Lance added, scanning the headlines without much interest.

Just then, the insistent ring of the doorbell broke the peace and tranquillity in the apartment. Lance looked up from his paper and Bob lifted his head as Bentley appeared from the kitchen and went to the front door.

'Telegram for the Honourable Lancelot Donaldson-Gilks,' said a stocky young lad in a cap.

Bentley took the envelope.

'Will there be any answer?' asked the boy.

'One moment. I will enquire. Please be kind enough to wait.'

Placing the envelope on a salver, Bentley brought it over to Lance. 'A telegram for you, sir. The boy wonders if there will be any reply.'

Lance set down his glass and opened the envelope. As he read, a furrow appeared on his forehead.

COME AT ONCE STOP
SITUATION VERY GRAVE STOP
WILL EXPLAIN ALL ON ARRIVAL STOP

REGARDS FATHER STOP

He handed the message to Bentley. 'What d'you make of that?'

Bentley read the telegram, his face betraying no emotion. 'Lord Cedrick appears to require your presence at Coombe End rather urgently, sir.'

'Yes, but why? What's all the mystery? We'll be motoring down to the old homestead next week for my brother's wedding. What's so dashed important it can't wait until then?'

'Do you wish to send a reply, sir? I have asked the boy to wait.'

Lance took a few moments to mull the situation over.

'For the life of me, Bentley, I don't understand the meaning of it. But I know Father wouldn't have sent a telegram if it wasn't urgent.'

'Just so, sir.'

Lance heaved one more world-weary sigh. 'Oh well, I suppose I'd better put in an appearance. Please ask the boy to send this reply.'

Bentley withdrew a notebook and pencil from his top pocket and began to write as Lance dictated.

'Will catch the 14:15 hours from Paddington tomorrow arriving Exeter St David's 16:30 hours. Please arrange transport. Regards, Lance.'

Bentley returned to the young lad and handed him the note. Once the boy had been paid and generously tipped, he touched his cap politely and ran off.

'I wonder what Father can be so bothered about,' Lance said when Bentley closed the front door. 'It's probably some sort of flap about Hugo's wedding – the wrong kind of flowers have been ordered or cook's had a fit and taken to her bed.'

'Will you require me to pack, sir?'

'Yes. I think the best course of action will be for me to travel down by train with Bob tomorrow afternoon. You can follow us down in the two-seater with the luggage.'

'Very good, sir. I will attend to it immediately,' Bentley said, leaving the room to prepare for their temporary transfer to Landacre Hall.

'Well, Bob, it looks as though we'll be spending rather more time on Exmoor than we'd planned,' Lance said. 'Come along, young pup, let's you and I go for a walk and while you're enjoying yourself in the park I can think the matter over.'

Hearing the magical word 'walk', Bob ran around in circles, his tail wagging furiously, barely able to contain his excitement. Lance lifted the dog's lead from the top of his desk, attached it to Bob's collar and, walking stick in hand, headed out the door, towed by an impatient Bob.

As they walked the short distance to Hyde Park, Lance couldn't help noticing two decidedly shady-looking characters loitering in the shadows of Belgrade Square. Why, he wondered, would anyone wear dark trench coats and heavy Fedora hats at the height of summer. But all thoughts of strange men in unseasonal garb left his mind as he shared in Bob's obvious delight at being outdoors on such a glorious day.

CHAPTER 2:
A NOSTALGIC JOURNEY HOME

Friday, June 6th 1919

THE FOLLOWING AFTERNOON LANCE alighted from a taxi at Paddington Station, his faithful canine companion by his side. He walked onto the cavernous concourse and consulted one of the information boards.

'Come along, young Bob, platform nine for us.'

They pushed their way through the crowds and arrived at the designated embarkation point just as the public address system crackled into life: 'The next train leaving platform nine will be the fourteen-fifteen to Plymouth,' boomed the voice overhead, 'calling at Reading, Swindon, Bristol Temple Meads, Taunton, Exeter St David's, Newton Abbott and Plymouth.'

Lance and Bob made their way towards a gleaming black engine, steam gently hissing from its pistons as it waited patiently to depart. They boarded and, finding his reserved seat in an empty first-class compartment, Lance settled down with his newspaper while Bob lay down at his feet.

At two-fifteen precisely the guard gave a long shrill blast on his whistle and the locomotive let out a piercing fizz of steam, then started to pull slowly out of the station.

Lance looked up from his paper just in time to see two men in Fedoras walk past to the next compartment. They seemed somehow familiar to him. Where had he seen them before? But he let these thoughts drift gently away as he shook open the broadsheet and immersed himself in the pressing events of the day.

An hour into the journey Lance laid the open paper in his lap and glanced out the window. The train was moving swiftly now, cutting through verdant English countryside basking in the summer sunshine. He found himself wondering for the umpteenth time what Lord Cedrick could possibly want to discuss so urgently. He really hoped it wasn't some serious issue with his brother's impending wedding. The happy couple had had enough setbacks as it was.

Lance was very fond of his younger brother, Hugo. He was a loveable chancer – thirty-three, tall, blond, brown eyes, a ladies' man, and irresistible to the opposite sex. Everything in life seemed to come easily to Hugo, a situation which only added to his belief that he didn't need to put much effort into building a solid career. His lax attitude to his future prospects had long been a constant source of irritation to their father, Lord Cedrick Donaldson-Gilks, the seventh Baron Westex, who believed in hard work and absolute dedication to King and country, qualities the Baron felt his second son sadly lacked. However, in spite of Hugo's relaxed manner, he had managed to carve out a very successful career as a sportsman, playing cricket for England and tennis at Wimbledon. He was a man about town, the sort of person everyone wanted at their party – affable, good looking and a *very* eligible bachelor.

Hugo had first met his fiancée, Clara Whytte, when he was just twenty-four and playing in the 1910 Wimbledon tennis tournament. She had simply breezed into his life at one of those shindigs held after a singles match. According to Hugo it was love at first sight for them both.

At the time Clara was also twenty-four and very beautiful. In January of that year, her father, the Texan oil millionaire Willard Whytte, had decided to send her to London in the hope that she would acquire some of her mother's English 'polish' to add to the accomplishments she had recently learned at her Swiss finishing school.

Their amour in full flight, Hugo and Clara had continued to meet that summer, enjoying what remained of the social season. The following year, Clara, completely besotted with Hugo, insisted he meet her parents and so on 14th June 1911, the two of them boarded RMS *Olympic* at Southampton for her maiden voyage to New York.

Hugo was still fond of recounting how he proposed to Clara. Overcome by the romance of life on board the ship, he dropped to one knee in Suite B-41 and popped the question. Clara hadn't hesitated to accept. Afterwards, as they'd reclined on the chaise longue in the warm afterglow of an intimate embrace, Hugo had taken out his pocket knife and carved their initials inside a tiny heart on the magnificent mahogany-panelled wall above an occasional table. Clara had been shocked at what she perceived to be

Hugo's vandalism of the ship's lavish interior. But Hugo insisted that it was the perfect way to mark their engagement

'It's a symbol of our thrilling new life together,' he explained. 'Wherever *Olympic* sails, this sign of our love will travel with her for all time.' Then he obscured his handiwork from plain sight by hiding it behind a large baroque clock that was standing on the table.

Hugo's trip to meet the Whyttes in America was a roaring success. The family had welcomed him with open arms; Hugo formally asked Willard for his daughter's hand in marriage and Willard readily agreed, only too delighted that Clara should be marrying into a titled English family. After Hugo had telegraphed the wonderful news to his family in England, all that was left to do was fix a date for the wedding and arrange for his prospective in-laws to meet his family in England.

However, back home, news of the engagement had not been greeted with universal enthusiasm. When Hugo returned to Landacre Hall a few months later, Lord Cedrick expressed his serious reservations at Hugo's sudden and unexpected decision to marry an American girl. His father felt this turn of events was *much* too impulsive; he had quite a different future mapped out for his second son, one that did not include marriage to the descendant of an untitled colonial settler. No, it was all much too hasty. They hadn't even been formally introduced to the Whyttes, nor had time to assess the American family's status before an official announcement needed to be made.

Hugo pointed out that Clara had already accepted; surely his father didn't want to bring the family into disrepute by reneging on his proposal. A man of Willard Whytte's financial standing wouldn't allow his daughter's reputation to be sullied in that way; he would undoubtedly sue for breach of contract.

Eventually, Hugo had convinced Lord Cedrick to meet the Whyttes before making any final decision, and it was agreed that Clara and her family would travel to England in early March the following year to stay for a month. Placated by his father's rather begrudging concession, Hugo felt sure that any reservations his family entertained would simply evaporate when both dynasties met.

So in March 1912, Willard, his English wife Ruth, their son Henry, and Clara made the trip over from New York. The visit got off to a slow start, but the wealthy Whytte family made a good impression, and after discussion Willard agreed to settle a substantial sum from Clara's trust fund on the happy couple as a wedding present.

With the nuptials set to take place on 14th June the following year, Hugo and Clara had been deliriously happy and Lord Cedrick wasted no time in announcing the engagement and forthcoming marriage in *The Times*.

Lady Cynthia, mother of the groom, had also been greatly excited by the forthcoming wedding. Hugo was the first of her three precious children to tread this path and she wasn't going to let the occasion slip by without the obligatory pomp and ceremony. She and Ruth, Clara's mother, drew up a guest list for what was to be *the* society wedding of the year, attended by members of the aristocracy as well as socialites from Britain and America.

The Whyttes' month-long visit passed quickly and on

Wednesday 10th April 1912, they boarded RMS *Titanic* in Southampton, homeward bound for New York. But in the early hours of Monday 15th, a number of incoherent news accounts slowly reached the astonished world: *Titanic* had been involved in a collision with an iceberg and was being towed to New York by SS *Virginian*. Then, after what seemed an eternity, it became clear that earlier reports had been mistaken – *Titanic*, the supposedly unsinkable ship, had sunk just south of Newfoundland with the loss of over fifteen hundred passengers and crew.

Frantic with worry, Hugo drove to White Star's offices in Southampton where, after being regaled with numerous confused reports, he learned that Ruth and Clara were alive and well and being treated for shock and minor injuries on board RMS *Carpathia*. A telegram from White Star later confirmed that Willard and Henry had been lost in the incident.

Hugo rushed to New York to be by his fiancée's side, but she became distant and withdrawn and he found it difficult to maintain their relationship, despite being gentle and sympathetic. What she needed, Hugo felt, was time to come to terms with the terrible circumstances. So reluctantly, the two families decided to postpone the wedding until Clara had recovered, as best she could, from the enormous loss of her beloved father and her brother.

For two years Hugo patiently maintained a correspondence with Clara, hoping for a signal that she was ready to discuss their wedding again. But then in July 1914, in light of the impending war with Germany, he enlisted as a captain in the army and was posted to France for the duration. Throughout the difficult days of the conflict he continued to write to Clara, and slowly but surely she began to show signs that she was returning to her old self. After Hugo was demobbed in December 1918, the pair were happily reconciled and the subject of their marriage arose again. Eventually, the wedding was re-scheduled for Saturday 21st June 1919, in just two weeks' time. It really would be bad luck if there was some new impediment to their marriage.

'Next stop Exeter St David's,' announced the guard loudly as he walked past Lance's compartment.

Lance folded away his paper and quickly rose to his feet. 'That's our stop, Bob.'

The dog jumped up and made a quick dash for the carriage door as the train slowed and pulled up to the platform, hissing and billowing steam.

They made their way out of the station to the parade where Lance, scanning the hustle and bustle of the crowd, saw a face he recognised. It was the family's long-time head gardener, standing next to the open rear door of a black Bullnose Morris saloon.

'Good afternoon, Digweed,' Lance said.

'Afternoon, Master Lance,' Digweed said, briefly touching the flat cap that seemed permanently glued to his head. ''Is Lordship asked me to collect you as 'ee's attending an appointment this afternoon and requires the service of the chauffeur.'

'Thank you, Digweed. I'm sorry to put you to the trouble of collecting me from Exeter, but the connecting train to Exhampton won't be leaving for at least an hour and I didn't want to wait.' Lance got into the back seat of the car.

'Tis no problem, sir. I've just dropped Lady Cynthia's maid at the station. She's going up to Liverpool to care for her sick mother,' Digweed explained.

Bob joined his master in the back, and Digweed shut the door carefully before ambling around to the driver's door and climbing in.

As the car drove slowly away from Exeter St David's, Lance caught a glimpse of the two men in Fedoras who had been on their train, but his attention was diverted by the strange noises coming from the car's engine as the ancient head gardener grappled manfully with the gearstick. He was more at home with an old-fashioned horse and trap than any kind of modern transport.

'Did'ee 'ave a good journey down, sir?' Digweed asked in a breezy conversational tone, stirring the gearstick like a Christmas pudding until the right gear was found.

'Yes, thank you Digweed. I hope Mrs Pierce hasn't been put to too much trouble because of my early arrival.'

'You know Mrs Pierce. Efficiency itself that 'un. She'll 'ave everythin' ready for you and Mr Bentley right enough, sir.'

Lance sat back in his seat enjoying the panoramic views as they made their way to Landacre Hall. Exmoor was particularly beautiful at this time of year, and the earthy rural smells filling the air reminded him of happier, more innocent times growing up in Coombe End with his best friend Robert 'Bob' Sixsmith. A sudden stab of grief mixed with guilt swept over him. It was difficult to think of his lost childhood chum without resurrecting the awful spectre of that tragic night in October 1918. He felt his eyes prick with tears and he stretched out a hand to stroke Bob's soft

19

black coat. The dog gazed lovingly into his face, his deep expressive eyes conveying absolute unconditional love. Everything will be all right, they appeared to say. I'm your best friend now. I'll look after you.

They drove through the village and on up the hill until at last, Digweed turned right, passing between the two huge stone pillars that marked the entrance to Landacre Hall. The driveway wound on for a further mile and a half before the house itself rose majestically from the stunning Exmoor landscape. The lavish nineteenth-century Gothic-style mansion, built on the site of a Tudor manor house, was the result of significant remodelling in 1830 by the late William Donaldson-Gilks, one of Lance's distant relatives who had made his fortune during the last days of the East India Trading Company.

As the Bullnose Morris rolled up to the entrance Digweed crunched the gears one last time and brought the car to an abrupt halt in front of the impressive carved stone portico. Levering himself out of the driver's seat, he sauntered around to open the passenger door, oblivious to the fact that his chaotic driving had left his passengers feeling as if they had been on a fairground ride.

Treadwell, the family's butler, stepped forward, looking as if he had just arrived from another century in his long-tailed, black, three-piece suit and tie with white gloves.

'Good afternoon, Master Lance,' Treadwell said, his formality adding to the sense of grandeur. 'I hope you have had a pleasant journey.' He glanced down his long nose disdainfully at Digweed who was about to wrestle the Bullnose Morris back to the garages behind the great house.

'Thank you, Treadwell,' Lance said, smiling. 'We've had a very pleasant trip, haven't we, Bob.' Bob took that as his cue to follow along merrily at his master's heels. 'How are you? All is well I hope?'

'Thank you, sir, all is well,' Treadwell said, standing back to allow Lance to manoeuvre himself with his cane into the entrance hall where Mrs Pierce was waiting. 'His Lordship has asked me to convey his apologies that he was unable to send his chauffeur to collect you from the station, sir. He had an appointment this afternoon that could not be postponed and he will not be returning until late this evening.'

'Thank you, Treadwell. Digweed indicated that Father's away.' Lance handed his hat to the butler. 'My man Bentley will be arriving sometime this afternoon. See he's taken care of when he arrives, will you?'

'Very good, sir.'

Lance turned to the housekeeper who had been waiting at a respectful distance. 'Good afternoon, Mrs Pierce, how are you?'

Mrs Pierce curtsied as best she could for a middle-age woman. Lance couldn't remember a time when she hadn't worked at Landacre. In his younger days he'd been a little frightened of her, but now, despite her pinched expression, she didn't seem nearly so terrifying.

'Good afternoon, Master Lance. I'm most well, thank you. I've your old rooms ready for you, and I've put your valet in the servants' quarters on the top floor. I hope you'll both be very comfortable.'

Mrs Pierce looked down at Bob who was staring up

at her expectantly, his tongue lolling from one side of his mouth and his tail wagging happily from side to side.

'This is Bob,' Lance said, noticing the direction of her gaze. 'He's been my constant companion since I returned from the war. Will you ensure there's a bed and a bowl of water placed in my rooms for him please, Mrs Pierce?'

'Yes, of course, Master Lance,' she said without taking her eyes from the dog. 'I'll see to it straight away.' She bobbed another small curtsey and glided away.

'Where is everyone?' Lance asked Treadwell who had been dutifully waiting while Mrs Pierce greeted Lance.

'Lady Cynthia is attending a charitable meeting with the local voluntary group, and Miss Tabitha and Master Hugo are out riding. The house guests are on a shopping trip to Exeter, sir.'

'Oh,' Lance said, moving to the foot of the grand staircase. 'In that case I think I'll take a short rest before dinner.'

'Very good, sir. Dinner will be served at eight. Will you require anything more, sir?'

'No thank you, Treadwell,' Lance said and he began his slow ascent of the stairs with the help of his cane, while Bob trotted up ahead of him.

CHAPTER 3:
A FAMILY DINNER

A T SEVEN O'CLOCK THERE was a quiet knock at the door to Lance's bedroom. Bentley entered carrying a glass of sherry and a large brown envelope on a silver salver.

'Good evening, sir. I hope you have had a pleasant rest after your journey. I have taken the liberty of putting out your white dinner jacket for this evening.'

'Thank you, Bentley,' Lance said, stretching from his slumber. 'How was your journey down from London?'

'Very uneventful, thank you, sir,' replied Bentley, bending slightly to proffer the tray as Lance sat up on the edge of the bed. 'Your aperitif, sir.'

Lance lifted the glass and frowned at the envelope. 'What's this?'

'It's the package that arrived yesterday, sir. I thought you would want to see the contents. It was not a bill as we first thought.'

Lance put his sherry on the bedside table, picked up the packet and pulled out the contents.

'What on earth!'

The envelope contained several sheets of paper and a dog-eared black-and-white photograph. The papers proved to be the manifest of the SS *Californian*, dated 5th April 1912, and recorded a cargo of three thousand woollen blankets and jumpers. The photograph was of a four-funnelled ship in port; on the other side were written the words 'Southampton April 1912'.

'Why on earth have I been sent these?' Lance asked 'They're dated more than seven years ago. Was there no covering letter or note with them, Bentley?'

'No, sir.'

'How very strange. I wonder who could have sent them.'

Lance completed his ablutions, fastidiously assisted into his evening wear by Bentley, all the while deep in thought about the envelope's mysterious contents.

'Do you know who'll be at dinner this evening?' Lance asked distractedly.

'I believe it will be Lady Cynthia, Master Hugo, Miss Tabitha, Miss Clara Whytte, her mother Mrs Ruth Hamilton-Whytte, and her new husband Mr Bruce Hamilton, sir.'

'Yes, I'd heard Ruth had remarried after the death of Willard,' mused Lance. 'I understand Hamilton is an American businessman of some kind.'

Bentley fussed silently with Lance's bow tie.

'Oh well, I suppose he'll be a good conversationalist at dinner,' Lance added and shrugged.

'I believe Lady Cynthia has also invited the Reverend Simon Eustace to dinner this evening, sir,' Bentley said, handing Lance his cufflinks. 'I understand he will be conducting the wedding ceremony for Master Hugo and Miss Clara.'

'Yes, that's right. Oh what a bore, having to endure such a stuffy affair on my first evening at Landacre!'

Bentley made no further comment as he helped Lance on with his dinner jacket and began brushing down the back and shoulders. 'I think that will be sufficient, sir,' he said, setting the clothes brush back on top of the tallboy.

Lance looked at himself in the wardrobe mirror. A tall, blond-haired man with intelligent ice-blue eyes stared back at him. Giving himself a satisfied nod, he turned to Bob who had been keeping an eye on all the activity from the bed provided for him by Mrs Pierce.

'What d'you think, Bob? All shipshape? Now, you be a good boy while I'm away and I'll take you for a nice walk before bedtime.'

The dog looked up at him, head cocked on one side as if to ask how long that would be.

'Not long I hope, young pup,' Lance said, patting Bob's head fondly.

It was around seven forty-five when, having summoned up the fortitude to face what he assumed would be an excruciatingly dull and tortuous evening, Lance set off for the drawing room where the other dinner guests would be gathering.

Since he had left the navy Lance hadn't attended many parties, the traumatic torpedo incident making it difficult for him to be convivial at such events. He hated the way people gathered in corners whispering, or the way they stared at him only to look away when he caught their eye. Most especially he couldn't abide being the object of their pity. That was the thing that Lance liked most about Bob. He never passed judgement and was blissfully untroubled by his master's character or mood; he just lived in the moment without one ounce of malice or spite. What wisdom the young pup possessed; what empathy in those dark eyes. Never mind those people, they seemed to say, let's you and I go for a walk.

With his heart thumping and a feeling of anxiety rising in his chest, Lance forced a smile and opened the door to the drawing room. His mother was already there, giving her last-minute instructions to Treadwell.

'Darling!' exclaimed Lady Cynthia when she spotted him. She sailed across the red Persian carpet in a cloud of powder and perfume, trailing tiny turquoise feathers from the hem of her evening gown. She put her arms around Lance in a motherly embrace. 'How lovely to see you. How are you?'

Lance drew back, slightly uncomfortable with his mother's flamboyant welcome. He wasn't one for overly demonstrative gestures from anyone, least of all his close family. 'I'm very well, thank you, Mother. Please don't fuss.'

'Of course I'm going to fuss, darling. After all, you're our very own war hero.'

'I'm nothing of the kind,' Lance said a little brusquely. He felt himself blush, and quickly went over to the drinks cabinet where he poured himself a sherry. He desperately needed a large glass of Irish malt whiskey but he knew his mother would have something to say about the impropriety of that.

'Let me introduce you to our guests, ' Lady Cynthia said, taking him by the arm and guiding him along gently but firmly.

Lance hadn't met any of the Whytte family yet. He had been away at sea for most of his naval career and absent from Landacre when the family first came over in 1912. Two men who had been in quiet conversation at the fireplace turned to face him.

'You know the Reverend Simon Eustace,' Lady Cynthia said. 'He'll be conducting Hugo and Clara's wedding ceremony on the twenty-first.'

A tall thin man in a white clerical collar smiled pleasantly at Lance. They had become acquainted some ten years earlier when the vicar had first arrived in Coombe End following a brief stint as a clergyman in America.

Lance returned a friendly nod. 'How nice to see you again, Reverend. I hope you're keeping well.'

'I'm very well, thank you. I hear you've had quite a difficult time recently. Are you fully recovered?'

Lance winced but forced himself to smile. 'I've been very fortunate, Reverend. I'm on the mend now.'

'And this is Bruce Hamilton,' interjected Lady Cynthia.

Lance turned slightly and held out his hand. 'I'm very pleased to meet you, sir,' he said.

Bruce smiled as he leaned casually against the carved stone fireplace, one foot resting on the raised brass surround. He was a portly man, well past middle-age, and sported a splendid handlebar moustache and bushy beard.

'So, this is Hugo's older brother,' he said in a rather heavy American drawl, shaking Lance's hand vigorously. 'I'm certainly very pleased to make your acquaintance, young sir.'

'Likewise,' replied Lance, trying to extricate his hand

and wondering if all Americans were so overly expressive. 'I understand you're a businessman.'

'Quite correct, young sir, although I'm retired nowadays.'

'What type of business were you in?'

'Mostly banking and shipping,' Bruce said, puffing out his chest. 'Spent several years at J. P. Morgan before adding International Mercantile Marine to my interests.'

'That must have been very exciting,' Lance said, attempting to summon up some polite curiosity.

'It has certainly been mighty lucrative, young sir,' Bruce said with an enigmatic smile and a twinkle in his eye. 'Yes, it's a fascinating—'

'Sorry, Bruce, I simply must introduce Lance to your wife,' Lady Cynthia said diplomatically, steering Lance away. 'He can be quite the bore if you get him talking about ships,' she whispered.

She led him over to the leather Chesterfield where Hugo was sitting between two ladies, one a much younger, slender version of the other.

'Lance, this is Ruth Hamilton-Whytte,' Lady Cynthia said, smiling.

The older lady rose from her seat. Ruth was a diminutive plump woman in her late fifties who had inadvisably chosen to wear an artichoke-green chiffon ensemble and a beaded headband from which a large blue feather protruded at a jaunty angle. Lance thought it made her look as if she were a small wobbling Conference pear.

'Pleased to meet you at last,' said Lance.

'Oh, how kind,' Ruth replied, her American accent not quite strong enough to hide her English origins.

'Do you hail from England, Mrs Hamilton-Whytte?' he asked.

'Oh, do call me Ruth, dear. How clever of you to spot I'm originally from England – from North Devon to be precise, although I've spent the last forty years in America, first with Willard in Manhattan and currently with Bruce on Long Island, so I suppose you could say I'm a naturalised American now.' She gave a short laugh.

'Are your family still in North Devon?' Lance asked.

'I have a brother, but we lost touch. Such a pity. I'm hoping to contact him while I'm in England. It would be wonderful to catch up with him again.

'You must let me know if there is anything I can do to help.'

'So kind, so kind,' Ruth twittered. 'You look so much like your brother, and I'm sure I shall be charmed by the same lovely nature.'

Hugo, who had been listening carefully to this exchange, squirmed in discomfort. 'Yes, but Lance is so terribly serious about things, aren't you, old chap,' he chipped in, getting to his feet. 'You should take a leaf out of my book and enjoy life a bit more.' He put a brotherly arm around Lance as if to impart some of his own bonhomie.

Lance twisted free of Hugo's grip and gave him a weary look. 'I will, Hugo, when the time's right.' He sighed and turned to Clara. 'And this must be your beautiful fiancée I've heard so much about. I'm especially pleased to meet you. You must be a *very* special person to have captured Hugo's heart so completely.'

Clara was indeed as arrestingly beautiful as Hugo had suggested.

'Hugo's an absolute darling,' Clara said, smiling nervously and holding out her hand towards Hugo for reassurance.

Just then, Tabitha, Hugo's and Lance's younger sister, raced into the drawing room adjusting her earrings as she ran.

'Sorry I'm late, Mother,' she said, flashing a smile around the room. 'I'm simply dying for a cocktail.' Spotting Lance she sprinted over and flung her arms around him practically squeezing him in two. 'Lance, you're home! How wonderful!' She absolutely worshipped her older brother putting him on a pedestal all her life.

Before he could utter a word the sound of the dinner gong reverberated in the hall and Treadwell appeared at the entrance to the dining room.

'Dinner is served,' he announced sombrely.

Dinner at Landacre Hall was a grand affair with plenty of staff on hand to ensure both family and guests were served smoothly and with great formality. The low hum of conversation and clinking cutlery filled the room. As the meal progressed the dialogue turned to the subject of Hugo and Clara's forthcoming marriage.

'Oh, I almost forgot to mention, Lance, we've an appointment tomorrow with a Miss Veronica Barnes from *The Exminster Chronicle*, our local newspaper,' said Lady Cynthia. 'She'll be reporting on the marriage for the social pages and will want to interview everyone.'

'Surely she's not interested in me, Mother,' said Lance irritably. There was nothing he'd detest more than being in the company of an inquisitive journalist intent on raking over events he'd rather forget. 'I'm not the one getting married. I'm only the best man.'

'Lance, dear, you must make an effort for Hugo and Clara's sake,' said Lady Cynthia, gently reproaching him across the table.

Lance pursed his lips. That helpless feeling he had endured as a schoolboy when he was scolded by the headmaster for failing to hand in his prep flooded back. He dreaded discussing his personal life with a complete stranger, and he certainly didn't relish the thought of his abridged biography being splashed across some local rag. But it seemed there was nothing to be done; his mother had decreed it and there was therefore little hope of avoiding the situation. Lance let out a dejected sigh.

After dinner, when the ladies had retired to the drawing room, Treadwell brought in the port and cigars. Lance smoked one of his father's best Cuban Havanas while vacantly staring down into a large brandy. Bruce and the Reverend were discussing America. Letting the trivial conversation wash over him, Lance found himself thinking about the mysterious documents he had received earlier. Then he remembered the ordeal he faced with the nosy journalist and wondered how he could extricate himself from it.

The other gentlemen started to drift back to the drawing room, and Lance was snapped out of his reverie by the roar of the gramophone.

'Tabitha, dear,' shouted Lady Cynthia, 'isn't it a bit loud?'

Al Jolson warbling 'Rock a Bye your Baby' from the large brass horn was not the sort of tune to inspire Lady Cynthia.

'Oh Mother!' exclaimed Tabitha, rolling her eyes.

Everyone settled down to enjoy what remained of the evening. Lance partnered the Reverend at bridge against Bruce and Ruth, Hugo played Canasta with Clara, Lady Cynthia settled down with her needlepoint and Tabitha continued to prance around the room to the strains of the jazz emanating from the gramophone, on several occasions almost colliding with the others engaged in more stationary pursuits.

It was around eleven o'clock when Treadwell entered the drawing room and gave an almost imperceptible cough.

'Detective Chief Inspector Quick from Exeter Police Station has called, m'lady. I have put him in the library.'

'Good grief!' exclaimed Lady Cynthia. 'Whatever can he want at this late hour. Lance, will you go?'

Lance nodded. He walked briskly to the library, uneasy at the sudden interruption to their private dinner party. When he entered the room, two men, one in a raincoat and trilby and the other in police uniform, rose from their chairs, their faces full of grim foreboding.

'Good evening, gentlemen. My name is Lancelot Donaldson-Gilks. Lord Cedrick's away at the moment. How may I assist?'

'Good evening, sir,' said the more senior of the two men, taking off his hat. 'I'm Detective Chief Inspector Quick from Exeter Police Station and this is Sergeant Bolt.'

The policemen held out their identification wallets.

Lance nodded. 'Is there something wrong, Chief Inspector?'

'It's about Lord Cedrick that I've called, sir,' said Inspector Quick, setting his hat on the table. 'I'm afraid there's no easy way of putting this, sir. Lord Cedrick and his chauffeur, Mr Edwin Speed, were killed in an automobile accident earlier this evening.'

Lance rocked backwards and sat down heavily in the nearest chair. His mouth went dry and he found himself breathing deeply.

'How did it happen?' he asked, his voice breaking.

'It's still under investigation, sir, but it seems likely that the driver lost control of the car and it hit a tree at the bottom of a steep incline.'

Lance blinked several times and started to tremble uncontrollably. Struggling valiantly to pull himself together he spluttered, 'Where did it happen?'

'Queen Dart Hill, just outside of Rackenford, sir.'

Lance knew that place; it was a very steep hill indeed. What on earth was his father doing *there*?

'Do you know what Lord Cedrick's destination was?' Inspector Quick asked.

'No, I'm afraid not, Inspector. I only arrived here myself this afternoon. Father had already left. What time did the accident happen?'

'It was reported to the Rackenford police station by a local farmer at around six o'clock this evening, sir. Because of the nature of the accident, the case was passed to Exeter and I have been appointed to investigate.'

'What do you mean "the nature of the accident"?' Lance asked, frowning.

'We have reason to believe it may not have been an accident in the true sense of the word, sir. There is evidence to suggest there may have been some kind of foul play. Of course, we must wait for the mechanical report before we can be sure.'

His head swimming, Lance rose unsteadily from his chair and poured himself a large glass of brandy from a decanter on one of the library tables. The sudden devastating news had driven him back into the dark abyss with which he was all too familiar. He knocked back the brandy and closed his eyes, waiting for the familiar warmth to permeate his body and numb his feelings. Lance let out a sigh of relief and pulled himself up straight.

'I'm very sorry to have brought you this bad news, sir,' the Inspector went on. 'Obviously, we shall want to interview all the members of the household, but I think it would be prudent to wait until the morning before we take matters further. Sergeant Bolt and I will return tomorrow when you've had time to inform the family. We can see ourselves out, sir.'

When the two policemen had left the room Lance slumped back in the chair, his breathing fast and shallow, his pulse racing. His father was dead? *Dead!* How on earth was he going to tell the family? He put his head in his hands and groaned. It was only two weeks before Hugo's wedding. Was it going to have to be postponed again?

CHAPTER 4:
THE AFTERMATH

Saturday, June 7th 1919

LANCE AWOKE THE NEXT morning still feeling groggy from the bottle of Napoleon brandy he had downed the night before. He lay in bed thinking for one hopeful moment that it had all been one of his dreadful nightmares. Only when Bentley brought him his usual cup of Earl Grey tea did reality strike; it *was* a nightmare but a horrible real waking one.

Informing the family, the evening before, of Lord Cedrick's demise had been horrendous. Lady Cynthia had fainted and had to be escorted to her rooms. Tabitha fled in floods of tears, letting out a series of sobbing shrieks, and Hugo's face had turned a deathly shade of white, Clara rushing to his side. Bruce and Ruth hurriedly conveyed their condolences and retired to their respective rooms while Reverend Eustace offered his sympathies and promised Lance he would return over the next few days to provide pastoral support and make arrangements for the funeral.

Lance blearily struggled out of bed, threw on his clothes, omitting his normal ablutions and any footwear, and went down to the dining room. Bob, who padded along quietly behind him, instinctively seemed to know that something was wrong.

The breakfast buffet was laid out on the dresser: eggs, bacon, sausages, kidneys, tomatoes, toast, marmalade and coffee. Rose, one of the parlourmaids, and a footman Lance had never seen before were standing by ready to assist, their drawn pale faces registering no surprise at Lance's dishevelled appearance. Rose placed a bowl of food on the floor for Bob and the dog tucked in eagerly.

Not so Lance. Usually, the enticing smell of breakfast would have had him salivating, but the death of his father had robbed him of his appetite and he couldn't face more than a good strong cup of coffee. Shaking as he carried it to the dining table he had to concentrate hard to avoid spilling any.

Thankfully, no one else had come down for breakfast. He sat in silence for a while, trying to come to terms with what had happened, his unkempt hair falling into his eyes, his unbuttoned shirt cuffs flapping against the tabletop. A number of questions were whirling around in his head. What had his father wanted to tell him? Where had he been going to or coming from? Who sent the mysterious package and was it connected to the accident? The appearance of the package at the same time as his father's urgent request to come down to Landacre seemed more than a coincidence. Perhaps the answers lay in his father's study.

Gulping down the coffee to bolster his resolve, Lance left the dining room, scarcely noticing the cold stone floor of the hallway under his bare feet. Bob followed him, his anxious eyes locked on to his master. Lance paused when he reached the study door, his determination temporarily weakening. Bob sat by him, patiently waiting for the next move.

Growing up at Landacre, Lance had learned not to enter Lord Cedrick's study without permission. It had always been a place of the utmost sanctity, a place where family members were only ever admitted by invitation. To be there now without his father present was a whole new experience for Lance and one that felt oddly uncomfortable.

He took a deep breath and opened the door. The long dark-green drapes had been drawn back to let in the early morning light through the glazed doors that opened out onto the veranda at the rear of the house. A number of valuable artworks in gold frames hung on the dark wood-panelled walls, and a large Chippendale desk dominated the centre of the room. His father's imposing green leather button-back chair hid a sizeable steel safe, and an Edwardian terrestrial table globe next to a towering bookcase only added to the sombre ambience of the room. The smell of antique mustiness immediately took Lance back to his childhood. How many times had he stood here quaking while his father reprimanded him for some minor misdemeanour? This was the room where Lord Cedrick oversaw family and estate business, a room that had witnessed important events. Lance stepped in and closed the door quietly behind him.

Bob began sniffing the furniture while Lance went behind the desk and gingerly sat down in his father's chair. Untidy piles of paperwork littered the desk, which

Lance quickly established were mostly unpaid bills and correspondence.

'Hmm, not much here, Bob.'

He pulled at the desk drawers but they were locked. He swung round and tried the safe door; also locked. Suddenly, there was a knock at the door. Lance gave a startled jump and was immediately filled with anxiety and guilt at being found rifling through his father's desk.

'Come in,' he croaked.

It was Treadwell, who on entering the room showed no surprise whatsoever at seeing Lance in Lord Cedrick's seat. 'Miss Veronica Barnes is here to see you, m'lord,' he said, presenting Lance with her visiting card. 'I have put her in the library.'

'Oh good grief! I'd forgotten she was coming this morning,' Lance replied, horrified by the intrusion of a visitor to the house so soon after receiving news of his father's death. 'I suppose I'd better see her to explain the situation and ask her to postpone the interview. Will you show her into the study please, Treadwell? I'll see her in here.'

A few minutes later Treadwell returned. 'Miss Veronica Barnes,' he announced as a slim, attractive woman in her late twenties walked into the room.

'Good morning. I'm Veronica Barnes from *The Exminster Chronicle*,' she said in clipped business-like tones, holding out a gloved hand towards Lance. She was smartly dressed in a dark-blue jacket and skirt and had a small navy pillbox hat perched insecurely on top of her head.

Lance stood up from behind the desk, suddenly keenly aware he was wasn't dressed to meet anyone, let alone someone from the press. Walking around to greet the visitor, he took her outstretched hand and gave it a firm shake.

'Good morning, Miss Barnes. I'm Lance Donaldson-Gilks. I gather you have an appointment this morning to interview our family regarding my brother's marriage.'

'That's right,' she replied with assured poise.

'Regrettably you'll be unable to go ahead with your interview as planned. I'm afraid there's been an accident. I'm so sorry you've had a wasted journey.'

Veronica walked determinedly towards one of the chairs in the room, removing her gloves as she went, and sat down. She glanced at Lance's bare feet, raised a perfectly shaped eyebrow and, taking a notepad and pencil from her capacious handbag, said, 'Oh, I'm sorry. What kind of accident?'

'I don't think you understand, Miss Barnes – my father's been involved in a motor vehicle accident and has been killed,' Lance replied in the authoritative tone he had successfully employed with his officers and crew on the *Panther*. 'My family are still in shock and are not in a position to be interviewed at present.'

'Good gracious! How simply terrible for you,' replied Veronica. She made a few notes on her pad and was about to ask Lance another question when there was another quiet knock on the door.

Treadwell entered the room, followed by Bentley who was carrying a pair of monogrammed slippers on his silver salver.

'Chief Inspector Quick and Sergeant Bolt are here to see you, m'lord,' Treadwell said. 'They are in the library, sir.'

Relieved by the interruption, Lance replied, 'Very good, Treadwell.'

'Your slippers, sir,' said Bentley, looking as if he had just sucked on a particularly sour fruit.

Lance took the slippers from the tray, avoiding any eye contact with his valet, and put them on before walking to the study door.

'I'm afraid I must attend to the Inspector now, Miss Barnes,' he said. 'Perhaps you would be good enough to postpone any further interview for the time being. Treadwell will show you out.'

Lance walked off down the hallway, Bob following hot on his heels, and went into the library where Inspector Quick was standing, his hat in one hand, looking around the room.

'Good morning, Inspector,' Lance said.

'Good morning, m'lord. I'm sorry to intrude on your family's grief so soon, but I'm afraid we've a certain procedure to follow and enquiries must be made.'

'I understand, Inspector. Protocol and all that. Do you have more information about the incident?'

'Yes, sir. I'm afraid the mechanical report on the vehicle your father was travelling in has revealed a number of discrepancies that need to be investigated,' the Inspector said, glancing at Sergeant Bolt who was standing by with his notebook and pencil.

'What kind of discrepancies?' asked Lance.

'Well, for starters, the brakes on your father's Rolls had been tampered with,' the sergeant blurted out.

'What Sergeant Bolt means, sir' – the Inspector threw Bolt an exasperated look – 'is that there's a question mark

over the state of the brakes at the time of the accident.'
He took a seat next to the sergeant. 'Now sir, if we could
make a start.'

Lance sat down in one of the reading chairs, Bob's head
resting on his newly slippered feet. 'All right, Inspector,
fire away.'

The Inspector asked Lance about his movements the
previous day. Lance told him about the mysterious telegram
that had prompted his journey from London and his arrival
at Landacre.

'So your father had already left when you arrived at
Landacre Hall, sir?'

'Yes, that's correct, Inspector.'

'Do you know where he was going or why?'

'No, as I said last night I have no idea where he was or
the purpose of his journey. And I'm none the wiser this
morning. I was rather hoping the answer to that question
would be in my father's study. I was having a quick look
around when you arrived, but a number of desk drawers
and the safe are all locked. I don't suppose you found any
keys on my father's body when it was recovered from the
accident?'

'We did recover a set of keys as a matter of fact, sir,' the
Inspector replied, removing them from his coat pocket.
'Perhaps we could see if they open anything.'

They made their way to the study where Lance took
the keys from the Inspector and began trying different
ones in the desk drawers. After several attempts one of
the locks gave a satisfying click and the left-hand drawer
slid out quietly. It contained an ink blotter, Lord Cedrick's

coat of arms carved into a fob wax seal, a gold signet ring engraved with the letters 'SIGILLVM TEMPLI' and a black leather-bound desk diary with his initials imprinted in gold leaf on the cover.

Lance picked up the diary, catching a faint whiff of antique leather. Flicking through the pages he could see his father's usual appointments – meetings in London at the House of Lords, others in Exeter with his banker and accountant, and at Landacre with the estate manager, and he had noted several local charity events. Lance turned to the current week where an entry for the day before – Friday 6th June – stood out from the rest. It read: '4.00 p.m. – JS – CM.'

'It seems he had an appointment yesterday at four o'clock, Inspector,' Lance said, handing the diary to the policeman. 'Unfortunately, it doesn't give any explicit information about his destination or the reason for his journey.'

The Inspector also flicked through the pages. 'There doesn't seem to be anything unusual or unexpected in it,' he remarked, setting the diary back down on the desk. 'Sergeant, take a copy of the notation under 6th June.'

Bolt made the necessary notes as directed.

Lance tried the rest of the keys in the remaining drawers; they all slid open in the same quiet manner as the first. There didn't appear to be much of interest in any of them.

Turning to face the safe, Lance tried all the keys in its lock. None of them were a fit.

'That's strange,' he remarked. 'I wonder why there's no key for the safe on this keyring. Were these the only keys you found at the scene of the accident, Inspector?'

'Unfortunately, it hasn't been easy to obtain items from the crash, sir. You see there was a fire ...'

'Oh, I see,' said Lance, not wanting to see at all. He preferred not to know about the grim details.

'We did recover the partial remnants of a photograph from the scene, sir,' the Inspector said, carefully producing a small package wrapped in tissue paper from his pocket. 'We were wondering if you could identify anyone.' He handed the delicate parcel to Lance.

Lance peeled back the tissue and stared at what remained of the photograph. It depicted a number of well-dressed men and women standing in what looked to be some kind of office.

'I'm afraid not,' he said, shaking his head.

'That's a pity, sir. Not to worry, I'm sure someone will know who those people are. Now, m'lord, I should like to interview the rest of your family and the household.'

'Of course, Inspector, please feel free to use the library as your interview room. I'll ask Treadwell to make the necessary arrangements.' Lance moved to the fireplace and rang the bell.

CHAPTER 5:
AN AGREEMENT IS MADE

S HE SAT BEHIND the desk in the now empty study Lance began to ponder where the key to the safe might be. Hearing a discreet click, he looked up to see Miss Barnes standing in the room. She strode resolutely over to the desk and sat down in the chair opposite.

'So, there's more going on here than you've led me to believe,' she said accusingly.

'I really don't know what you mean,' Lance stuttered, somewhat taken aback.

'Oh? The police are investigating a suspicious accident involving your father and his chauffeur and you're doing your best to convince me nothing irregular is happening,' she said primly. 'There's more going on here than meets the eye and my fine reporter's nose is telling me it's fishy.'

'I think you may be under a misapprehension, Miss Barnes,' Lance said.

'I think not,' she replied firmly. 'I've been standing in the hallway for the past half hour and I overheard Inspector Quick's remarks. It's clear he isn't happy about certain aspects of the incident.'

'I thought you'd left after our earlier meeting!' exclaimed Lance, appalled that this meddlesome journalist was insinuating herself into his family's affairs.

'Oh, I only allowed you to think I'd departed so I could get a better perspective on matters. A good investigative reporter is always alert to a decent story. I thought something interesting might be about to break when Inspector Quick was announced. I simply made it my business to find out what that "something" might be.' She shrugged.

'But you're *not* an investigative reporter are you, Miss Barnes,' Lance said pointedly. 'You only report on social events of little consequence.'

She sniffed. 'Yes, but the *Chronicle* encourages me to use my discretion, and that's exactly what I'm doing now.'

Bob stood up and went over to Veronica, his tail wagging in a friendly fashion.

'Oh what an adorable dog!' she gushed. Bob's tail picked up speed as she tickled him behind his ears. 'What his name?'

'Bob. Now, if you don't mind, Miss Barnes ...'

'Oh Bob, you're a real sweetheart, aren't you.' Veronica was rewarded with a sloppy big lick on her hand. 'How old is he?'

'Look, Miss Barnes, this really isn't ...'

'I'd say he's still quite young. He's still got those big puppy paws and ...'

'MISS BARNES,' Lance said loudly.

Bob's ears went back.

'Miss Barnes,' Lance repeated a little more calmly, 'while I'm glad to see that you get on so well with my dog, this is not a good time for my family and I'd appreciate it if you would leave. I know as little about my father's death as you do, and I need to put all my energy into getting to the bottom of it. Chaperoning a society reporter through a police investigation is not part of the plan.'

Bob nuzzled her hand. She looked directly into Lance's eyes speaking softly. 'You know my true ambition is to become one of the best reporters in the business, you've absolutely no idea how difficult that can be when you're female.'

Lance inclined his head acknowledging her difficulty.

'This opportunity may be the only chance I'll have to show people that matter in my profession how good a reporter I can be.' She shook her head sadly. 'For some unfathomable reason you seem determined to deny me my big break.' She continued to stroke the dog's head and he wagged his tail again. 'Besides Bob approves of me, don't you, boy?'

Against his better judgement Lance found himself smiling. 'Miss Barnes ...'

'Please, call me Veronica. Since you were in a state of underdress when we met earlier I think we can dispense with formalities, don't you?'

'Veronica ... it's not my responsibility to give you a leg up in your career. Furthermore, and more importantly' – Lance winced at the sound of his own pomposity – 'my family are deeply traumatised by the news of Lord Cedrick's death, the last thing they need is a stranger poking about.'

'But I'm not a stranger any more, Lance. See? We're on first-name terms already. It's perfectly acceptable for people on first-name terms to embark on a course of action together to solve a mystery, don't you agree?'

'Why on earth would I want to enlist your assistance in solving this mystery?'

'Ah! So you admit there's a mystery to solve then.'

Lance found himself smiling again. 'Well, perhaps there are some questions that require an explanation, but it's all rather gruesome – not really the kind of thing for young ladies to be embroiled in. Take it from me, you'd be far safer reporting harmless local events.'

'But I don't want to be safe. You really don't understand what it's like to be constantly overlooked professionally because of your gender, do you? I expect your life has been completely mapped out,' Veronica said. 'You men just step into positions that are made available to you. Women, on the other hand, have to work twice as hard as men to achieve a tenth of their status, and that's if they're even given a chance in the first place. I'm simply fed up with being passed over for promotion by men who aren't competent. I want to be taken seriously. I want to be the best investigative reporter there is, regardless of my gender. I don't want to be considered just a pretty face who reports on society gossip and trivial occasions.'

Lance was taken aback by the ferocity of her little speech. Exasperated and bemused all at once, he ran a hand through his hair. How should he handle this feisty spitfire?

'In any event, you'll probably need my skills and connections to help you get to the truth,' Veronica added with another little sniff.

'Oh yes, and what would those be?' Lance asked, warming to her bold self-confidence.

Veronica leaned forward, resting her arm lightly on the desk. 'You know' – she looked directly into his eyes again and smiled, her voice coquettish and soft – 'my womanly guile and contacts in the newspaper trade.'

'What contacts?' Lance asked with a faintly amused air. 'The local ladies that lunch?'

'A good reporter never reveals her sources,' she retorted.

Lance had to concede that it might be helpful to have someone on hand who was experienced at wheedling information out of people. And it would be especially helpful if that someone was a woman since women were generally not taken seriously in formal situations, often engendering loose lips.

As if to settle the arrangement, Bob walked around the desk and sat in front of Lance. 'Well, young pup, what do you think?'

Bob wagged his tail.

'Well, you have Bob's seal of approval,' Lance said, looking at Veronica, 'but you must promise me you'll not publish anything in your newspaper without my first agreeing to it,' he added sternly.

'Okay, I agree to that,' she snapped back before Lance had an opportunity to change his mind. 'Where shall we start?'

'How much did you overhear?'

'Well, I know the car your father was travelling in had something wrong with the brakes and I know you're missing the key to the study safe. The question is, who would want to kill your father and why?'

'You're right, that's the crux of the matter and I'm afraid I'm at a complete loss. What you won't be aware of is the mysterious envelope I received in the post on Thursday. I'll ask Bentley to bring it down from my room and we can take a closer look at the contents.'

He walked over to the fireplace and rang the bell. Treadwell appeared moments later. 'You rang, m'lord.'

'Yes, Treadwell, would you ask my valet to bring to the study the packet I received in the post on Thursday morning please.'

'Certainly, sir.'

The butler was about to leave the room when Lance said, 'Incidentally, do you know where my father kept the key to the study safe?'

'No sir, I'm afraid not. Your father was not in the habit of confiding its whereabouts to me,' Treadwell said impassively before leaving to carry out his errand.

Lance and Veronica looked at one another.

'I wonder where it can be?' Lance said.

'Well, if it wasn't on him in the accident it must be somewhere in the house.'

'Yes, but where.'

'In all good thriller stories things are usually hidden in secret drawers and such like.'

'My dear girl, we're not in some kind of mystery play. Besides, I never remember my father talking about secret drawers in the house.'

'Perhaps he chose to keep it to himself. Secret drawers might have been very useful to him.'

There was a gentle tap at the study door and Bentley entered. 'The envelope you requested, m'lord,' he said, handing it over to Lance. 'Will there be anything more, sir?'

'No, that will be all for the moment, thank you.'

As Bentley left the room Lance tipped the contents of the envelope onto the desk. He picked up the photograph of the four-funnelled ship and turned it over.

'It says "Southampton April 1912" on the back,' he said, handing it to Veronica.

She turned it from back to front and studied it for some minutes. 'It appears to be one of the new superliners operated by Cunard or White Star – you know, like the *Mauretania* or the *Olympic*. If we could find out who took the photograph perhaps we could learn the name of the ship. That might help us work out what this is all about.'

'Yes, but how are we going to do that?'

'I'll go back to my newspaper office and make enquiries. I'm sure I'll be able to find out something of use. You see, you need me already!' Veronica winked playfully.

Lance picked up the other document, trying to ignore her improper behaviour. 'This looks like a ship's manifest,' he said, handing it to her.

Veronica took the paper and glanced over the content, a quizzical look creeping over her face. 'You're right. It's a ship's manifest for the SS *Californian*. I wonder why that name seems vaguely familiar to me. This manifest's dated April 1912. That can't be a coincidence, can it? Both the manifest and the photograph dated April 1912. It must mean these items are linked in some way, but how are these connected to your father?'

'I haven't the foggiest. As far as I know Father's never had anything to do with shipping. Then there's this.' Lance lifted Lord Cedrick's diary from the desk, flicked through to the entry under 6th June and set it in front of Veronica.

'Hmmm, "4.00 pm – JS – CM",' she read aloud. 'That's quite cryptic. It doesn't give us much to go on.' She skimmed through the rest of the pages. 'Your father seems to have had a habit of making short entries. Look at these.' She pushed the diary back to Lance and tapped the pages. Under various dates in April and May was inscribed 'SE – MC.'

Lance shook his head. 'I wish my father had been more explicit in his notations,' he said.

'I see he had a number of entries for the House of Lords and other estate appointments,' said Veronica. 'I suppose since you're now the eighth Baron Westex you'll be taking up those duties.'

The shocking realisation made Lance sit bolt upright. The fact that he had inherited the Landacre estate and his father's titles hadn't occurred to him until now. 'In all honesty,' he said, with a pang of alarm, 'I haven't had time to think about it. Things have been happening so quickly.'

A cold shiver ran down his back and his mind raced through the implications. The weight of unfamiliar onerous duties as the eighth Baron would be difficult for him to bear. It would mean making Landacre his primary residence and forgoing his old life. How would he manage these new responsibilities so soon after his recent traumatic encounter at sea when he was already at breaking point trying to cope with his current unhappy existence?

'We should ask Bruce Hamilton if he knows anything about the SS *Californian*,' Veronica was saying, bringing him back to the present. 'I seem to remember from my background research for my piece on your brother's wedding that he's in shipping, isn't he?'

'Yes, before he retired. I'll ask him over lunch if he knows anything about it.'

'In the meantime, I'll get back to the office and see if I can find out anything about the photograph and the manifest. A good investigative reporter doesn't let the grass grow under her feet.'

'All right, why not come for dinner this evening and we can compare notes,' Lance suggested.

'That would be wonderful. Thank you.'

'Dinner will be at eight,' Lance said, opening the door to the study and walking with Veronica to the main entrance. 'How did you get here this morning?'

'Oh, I always travel by bicycle.'

'You haven't cycled up from Exeter, have you?'

'No, of course not.' She laughed. 'I got the train from Exeter to Exhampton and rode from there. It's not far — just a few miles.'

'I'll send the car for you tonight. You can't ride your bicycle this evening.'

'All right. Please ask your driver to call for me at Deacon Heights in Exeter. Shall we say around seven fifteen?'

'Until then,' Lance said.

He watched Veronica peddle away down the long winding drive unsettled by a flutter of exhilaration that pulsed through him. Quelling these feelings he walked back to the study where he rang the bell by the fireplace. Just then he noticed his dog had something between his paws, vigorously chewing and tearing.

'What have you got, Bob?' Lance asked, bending down to pick up what turned out to be mangled fragments of paper. He did his best to flatten out the creased scraps trying to decipher the content. It was no good the writing was almost completely illegible.

'Oh Bob, what have you done!'

There was a soft knock on the door and Treadwell came in. 'You rang, m'lord.'

Lance quickly stuffed the shredded paper into his pocket. 'Yes, Treadwell, can you tell cook there'll be one extra for dinner this evening? I've invited Miss Barnes to dine with us tonight.'

'Yes, sir. I'm sure Mrs Hughes can easily accommodate her.'

'Please also ask Digweed to collect Miss Barnes by car from Deacon Heights in Exeter at seven fifteen this evening.'

'Certainly, sir. Will there be anything further?'

'Yes, how are Inspector Quick and Sergeant Bolt getting on? Have they finished their interviews yet?'

'I believe they have interviewed the family members and some of the guests, sir.'

'Oh, who have they still to interview?'

'Mr Hamilton left the house very early this morning, sir, before anyone was down for breakfast and before Inspector Quick and Sergeant Bolt arrived. He has yet to return, m'lord.'

'How strange,' Lance said. 'Is there anything else I should know, Treadwell?'

'I gather the police will be interviewing the household staff after lunch, sir. And your mother has sent for her sisters, Lady Maud and Dame Lettice.'

'Very well, Treadwell, that will be all. Thank you.'

Lance was relieved that his mother had invited her sisters to stay. They would prove a great comfort to her at this terrible time allowing Lance to help the police with their enquiries. He looked down at his slippered feet and realised that he still hadn't dressed properly.

'Come on, young pup. Let's make ourselves respectable before Bentley blows a fuse.'

CHAPTER 6:
THE SAFE KEY

AFTER A SUBDUED LUNCH Lance wanted time to think, and decided that a long walk with Bob was just what he needed to blow away the gloomy cloud that hung over them all in the great house. The therapeutic effect of chattering aloud to his canine confidant was guaranteed to lift his mood.

As a light breeze wafted through the air, bringing with it the delicate perfume of wild flowers, the remnants of his throbbing headache began to melt away and his soul was lulled by the hypnotic hum of darting insects and the harmonious call of song birds. The soothing effect permeated every cell of his body, and without realising it his mind drifted to the subject of Veronica Barnes.

'What an impertinent young lady, Bob, winking at me like that! And refusing to take no for an answer, today of all days. I've never met a girl like her. Quite extraordinary. Quite extraordinary.'

His mind was filled suddenly with the image of her face – flawless skin, violet eyes, cupid-bow mouth, a sprinkling of freckles across her nose. She didn't stand on ceremony and he liked that; it was a refreshing change from the callow females who moved in his own hidebound circle. And Bob liked her too.

The late-afternoon air was starting to cool when Lance strode in through the main entrance of the house, Bob trotting along merrily behind, damp and muddy from his recent foray chasing rabbits and fetching sticks from the streams that criss-crossed the estate. As Lance went towards the boot room, Treadwell materialised from the servants' quarters.

'The Inspector has requested to see you before he leaves for the day, m'lord.'

'Thank you, Treadwell. Is he still in the library?'

'Yes, sir.'

'Fine, I'll pop along now. Please take Bob and arrange for someone to clean him up.'

'Very good, m'lord,' the butler replied, awkwardly guiding the wet dog along the passage towards the back of the house.

Outside the library, Lance could hear the sound of muffled voices. He stood there for a few minutes straining to overhear what was being said. The Inspector and his sergeant were deep in discussion. Hugo's name floated through the air. After a few inaudible sentences he heard the name Seb Smithers; Smithers was the head groom at Landacre. What were they talking about? Damn these solid doors, he thought as he turned the handle.

As soon as Lance entered the room the two policemen abruptly stopped talking.

'Good evening, m'lord,' said Inspector Quick.

'Good evening, Inspector. I trust your investigations have been fruitful?'

'We're making progress, sir,'

'Have you found the missing safe key, Inspector?'

'No, I'm afraid not. We've had a look around the study and your father's suite on the first floor but we've failed to find the key in any of those rooms.'

'That is peculiar. I'm sure it must be here somewhere,' Lance replied, his brow furrowing.

'Indeed, sir,' said Inspector Quick. 'We'll soon be leaving for the evening, m'lord, but in order to expedite matters we shall return tomorrow morning, bringing a locksmith. We'd like to look inside your father's safe without further delay.'

'I see. And what do you expect to find there, Inspector?'

'We don't expect to find anything in particular, sir, but we must follow every line of enquiry. The safe may contain valuable information.'

'Of course.'

'I'd be obliged, m'lord, if you'd ask members of your family and the household staff to refrain from entering your father's suite on the first floor. We wouldn't want any evidence disturbed, would we, sir.'

Lance nodded.

'I've asked Mr Treadwell to ensure the rooms are kept locked. I hope that's in order, m'lord,' the Inspector said, his tone suggesting it was a *fait accompli* rather than a request for permission.

'Certainly,' Lance said. 'What about my father's study, Inspector?'

'I'd be grateful if you would desist from entering that particular room for the time being, sir … just until we have opened the safe.'

'Very good, Inspector.'

'Well, goodnight, m'lord,' Quick said, signalling to his sergeant that he was ready to leave.

The pair departed from the library and left in the police car waiting for them in front of the big house.

Lance made his way up to his own rooms on the first floor. Inside, Bentley was attending to his dining attire.

'I have laid out your black dinner jacket with the satin lapels for this evening, m'lord.'

'Thank you, Bentley.'

Bob had been returned clean and dry and was watching the evening's robing ritual from his bed when the bedroom door burst open.

'Hello, Hugo,' Lance said, glancing with concern at his brother's lined, ashen face. 'You all right? I haven't had a chance to speak to you since Pa's accident.'

'God, this is awful,' Hugo said, slumping down onto the bed. 'Ma's putting on a brave face, but Tabby's finding it awfully hard to cope.'

'I know, Hugo, I know. You just learn to deal with it as best you can,' murmured Lance, having discovered this pearl of wisdom through his own recent experiences. 'What did you say to the Inspector when he interviewed you?' he asked, remembering that Hugo's name had been at the forefront of the Inspector's discussion with Sergeant Bolt.

'What could I say,' Hugo said, the pitch of his voice rising to a wail. 'I don't know anything. I was out riding all yesterday afternoon with Tabby. I wasn't here when Pa left!'

'All right, old chap, you can only tell what you know,' Lance said, seeking to ease his younger brother's angst. 'Did Pa seem different to you in the last few days?'

'Different? In what way?'

'You know, distracted, upset, worried ... that kind of thing.'

'Well now you come to mention it, he did seem somewhat preoccupied over the last few days, as if he had something on his mind. He didn't mention what it was to me.'

'Are you sure he didn't say anything out of the ordinary?'

Hugo paused to reflect. 'Well, he did ask me if everything was all right between Clara and me. At the time I thought he was just concerned that I might be suffering from pre-wedding nerves. I didn't think there was anything more to it than that.'

'And are you? Had you given Pa any sign you were experiencing something of the sort?'

'No, of course not,' Hugo retorted indignantly. 'Everything in that department's first-rate.'

'How's Clara taking things?'

'She seems to be coping well enough.'

'Have you decided what you want to do about your wedding in light of Pa's death?'

'I know it may seem callous, Lance, but Clara and I want it to go ahead as planned.'

Lance raised an eyebrow. 'You don't think it would be wiser to postpone for a while?'

'NO!' barked Hugo. 'We've already delayed for far too long. We've talked it over and Clara wants the wedding to go ahead as arranged.'

'All right, old chap, as you wish,' Lance said. He put a reassuring hand on Hugo's shoulder. 'Come on, we'd better go down and face the music.'

Dinner was going to be testing for everyone that night, Lance thought as the brothers descended the staircase. He mentally girded himself to handle the ordeal, then remembered that Miss Barnes – Veronica – would be there. An unfamiliar and rather inappropriate tingle of excitement coursed through his veins, at odds with the melancholic atmosphere in the house.

Hugo and Lance entered the drawing room where Lady Cynthia was already seated. They each gave her a peck on the cheek. It was as if she had aged ten years overnight. Her face was pinched and drawn, and the sparkle was gone from her eyes. But she was not about to let standards slip in the face of personal tragedy and had made it known that she expected the family to observe strict social protocol as usual.

Presently, the door to the drawing room opened and Treadwell entered. 'Miss Veronica Barnes,' he announced.

Veronica floated gracefully into the room, a much-needed breath of fresh air. Lance strode eagerly over to greet her.

'Good evening, Veronica,' he said, a spike of excitement rising in him as he gently clasped her arm and guided her forward. 'I hope you had a good journey from Exeter.'

'Yes, thank you,' she replied, a faint smile dancing around her lips. 'I must say, your driver certainly has a way with vehicles!'

Lance couldn't help but smile back. He guessed Digweed had fought against the 'new-fangled' contraption all the way from Exeter. 'I'd like you to meet my mother, Lady Cynthia,' he said, walking Veronica over to the Chesterfield.

Veronica held out her hand. 'I'm so sorry for your loss, Baroness. In the circumstances it's very good of you to invite me this evening.'

Lady Cynthia took her hand. 'Thank you. That is most kind. It's a great pity we couldn't have met in happier circumstances, but do please carry on as normal. The Donaldson-Gilks family would not want our personal loss to interfere with our duty.'

Lance guided Veronica over to the drinks table where his brother was pouring himself a large whisky.

'This is my brother Hugo.'

Hugo glanced up at Veronica and flashed a feeble smile in her direction. 'Hello,' he said, trying to sound cheery.

'Nice to meet you, Hugo.'

'Would you like a drink? I'm having a double. I suggest you have a large one too. You may need it before this torturous evening's out.' He took a swig from his glass.

'It's all right, Hugo, I'll help Veronica with her drink,' Lance said quietly. 'What would you like, Veronica? Sherry, gin, vodka, whisky or perhaps you'd like a cocktail?'

'A vodka with soda would be lovely, thank you.'

Lance set about pouring the drinks as Clara came into the room looking somewhat flustered. She practically sprinted over to Hugo who was downing the dregs from his glass before pouring a second.

'You must come at once and speak to Mother, Hugo. She's in a dreadful state,' she said breathlessly.

'What's up, darling?' Hugo asked, his voice tinged with sudden alarm.

'It's Bruce. He hasn't returned from Exeter and Mother's very distressed.'

Lance handed Veronica her drink.

'Bruce hasn't returned?' Lance asked, pouring himself a sherry. 'What time should he have been back?'

'Sometime late this afternoon, I think,' Clara said.

'What was he going into Exeter for anyway?' Lance asked.

Clara became even more agitated. 'I've really no idea.'

'Does Ruth know why he was going to town?' Lance asked.

'No, I don't think she does. Oh Hugo, you must come at once, please,' she pleaded, grabbing his hand and pulling him towards the drawing-room door.

Hugo set his half-empty glass on an occasional table and left the room with Clara. On their way out they passed Tabitha who was just arriving. She looked tired and had red rims around her eyes from crying.

'What's all the fuss?' she asked, casually walking over to the drinks table and helping herself to a cocktail.

'It's Bruce. He hasn't returned from Exeter and Ruth's in a terrible state about it,' Lance explained. 'Hugo's going to see if he can assist.'

Lance introduced Veronica to his sister and left the two girls to chat while he fetched himself another drink, something a little stiffer this time.

A few minutes later Hugo returned, a worried look on his face. 'Ruth's insisting that I call the Inspector and report Bruce missing,' he whispered to Lance so as not to alarm the others.

'All right, the nearest telephone is at the post office in Coombe End,' Lance said. 'I'll get Bentley to bring the two-seater round and we can drive down together.'

'No need for that, old man, I'll go myself. I don't want to spoil your evening with Veronica. I'll get Digweed to run me down.'

'Well, if you're sure.'

'Yes, that'll be fine. Just tell Treadwell that Clara and Ruth will take dinner in their rooms this evening. They're not up to facing everyone tonight.'

Hugo hurriedly left the drawing room to find the gardener.

Dinner that night was a sombre affair. Although Mrs Hughes had provided the usual high calibre fare, those partaking of the meal merely pushed the food around their plates, their appetites diminished. As soon as the agony was over, Lance took the opportunity to escape with Veronica to the study, where he unlocked the door using a duplicate key kept in the butler's pantry.

'Lance! Are we supposed to be in here?' Veronica whispered. 'I thought you said at dinner that the police didn't want anyone in this room until they'd opened the safe.'

'It's all right, calm down. We're not going to do any damage. We'll leave it just as we found it. You know how the police are – belt and braces.'

'Are you sure? I don't think Inspector Quick will be very happy if he finds out.'

'We'll just have to make sure he doesn't find out,' Lance said, closing the door quietly behind them. 'I'm sorry it's been such an unpleasant evening for you.' He indicated an easy chair next to the cold fire grate.

'There's no need to apologise. The evening was much as I'd expected. There's been a death in the family. I think your mother's been marvellous allowing me to dine here at all. There aren't many families that would have been able to face strangers so soon after a tragedy.'

'That's part of the Donaldson-Gilks make-up – a strong backbone and stiff upper lip is in our genes.'

Veronica laughed.

'Would you like a nightcap?' Lance asked.

'A brandy would be nice.'

Lance poured the drinks and handed a glass to Veronica before sitting in the easy chair on the other side of the fireplace. 'Now let's get down to business,' he said. 'I've been dying to ask you all evening how you got on with the photograph and manifest.'

Veronica slipped off her shoes, sighed and wiggled her toes. 'Well, let's see. The photograph I've lent to a photographer friend of mine at the *Chronicle*. He's been around the newspaper business for some time and says it looks as if it was taken by a professional photographer, possibly one who works for a newspaper. He says he may be able to find out who took it. He's going to let me know as soon as he has something.'

'What about the manifest?'

'He had a good look at it but couldn't be of any help in that direction. I'm going to have a rootle around in the paper's archives. Something may crop up. What about you? Anything new?'

Lance put his hand in his pocket and pulled out his folded handkerchief. He walked over to the desk and tipped a number of paper fragments onto its surface.

'I found Bob chewing these after you left this morning,' he said. 'I think they may have fallen from father's diary.'

Veronica got up to study the pieces. 'It's a bit like doing a jigsaw,' she remarked excitedly as she moved the mangled scraps around.

They worked feverishly until all the parts fitted.

'There,' said Lance as he put the last bit in place. 'It seems to be a letter to someone called "Seymour" of 1 West Quay Road, Southampton.'

They stared at each other in amazement.

'Am I seeing things?' Veronica asked. 'Does that say 10th April 1912?'

'Yes, I think it does,' Lance replied, peering intently at the spidery handwriting that had become difficult to read as a result of Bob's earlier attentions. 'It's uncanny – everything seems to point to something significant happening in April 1912. But whatever it was, how on earth can it have anything to do with my father seven years later?'

They scrutinised the body of the letter, trying to make out the content; Bob had done an excellent job of obliterating many of the words.

'*And I still don't like this ship*,' Lance read aloud.

'Hmm,' mused Veronica. 'Let's assume this letter was sent from someone on board one of the superliners like the one in the photograph.'

'All right, let's say it was. Where does that get us?' Lance asked.

Veronica walked over to the table globe in the corner of the room and spun it, stopping it abruptly when the Atlantic Ocean faced her. 'You know, Lance, most of the superliners travel the Atlantic route from Southampton to New York.'

Lance wondered if this information was significant.

Absentmindedly she spun the globe in the opposite direction. As she did so a small hidden drawer silently slid out from the side of the framework.

'Good grief!' she exclaimed, stepping back in surprise. 'What did you do?'

'I don't know!'

Lance raced over and they stood in breathless excitement peering into the small dark drawer. Glinting gently in the subdued light lay a key.

'Gosh, is that what I think it is?' Veronica said.

'It must be the safe key we've all been looking for,' Lance replied, lifting it from the drawer. 'Let's see if it fits.'

He went to the safe behind his father's desk and, sliding aside the metal flap covering the keyhole, he inserted the key into the lock and turned it clockwise. The locking mechanism bolts made a discreet clunk as they were drawn back. He twisted the handle and heaved open the heavy metal door to reveal a number of large leather-bound ledgers inside.

'These must be the estate account books,' he said, lifting them out with a grunt and placing them on top of the desk. There was also a petty cash tin, three brown foolscap envelopes and a red leather embossed jewellery case.

'What's in the envelopes?' Veronica asked with excitement.

Lance picked up the first one and read out the words '*Coombe End Memorial Committee*' printed in green ink on the front. Opening the unsealed flap, he emptied the contents out onto the desk and rifled through the papers that fell out.

'These appear to be a set of accounts and associated documents,' he said.

They examined the neat figures listed with precision under a number of headed columns.

'According to the paperwork, the Memorial Committee has been receiving some generous donations from leading figures in the village,' Lance said. 'They appear to be raising funds to put up a memorial for those families who lost loved ones during the great conflict of 1914–18.'

'Who's on the committee?'

Lance flicked through the sheets of paper. 'There seem to be three other people in addition to my father: Simon Eustace, the vicar, George Bagshott, who runs the Exmoor Hunting Lodge Hotel – I don't think I'm acquainted with him – and Jacob Snyder. He's the local apothecary and sits on the Parish Council.'

Veronica made a note of the names in a small jotter she fetched from her bag.

'Wait a minute, look at these,' Lance said, thumbing through a number of cheques drawn on the Memorial

Fund bank account. 'These cheques have all been made out to cash!'

'Is that unusual?' Veronica asked.

'I would say so. It's not normal to draw out that much cash unless the fund had a lot of bills to pay all at once. Yet there doesn't appear to be any merchants' bills indicating such a circumstance.'

'What's in the other envelopes?'

Excitedly they opened the second. It contained a replica of the photograph that the police found at the scene of Lord Cedrick's accident but this one revealed the individuals obliterated in the fire-damaged copy.

'Good Lord, that's Father!' Lance exclaimed.

Veronica peered closely at the group of men and women in the picture.

'That's odd,' he murmured. 'The figure standing next to him in the dapper suit looks like Bruce, except he's much younger there. I wonder who the others are and why Father had a duplicate in his safe.'

Lance opened the third envelope and pulled out a complete set of the same documents he had received in the post the previous Thursday.

'So ... he had a spare set of these too,' Lance mused. 'I wonder if it was him who sent me the copies. But if so, why?'

'Perhaps he sent you a copy just to be sure he could put his hand on an identical set if the originals were stolen or destroyed.'

'All right, let's accept that premise. The paperwork doesn't appear to be very incriminating. Who'd want to steal them or destroy them? What would be the point?'

'I don't know, but when we find out the answer to those questions we shall be a lot closer to the truth.'

'We'd better put everything back as it was,' Lance said. 'Inspector Quick will be here in the morning with his locksmith and won't be best pleased to discover that we've disturbed the contents of the safe before he's had a chance to view them.'

Veronica stood stock still, a glazed look on her face. She reached over and picked up the diary sitting on top of the desk.

'Just a minute, I think I may have discovered a clue,' she said. 'Did you say Simon Eustace was on the Memorial Committee?'

'Yes, that's right.'

'Well, don't you see – Simon Eustace, "SE" – on the Memorial Committee, "MC"? That was the notation in your father's desk diary, "SE – MC",' she said pointing excitedly to one of the notations.

'My goodness, so it is. So perhaps Father had an appointment with Simon Eustace to discuss the new memorial. We must ask the Reverend about it. He's coming back to the house in a few days to discuss arrangements for Pa's funeral. I'll ask him then.'

'Yes, but don't you see?' Veronica quickly turned the pages of the diary until she got to the one marked 6th June and jabbed her finger repeatedly at the notation. 'If this was the standard way your father made his notations, all we have to do is find someone with the initials "JS" relating to something with the initials "CM". Then we shall know where your father was going yesterday.'

'Of course!' said Lance. 'How clever of you, Veronica.' He took a step forward to clasp her hands in an act of spontaneous jubilation but at the last minute stopped himself. Instead he merely said, 'Well done, you.'

Veronica looked extremely pleased with herself.

'Of course, Jacob Snyder could be "JS",' Lance said. 'I wonder if that's who Father was referring to.'

'Yes, but what does "CM" stand for and does it have anything to do with Jacob Snyder? Did your father belong to any other committees or societies?'

'Not that I know of.'

'Well, it is the initials of the Memorial Committee reversed,' mused Veronica. 'We must interview Jacob Snyder. Let's ask him what he knows. Perhaps he can shed some sort of light on the initials "CM". Where can we contact him?'

'Slow down, Veronica,' Lance said, trying to marshal his thoughts calmly.

Veronica sighed.

'Snyder has an apothecary establishment in the village. We'll drop in during opening hours on some pretext or another and ask him a few casual questions. We mustn't be too obvious about things, otherwise he'll clam up.'

Veronica tapped her lips with her pencil.

'In fact it might be better if only one of us visits Snyder,' Lance continued.

'Yes, you're right. We need to go about this in a very artful way if we're to get to the bottom of things,' Veronica said.

'Perhaps I should pop in on the pretext of getting a few headache powders. A reporter from the *Chronicle* would certainly raise his hackles,' Lance said.

To his surprise Veronica reluctantly agreed. 'One of the difficulties that reporters have is that you have to be very quick off the mark, not only in getting to locations, but also in asking very direct questions. It puts a lot of people off. I must learn to be a bit more circumspect in future.'

Lance gathered up the account books and envelopes and placed them back in the safe, carefully locking the door. 'I'll give Inspector Quick this key tomorrow. I expect he'll be a bit miffed about bringing a locksmith out to the Hall when he won't be needed.'

'We should tell him of our discovery about the notation in your father's desk diary. He may be able to help. At any rate, we shouldn't keep something like that from him.'

'You're quite right, Veronica. I'll tell him as soon as he arrives.'

'What about the letter Bob chewed? Shouldn't we tell him about that as well?'

'Let's just keep that to ourselves for the moment. I think we ought to take a trip down to Southampton and visit this "Seymour" person ourselves. Let's see what he or she has to say first before we tell the Inspector. After all, it may just be a red herring.'

'All right. When shall we go?'

'There's no time like the present. Let's pop down tomorrow. We could motor down in my two-seater. It'll probably take us around four hours to get there, so we should be able to conduct our interview and get back in one day.'

'Fine. We'll need an early start then. What time shall we leave?'

Lance thought for a minute. It would be very inconvenient for Veronica to have to go home this evening and come back early in the morning. 'Why don't you stay over at the Hall?' he suggested. 'I'll get Mrs Pierce to make up a guest room. That way we can leave as soon as we've spoken to the Inspector in the morning. What d'you say?'

'What about my clothes? I can't very well go gallivanting off to Southampton in my evening wear!'

'Oh, that's all right. Tabby can lend you some of hers. She's got a wardrobe full of things she hardly ever wears and you're both about the same build,' Lance said, determined to dismiss any objection Veronica could raise.

It was settled then. Lance gave his instructions to Mrs Pierce, and after another nightcap they said goodnight and retired to their rooms.

* * *

The next morning Lance rose with a spring in his step. He felt oddly conflicted. His father was dead, probably murdered, and the loss and the manner in which it had occurred deeply troubled him. In addition, the consequences for his family and the responsibilities that would subsequently befall him weighed heavily. Yet the presence of Veronica and the mission that bound them together made him feel elated and alive, sensations that had been missing from his life since his return from the war.

Leaving instructions with Bentley to look after Bob for the day, Lance went down to breakfast. Rose, the parlourmaid, and the footman whom Lance had since learned was named Evans were in attendance at the breakfast buffet as usual, silently watching Hugo and Clara attempting to keep up appearances.

'Good morning, Clara, Hugo,' Lance said, nodding to them as he entered the dining room. 'Any news of Bruce?' He helped himself to some eggs, bacon and coffee from the buffet on the dresser.

'I'm afraid not,' Hugo said. 'I telephoned Exeter Police Station last night and asked if they'd received any information of an accident, but they said nothing had been reported. They took down some details about Bruce's weight, height et cetera, and said they'd let us know if anything developed.'

'I take it Bruce hasn't returned yet, then,' Lance replied.

'No. No one has heard from him since he left the house yesterday morning,' Clara said, her voice trembling.

'Well, look on the positive side,' Lance said. 'No news is good news. Nothing terrible could have happened, otherwise we'd have heard about it by now.'

Clara smiled half-heartedly as Lance sat down at the dining table and began to eat.

Just then, Veronica and Tabitha came into the dining room and wished everyone a good morning. They made their way over to the dresser and helped themselves to bird-sized portions from the buffet.

'I see you girls have sorted out something for Veronica to wear,' Lance said, admiring her choice of pale blue summer dress with satin sash at the waist.

'Oh, that old thing,' Tabitha said. 'I haven't worn it for ages but I must say it looks better on Veronica than it ever did on me.'

Breakfast was almost over when Treadwell entered the room. 'Inspector Quick and Sergeant Bolt have arrived, m'lord. They have a *tradesperson* with them,' he announced in his most superior manner.

'Thank you, Treadwell,' Lance said, dabbing a napkin at the corners of his mouth and rising from his chair. 'I'll come out.'

Lance greeted the party in the hall. 'Good morning, Inspector. I think I may have some good news for you,' he said.

'Good news will be most welcome, m'lord,' replied Inspector Quick.

Lance recounted the events of the previous evening and produced the safe key from his pocket, handing it over to the Inspector as he spoke.

The Inspector took the key. 'Have you opened the safe, sir?' he enquired casually, turning the key over in his hand.

Lance shuffled uncomfortably from foot to foot. 'Yes, Inspector, we did have a quick look inside.'

'I see, m'lord. I thought I'd made it plain before leaving yesterday that the study was out of bounds. It's customary, and certainly preferable, to allow the police to make their investigations without disturbing the evidence.'

'Oh, we didn't disturb anything, Inspector. We put it back exactly as we found it,' Lance said.

'It's not just a question of disturbing the contents of the safe, you understand, sir,' continued Inspector Quick gravely. 'There are the external circumstances to be taken account of. Your actions have quite possibly rendered evidence of any kind invalid.'

'Gracious! I'm so sorry. We never gave it a second thought.'

'Quite so, m'lord,' the Inspector said, his irritation unmistakeable. He handed the safe key to Sergeant Bolt. 'Well, there's nothing to be done. We'll go and see for ourselves. We may be able to glean something useful from the scene.'

'Before you go, Inspector,' Lance added, hoping his next revelation would put him back in the Inspector's good books. 'Miss Barnes thinks she may have discovered a clue to the notations in my father's diary.'

Lance explained in detail about Simon Eustace and the Memorial Committee and how the initials matched the entries in the diary.

'Very bright, your friend Miss Barnes. Quick on the uptake,' the Inspector conceded, absentmindedly scratching the side of his face with a bony finger. 'Make a note of that, Sergeant Bolt,' he said briskly.

Bolt took out his notebook and pencil and did as he was asked.

The Inspector had just started to walk down the hallway to the study door when he stopped and called back to Lance. 'Incidentally, was your father involved in any government work?'

Lance frowned. 'Not as far as I'm aware, Inspector. Does that have some kind of relevance?'

Inspector Quick sighed. 'I've been informed that Chief Superintendent Schilling from Scotland Yard will be arriving this morning. He'll be taking over the investigation, under instruction from the Home Office.'

CHAPTER 7:
A TRIP TO
SOUTHAMPTON

Sunday, June 8th 1919

THE TRIP DOWN TO Southampton was uneventful, and at around one o'clock Lance pulled into West Quay Road in his red Aston-Martin two-seater, Veronica in the passenger seat keeping an eye out for No. 1.

'This is it,' she shouted and he stopped the car, noisily pulling on the handbrake.

It was an end-of-terrace red brick house with stone steps leading up to a sturdy black front door. They got out of the car and climbed the steps.

Lance rapped the door knocker loudly. Nothing happened. He rapped again. Still no answer. With his hand to his forehead to keep out the glare of the sun he peered in through the front window. 'I can't see anyone.'

Just then an elderly woman walked along the pavement and up the steps to the house next door. She looked over at the pair and called out loudly, 'Can I help you?'

'We're looking for the Seymours,' Lance said. 'D'you know if they're in?'

The elderly woman shook her head. 'You won't find the Seymours there any more, m'dears. Florence Seymour moved away when her brother died – must 'ave bin five or six years ago now.'

'Oh,' Lance said, slightly taken aback. 'D'you know where she moved to?'

'Combe Martyn ... 'tis a small village just afore Southampton.'

'You wouldn't have her current address would you?'

The woman eyed them suspiciously.

'We've come about a letter we found that was addressed to her,' Veronica added. 'It would be very helpful if you could tell us her whereabouts.'

After a second or two of further scrutiny the woman relented. 'If you'll wait a moment I'll just pop inside and find her details. Funnily enough she's had a couple of other callers recently so I shan't have to look far.'

A few minutes later she returned with a torn piece of paper in her hand. 'Here you are. Her new address is Rose Cottage, Sandy Lane, Combe Martyn,' she said, handing the crumpled note to Lance.

'Thank you, you've been most helpful.'

'That's okay, m'dears,' the woman said. 'When you see Flo, tell her Aggie sends her best,' and without another word she disappeared back into her house.

'Well,' said Veronica, 'I didn't expect that. I wonder who the other callers were and, more to the point, why they called.'

The pair exchanged a fretful glance.

'I've just had a thought,' Veronica said and grabbed Lance's arm. 'Combe Martyn – "CM" – the initials in Lord

Cedrick's diary for 6th June. D'you think your father was coming here on the day of his accident?'

'By Jove, you may have hit on something, Veronica, and Seymour could be the surname related to the "JS" initials.'

'Yes, but *Florence* is wrong all together – the initials in the diary were "JS", not "FS". I wonder what her brother's Christian name was. If it began with a "J" then we could be in business.'

'You're right. We'd better get over to Combe Martyn and find out what we can,' Lance said.

They got back into the red two-seater and quickly drove over to Combe Martyn. Rose Cottage was at the end of a narrow lane set slightly apart from the rest of the village. Lance and Veronica walked up the path to the pretty house, observing how aptly it had been named as they ducked under a profusion of pink roses in full bloom that arched over a dilapidated porch.

Lance knocked. A short while later the door was opened by a young woman in housemaid's uniform.

'Is Miss Seymour in?' enquired Lance politely.

'Who's callin'?'

'Please inform Miss Seymour that the Honourable Lancelot Donaldson-Gilks and Miss Veronica Barnes are without and wonder if it would be convenient to have a brief word,' replied Lance, giving the girl his calling card.

Her eyes grew large as she read the embossed detail. 'Wait 'ere, sir. I'll see if the mistress is in,' she said curtly before scurrying away down a dark passageway.

A few minutes later she returned. 'The mistress will see you, sir, ma'am. Follow me please,' she said leading them along the dimly lit hallway into an equally drab drawing room.

'Good afternoon, Miss Seymour,' Lance said, stepping forward with an outstretched hand. 'I'm Lance Donaldson-Gilks and this is Veronica Barnes.'

Miss Seymour was a lady of advancing years. She wore a long dark grey dress with a hickory-coloured woollen shawl pulled tightly around her shoulders, and her grey hair was rolled into a tight cylinder around a knitted skull-cap held in the centre. A pair of sharp eyes peered inquisitively over her pince-nez as she greeted the unexpected guests.

Miss Seymour gestured to them both to take a seat. 'Would you like some tea?' she asked. She arranged for light refreshments to be brought in and, when the maid had left the room, turned a steady gaze back to her visitors.

'Now then,' she said making herself comfortable in an armchair. 'How can I help you?'

'We wondered if we could discuss a letter that was sent to you in April 1912.' Lance pulled from his pocket the chewed pieces of the letter and laid them on the low table in front of them.

'We found it among my father's possessions. We wondered if there was anything you could tell us about it, in particular how it may have reached my father.'

Miss Seymour examined the pieces Lance had arranged on the tabletop and she gave a little nod. 'Oh, it's that letter again,' she said taking off her pince-nez and looking directly at Lance. 'Your father must be Baron Westex then.'

'Thank you. Yes, that's correct,' Lance said, a little surprised that Miss Seymour had recognised his family name.

'I met the Baron when he visited recently.'

'Good Lord!' exclaimed Lance, looking across the room at Veronica. 'When did he call, Miss Seymour?'

'Oh, some time in the last week or two,' the old lady replied. 'Was it a Wednesday? No, no I don't think it was. It may have been a Thursday or a Friday. I'm sorry, I don't remember exactly what day. My memory isn't what it used to be.'

'Can you tell us why he called on you?' Lance asked.

Miss Seymour hesitated. 'It's rather delicate. May I ask what this is in connection with?'

'We're investigating the circumstances surrounding his tragic accident—'

'What tragic accident?' Miss Seymour asked, all colour draining from her face. 'Your father is well, I hope.'

'No, I'm afraid not, Miss Seymour. He was killed last Friday evening in a motor accident.'

Miss Seymour sat down; she was trembling a little. 'Oh dear, oh dear.' She frowned at the rug, then looked back up at Lance. 'I'm so sorry for your loss. This must be a very difficult time for you. Under the circumstances, I'm happy to help in any way I can.'

Lance told her how their visit to Southampton had come about. Miss Seymour listened carefully, nodding as Lance explained that murder was being considered as a possibility.

'Your father told me that I would receive other callers wanting to know about our meeting,' she said. 'He asked me to keep the details of our conversation confidential. That's why I was hesitant to speak even to you. But since he's no longer with us … Oh dear, oh dear. How awful.'

Lance smiled reassuringly. 'Thank you, Miss Seymour.'

'Your father came here to talk to my brother John,' Miss Seymour said, recovering somewhat.

'Your brother's name is John?' Veronica blurted out.

'Yes, that's right.' said Miss Seymour looking puzzled.

'I see,' Lance said, somehow remaining calm. 'Do you know what he wanted to talk to John about, Miss Seymour?'

'I'm afraid the Baron wasn't very explicit on the matter. I do remember him intimating that something was amiss at his country seat. Something suspicious had happened, quite recently too, I gathered – something that had completely shaken him. He seemed very agitated, and I rather think he was hoping that John would know something to clarify the situation.'

'Did he say what that something was?'

'No, I'm afraid he didn't. He did show me a photograph, dated April 1912, of a group of people and asked me whether I knew who they were. Sadly I wasn't able to help – that is to say, I wasn't able to help with most of them. One of them, though, was the gentleman who'd given John his award just before he died.'

'Award?' Lance asked.

'Yes, for exemplary service.'

Lance cast a knowing look at Veronica, hoping she was thinking what he was thinking: that the photograph his father had shown to Miss Seymour was the one they had found in his safe.

'I showed him the last letter I'd received from John, sent around that time,' Miss Seymour continued. 'This letter.' She tapped the fragments on the table. 'Your father seemed very upset by it. He asked if he could make a copy.'

'Ahhh, so that's how he came to have it,' Veronica said. 'Do you still have the original? As you can see, our dog rather mangled his copy.'

Lance felt a unexpected glow of pleasure at her reference to 'our dog'.

'I'm afraid not,' Miss Seymour said. 'Just after the Baron called I received a visit from two Home Office officials. They requisitioned the letter and left me with a receipt. They asked me not to talk to anyone about the matter, but I don't suppose discussing it with you will do any harm.'

Miss Seymour got up from her chair and moved slowly over to her writing bureau. She folded down the front and took a small envelope from the top drawer. She gave it to Lance who withdrew the enclosed receipt and read it carefully before handing it to Veronica.

Official Receipt from HM Government
Home Office
Received from Miss Florence Seymour one personal letter from
Third Officer John Seymour dated 10th April 1912.
Signed: B de Bretagne
Date: 4th June 1919

'Hmmm,' mused Lance. 'That's very strange. Did they give you any reason why they wanted to take the letter away with them?'

Miss Seymour shook her head slowly. 'Not really. They just said it contravened the Official Secrets Act.'

'The Official Secrets Act?' Lance said, alarmed.

'Yes, that's right. I thought it a bit odd myself. I can't think why they thought it had anything to do with official secrets. As far as I could see it was just one of my brother's typical unremarkable letters home.'

'Can you remember the content, Miss Seymour?' Lance asked anxiously. 'It could be very important.'

'Well' — Florence cocked her head to one side — 'he just said he was taking the opportunity to write to me after his ship had docked in Southampton on her way to New York. He said he was happy that his fellow officers were old friends he'd sailed with many times before and that Edward Smith had been appointed captain on that trip. He said he was looking forward to an uneventful tour of duty and returning home for a short break after the voyage.'

'I see. And what rank was John in the navy, Miss Seymour?' Lance asked.

'Oh no, John wasn't in the navy, Baron Westex. He was an officer on those big passenger ships. He worked for the White Star Line.'

Lance and Veronica exchanged another meaningful glance as Miss Seymour continued.

'They're a really prestigious company with some of the largest and grandest passenger liners in the world. John was always very proud of the fact that he'd served in their fleet. He told me he'd met some of the wealthiest people on the planet aboard those vessels.'

'Do you have any idea what he might have meant when he wrote "I still don't like this ship"?' Lance asked, pointing at a shred of the letter that had not been chewed to destruction by Bob.

'I'm not sure really,' Florence replied. 'It was unusual for John to make such a comment. He'd sailed many times before and I'd never heard him say anything of that kind. Thinking about it I suppose I'd have to say he'd had some kind of deja vu experience.'

'Did he write anything in his letter to give you that notion?' Veronica asked.

'Not explicitly, but he did record an uneasy feeling that he'd sailed on her before.'

'What made him think that?' asked Lance.

'I really don't know. I don't think John could quite put his finger on what it was.' Miss Seymour shook her head.

Just then the door to the drawing room opened and the maid brought in the tea-tray. Putting it down on the table, she bobbed a small curtsey before leaving the room.

Miss Seymour poured the tea and offered Lance and Veronica milk or lemon. 'Would you like a cake or a biscuit?'

Veronica lifted a small butterfly sponge with yellow icing from the cake stand and took a bite. 'Oh, these are lovely cakes,' she said, pushing the rest of it into her mouth.

'Thank you, my dear,' Miss Seymour said. 'Tilly's a bit dour but she does make such good cakes. Please ... have another.'

They both tucked into the display of colourful fairy cakes.

'We went to your old address in Southampton,' Veronica said between mouthfuls. 'Your neighbour Aggie told us you'd moved. She very kindly gave us your new address.'

'Oh Aggie! How is she?'

'She was a bit worried about telling us where you were at first, but she did ask us to pass on her best wishes once she'd made up her mind to help,' Lance said.

'Yes, Aggie's a very careful person. I haven't seen her since I moved here.'

'How long ago was that?' Veronica asked.

'It must be well over six years ago now – just after John died. I couldn't keep up the old place on my own so I decided to move into something a bit smaller, away from all my memories. The last time I saw Aggie was at John's memorial service.'

'That must have been very traumatic for you,' Lance said sympathetically.

'Yes, it was. You see we'd been together all our lives. As brother and sister we looked after each other. His loss left quite a void in my life. Of course, I was quite used to being on my own for short periods because John was often away at sea, but we always had each other to rely on. Now it's just me.' Miss Seymour gave a little sniff. 'He had a very good send-off though. A number of John's old shipmates attended the service.'

Suddenly her face lit up. 'Of course, why didn't I think of it earlier? There'd been rumours amongst the crew that the new ship wasn't safe. He said as much at the memorial.'

'Who did?' Lance asked, perking up again.

'A pleasant young man who attended the memorial,' Miss Seymour replied. 'He said he'd discussed it with John when she docked in Southampton. Quite upset about it, he was. Said he'd tried to persuade John not to sail on with her.'

'What did he say exactly?' Lance asked.

'Well, he said there had been a fire in one of the boiler rooms before she sailed to Southampton, which a lot of the crew thought was causing the ship to list to port. He said most of them got off after she docked in Southampton and refused to sign on again for the onward trip to New York. John wrote as much in this last letter, this one your father took a copy of.'

Lance and Veronica glanced at one another.

'Go on,' Lance said.

'As I remember it came out at the subsequent inquiry that a number of boiler men felt the fire may have caused the steel of the hull to weaken. Is that important?' asked Florence.

'I think it may be,' said Lance. 'Do you remember the man's name?'

'Yes, I think so. I believe it was Peter Hopwood, but I couldn't be absolutely sure about that.'

The name seemed familiar to Lance somehow but he couldn't place it.

'Was he a fellow officer?' Veronica asked.

'As I said, he attended John's memorial service. He may have been a fellow officer but I don't think so somehow – he didn't seem to have the polish. A nice man, I thought – well built, quietly spoken.'

'A steward perhaps?' Veronica said.

Miss Seymour thought hard. 'Oh, old age is such a thief. I really can't remember. I think it more likely he was a crew member from another section of the ship – you know, a deckhand or engineering crew. I was quite surprised at the time that he'd actually taken the trouble to attend the service since I don't believe he lived locally.' Miss Seymour paused. 'I'm afraid I'm feeling rather drained now. If you have any other questions, I'd be grateful if you could leave them for another day. It's all quite difficult, thinking about John again. And it's been a shock to learn of your father's death, Baron Westex.'

'Yes, of course.' Lance stood up. 'Our apologies for upsetting you.'

'May I ask one final question?' Veronica said, getting up. 'What was the name of the ship John was referring to in his letter?'

'Oh, I thought you knew. It was the *Titanic*. John went down on the *Titanic*.'

Lance and Veronica bade farewell to Florence Seymour, thanking her for the information and the courtesy she'd shown them.

On their way back down the hall passage Lance looked for the parlourmaid. He wanted to ask her if she could remember when his father had called.

'I'm afraid Tilly has the rest of the day off,' Miss Seymour said as she walked the pair to the door. 'She visits her family on Sundays.'

Once outside Veronica could contain herself no longer. 'Well I never! This must have been where your father was on the day of his death,' she said excitedly. 'It accounts for his diary entry "JS – CM" ... John Seymour – Combe Martyn.'

Lance frowned. 'Yes, I see what you're saying, Veronica, but father's accident was in Rackenford. That's in completely the opposite direction to Southampton. Why would he be driving through Rackenford to get to Southampton? It just doesn't make any sense. If Father didn't know that John Seymour was dead before his visit, surely he would have written "JS – S" for Southampton. John Seymour never lived in Combe Martyn. Conversely, if he *did* know John had died and that Miss Seymour had subsequently moved to Combe Martyn why didn't he write "FS" for Florence Seymour in his diary? No, it just doesn't fit. I'm not convinced Father was coming here on 6th June. It's a great pity we couldn't have spoken to Tilly.'

'But it's reasonable to assume that Lord Cedrick's death has something to do with *Titanic*, don't you agree?' Veronica said sounding disappointed. 'The picture of the four-funnelled ship you received in the post … it's got to be *Titanic*.'

'We can't be certain of that,' said Lance.

On the journey back to Landacre they each sat deep in thought, evaluating the information they'd uncovered.

Eventually Veronica broke the silence. 'So, where does that leave us then?'

'I'm not sure. Let's go back over what we know.'

'Well, Lord Cedrick visited Florence Seymour, although we're not clear on what day. What did he want to know? Did it have anything to do with *Titanic*'s maiden voyage? If so, what relevance did it have to your father?'

'Yes, and I wonder why HMG requisitioned her brother's last letter on the pretext of "official secrets"? As far as I can tell there was nothing in the original warranting that kind of action.'

'HMG must have thought so, otherwise why go to those extraordinary lengths?' Veronica asked.

'I haven't the foggiest. But it may explain one thing.'

'What's that?'

'Well, ever since I received Father's telegram I've had the strangest feeling I'm being watched. Perhaps it's HMG.'

'Why? What possible reason would they have to watch you? You're as much in the dark as anyone over the tragic events of the last few days.'

'*We* know that, but they don't, do they? Perhaps they think I'm mixed up in the affair and just want to keep an eye on what I'm doing. They may think I can lead them to information of some kind, whatever that may be.'

'I think you're being just a little paranoid. I can't see it myself. It seems so far-fetched.'

'Perhaps you're right,' Lance said, suddenly overcome by a feeling of complete mental exhaustion.

They settled back into a comfortable silence, continuing their long journey back to the West Country.

As they neared Exmoor Veronica said, 'Will you drop me back to my apartment please? It'll be very late when we get back and I have to be up early in the morning for work. I must put in an appearance at the office. I don't want to give them an excuse to get rid of me.'

'Of course. Will I see you tomorrow?'

'I really must do some work for the paper,' Veronica said, 'but I'll continue to search the archives during my breaks. Perhaps you'd like to have supper at my apartment tomorrow and we can have another go at trying to fathom out what's going on.'

'I'd love to. Shall we say seven thirty? We can compare notes when we meet up.'

* * *

It was around nine o'clock that evening when Lance eventually arrived back at Landacre. He was greeted at the main door of the Hall by Treadwell.

'Good evening, m'lord. I trust you had an excellent day.'

'Very good, thank you, Treadwell. Has anything occurred since I've been away?'

'Your aunts, Lady Maud and Dame Lettice, arrived this afternoon, sir. Mrs Pierce has put them in the guest rooms on the first floor to be near your mother.'

'Very good, Treadwell. Anything further?'

'Chief Superintendent Schilling from Scotland Yard called this afternoon, sir. He was most disappointed you were not available. He will return in the morning when he hopes you will find it convenient to meet with him.'

Lance sighed. 'Oh very well.'

'In addition, Reverend Eustace visited this afternoon,' Treadwell continued. 'I gather he also intends to return tomorrow, sir.'

'I see. Thank you,' Lance said gloomily. He had been able to put the practicalities of his father's death to the back of his mind while he was in Southampton with Veronica and now it all felt like too much.

'Will you require anything more this evening, m'lord?'

'Yes, please ask Mrs Hughes to put a plate of something together for supper. I'll have it in my rooms.'

'Very good, sir,' replied Treadwell, retreating towards the kitchens.

Exhausted, Lance ascended the grand staircase and made his way to his suite. Bob jumped up from his bed and greeted his master enthusiastically, his body wriggling from side to side propelled by his wagging tail.

'Hello, young pup,' Lance said, stooping to pat the dog affectionately on his head. 'Have you had a nice day?'

Bentley was placing clean laundry in the tallboy. 'Good evening, m'lord.'

'Good evening, Bentley,' Lance replied, walking over to the bed. He loosened his collar and took off his jacket, discarding them both carelessly on the bedspread. Thankful to be relaxing at last, he sat down in the easy chair next to the bed.

'May I arrange supper for you?' Bentley asked, instinctively going towards Lance to remove his sturdy brown boots.

'It's all right, Bentley. I've already asked Treadwell to organise something for me, thank you. Has Bob been a good boy today?'

'He has certainly missed you, sir,' Bentley replied, fussily attiring Lance in a smoking jacket and slippers.

There was a quiet tap at the door and Treadwell entered carrying a silver tray containing a platter of Mrs Hughes's finest. 'Your supper, sir,' the butler said as he placed the tray on the table next to Lance.

'Thank you, Treadwell,' Lance replied, suddenly feeling a tad overdressed to eat a meal alone in his rooms. He'd have been happy just to sit in his shirt tails, but that was not Bentley's way. As his valet melted away Lance began to unwind with a glass of fine wine and a plate of excellent food, and contemplated his visit to Southampton. Suddenly the door was thrown open and his brother appeared.

'So you're back at last,' Hugo said crossly.

'Good grief, Hugo, you'll give me indigestion bursting in like that! What's all the hullaballoo about?'

'It's Bruce. He's still missing, and Clara and her mother are in such a state about it.'

'Well, I'm not sure what more we can do. You've informed the police. I'm sure they'll contact us when they've something to report.'

'I know. I just feel so helpless. It upsets me to see Clara and her mother so unhappy. I want to do something. Anything.'

Lance thought for a minute. His brother had obviously spent the day building up a head of steam over the matter. How could he alleviate his torment?

'Would it help if we organised a search of the grounds?' Lance asked without enthusiasm. He was pretty sure it wouldn't turn up anything of use.

'Yes, that's it! What a good idea,' Hugo replied with gusto. 'At least it shall make me feel like I'm doing something to help Clara and her mother.'

'All right then,' Lance said. 'I'll get Treadwell to organise the groundsmen to assist with the search tomorrow morning.'

'Thanks, Lance. I knew you'd know the right thing to do,' Hugo said. 'Sorry for pestering you,' he added with a sheepish grin.

'It's all right, old chap. I know you're going through a testing time at the moment. We all are. Try and get some rest tonight and we'll start a search bright and early in the morning.'

CHAPTER 8:
THE SEARCH

Monday June 9th 1919

O N MONDAY MORNING LANCE rose early and had a light breakfast. Sipping a strong cup of coffee in the study afterwards, he'd given instructions to Treadwell to arrange for the groundsmen to assist in a search for Bruce around the estate. Hugo had taken charge, organising the men as they gathered outside the main entrance to the Hall.

Lance was pleased his brother was rising to the responsibility of being a Donaldson-Gilks. Their father would have approved of Hugo's newly found commitment to duty and his surprising display of strong leadership qualities. It was Lance's intention that this search activity should go some way toward helping Hugo regain his natural equilibrium, something that had been conspicuously absent over the previous few days.

As the search party moved away from the Hall out into the extensive grounds, Lance sat on in the study, reviewing the information he and Veronica had gathered the previous day and attempting to piece it all together. Why had the letter from John Seymour caused his father such concern? What was his father doing driving through Rackenford? How were these things connected to *Titanic*?

His train of reasoning was abruptly halted when Treadwell knocked on the door. 'Reverend Eustace is here to see you, m'lord,' he announced.

Frustrated by the disturbance, Lance sat back in his chair, letting out a deep sigh. 'Thank you, Treadwell. Please show him in.'

'Good morning, m'lord,' the Reverend said, striding into the room and taking Lance's proffered hand, encasing it with his other to demonstrate his sincerity. 'How are you coping?'

'Hello, Reverend. Please, just call me Lance. Truth be told it's been pretty hard going, but the Donaldson-Gilks family are made of stern stuff.'

'Quite,' the Reverend said. 'I looked in on your mother yesterday. She's quite extraordinary, a truly formidable lady. Hugo and Tabitha seem to have taken things very hard though.'

'Yes, I think they're both finding it extremely difficult, especially Tabby. She was very close to Father. She was always his "little girl".'

The Reverend nodded sympathetically. 'Your mother has suggested that as you're now the eighth Baron Westex it's your responsibility to take charge of organising your father's funeral. That's why I've called this morning. I was wondering if you'd have time to discuss the matter now.'

Lance winced imperceptibly. Having to talk about his father's funeral made his death so real, and drew a firm line between Lord Cedrick's tenure at Landacre Hall and Lance's. He gave the Reverend a weak smile. 'Of course,' he said.

The vicar began to run through his suggestions for the Order of Service and the etiquette to be observed throughout the process. But Lance found it difficult to concentrate. He nodded here and there in agreement with the Reverend's recommendations, but the clergyman's hypnotic voice droned on and on. By the time he had got deep into the minutiae, Lance was gazing out through the window of the study, his consciousness floating over the beauty of Exmoor in the distance.

'Of course, the family should indicate which hymns will be required during the service and any readings to be included,' the Reverend continued.

With some effort Lance brought himself back into the room. He felt weary. 'I'll discuss the question of hymns and readings with the family and let you know what their preference is.'

'Very good. Have you decided on a date for the funeral?'

'Not yet. The police haven't released Father's body and we've no way of knowing when they will. I'll ask Chief Inspector Quick about that.'

'I'm assuming you'll want your father's remains interred in the family mausoleum here at Landacre.'

'I believe that was his wish.'

'Perhaps it would be possible to go down there now. It would be extremely helpful in planning my address at the service.'

'Of course. I'll ask Treadwell to accompany us with the key.' Lance limped over to the fireplace – his leg was giving him a slight twinge – and rang for the butler.

Treadwell appeared momentarily. 'You rang, m'lord?'

'Yes, Reverend Eustace and I are going down to the mausoleum. Will you kindly bring the key to unlock the door? I'd be grateful if you could accompany us there.'

'Very good, sir.'

The butler disappeared and returned a few moments later with an enormous ornate wrought-iron key. Then the three of them made their way out through the study's patio windows and across the park. It was filled with wild blooms and the occasional grazing deer, and Bob, who went with them, enjoyed himself immensely chasing butterflies and sniffing the hedgerows.

As they approached the lake, the great mausoleum built of Bath stone came into view. Set back from the water, it was an oasis of tranquillity, a perfect final resting place for countless generations of the Donaldson-Gilks family.

They ascended the stone steps and walked along the colonnaded porch flanked by classical Greek columns, which supported the majestic vaulted roof of the building. A great studded door, its black paint peeling from the rusty iron, stood before them, solidly barring entry.

Bob stiffened and the hairs on his neck and back rose. He put his nose to the stone floor and snuffled at the door's base. Issuing an urgent bark, he pawed at the ground near the door, his black claws rasping noisily on the stone.

'Good Lord,' the Reverend said. 'Bob's making quite a fuss. Is that normal for him?'

'No, it is not,' replied Lance. 'What is it, young pup?'

Bob continued to scratch at the floor and whined.

'I think we should open this door quickly, Treadwell,' Lance urged.

The butler placed the large key into the ancient lock and turned it anti-clockwise. The bolt mechanism groaned.

'That's strange, m'lord. It seems the lock has been oiled recently.'

Lance and the Reverend looked at each other in alarm.

'Has anyone been down here in the last few days, Treadwell?' Lance asked.

'Not to my knowledge, sir.'

The door creaked open a little, the bottom rubbing a groove in the stone floor, as it had done for centuries.

'Give it a good push, Treadwell,' said Lance.

'I am, sir. There appears to be something preventing it from opening.'

The three of them pushed but still it resisted all attempts to give way. Finally they put their shoulders to it and the portal yawned wide.

Bob rushed inside, the men following him. Lying on the cold hard stone floor was the body of a man in brown tweeds.

Treadwell, who had some basic medical knowledge, felt for a pulse in the man's neck. After a few moments he shook his head and looked up at Lance.

'Good Lord!' the Reverend exclaimed, bending over the corpse and making the sign of the cross.

'We shouldn't touch anything,' Lance said, still feeling scorched by Inspector Quick's reprimand for disturbing evidence. 'Chief Superintendent Schilling will be here directly. We'll inform him immediately he arrives.' He peered around to see if he could detect any clues that might identify the body or suggest how it came to be there.

'Do you recognise him?' the Reverend asked, a tremor in his voice.

Reluctantly, Lance took a closer look at the man. 'His face is covered in blood – he's obviously taken a number of savage blows to the head – but my best guess is that we've just located the missing Bruce Hamilton.'

Reverend Eustace knelt down beside the corpse and began whispering a short prayer while Lance and Treadwell stood in respectful silence.

CHAPTER 9:
A PLAN IS HATCHED

L ANCE AND REVEREND EUSTACE hurried back to the Hall, leaving Treadwell to stand guard over the body with Bob. They arrived just as Mrs Pierce was supervising luncheon preparations in the dining room and she stepped out into the hallway to see what all the hubbub was about.

'Is everything all right, Master Lance?'

'I'm afraid everything is NOT all right, Mrs Pierce,' Lance replied, leaning heavily against the hallstand for support. 'Has Chief Superintendent Schilling arrived yet?'

'He arrived twenty minutes ago, sir. Treadwell is nowhere to be found, so Evans put him in the library with Chief Inspector Quick and Sergeant Bolt.'

'Thank goodness,' Lance said, casting a relieved glance at the Reverend.

The two men collected themselves and hurried past Mrs Pierce and into the library. There, they outlined their discovery and the three policemen hastened down to the mausoleum to observe the crime scene at first-hand, followed by Lance and the Reverend.

Swiftly assuming authority, Chief Superintendent Schilling issued a number of brisk orders and it wasn't long before the weighty cogs of the official police inquiry began to grind into action.

Minutes later Hugo came charging into the building, his gaze instantly falling on the lifeless body lying on the stone floor. Lance put a brotherly arm out to prevent him from coming any further.

'I've just heard ... from some of the grounds staff ... a body's been found,' Hugo said, gulping huge lungfuls of air.

'Yes, that's right,' Lance replied, attempting to walk his brother away from the scene and spare him unnecessary pain.

'Let me see,' wailed Hugo frantically. 'Is it Bruce?'

'It's not immediately apparent who it is because of the injuries.'

'What injuries? Let me see. Let me see, Lance. Please,' his brother cried, struggling to free himself.

Lance stood aside.

Hugo went slowly towards the body, then stood in silence for a minute or two. He swallowed hard and said softly, 'He's the same size and weight as Bruce. He has the same colour of hair.'

'I must ask everyone to leave the crime scene,' snapped Chief Superintendent Schilling with brusque efficiency.

Inspector Quick and Sergeant Bolt began to usher the gathering out through the mausoleum door.

'Please ask everyone to remain on the estate for the time being,' barked the Superintendent. 'We shall want to interview them all.'

The Reverend, Treadwell, Lance and Hugo made their way slowly back to the house, Hugo seeming to have lost all bodily strength and finding it difficult to walk.

'Let Treadwell help you,' Lance said.

'It's okay, Lance. I'll be all right in a minute. I just need to catch my breath.'

Back at the Hall a melee of staff had gathered on the gravel drive outside the front portico. Word had obviously got around that a body had been discovered in the grounds and the news had not unnaturally spooked the staff.

'Be it right, sir, that Bruce Hamilton's body's bin found?' Digweed asked anxiously.

'A body has been found,' Lance replied calmly, 'but identification hasn't been made yet.' A murmur rippled through the staff. 'The police will want to interview you all,' Lance continued. 'Please make your way around to the staff quarters and I'll ask Mrs Pierce to provide good strong cups of tea while you're waiting.'

Everyone turned to walk around to the back of the Hall, a low hum of conversation accompanying them.

Lance, Hugo and the Reverend went in and were met by Tabitha, a look of fretful concern clouding her face.

'What's happening, Lance?' she asked.

'Let's get everyone into the drawing room and I'll explain everything,' Lance said, adopting the familiar commanding tone that he'd been accustomed to using onboard the *Panther*.

A few minutes later Lady Cynthia, Lady Maud, Dame Lettice, Tabitha, Hugo, Clara, Ruth Hamilton and the Reverend were all in the drawing room, the atmosphere thick with dread.

Lance apprised the assembly of the morning's events and explained what action Chief Superintendent Schilling was taking. A stunned silence filled the room.

'Is it Bruce?' Clara asked, her reedy voice quavering.

'It's too early to say,' Lance replied, 'but I'm afraid we must be prepared for the worst.'

Ruth looked crushed. 'So much loss over the last few years,' she half whispered, her vitality and strength visibly evaporating. 'It's just too, too hard to bear.'

Clara put a comforting arm around her mother's shoulders. 'We'll be in our rooms if Superintendent Schilling requires us,' she said, gently assisting her mother out through the drawing-room door.

The remainder of the day was a lengthy one for everyone at Landacre. The police diligently carried out their duties under the watchful eye of the Superintendent. Once the mausoleum was cordoned off, an immediate search of the area commenced, proficiently carried out by an influx of additional constables from Exeter Police Station. As the pace of the inquiry gathered momentum, Superintendent Schilling embarked on a series of interviews with members of the family and household staff.

* * *

After what ranked as one of the most stressful and tedious afternoons in Lance's recent memory, it was with some relief that around seven thirty he entered Deacon Heights in Exeter.

Nodding to the concierge, he made his way up the staircase as enthusiastically as he could with a bad leg and a cane until he was standing outside Apartment 2b. He was eager to see Veronica and looking forward to spending some time with her, just the two of them. He drew himself up, straightened his tie and knocked.

When Veronica opened the door, Lance stood for a moment breathing in the soft delicate fragrance of her perfume before stepping inside and following her along the wide hallway towards the drawing room. As he did so he couldn't help appreciating her shapely figure.

'Please do go in,' Veronica said, indicating the door at the end through which a large room with a high ornate plaster ceiling beckoned.

Stepping through the doorway, Lance found himself in a bright Art Nouveau-styled room overlooking the Cathedral Green, the décor a feminine palette of muted violet and cornsilk.

'What an exquisite room this is!'

'Yes, I like it too.'

At the sound of a man's voice, Lance twisted around, catching in the reflection of the mirror hanging above the fireplace the figure of a young man reclining casually on one of the sofas. He faced the man fully, who proved to be in his early thirties and had unusually dark eyes and long floppy hair.

'This is David Price,' Veronica said airily. 'He's a photographer at the *Chronicle*.'

David stood up and shook hands with Lance. 'Good evening.'

'Good evening,' Lance replied, trying to conceal his bitter disappointment at finding a third person, and a man at that, present.

'David's been helping me with the laborious task of sifting through the mountain of archives,' Veronica said. 'I thought it would be helpful if he came to supper this evening so we could discuss our findings.'

'Fine,' said Lance offhandedly, dropping down awkwardly into one of the easy chairs opposite David.

Veronica bustled around making drinks for her guests. 'Well ... you go first,' she said after she had handed Lance a sherry. 'I'm dying to know your news.'

Lance, who was part way through taking a sip from his drink, stifled a sardonic laugh. 'Your choice of words is quite prophetic in the circumstances, Veronica. I think you should prepare yourself for a shock. We found the "missing" Bruce Hamilton at Landacre this morning – at least we assume it's him – and he wasn't alive,' Lance said grimly.

'You mean he was dead!' exclaimed Veronica.

'Not alive usually means dead,' Lance said with a smile.

David let out a long whistle. 'Who'd have thought it? How was he found?'

Lance explained how the events of the day had unfolded, right up to the police interviews. 'There was one strange thing,' he said with a frown. 'After my interview with Superintendent Schilling he asked me to sit in on the rest of the interrogations.'

'That *is* strange,' Veronica said. 'I'm sure it's not usual.'

'That's what I thought, but I went along with it anyway.' Lance shrugged.

'Did you learn anything that would be helpful?' David asked.

'It's difficult to tell at the moment. It probably won't become clear what's important and what's not until something else happens. And of course it's sometimes what's left *unsaid* that matters.'

'Yes, that's quite true,' mused Veronica.

'Well, what's your news?' Lance asked.

'Oh, we spent considerable time sifting through the archives at the paper,' replied Veronica. 'You wouldn't believe the number of files they keep.'

'Yes, and they were all thick with mould. I shouldn't think anyone's been down in the vault for years,' David chipped in. 'Not good for my asthma at all.'

Veronica ushered the two men into the dining room where they began to eat a small supper she'd carelessly thrown together earlier in the evening. Cooking didn't seem to be her strong suit, Lance noted as he put a forkful of limp lettuce into his mouth.

'Did you find anything interesting in the files?' he asked, washing the tasteless meal down with an equally indifferent wine.

'Well,' David said, 'there was a copy of the photograph of the four-funnelled ship you received in the post and luckily the photographer's name was printed on the back.'

'Gracious! That was fortunate!' Lance exclaimed. 'What was the name? We should contact them shouldn't we? Perhaps they can throw some light on the situation.'

'His name is Matthew Lock, and we've already contacted him,' Veronica said triumphantly. 'He was a colleague of David's when they worked together on the *Southampton Messenger* a few years ago. We telephoned him from the *Chronicle*'s office and you'll never guess what he said?'

Lance shook his head. 'What?'

'He said he took the picture on the morning of 10th April 1912 at Southampton docks just before she sailed,' Veronica replied.

'Before who sailed?'

'The *Titanic*!' David said jubilantly.

'So you were right then, Veronica – the photograph is of *Titanic*,' Lance said quietly. 'And she was just about to set sail on her fateful maiden voyage.'

'Yes, but there's more,' Veronica said. She looked like she was about to burst.

'Yes,' David added, 'Matt remembers there was a terrible scene on the dock that morning.'

'Really?'

'Apparently, one of the firemen sailing with her from Belfast was down by the ship's gangplank attempting to persuade the crew *not* to sail on to New York with her,' David continued. 'He was rambling on about a serious fire that was causing some of the boiler room's bulkheads to buckle. It seems he made quite a fuss until he was escorted away by some of the shipping company's security staff.'

'Does your friend Matt remember the fireman's name?' asked Lance.

'No, I'm afraid not – just that he was one of the firemen who had sailed with *Titanic* from Belfast and under no circumstances was he willing to sail on to New York with her while the fire was still raging,' David replied.

'That's a pity,' Lance said. 'It would be a good idea to talk to him if we could find out who he was.'

'Surely the shipping company in Southampton would have his records,' interjected Veronica, her eyes shining with intrigue. 'I could visit their offices on the pretext of doing a piece for the *Chronicle*. David could come with me to take a few pictures and add some authenticity to the ruse.'

'I'm not sure that's a good idea,' Lance snapped, surprised to discover that he didn't like the thought of Veronica being with David for a whole day. 'How would you find out this particular fireman's name? You can't just walk into the shipping office and simply ask the manager?'

'Why not?' asked Veronica. 'I'm a reporter after all.'

Lance thought for a minute or two, unable to find a suitable response. 'I suppose you're right – going undercover as a reporter is quite a clever double deception, but you'll have to approach the question in an adroit way if you're to obtain an answer.'

'Oh, I'm more than capable of extracting the information we require,' Veronica said, smiling in her most beguiling manner.

Lance now found that he didn't like the thought of Veronica schmoozing a faceless office manager either, but what could he say. He felt sure she wouldn't appreciate his views on the matter.

It was agreed then. Veronica and David would travel down to Southampton the next day to interview the shipping office manager and learn the name of the fireman who had caused such a scene on the docks before *Titanic* sailed.

'It's getting late,' David said, looking over at Veronica. 'I'd better go, Ronnie. We've got an early start in the morning. I'll drop by and pick you up about seven thirty, okay?'

'Yes, that's fine, David. I'll be ready.'

'Thanks for a lovely evening,' he said as he got up from the dining table.

He walked over to Lance, who by that time had also stood up, and shook him firmly by the hand.

'Goodnight, Lance,' David said cordially. 'We'll get together again when we return to see if we can progress matters.'

Lance sauntered into the drawing room while Veronica accompanied David to the apartment door. From his position in one of the easy chairs Lance could see David putting on his overcoat and hat. Just before Veronica opened the front door, David bent down and kissed her gently on the cheek.

A jolt of electricity shot through Lance's body. It took him by surprise, but after a moment's thought he had to admit that he was jealous. He hadn't even been conscious of being attracted to her. There had been so much going on since they had met. He'd had other things on his mind.

'Would you like a nightcap?' Veronica asked when she returned to the drawing room.

'I'll have a whisky, thanks.'

While she poured the drinks Lance asked casually, 'How long have you known David?'

'David?' She handed Lance his drink. 'Oh, I've known him for a number of years – ever since I started at the *Chronicle*. He's always been terribly kind and helpful.'

I bet he has, thought Lance. 'He seems very nice,' he said.

'Yes, he is, and he's an excellent photographer – always gets the right shot. He does very good portraits too, if you know anyone who wants their picture taken.'

'I'll bear that in mind,' Lance said without feeling.

On his drive back to Landacre that night his brain whirred. Trying to mull over the information about the *Titanic* and the events of that day at the Hall was futile. Uncomfortable thoughts of Veronica and her close relationship with David constantly bombarded him, along with the surprising discovery that he seemed to be rather taken with her himself. Driving back across Exmoor, pangs of jealousy tinged with old familiar feelings of despair and hopelessness coursed uncontrollably through his mind.

CHAPTER 10:
THE APOTHECARY

Tuesday June 10th 1919

THE NEXT MORNING LANCE woke with a start. He
lay in his bed, oblivious of time, trying to grasp
onto the last vestiges of a dream floating though
his unconscious and overwhelmed by a powerful feeling
of unease. Was his head playing tricks on him or had he
been having one of his terrible nightmares? He tried in
vain to recall the disturbing images but it was useless. Was
it the terrible events of the last few days that caused this
disquiet or was it the unexpected feelings he seemed to
have developed for Veronica? He wasn't sure what troubled
him more: the fact that he had feelings for Veronica Barnes
at all, or that those newly discovered feelings might be
nipped in the bud by the attentions of another admirer.

Gradually Lance became aware of a presence beside his
bed. It was Bentley holding a silver salver with his morning
cup of Earl Grey.

'Good morning, m'lord. I trust you slept well?'

'I'm not sure,' Lance responded. 'I think I may have
had a bad dream.'

Without changing the timbre of his voice Bentley replied, 'I'm sorry to hear that, sir. The weather is quite clement this morning. I have laid out your flannel suit.'

Lance washed, dressed and went down to breakfast, Bob skittering down the stairs behind him. Hugo and Clara were sitting at the dining-room table deep in earnest conversation and they stopped abruptly when Lance came in.

'Good morning, Hugo, Clara,' he called out before moving to the dresser where he helped himself to some bacon and eggs.

'Morning,' replied Hugo and Clara in unison. They looked haggard and hollow-eyed.

'How's Ruth?' Lance asked, settling down at the table and snapping a crisply pressed white damask napkin across his legs.

'She seems to be coping well enough, considering,' Clara said. 'I think she'll be getting up later.'

'Damn it all, Lance!' thundered Hugo. 'When will this stop? What's it all about?'

Lance looked up at Hugo, his face full of reproach at his brother's outburst in front of Clara. That was not the Donaldson-Gilks way.

Hugo shot a glance at his fiancée. 'Sorry Clara,' he mumbled.

Lance was worried about Hugo. He was not handling recent events well at all. His usual bonhomie had vanished and seemed to have been replaced by a short fuse; he was very much on edge.

'Superintendent Schilling has matters well in hand,' Lance said in an attempt to pacify him.

'I'm not sure that I agree with you there,' Hugo replied curtly. 'He hasn't given us any indication that they're making significant progress with their investigation. And when are they going to release Father's body? We'll be having two funerals and a wedding on the same day at this rate!'

'I think we should leave things to the experts,' Lance replied calmly. 'I'm sure they know their business better than we do.'

Earlier, while in bed sipping his tea and looking for a way to distract himself from thoughts of Veronica and David on their long journey to Southampton, Lance had decided he would walk the two miles from the Hall to the apothecary's premises in the village with the aim of engaging Jacob Snyder in conversation. He might be able to garner some useful information regarding Snyder's connection with the Memorial Committee. The walk would also give him a chance to test his injured leg.

After breakfast Bob stood in the vestibule wagging his tail energetically, his body wiggling excitedly from side to side.

'Come along, young pup,' Lance said. 'Let's you and I walk into Coombe End.'

Grabbing his walking cane and Bob's lead from the hall stand, Lance opened the main doors and the two of them set off down the long drive toward the village, nestled in a narrow gorge at the foot of the moor.

It was a glorious morning; the sun was already high in a clear blue sky and a gentle balmy breeze ruffled the uncut grass and wild flowers, producing a subtle hypnotic rustle. Bob sauntered along nearby, stopping occasionally to investigate an interesting smell or some wildlife moving in the undergrowth, but never losing sight of his master. His mind still in turmoil, Lance unconsciously soaked up the environment around him – the call of the songbirds, the clattering of jackdaws high in the trees, the gentle hum of bees unhurriedly gathering nectar while insects darted from bloom to bloom. The full glory of the moor gradually seeped into his soul and as he walked on, he detected a lift in his mood.

After a while his leg became painful and he stopped for a minute to rub his thigh. Damn this leg, he thought, will it never get better? The ache eased somewhat but as he resumed his stroll he found his pronounced limp had returned. Eventually he removed his jacket, draping it casually over his shoulder, and ambled into the village feeling uplifted and almost carefree.

Coombe End, a small picturesque village mentioned in the Domesday Book, had its fair share of interesting establishments. In addition to the apothecary, there was a blacksmith's forge, a butcher's, a post office, the Blue Boar Inn, a draper's, a saddlery, a bakery, a greengrocer's, and a hardware store, as well as dentist's and a doctor's. At the far end of the village, sitting within a well-kept graveyard, was the ancient church of St Peter, originally built in the early twelfth century. The rectory and village hall stood either side of the church. Opposite the rectory was the primary school where the local children learned their ABCs under the tutelage of Miss Helena Fairfax.

'Morning, Ned,' Lance shouted over as he passed the blacksmith's workshop where Ned Cooper was beating out horseshoes for the bay mare that stood tethered up at the railing.

'Mor'nin, m'lord,' replied the blacksmith, looking up briefly without interrupting his work.

Lance walked on down the lane towards the main square where on the third Thursday of each month the parish held its livestock and produce market. The apothecary overlooked the square. A diminutive red sign in the window read 'Open', and Lance went up the steps and opened the door. A tiny bell tinkled, announcing his presence.

The interior of the shop was dimly lit and sparsely furnished; a faint odour of herbs and medicines infused the small room. A wooden counter ran the length of the pine floor in front of a large Welsh dresser that displayed numerous glass jars, all carefully labelled.

Jacob Snyder was already serving a customer, Mr Bert Beamish, landlord of the Blue Boar, explaining how to use the contents of a small white folded paper he'd just handed him.

'Just empty the contents into a glass of water before bedtime, Mr Beamish, and drink it all down in one go,' Jacob was saying. 'I'm sure it will have the desired effect.'

Mr Beamish thanked Jacob and turned to leave.

'Good morning, m'lord,' the landlord said, tipping his hat as he passed Lance.

'Good morning, Mr Beamish,' Lance replied cordially, watching him leave.

Jacob Snyder was a stout man in his mid-fifties with a sweaty sallow complexion and wispy red hair combed over his balding crown from the left side of his head. His rheumy eyes looked out eagerly from behind horn-rimmed glasses perched precariously on his wide purple nose.

'Good morning, m'lord,' Jacob said, rubbing his hands together. 'How may I help you this morning?'

'I was wondering if you had anything for a headache.'

'Certainly. Is it for yourself?'

'No, it's for my mother, Lady Cynthia.'

'Of course,' Jacob replied, nodding. 'We heard your sad news. May I, on behalf of the Parish Council, offer our condolences to you and your family on the death of Lord Cedrick.'

'Thank you, Jacob. Your kind words are much appreciated. I shall pass them on to my family. I must say it has been a dreadful business, especially for Mother.'

'Quite so, quite so,' the apothecary said as he busied himself behind the counter mixing up a small quantity of white powder in his pestle and mortar and tipping it into six individual white papers.

'Have the funeral arrangements been confirmed, m'lord?' he asked as he folded the papers. 'I know a number of prominent figures from the village would wish to attend.'

'I'll ask the rector to let the village know when the funeral is to take place. The police have yet to release Father's body.'

'Oh,' the apothecary said, stopping what he was doing. 'That's a bit unusual isn't it? Why are the police delaying?'

'It seems there may be special circumstances surrounding Lord Cedrick's death,' Lance replied, studying Jacob's face to see if there was any reaction to this news. For a moment Lance thought he saw a flicker of anguish flash across the apothecary's normally expressionless face.

'Really?' Jacob replied, his eyes like saucers behind the lens of his glasses.

'Yes, it seems there may have been "irregularities". I understand the police are looking into all Father's most recent undertakings,' Lance said. 'I think they're particularly interested in the Memorial Committee,' he added, hoping it would rattle Jacob into confiding something that might be useful.

'Why should they be interested in that?' Jacob asked indignantly. 'I'm a member of the committee and I can assure you that to my knowledge nothing "irregular" has taken place!'

'I'm afraid I couldn't tell you what their motives are. All I know is they've taken a particular interest in some of the paperwork in Lord Cedrick's safe and have had copies made of some of the documents.'

'I see,' Jacob said. 'Landacre certainly has had a number of troubling incidents recently. There was a terrible din yesterday morning when a mayhem of police cars sped through the village on their way up to the Hall, their bells ringing to kingdom come. Mrs Procter at the post office heard that a body's been found on the estate.'

So Jacob was on a fishing expedition of his own, Lance thought. That was one of the main drawbacks of living in such a small community – everyone knew everyone else's business. There was nothing they enjoyed better than a good gossip over a pint of ale at the Blue Boar.

'I believe there was some kind of disturbance yesterday,' Lance said as coolly as he could. 'Alas, the matter is in the hands of the police who've asked the family not to discuss the affair for the time being.'

'I see, I see,' Jacob said.

'I presume that since I'm now the eighth Baron Westex it will fall to me to step into Father's shoes on the Memorial Committee,' Lance said, attempting to bring the conversation back to the subject.

Jacob made no reply but continued preparing the headache powders.

Lance pressed on. 'In the circumstances I suppose I should know what the main purpose of the committee is.'

'Oh, I thought everyone in the parish was aware of the project,' Jacob said.

'Sorry, not me. I've been away at sea for some time, and I've been living in London since I got back,' Lance said. 'I'd be grateful if you could fill me in.'

'Well … we're raising money to erect a memorial to all our brave lads lost in the last great conflict. Lord Cedrick and other prominent local businessmen wanted to honour their sacrifice with something appropriate that would last for centuries to come. We're going to have it placed in the village square where it can be seen on a daily basis,' Jacob explained.

'Oh, I see,' Lance replied, nodding appreciatively. 'And Father's contribution to the committee was …?'

'Lord Cedrick was the chairman. He was arranging for a drawing and written details of the proposed memorial to be produced. You know the kind of thing – what it will look like, what type of materials are to be used, the cost and time it will take to erect and so on. These matters were to be discussed and agreed at our next meeting before the work was commissioned.'

'The design and cost haven't been agreed then?'

'Not yet. Lord Cedrick was still in discussion with the stonemason, old Bill Parks over at Stapleford, about that. A committee meeting has been scheduled to take place at the end of the week to confirm all the details. A figure of one hundred pounds has been mentioned, but we don't have a definitive sum yet.'

'But I understand the committee has begun to raise the money needed for such a project.'

'Well … yes,' Jacob said hesitantly. 'We are some little way towards our target. The people of the parish have organised a few local events.'

'Who's the treasurer for the committee?'

'Well, I suppose that would be me since I deposit the money at the bank and enter the donations in the ledger.'

'Oh, then I'm sure the scheme is in good hands,' Lance replied, giving him a polite smile. 'Incidentally, what day will the committee meeting be on? I plan to attend in lieu of my father.'

'We had planned to go ahead on Friday evening. We usually meet at the village hall around seven thirty,' Jacob said, a little taken aback. 'Though in the circumstances I thought … that is to say, the committee thought the venture should be put on hold for the time being.'

'I'm sure there'll be no need for that,' Lance replied swiftly. 'Please inform the other members of the committee that they may expect me in attendance on Friday evening.

I'll speak to Bill Parks before the meeting so I can update them on the current status of the scheme.'

'Very good, m'lord,' Jacob replied, his watery eyes blinking rapidly.

Lance felt strangely satisfied to see that Jacob was rather discombobulated by this turn of events. 'You might also want to warn the other members of the committee that they will be receiving an official visit from the police. I do hope they'll be able to give them their full co-operation.'

'Thank you, m'lord. I'll do that,' Jacob replied, handing Lance a small cardboard box containing the headache papers. 'Please instruct Lady Cynthia to take the contents of one paper diluted in a glass of water when the need arises.'

'Thank you, Jacob,' Lance said. 'I'd be obliged if you would put that on the Hall's account.'

'Certainly, m'lord. Will there be anything else?'

'No, I think that's all for now.'

'Then I'll bid you good morning, m'lord.'

'Good morning, Jacob, and please remember me to your good lady wife,' Lance said, turning swiftly on his heels and leaving the shop.

Back in the bright sunshine again, Lance untied Bob's lead from the railings and gave the patient dog a pat on the head.

'Well, Bob, that was rather interesting,' Lance said as they sauntered off. 'Let's pop down to St Peter's and see the rector. I want to talk to him about the Memorial Committee.'

They walked down the main thoroughfare and crossed the lane that ran parallel to the church. As they went up the path to the lychgate, Lance suddenly shivered, despite the rising temperature, and, turning around quickly, caught the apothecary watching him intently from the front window of his business.

CHAPTER 11:
AN ECCLESIASTICAL MEETING

L ANCE AND BOB WALKED through the churchyard, where a plethora of ancient gravestones stood in silent remembrance, and made their way along the winding gravel path to the south entrance of the church. Lance lifted the latch of the heavy wooden studded door and let himself in.

The church was small by town standards but it was quite grand for a village. It had rows of plain oak pews facing a raised, carved stone pulpit from where Reverend Eustace regaled his congregation with his interminable pious sermons. Behind the dais was a small wooden organ, donated to the church several years earlier by an adjoining parish, and the choir stalls. An altar, covered with a cloth of red and gold, displayed a large brass cross, two brass candlesticks and a colourful arrangement of flowers recently left by the ladies of the WI.

The aroma of bygone centuries filled Lance's nostrils, almost overwhelming him. It imbued a sense of peace and veneration, a feeling further enhanced by shafts of sunlight streaming through the exquisite stained-glass window set high in the east wall, casting the entire church in an otherworldly multicoloured glow. He walked soundlessly down the nave past numerous wall-mounted plaques dedicated to his ancestors and other noteworthy villagers towards the apse where Reverend Eustace was kneeling in prayer. Lance stood respectfully for a few minutes, giving the clergyman time to complete his devotions before coughing discreetly.

The vicar looked round. 'Oh, hello Lance, what a pleasant surprise,' he said, his voice reverberating high in the vaulted ceiling. He put his hand on the altar rail to help himself up.

'Hello, Reverend. I've just been into the village for some headache powders for Mother and thought I'd drop by for a quick word about the Memorial Committee.'

'Oh!' the Reverend replied, mildly surprised. 'What about it?'

'When we opened Father's safe we found an envelope containing some details – you know the type of thing, financial accounts, a list of names.'

The Reverend nodded. 'Lord Cedrick was the chairman of the committee, Lance. It wouldn't be unusual for him to have paperwork of that kind in his keeping.'

'Your name was on the list, together with George Bagshott and Jacob Snyder.'

'Yes, that's right. We're the nominated officials.'

'Father had made a series of entries in his desk diary. We think they may refer to meetings he had with you about the committee. Did he say anything to you prior to his death which in retrospect you think could have had a bearing on his accident?'

'It's strange you should mention that,' the Reverend replied. 'I've been wrestling with my conscience about an issue Lord Cedrick raised.'

'So he *did* have some fears then.'

The Reverend frowned. 'It's quite a difficult situation. I think your father thought there might be some jiggery-pokery going on regarding the fundraising for the memorial. Not that he had any concrete proof, you understand. He just felt that something wasn't quite right.'

'Did he say as much?'

'That's what our meetings were about. He was extremely worried by the lack of financial information being provided by Jacob Snyder, the treasurer. He wanted to ask my opinion about whether he should publicly raise the issue at the next committee meeting.'

'And what did you advise?'

'I suggested he obtain some evidence of wrongdoing before going public and I've been worried ever since that he may have stumbled upon something that led to his accident. I tell you, Lance, it's been weighing heavily upon my mind, and I'm glad, finally, to be able to talk to someone about it.'

'Tell me about the committee, Reverend.'

'What do you want to know?'

'When it was formed and who's on it would be a good start.'

The Reverend took a deep breath and let it out in a loud sigh. 'Well … it was formed at the beginning of the year after a number of people in the village felt it right and proper that we did something to memorialise all the local lads who'd lost their lives in the fourteen-eighteen war. A public meeting was held and Lord Cedrick was elected chairman of a newly formed committee to establish the feasibility of the task. I was elected secretary, Jacob Snyder, treasurer and George Bagshott, committee fundraiser.'

Lance nodded.

'A number of others were elected but not given specific roles. They were Helena Fairfax, the school teacher, Ned Cooper, the blacksmith, Amelia Procter, our post mistress, Bert Beamish, landlord of the Blue Boar Inn, and Edna Sutton, the chairwoman of the Women's Institute.'

'I see,' said Lance. 'And what did Father think was going on?'

'It all started about six weeks ago. A second public meeting was held where members of the parish were invited to learn of our progress. We were expecting to have a full report on the finances from Jacob, since countless fundraising activities had already taken place over the preceding months and the committee wanted to know how much money had been raised so far.'

'Sounds perfectly reasonable to me.'

'That's just it, Lance. Jacob didn't produce any proper accounts, or even an official bank statement. Nothing! As he spoke, he referred to a sheet of paper with a few vague handwritten entries scrawled on it. But honestly, it looked as though it had been torn from an old exercise book. Anyway, despite being pressed to do so, he was unable to give any detailed information about how much had been raised at each event, what expenses had been incurred or how much had been banked. He was extremely evasive about the amount of money raised. He merely said it was in the region of ten pounds, give or take a few shillings. His explanation was littered with financial jargon and misdirection. Nearly everyone at the meeting felt uneasy about his assurances. The villagers considered him arrogant and disdainful, deliberately trying to bewilder simple country folk with figures.'

'Gosh,' said Lance. 'Was that what triggered Father's interest then?'

'Partly, but not only that. After the meeting the widow Bird approached Lord Cedrick and asked to speak to him confidentially. She explained that the figure of ten pounds, which Jacob insisted was the amount raised by the committee so far, simply couldn't be right.'

'What gave Mrs Bird that idea?'

'Because she had made a donation to the fund not four weeks earlier of exactly that amount. Since then there had been at least six fundraising events held in the village. Mrs Bird wondered why Jacob was adamant that no more than ten pounds had been raised to date.'

Lance scratched his head. 'On the face of it, it does seem rather strange, especially since he must recall Mrs Bird's donation. Jacob seems to be implying that all the other fundraising activities haven't raised a penny.'

'That's what your father thought. We discussed the matter at several private meetings and decided to press Jacob on the matter. He was asked on a number of occasions to produce the financial information but always had a reason for being unable to do so.'

'What were his explanations?'

'Oh, they were all pretty weak. On the first occasion he said his elderly mother was ill and he had to visit her. The second time he couldn't attend the scheduled meeting at the last minute and sent Edna Sutton to offer his apologies and explain that a tenant of his had a problem. On the third and last occasion he complained of illness and sent his wife Sylvia along. Of course, she couldn't answer for him. Lord Cedrick lost patience with his continued evasion and decided to approach the bank in Exeter, where the account is held, to discuss the matter with the manager.'

'And did he?'

'He made an appointment, but sadly fate had other plans before he was able to report back, so I don't know the outcome.'

'I see,' Lance said. 'What do you think has happened to the money, Reverend?'

'Well, without any proof it's difficult to make any definite accusations,' he responded guardedly. 'Although ...'

'Yes?'

'There have been rumblings in the village,' the Reverend whispered. Glancing around the church to assure himself they weren't being overheard, he continued, 'I know as a man of the cloth I shouldn't repeat gossip, but as you're a family friend and out of respect for your father, the word is ... Jacob has a problem with money.'

'Oh! What sort of problem? It's not another woman is it?'

The Reverend laughed. 'I don't think it's anything like that. Let's just say I think he does a lot of business with the turf accountant over at Haldon Hill Racecourse.'

Lance let out a low whistle. 'So the thinking is he's dipping into the Memorial Fund to finance a gambling habit then.'

'That's about the size of it, although at the moment we've no actual evidence. Of course, there are those on the committee who think Jacob is an absolute paragon of virtue and hang on his every word as some kind of "golden droplet of wisdom".' The Reverend smiled.

'Who thinks that?'

'I'm afraid Edna Sutton rather makes a laughing stock of herself when she's in his company.'

'Edna Sutton!' Lance pictured the dumpy middle-aged woman with buck teeth and jam-jar bottom glasses and shook his head.

'Yes, it is rather comical, I know,' the Reverend replied. 'But there you are. I've seen it for myself at the committee meetings. She has a certain way of looking at him – you know, with large doe eyes. It's as though he's cast some kind of spell over her, and she makes a point of agreeing with everything he utters.'

'Do you think Jacob returns her affections?'

'No, not as far as I know. He doesn't have an eye for the ladies. He's not the attentive sort unless they can assist him with his social climbing. No, Edna Sutton wouldn't even register with him. She comes from a very poor family in the next valley and is married to a simple hill farmer without any social graces. I suspect poor old Edna has been mesmerised by Jacob's perceived standing in the village and is just making a silly spectacle of herself. He's no oil painting himself, but they do say status is a powerful aphrodisiac.'

'Well, I haven't noticed its effects,' Lance said wryly, thinking for a moment about Veronica and his failure to make an impression on her despite being heir to Landacre. 'I understand the next committee meeting is scheduled to take place this Friday evening. I've told Jacob to inform the members to expect me as Lord Cedrick's representative.'

'That's sure to put the cat amongst the pigeons. What did he have to say about that?'

'He showed no obvious sign that it perturbed him, but I rather formed the impression that he was *very* concerned.'

'What do you plan to do?'

'I'm going to see the bank and old Bill Parks to discuss the matter before Friday evening. With any luck I'll get some useful information from those two sources. If Father did know that Jacob had been helping himself to the committee's funds, I think that would give Jacob a very good motive to silence him, don't you?'

'Yes, I can see it would make sense. But how does that relate to the discovery of Bruce Hamilton's body at Landacre? I don't see any connection there.'

Just then a sound came from the south end of the church. Bob looked up from where he'd been lying and growled quietly.

'What's up, lad?' Lance asked.

The dog got to his feet and raced to the south door. The Reverend and Lance dashed after him and pulled the door wide open but there was nothing to see; all they heard was the sound of gravel being crushed heavily under foot as someone hurried away down the path.

'It seems we've been entertaining an eavesdropper,' Lance muttered.

CHAPTER 12:
TEA AND CAKE

LANCE TOOK HIS LEAVE of Reverend Eustace and walked slowly back to Landacre with Bob, the long arduous trek up the hill out of the village taking its toll. That was probably a bit too far to walk in one morning, Lance thought. As he limped through the front door of the Hall, Treadwell approached from the kitchen quarters.

'Good afternoon, m'lord. Lady Cynthia has asked if you would join her for tea in the conservatory when you return, sir.'

Exhausted, Lance put his walking cane into the hall stand and made his way unenthusiastically to the conservatory, Bob trotting along behind.

Sitting around a low rattan table laid out with dainty morsels and surrounded by numerous hot house plants were Lady Cynthia, her sisters Lady Maud and Dame Lettice, and Tabitha.

'Oh, there you are!' exclaimed his mother, her voice full of reproach. 'We wondered where you were.'

Lance bent down to kiss her dutifully on the cheek.

'Sorry, Mother, I've had some business in the village to take care of this morning,' he said.

'You've been very inattentive to your aunts, Lance,' she said.

'I know, Mother. Let me make it up to you now.' Lance looked at his aunts and smiled politely. He sat down next to Tabitha on the white rattan sofa, grateful to be taking the weight off his leg.

'Hello, big brother,' she said, giving him a nudge with her elbow. 'I'm afraid your absence has been noted.'

'All right, little sis, don't labour the point,' Lance said, nudging her back. 'I'm already in enough trouble as it is.'

'What I should like to know,' boomed Lady Maud, 'is what's so important that it's kept you away from Landacre all morning, Lance? I'd have thought you'd have more consideration for your mother at this terrible time.'

Lady Maud was the eldest of the three sisters and the most austere, her large bosom serving as a resting place for the lorgnettes that were meant to dangle from the gold chain around her neck. She always made Lance think of a galleon in full sail.

He decided the best form of defence was charm. 'Good grief, Aunt Maud, you don't look a day older than the last time I saw you. How do you do it?'

Lady Maud put her nose in the air and looked down it, harrumphing.

Feeling a tad peckish, Lance helped himself to a selection of the tiny cucumber sandwiches on the tea table. His mother poured him a cup of Lapsang Souchong from the large crested silver teapot.

'And how's my favourite explorer,' Lance said to Dame Lettice between mouthfuls.

Dame Lettice, the youngest of the sisters, appeared smaller and more fragile than her siblings, but her delicate exterior belied a steely temperament that had given her the stamina to accompany her husband, Lord Randolph Rolf-Sylvester, on numerous difficult expeditions in Africa. Indeed, she had been made a Dame of the British Empire for bringing basic healthcare and hygiene to some of the remotest parts of the continent.

'Well enough, thank you, Lance,' Dame Lettice said with a sad smile. 'We've all been so upset by the events of the last few days. I do hope our company will help your mother through these difficult times.'

Lance looked tenderly at his mother. 'Thank you, dear Aunt Lettice. I'm sure Mother appreciates your support.'

Lady Cynthia smiled weakly.

'By the way, I bumped into the Reverend this morning, Mother,' Lance said, keen to change the subject. 'Did Pa mention anything to you about the memorial the villagers want to erect in the square?'

'I've heard about it, but I don't think your father mentioned anything specific. Why do you want to know?'

'I'll be standing in for him at a committee meeting about it on Friday evening and I wanted to get up to snuff on the subject.'

'Have the police said when they'll release your father's body for burial?' she asked.

'Not yet. It seems they have reason to believe there is more to his accident than they first thought. I gather that's one of the reasons they've delayed.'

Lady Cynthia looked horrified.

'Good gracious!' Lady Maud and Dame Lettice exclaimed in unison.

'You surely don't believe your father's death was anything other than an accident, do you, Lance?' Lady Maud asked.

'I think the police do,' Lance said.

'Well, whatever next!' she said. 'It's an absolute disgrace the way the police are preventing the family from having a decent Christian burial. I shall speak to the Commissioner about it.'

'Surely, dear, you shouldn't meddle in police matters,' Dame Lettice said quietly to her sister.

'It's not meddling, Lettice,' Lady Maud roared. 'We would all be better served if the police concentrated their intelligence, such as it is, on the proletariat and stopped interfering in the funeral arrangements of the nobility.'

'I don't think the Commissioner would see it in that light, dear,' Dame Lettice replied.

'Then the man's a fool,' thundered Aunt Maud. 'I shall certainly discuss the matter with him if it means that Cynthia doesn't have to bear any further ignominies!'

Lance set his empty plate back on the table. 'Where's Hugo?' he asked casually.

'He's gone in to Exeter with Ruth and Clara,' replied Tabby.

'What's happening in Exeter?'

'Chief Superintendent Schilling called this morning and asked them to accompany him into Exeter to identify Bruce Hamilton's body,' Lady Cynthia explained. 'Hugo's gone with them for moral support.'

'Why has no one been asked to identify Father's body?' Tabby asked.

'Because of the fire. I don't think there was much left to identify,' Lance said softly.

'It must be a *very* grim experience to identify one of your loved ones,' interjected Dame Lettice. 'I wouldn't want to do it and I've experienced some very rough situations in the Congo.'

'No, indeed. From my limited conversation with Ruth I'd say the poor creature doesn't have the constitution for such a task,' Lady Maud said grimly. 'And Clara's not much better. From what I can see neither of them have been graced with an abundance of fortitude or intelligence.'

'Maud, dear, that's not a very gracious thing to say,' admonished Dame Lettice. 'These are difficult times.'

Lady Maud snorted. 'Gracious or not it's the truth,' she said. 'The vulgarity of new money is no substitute for a wealth of good lineage!'

'I thought you said Bruce's face had been disfigured, Lance,' Tabby said. 'That's going to make it difficult to identify him, isn't it?'

'Yes, that's true,' Lance replied. 'But there are other things that can identify a body, Tabby. Like birthmarks.'

'Did Bruce have any birthmarks then?'

'That's the sort of thing only a wife would know, Tabby dear,' her mother said gently.

There was an uncomfortable lull in the conversation before Dame Lettice asked the question on everyone's lips: 'Are Hugo and Clara still going ahead with the wedding? I mean there've been so many distressing events. Surely it would be better to postpone until everything has been cleared up by the police.'

'I agree, Lettice,' Lady Maud said. 'It's most unseemly to press ahead in the light of recent tragic events. Cynthia, you should speak to the young people about it – tell them it would be better to wait.'

'I think Hugo and Clara are set on continuing with the wedding as planned,' Lance said. 'They told me as much the other day.'

'But it's not decent,' said Lady Maud. 'It wouldn't have been allowed in my youth! People had more consideration for social etiquette then.'

'I'm afraid I don't have that much influence over Hugo these days,' Lady Cynthia said. 'What can I do? He's a grown man. I wish Cedrick were here. He'd know how to handle the situation.' She pulled an embroidered handkerchief from one sleeve and dabbed at her eyes.

Lance stood up. 'Sorry to eat and run, but I must see old Bill Parks over at Stapleford.'

'But you've only just returned from the village,' Lady Maud complained. 'You really should show more concern for your mother.'

'Sorry, but it must be done. I need to prepare for that meeting on Friday if I'm to fill Father's shoes as chairman. I'll leave you in Tabby's capable hands.' Lance looked down at his sister with a twinkle in his eye.

Tabby scowled back at him.

* * *

Speeding through the lanes to Stapleford in his two-seater, Lance reflected on the temporary nature of life. He deeply regretted not taking at least one of the many opportunities he'd had to really talk to his father, to express his deep appreciation for all he had done and tell him how much he loved him. There was so much left unsaid, so much Lance would have liked him to know. It was too late now. Never again would he be able to seek him out for advice about this and that. How he would miss his father's reassuring presence.

Lance also wished he'd taken more of an interest in the running of Landacre. He was going to find it difficult to take up the reins without his father's sage guidance to keep him on track. The crushing weight of recriminations and despair he'd experienced since leaving the navy had proved almost too much to bear. Would the added responsibility of running Landacre be the final straw?

It was late afternoon and the sun was beginning to slip lower in the sky. He put his worries aside as he pulled into Stapleford and drove slowly through the village. Bill Parks's tiny cottage was the last dwelling on the right past a couple of oak trees. Its front door opened directly onto the lane, and it looked shabby and uncared for. Lance brought the car to a standstill, hopped out and rapped loudly on the knocker.

Lance heard a faint rustling coming from within, followed by the tap-tap of footsteps on a flagstone floor. Then the door creaked open to reveal a small round middle-aged woman.

'Yeeees?' enquired the woman.

'My name is Lance Donaldson-Gilks. Is Mr Parks at home?'

''Ee's just come in from work, sir,' replied the woman wringing her hands through the dirty apron she wore around her waist. ''Ee's a havin 'is tea,' she added helpfully.

'Oh! Would you mind if I wait?'

'Suit ya'self.' The woman shrugged and ambled back down the passage, disappearing into the gloom.

'Bill ... Bill ...' she shouted, 'there's some'un to see ya.'

'All right, all right,' answered a deep baritone voice at the end of the hall. 'Can't decent God-fearing folk eat thur tea in peace?'

The kitchen door opened and a gnarled, wizened old man hobbled up the dark passageway.

'Mr Parks?' Lance enquired.

'Aye.'

'My name is Lance Donaldson-Gilks. I believe you knew my father.'

'Aye, sir, I did. Nasty business that. I'm sorry fur ya loss.'

'Thank you, Mr Parks. I wonder if I may come in and talk to you about the Coombe End memorial. I believe you were helping Lord Cedrick with the matter.'

Bill Parks stood back from the front door and indicated a door to his right. Lance entered the dimly lit cottage and went into the front room. It was obvious from the extremely spartan, uninviting interior that Mrs Parks's parlour was rarely used. Lance decided to remain standing.

'Now, m'lord, what can I be a doin' fur y'ur?' Bill asked gruffly.

'I understand you were in discussion with my father regarding the memorial for Coombe End,' Lance said. 'As heir to Landacre I feel it's my duty to assume his committee responsibilities and ensure continuity.'

'Y'ur perfectly right, sir. Lord Cedrick was a planning the thing.'

'How far had you progressed with the designs?'

Bill drew in a deep breath. 'Well, let's see. I'd thought granite for the monument. Good stone, granite is – t'will last for years and years to come. Won't 'ave no problem with that, 'ee won't. Lord Cedrick seemed happy with the notion. 'Ee gave me a drawin' of the thing an' asked me for a price to complete the work. I told 'im with materials and labour t'would be in the region of one hundred pounds. He seemed to accept that, said 'ee'd just need to agree it with committee, then 'ee'd give me the go ahead like.'

'Did Lord Cedrick make any payment?'

'Aye, he gave me a few bob for me trouble.'

'Exactly how much did he give you?' Lance asked, wanting to be sure of the precise financial situation.

'T'was three bob, sir.'

'And did he make any other down payment?'

'No, sir. I was still awaitin' to hear from 'im.'

'All right, Mr Parks, thanks for your help. I won't keep you from your tea any longer. I'll be attending the committee meeting on Friday. I assume you will be too.'

Bill nodded his head. 'Aye.'

'The committee should be in a position to let you know the outcome at that meeting,' Lance said, thankful to be swapping the chilly room for the sunshine outside.

Bill followed Lance out. 'Nice car that,' he said appreciatively as Lance jumped into the driver's seat.

'Thanks, Mr Parks. She's a beaut all right. See you Friday.'

With that Lance turned the car around in the lane and headed back home.

So Bill Parks had only received one very small payment. As far as Lance could recall there was no entry in the accounts to show that his father had claimed this payment from the fund. Presumably he'd intended to request the money from the committee later. He mulled it all over as he raced back to Landacre.

CHAPTER 13:
A VISIT TO THE BANK

Wednesday June 11th 1919

THE NEXT MORNING LANCE rose with a spring in his step. He would be seeing Veronica later that evening and found himself excited at the prospect of being in her company once again. He'd also be interested to learn what she and David had discovered as a result of their undercover jaunt to the shipping line's offices in Southampton.

He went down to breakfast where Tabby was already drinking her coffee. As usual, Rose and Evans were standing in silent vigil next to the breakfast buffet.

'Morning, Tabby,' Lance said, helping himself from the dresser.

A few minutes later their brother came in.

'Morning, Hugo. Everything all right?' Lance enquired.

'Fine,' Hugo responded in a flat monotone.

'No Clara this morning?' Lance said in an attempt to jolly the conversation along.

'I expect she'll be down later,' Hugo replied, sitting down at the table with a small plateful of scrambled eggs.

'She had a very harrowing day yesterday and she has such a delicate disposition. I really don't know quite how she bears it all, I simply don't.'

'Yes, how did you get on at Exeter Police Station with Ruth and Clara?' Tabby asked, getting straight to the point.

'It must have been very traumatic for you all,' Lance said softly, endeavouring to tone down Tabby's directness.

'It was ghastly, if you must know,' Hugo replied. 'They took us into a small room where the body, covered only by a sheet, was laid out on a metal table. It was so cold, so impersonal. What an awful job that must be, cutting up ...' His voice trailed off.

'Who made the identification?' Lance asked gently.

'Ruth did.'

'Yes, but HOW?' Tabby asked, her eyes as round as saucers. 'After all, his face had been so disfigured.'

Lance worried that his little sister was developing an unhealthy interest in the more gory side of the tragic event.

'They lifted the sheet and Ruth looked at him,' Hugo said, shrugging.

'But his face?'

'The pathologist had cleaned it up well before Ruth was allowed in.'

'Yes, yes, but was she able to say it was *him*?'

'I'm sure she must know her own husband, Tabby. Anyway, I believe Scotland Yard has sent to America for his dental records just to be certain.'

'Oh,' Tabby said.

Hugo went on. 'They gave Ruth a bag containing all of Bruce's personal effects. It was horrible. Ruth asked me to give it to Treadwell. One of the footmen has been instructed to pack up all his belongings for shipment back to America after the wedding.' He threw down his knife and fork and pushed his half-eaten eggs away. 'I think I'll go out for some fresh air,' he said. 'It might perk me up a bit.'

'I'd offer to go with you,' Lance said, 'but I've an appointment to attend. Why don't you keep him company, Tabby?'

Tabby scowled at Lance but put her hand on Hugo's arm. 'Come on, sourpuss. Let's go for a ride.'

After he had finished his breakfast Lance got ready to visit the bank manager in Exeter. Determined to get to the bottom of the Memorial Fund's financial situation, he collected the envelope containing the papers from the safe and jumped into the two-seater. Bob sat in the passenger seat, his ears flapping in the stiff breeze as the red sports car zipped along the narrow country lanes towards the city.

Forty-five minutes later they were standing on the pavement in a bustling high street looking up at the grand building that housed the Exminster National Bank, an institution that had upheld the highest principles of banking since the eighteenth century.

'Come along, young Bob,' Lance said. 'Let's see what we can learn inside.'

Entering through a revolving door Lance found the interior of the bank positively palatial. An expansive floor of black-and-white Carrara marble gleamed in the morning light streaming through the colossal Georgian windows. Splendid Tuscan columns supporting a high baroque plaster ceiling kept silent watch over proceedings, while a number of the well-to-do of Exeter went about their daily banking business in hushed tones at polished mahogany counters.

Lance and Bob made their way through the busy throng to a reception desk to the right. An ebony screen behind it allowed the tellers and clerks to go about their business unseen by the bank's clientele.

'I wonder if the manager could spare me a moment of his valuable time?' Lance enquired of a spotty youth sitting behind the desk.

'Have you an appointment, sir?' the clerk asked, his mature tone at odds with his boyish appearance.

'No, I'm afraid I haven't, but my business with him will just take a minute. Would you inform him that Lord Westex requests a consultation?' Lance handed the young man his calling card.

'If you'll wait here a moment, sir, I'll see if Mr Dacres is available.'

The clerk disappeared behind the screen. A few moments later he returned. 'The manager will see you now, sir.'

Lance and Bob followed the clerk around the screen where they were presented with a long carpeted passageway punctuated at intervals with doors on either side. Directed to the end of the corridor, they were confronted by a large mahogany door upon which the words 'Mr George Dacres, Manager' were inscribed in gold leaf.

Lance knocked.

'Enter,' said an authoritative disembodied voice from within.

Lance turned the polished brass knob and walked in.

'Good morning, Mr Dacres,' he said with a cordial nod of his head. 'Thank you for agreeing to see me at such short notice.'

The manager, a thin man with grey hair dressed in a smart black pinstriped suit, smiled pleasantly and stood up from behind his enormous desk.

'My name is Lancelot Donaldson-Gilks – Lord Westex. I'm here about the Coombe End Memorial Fund, for which I understand your bank holds an account.'

Mr Dacres shook Lance's hand vigorously. 'Good morning, m'lord. Do sit down.'

'Thank you,' Lance said, moving towards the chair indicated by the manager.

The manager resumed his own seat and studied Lance and Bob over the top of his gold half-rimmed spectacles. 'Now, how may I assist you with the fund?' he asked.

Lance opened the envelope he'd brought with him and laid the contents out on the desk. The manager glanced at them.

'You may be aware that Lord Cedrick died recently,' Lance said.

'So I believe. I'm very sorry for your loss, Lord Westex.'

'Thank you. Unfortunately, the police believe the accident may not have been without some sort of earthly assistance, as it were.'

A look of unease crossed the manager's face.

Lance pressed on. 'Since I'm heir to my father's land and titles I've taken up his responsibilities, some of which include the Memorial Fund. I've subsequently learned that Lord Cedrick visited you recently, possibly because he was worried about the account.'

Mr Dacres sat motionless, betraying no indication that Lance's assumptions were right or wrong.

'I feel it my duty to discover the truth, and to that end I'm wondering if you can assist me. Did Lord Cedrick visit you recently? Was he concerned about the fund?'

The manager leaned back in his chair, putting his fingertips together as he contemplated his response. 'Yes, Lord Cedrick did attend an appointment to discuss the fund. I thought he seemed quite troubled at the time.'

Lance leaned forward. 'Did he say what he was troubled about, Mr Dacres?'

'Lord Cedrick was interested in the deposits and withdrawals. He brought with him a number of cheques. As I recall there were three, each made out to cash. But one moment, let me see if I can confirm that for you.'

The manager pressed a small black button on his intercom. 'Miss Disney, please ask Mr Hubbard to bring in the ledger containing the Coombe End Memorial Fund postings please.'

'Right away, Mr Dacres,' replied a woman with a reedy voice.

A few minutes later there was a soft tap at the door.

'Come.'

A small mousey-looking man appeared carrying an enormous brown leather-bound book opened mid-way. He set the heavy tome on the desk in front of the manager.

Mr Dacres ran his finger down one of the columns in the ledger and then abruptly stopped. 'Just as I thought,' he said. 'There were three cheques, each one made out for one pound ten shillings.'

'I think these must be the cheques,' Lance said, pulling them from the paperwork he'd tipped out on top of the desk.

Mr Dacres compared them one by one against the entries made in the ledger. 'Yes, they're the ones,' he said eventually. 'The cheque numbers are the same as those entered in the withdrawal column.'

'What is the balance of the account today, Mr Dacres?'

'It's five pounds in credit, m'lord.'

'That's rather less than I'd expected. Can you tell me on what date the account was opened and how much has been deposited since that time?' Lance continued.

The manager ran his finger down the deposit column. 'The account was opened in January of this year, and five deposits have been made over that period amounting to nine pounds ten shillings.'

'And these cheques are the only drawings on the account so far?'

'That appears to be the case.'

'I see they are countersigned by two people, Mr Dacres. Who has authority to sign them?'

The manager turned over a number of pages to the front of the ledger. 'Lord Cedrick, Mr Jacob Snyder, Reverend Eustace and Mr George Bagshott.'

Lance glanced at the cheques. 'These three appear to have been signed by Jacob Snyder and George Bagshott.'

'Quite so, m'lord,' murmured Mr Dacres.

'But it just doesn't make any sense,' Lance said. 'Reverend Eustace informed me that Mrs Bird donated ten pounds to the fund, and the village has held several fundraisers in addition to the donation, yet the amount banked is less than Mrs Bird's donation.'

The manager didn't seem to feel compelled to offer any answers and sat impassively behind his desk.

'Something's not right,' Lance went on, shaking his head. 'Something very improper appears to have taken place, Mr Dacres, and I don't like the look of it.'

Snapping into action, Lance stood up and held out a purposeful hand. 'Thank you for meeting with me. I'm sure you're a very busy man so I won't detain you any further. It's obvious I need to go back to Coombe End and make further investigations.'

'If you require any further assistance, m'lord, please don't hesitate to contact me again,' Mr Dacres said, rising to his feet and shaking Lance's outstretched hand. 'We at the Exminster National Bank pride ourselves on our customer service,' he added cordially.

Lance and Bob made their way back to the car again and set off on the return journey to Landacre.

'There's something seriously amiss with the Memorial Fund, that's for sure,' Lance said to Bob, sitting beside him in the passenger seat. Not getting any response, he patted the dog's head. 'Let's see if we can get to the bottom of it, young pup.'

CHAPTER 14:
AN AIR OF ROMANCE

AS HE CHANGED FOR dinner that evening, Lance was in good humour. He was very much looking forward to an enjoyable supper in Veronica's company and he had plans that evening, romantic ones.

He'd spent hours that afternoon contemplating how he'd broach the subject. He'd tell Veronica how he felt about her and she'd immediately fall for his fatal charm. Nothing to it, he thought, humming a melodic ditty as he combed his hair. It was just like planning an attack at sea really.

Having laid out a dinner suit with his usual diligence, Bentley was busy attending to his sartorial duties while Bob watched from his bed. Lance sensed an uneasiness gradually permeating the room, as if there was something his valet very much wanted to communicate but felt uncomfortable raising.

'Is everything all right, Bentley?' Lance asked.

'Everything is most satisfactory, m'lord.'

Undaunted by his valet's hollow reply, Lance decided to take another tack. 'How are the servants taking the events of the last few days? I'm sure it's been a most unsettling time for everyone.'

Bentley gave a small apologetic cough. 'If you will permit me, m'lord,' he replied with a hesitant solemnity, 'I will admit that recent events have indeed been on the minds of the staff, sir. There has been a great deal of gossip and speculation below stairs. I don't mind saying some of the talk in the servants' quarters has caused me a certain amount of disquiet.'

'Really Bentley? What's the root of this unease? Someone been putting salt in the sugar?' Lance asked with a smile.

'No, m'lord,' Bentley replied, straight-faced. 'It seems there's some kind of discrepancy regarding Mr Bruce Hamilton's effects, sir.'

'What kind of discrepancy?'

'I think you should have a word with Evans, the second footman, sir. He seems very troubled. I think he may possess information which could have significant bearing on Mr Hamilton's unfortunate demise, sir.'

Lance raised an eyebrow. 'Evans? Is that the new footman who has been attending the breakfast room?'

'It is indeed, m'lord.'

'Very well, Bentley. I'll make a point to discuss the matter with him at the earliest opportunity.' Lance adjusted his shirt cuffs to ensure they showed below the sleeves of his dinner jacket.

'Thank you, m'lord. I'm sure that will be for the best. May I also recommend you talk to Rose, the parlourmaid. I'm sure she has something on her mind too. This morning she put the marmalade away in the meat pantry.'

'Is that significant?'

'Why yes, sir. The marmalade should be stored into the dry pantry.'

Lance couldn't help smiling at Bentley's idea of an egregious crime. 'The point being?'

'The point being, m'lord, that something is worrying her so much that she isn't thinking straight.'

'I see, Bentley. Thank you for mentioning it. I'll have a word with her.'

'Thank you, sir.'

Lance made his way down the main staircase and stopped by the hall stand, where Digweed had left an enormous bouquet of roses, peonies, sweet peas, and cornflowers, all picked from their own garden. He stood for a moment, his nose buried in the flowers, enjoying the fond boyhood memories their delicate fragrance evoked. At one time Landacre had been renowned for its award-winning exhibits at all the county flower shows. He was confident that Veronica wouldn't mistake the message he intended the flowers to convey.

A while later, bouquet in arms, Lance ascended the staircase to Apartment 2b, Deacon Heights. He took a deep breath and rapped the door.

Nothing happened. Lance exhaled. She seemed to be taking an age to answer. He could feel a hot prickling sensation rise up to his face. A uncharacteristic tension enveloped him. He was just about to knock again when she suddenly opened the door.

'Oh hello, Lance. Come in, do,' she said nonchalantly, taking a step back to allow him entry.

He thrust the enormous bunch of flowers awkwardly into her arms. 'These are for you,' he stammered.

'Oh, how lovely. I'll put them in water later. Please, go on through to the drawing room,' she said, leaving the bouquet on the hall stand without giving it a second glance.

Lance felt as if he had been doused in cold water, and a pang of torment surged through him as his carefully crafted fantasy popped like a balloon. Was his simple romantic 'bomb-proof' plan showing early signs of being holed below the waterline? How could she fail to grasp the meaning? Surely she recognised this obvious sign of his affection. A swirl of contrary emotions pulsed through his body. Pull yourself together man, he told himself. He'd commanded the *Panther*, for heaven's sake. All that was required in the face of this unexpected reaction was a swift change of plan, something he'd done a hundred times in the navy. He decided he'd bring the conversation round to the subject over supper and compel her to understand his intentions. With rekindled resolve and a hastily concocted new plan, he removed his gloves and placed them with his hat on the hall stand next to the discarded flowers.

The smell of supper wafted through from the kitchen as he walked into the drawing room.

'Good evening,' David said quietly and got up from one of the fireside chairs to shake Lance by the hand. 'Drink?' he asked. 'You look as if you need one.'

Lance's heart sank like a stone as yet another part of his illusion was shattered. He had expected to be alone with Veronica this evening. With David in attendance his hurriedly amended romantic plan was completely dead in the water. He slumped down in the nearest chair.

'Everything all right, old man?' David asked.

'Yes, fine thanks,' he muttered. 'I'll have a whisky, thanks.'

Over supper Lance regained his equilibrium somewhat and regaled David and Veronica with accounts of his visit to the apothecary, the discussion with Reverend Simon Eustace and his subsequent visit to the bank.

The barely edible meal over, the three moved back to the drawing room, each with a large brandy.

'You know,' Lance said, looking broodily into his brandy balloon and gently swilling the copper-coloured liqueur around the glass, 'I think this affair could very well hinge on the fact that the Memorial Fund is almost certainly being systematically defrauded. Jacob Snyder has a certain social standing in the village. He's a parish councillor as well as a businessman. If he's embezzling money, he wouldn't want it to be known that he's a fraudster. So perhaps he decided to shut my father up permanently to stop it getting out.'

'Good Lord, Lance,' Veronica said. 'That's quite a serious accusation to make without concrete proof. You don't even know it *is* Jacob Snyder doing the defrauding. It could be someone else.'

'Yes, I know, but there was something about his demeanour I didn't like. As soon as I mentioned the Memorial Fund he became wary, tight-lipped. And what about all the fundraising and donations? Mr Dacres is sure no more than nine pounds ten has ever been deposited at the bank. We know that figure can't be right. Who would have the easiest opportunity to embezzle the funds if it wasn't the person responsible for handling the money?'

'Does anyone else manage the cash before Jacob gets to it?' David asked.

'Well, George Bagshott is responsible for committee fundraising, so I suppose he might have an opportunity to palm some of the proceeds before he hands them over to Jacob,' Lance replied.

'Who do you think you heard running down the church path?' David asked.

'I don't know, but I'm sure I'm being watched. Perhaps it's the same people.'

'But you said that started outside your London apartment,' chipped in Veronica. 'You weren't aware of the problem with the Memorial Fund at that stage. Why on earth would anyone want to shadow you because of a small local memorial fund? It just doesn't make any sense.'

'It would be more plausible if Jacob Snyder were outside the church,' David said. 'You said he watched you walk in that direction after you left his shop. Perhaps he was worried that Simon Eustace could reveal something to point you in his direction.'

'Yes, but how does Bruce Hamilton come into the equation?' Veronica asked. 'He doesn't seem to fit into the Memorial Fund scenario at all.'

'That's a tricky one,' replied Lance, nodding. 'Perhaps he heard something or saw something and Jacob had to kill him off.'

'It's possible, but I don't think it's very probable, do you?' David said.

The three of them were silent for a few minutes as they mulled it all over.

'How did you get on in Southampton?' Lance asked, breaking the sombre mood.

Veronica beamed. 'I think we did rather well,' she said looking over at David.

'Tell me all about it,' Lance said, keen to pick up on any hint of a deepening relationship between David and Veronica.

'We took the train—' David began.

'Yes, we took the train down to Southampton,' Veronica cut in excitedly, 'and we were met at the station by Matthew Lock.'

'Who's Matthew Lock?' Lance asked.

'Matt's an old friend—' David said.

'You know ... he's the photographer that works for the *Southampton Messenger*,' Veronica butted in. 'The one who helped us identify the photograph in the envelope.'

'Oh yes, of course. I remember now. Why did you arrange to be met by him?'

David tried again. 'We thought—'

'We thought it would be a good idea to talk with Matt first,' Veronica interrupted. 'He knows the lay of the land down there, and he was able to fill us in with some useful local knowledge.' David sat back in his chair and Veronica carried on. 'He met us at the station, and over a cup of tea he briefed us on the background of the shipping company. He advised us that the person we should see was the manager, a Mr Robert Mayflower at the offices in Ocean Road. Apparently, he's been the manager there for nearly twenty years. He also brought with him copies of his newspaper's reports relating to *Titanic*'s sinking.' Veronica set a manilla folder on the coffee table. 'David and I have pored over them, but there doesn't seem to be anything that is immediately striking as pertinent to our investigation.'

'Let's not leap to conclusions,' Lance said. 'I'd like to look through them myself before we write them off completely.' He lifted the folder and glanced through the clippings. He stopped to look at one more closely. 'That's interesting.'

'What's that?' asked Veronica.

'This article dated 17th April 1912 – it gives a list of passengers who survived the disaster.'

'Yes, we saw the names,' David said. 'Is there something in that?'

'According to the report, one of the passengers who survived was Lady Grace Agnew. She's a very good friend of mother's.'

'We should interview her,' Veronica said. 'Perhaps she can shed some light on the matter.'

'Well, that ought to be easy. I believe she's invited to Hugo's wedding. She'll probably be coming to stay at Landacre in the next few days. I'll ask Mother about it.'

'Anyway, getting back to our trip to Southampton,' Veronica said. 'After we met Matt, David and I trotted along to the shipping office. They were surprised to receive a visit from the *Chronicle* I can tell you.'

'I bet they were,' Lance said.

'Matt's information was spot on …' David said.

'Yes, Mr Mayflower was very reluctant to help us with our questions at first,' Veronica said, 'but I soon had him eating out of the palm of my hand.' She smiled beguilingly at Lance.

'Oh yes, and how did you ingratiate yourself with him?' Lance asked.

'You either have it or you don't,' she teased. 'And I have it!'

'Of course you do, my dear girl,' Lance said, laughing.

Veronica stared at him sternly, then carried on. 'Anyhow, we asked him about the day that *Titanic* was in Southampton signing up crew for her maiden voyage. Mr Mayflower remembered it well. He said there'd been a great deal of bother when one of the ship's company had disembarked from her Belfast sailing and constantly harangued anyone thinking of signing on for the run to New York with details of a fire in her coal bunker.'

'Now that's interesting. It confirms what Florence Seymour said,' Lance commented.

'Apparently the disruption caused quite a stir at the time,' Veronica continued, 'and members of the press with photographers in tow descended on the quay to interview him. Mr Mayflower said the senior management of the shipping line were incandescent with rage at this unwelcome attention. They felt the bad publicity would damage the reputation of the company and have disastrous financial consequences for the shipping line. As a result the directors were anxious to prevent details of the fire from leaking out to the public. Mr Mayflower was ordered to arrange for the company's security staff to escort the troublemaker from the dock before he could give any details of his accusations to the press.'

'I'll be damned,' Lance said, then threw an apologetic look at Veronica for his language.

Veronica appeared not to notice. 'Mr Mayflower said he has subsequently suffered many sleepless nights, realising he was party to stifling an issue that may have had a substantial bearing on *Titanic*'s sinking.'

'I bet he has!' Lance exclaimed. 'It must be very difficult for him to live with the knowledge that he knew something was wrong with *Titanic* before she sailed only to learn later of the horrendous loss of life.'

'Yes, indeed,' David said.

'Do we know the name of the person on the quay who was escorted away?' asked Lance.

'Mr Mayflower said his name was Peter Hopwood,' Veronica replied triumphantly.

'Peter Hopwood? Where have I heard that name before,' Lance muttered to himself.

'You remember, that was the name Miss Seymour mentioned to us,' Veronica said. 'He attended her brother's memorial service. He was the person she said spoke to John Seymour about *Titanic*.'

'Ah yes, of course.'

'Mr Mayflower was kind enough to check his files for a forwarding address and you'll never guess where he is now.'

'Do I *have* to guess?' Lance asked. 'Can't you just tell me like any normal person?'

'Okay, okay, but let me have my moment of brilliance,' she said and paused. 'He's currently working at Landacre Hall!'

Lance's mouth fell open. 'I thought I recognised the name,' he said. 'He's our gamekeeper.'

CHAPTER 15:
A SALTY TALE

Thursday June 12th 1919

NEXT MORNING, LANCE BREAKFASTED in his room; he needed to clear his head without the constant chatter of house guests fogging his thoughts. Finishing his toast and marmalade, he looked down at Bob who stared back at him reproachfully as if to say 'Where's my titbit?'

'Let's go for a walk, young pup.'

On hearing the word 'walk', Bob immediately forgot about sulking and started to turn somersaults and wriggled excitedly in and out between Lance's legs.

'All right, all right, lad,' Lance said, laughing. 'Calm down. Let's go to the boot room and get our walking gear.'

As Lance made his way down the passage to the rear of the house, he encountered Treadwell on his way to the wine cellar where each morning he selected with appropriate solemnity the libations that were to accompany the family's evening meal.

'Good morning, m'lord.'

'Good morning, Treadwell,' Lance replied breezily. 'Bob

and I are just off for a walk around the estate. I'm expecting Miss Barnes later this morning. If she arrives before I return please make her comfortable in the study.'

'Certainly, sir.'

'I should also like to talk to Peter Hopwood. Please ask him to make himself available around mid-morning.'

'Very good, sir.'

'Oh, and I shall also want to have a word with Evans, the second footman, at some point,' Lance added, remembering Bentley's earnest conversation from the night before.

A look of concern flickered across the butler's normally expressionless face. 'Begging your pardon, sir, if it's about the recent lapse in his duties, I've already spoken to him about that particular matter,' Treadwell said.

Lance hesitated. He knew nothing of any transgression by the second footman. 'Is it something I should be aware of, Treadwell?'

'It's nothing really, sir,' responded the butler. 'Evans has been missing from his post on a few occasions. He appears to have slipped away without saying anything to anyone. When I spoke to him about it he refused to inform me where he'd been or give me reasons for his absences. Obviously I cannot allow that situation to continue unchecked. The effect on the rest of the staff would be most unsatisfactory.'

'Quite so,' replied Lance, relieved to know that Treadwell had dealt with the issue. 'No, it's a quite different matter I wish to discuss with him.'

'Very well, m'lord. I shall ensure he's available at your convenience, sir.'

'Thank you,' Lance said as he and Bob continued down the passage to the boot room.

Around eleven o'clock they returned from their walk in good spirits. As they entered the main door to the Hall, Treadwell approached.

'Miss Barnes has arrived, m'lord. I have put her in the study as you directed, sir.'

'Thank you, Treadwell. Please ask one of the footmen to see to Bob.'

Treadwell gave Lance a small nod of acknowledgement and retreated down the hallway towards the servants' quarters, Bob following obediently along behind.

On his way to the study Lance recalled his amateurish attempts at romance the previous evening and he winced, a prickly hot panic sweeping through him. Not for the first time he wished he was more like Hugo. His brother was quite at ease with the opposite sex and they fawned all over him. David, too, was so very sophisticated and relaxed in Veronica's company. A strange mixture of excitement and anxiety rose inside him as he opened the study door.

Standing by the window gazing out over Exmoor, Veronica turned to face him. 'Oh, hello, Lance. What a lovely view of the moor you have from here,' she said.

'It is rather beautiful, isn't it,' he said, relieved to be making small talk.

Before leaving her apartment the night before, Lance had volunteered to speak to Peter Hopwood about his time on the *Titanic* and report back to Veronica and David. But Veronica had had other ideas and insisted on being present at the meeting. 'After all, Lance, we're in this together.

Equal partners, remember?' she'd exclaimed. As a result, it had been agreed that they would both discuss the matter with the gamekeeper.

'All ready for the great inquisition?' Lance asked, smiling and rubbing his hands together.

'This is serious, Lance. You shouldn't be taking it quite so lightly. I'm certainly not. If what your gamekeeper says turns out to be pertinent, we may have to inform Chief Superintendent Schilling about it later.'

'I'm only having a bit of fun, Veronica. Don't you have a sense of humour?'

'Not when I'm working. This could be very important for my career. I'm not here for your amusement, you know.'

'No, of course not,' Lance said, suitably chastened. He walked over to the chimney breast and rang the bell for Treadwell.

A few moments later there was a soft knock at the door and the butler glided into the room as if on castors. 'You rang, sir?'

'Will you ask Hopwood to come in now, please?'

The gamekeeper entered the study nervously twisting a flat cap between his hands. His attire was entirely functional: sturdy country shoes over woollen socks, brown corduroy plus fours, a green waistcoat, plaid shirt, his shirtsleeves rolled up to his elbows, and an open collar to reveal a red neckerchief. He stood awkwardly beside the desk, half turned towards the door as if he might bolt from the room at any moment.

'Mornin', m'lord ... Miss,' Hopwood said, his deep gravelly voice both respectful and guarded.

'There's no need for concern, Hopwood. Miss Barnes and I just want to have a word with you about your time on *Titanic*.'

If Lance had hoped his last sentence would put the gamekeeper at ease, he was disappointed. If anything, Hopwood become rather more agitated.

'We understand you sailed with *Titanic* from Belfast before her maiden voyage to New York in April 1912. Is that correct?' enquired Lance.

'An' if I did, what of it?' Hopwood replied.

Lance was a little taken aback by the man's defensiveness. 'Nothing, nothing at all,' he said softly. 'It's just that it would be helpful if you could answer a few questions Miss Barnes and I have relating to your experience on board.'

'I dunno nufin' 'bout 'er sinkin'.'

'No, of course not,' Lance said. 'We just want to ask you what you know about the fire.'

The gamekeeper glanced around anxiously as if he was expecting someone to jump out from behind the curtains.

'You're not in any trouble, but it's very important you tell us what you know,' Lance said, starting to feel quite alarmed at the man's reaction to his questions.

'I'm not supposed to tell.'

'What d'you mean you're not supposed to tell?' Veronica demanded.

Hopwood looked startled and visibly shrank back at her intervention.

'I think what Miss Barnes means is … you have our word that anything you say to us will not go beyond this room,' Lance said, glaring in her direction. 'The thing is, we think you can help us. As you know, Lord Cedrick died recently and we have reason to believe his accident may have had something to do with *Titanic*.'

''Ow's that then?'

'It's a long story. All you need to know is that we think you might know something that would be helpful in discovering the reason for my father's last car journey.'

The gamekeeper looked puzzled. 'Dunno nufin' 'bout that.'

'No, we know that. But you do know about the *Titanic*,' Veronica jumped in. 'We know that you disembarked *Titanic* in Southampton after her trip from Belfast and were interviewed by the press on the quayside. It seems you were trying to persuade your fellow crewmates not to sail on to New York with her.'

'What if I was?'

Veronica let out a loud sigh. Lance scowled at her. 'Well, can you tell us *anything* about the fire on board *Titanic*?' he asked kindly.

Hopwood glanced around the room again. Having assured himself that no one else was present he said, 'Well ...'

'Yes,' said Veronica impatiently.

'It's like this, m'lord,' Hopwood said, keeping his eyes on Lance. 'I signed on with *Titanic* in Belfast as a fireman stoker. The coal for 'er journey 'ad been delivered to docks 'bout three weeks afore she sailed and was loaded in 'er coal bunkers.'

'Is it usual to have the coal delivered that early?'

'Oh yes, m'lord. Most ships leaving the yard for the first time usually load with coal well in advance.'

'Go on,' Veronica said eagerly.

'Well, as soon as we was aboard like, a fire was discovered in 'er coal bunkers – t'were numbers nine and ten. Roarin' away fierce it were, an' 'ad turned the steel of the bulkheads in boiler room six red 'ot.'

'What happened next,' Lance asked.

'Well, as we got under steam from Belfast, the gaffer ordered us to rake out 'ot coals from bunkers and shovel 'em into the boilers, but t'was no good like. As fast as we was a shovellin', the more the coal burnt. T'was hard work too, cause *Titanic* seemed to be listing to port. Made the work bleedin' difficult. Then as we docked in Southampton, t'was clear to me that the fire was causin' the ship's steel to buckle in the boiler room. T'wasn't safe that, not with 'er listing an all.'

'No, of course not,' Lance said. 'What did you do then?'

'Well, I told gaffer she wasn't safe and I wouldn't be signing on for the rest of trip. As rumours spread around the ship, a lot of the others felt same as me and we all got off in Southampton. I tried to tell the officers 'bout it, but afore I knew where I was, a crowd of them reporters and photographers came a swarmin' round like locusts. Next thing I knows is I'm being forcibly taken off the dock.'

'Did you speak to John Seymour about it?' Lance asked.

'Hmm …' Hopwood put his big hand to his jaw and a wrinkle appeared on his forehead. 'Was 'e the Third Officer aboard?'

'Yes, that's right,' Lance said. 'Did you speak with him?'

'Yep, I did speak to a junior officer, briefly like, just afore they marched me off the dock.'

'Did he seem worried to you?' Veronica asked.

'Now you mention it 'e seemed more puzzled than worried.'

'What gave you that impression?' asked Lance.

'He kept saying somethin' 'bout the floor coverings being changed, and 'e mentioned that a large number of first-class passengers had cancelled their bookings at the last minute. Seemed like gobbledegook to me. There was one strange thing, though.'

'What was that?' Veronica asked, leaning forward.

'Well, as soon as we docked in Southampton, *Titanic* was taking on stuff – you know provisions, luggage, cargo and so on, but my mate in the cargo hold reckoned that afore she sailed, a last-minute order came through to offload a number of crated bronze statues belonging to a well-to-do passenger in first class. Queer that, I always thought. Why would you want to offload cargo that's just bin loaded? Caused a lot of bleedin" – Hopwood glanced at Veronica – 'caused a lot of trouble for the cargo handlers, that did.'

'Can we talk to your friend?' Lance asked.

''Fraid not,' the gamekeeper said quietly. 'Ee was one of the unlucky ones. Sailed on to New York with 'er, he did, and was lost.'

'I'm sorry,' Veronica said sympathetically.

'Yes, Hopwood, we're sorry for the loss of your friend. Did he happen to say who the well-to-do passenger was who wanted his bronze statues offloaded?'

Peter Hopwood thought long and hard. 'I think he said they belonged to J. P. Morgan, m'lord.'

Lance stared at the top of the desk, nodding thoughtfully. Then he looked up at the gamekeeper. 'Thanks for helping us with our enquiries, Hopwood. I know it's been very difficult for you,' he said.

'I won't get into any trouble like?' Hopwood asked anxiously. 'They made us sign them official secrets, they did. Said as 'ow I should be put away if I mentioned anything about *Titanic* to anyone, m'lord.'

'Who made you sign the Official Secrets Act?' Veronica asked sharply.

'Them two men from the government. Came round to my boarding house they did. Said as they was from the Home Office.'

'What did they look like?'

'That's just it, Miss, I don't know. They was kind of invisible like. They 'ad long dark overcoats with hats pulled down over their faces.'

Lance immediately thought of the two men who had followed him from London. 'You're quite safe, Hopwood,' he said. 'Everything you've said will remain between us. Now, if there isn't anything else to add you may return to your duties.'

Hopwood nodded toward Lance, touching his forelock with the cap in his right hand, and hastily left the room.

'Well, what d'you make of that, Lance?' Veronica said, blowing out her cheeks.

'His account certainly confirms what Florence Seymour told us. There was obviously a serious fire on board *Titanic* when she set sail.'

'And it seems someone is very anxious to keep the story under wraps,' Veronica said breathlessly, 'requisitioning Miss Seymour's letter and putting the frighteners on

Hopwood to sign the Official Secrets Act. I wonder why? What possible reason could there be for all this cloak-and-dagger stuff?'

Lance summoned Treadwell and ordered a pot of coffee. Then he and Veronica spent a very pleasant hour talking over what they had learned. Before Veronica returned to work at the *Chronicle*, she agreed to meet Lance at the village hall the following evening to witness the goings-on at the Memorial Committee meeting.

CHAPTER 16:
RUCTIONS

Friday June 13th 1919

A T APPROXIMATELY SEVEN FIFTEEN the next evening, Lance drove down to Coombe End and parked his two-seater outside the picket gate to the village hall.

'Come along, young Bob,' he said as they strode up the path to the entrance porch, Lance clasping the Memorial Fund folder from the safe.

The village hall was a big barn-like building with a corrugated tin roof and pine floor. Lance imagined the building would be noisy when it rained and rather cold in winter since there was no obvious form of heating. Thank goodness it was summer, he thought, as he and Bob negotiated their way through row upon row of chairs put out for members of the public to attend the meeting.

At the top of the room was a raised platform which served as a stage for local pantomimes, plays and recitals. Today, three trestle tables had been set out. Behind them stood Reverend Eustace deep in conversation with a rather corpulent man in his mid-sixties. Lance ascended the small wooden steps to the left of the platform and walked over to the pair.

'Hello, Reverend.'

'Oh, hello Lance. You made it then.'

'Yes, we did,' Lance said, glancing down at Bob.

'Have you met Colonel George Bagshott? He runs the Exmoor Hunting Lodge Hotel a few miles from Landacre.'

George Bagshott and Lance casually ran an eye over each other. Lance was the first to speak. 'I don't think we've ever met, have we?'

'I don't think so, sir,' Colonel Bagshott replied, his parade-ground voice reverberating in the rafters. He shook Lance's hand in brisk military fashion.

'I'm very pleased to meet you,' Lance said.

'Likewise, I'm sure, m'lord.'

'Please, call me Lance.'

'Lance has assumed Lord Cedrick's responsibilities since his terrible accident,' the Reverend explained.

'Yes, awful business that,' barked the Colonel.

'Where do you want me?' Lance asked.

'As you're taking over from Lord Cedrick, you should sit at the centre table and ensure the meeting doesn't get out of hand.' The Reverend laughed.

'We're not expecting any trouble, are we?' Lance asked, concerned by the vicar's throwaway remark.

'Public meetings are always so unpredictable, don't you find? Anything can and usually does happen. Though I'm quite sure you're more than capable of handling any awkward situation after your time as a captain in the navy,' the Reverend said with a twinkle in his eye.

Lance suddenly felt vaguely apprehensive. It hadn't occurred to him that the meeting could become unruly or difficult to manage. He would rely on good old common sense and decency to guide him through.

The sound of footsteps echoed around the hall as villagers began to arrive. They made themselves as comfortable as they could on the steel-framed chairs and waited patiently for the meeting to start. Above the general din Lance heard Veronica's voice at the doorway. He turned and watched her walk resolutely down the centre aisle clutching her capacious handbag, her hair tousled and windswept.

Lance came down the little wooden steps from the platform to greet her. 'Hello, old thing,' he said, noticing a flutter of excitement in his stomach.

'Hello, Lance. I was afraid I'd be late,' she said, somewhat out of breath.

'You haven't missed anything. We haven't started yet.'

The hall was very full now. The remaining members of the Memorial Committee made their way up onto the platform and took their seats at the tables with one notable exception.

'Who's missing?' enquired Veronica.

'I can't see Jacob Snyder,' Lance said, quickly glancing around the hall to see if the man was somewhere in the room.

'D'you think he'll turn up?'

'It doesn't look like it,' Lance replied, a sense of vague irritability starting to grow.

'There's still time for him to make an appearance,' Veronica said reassuringly. 'I'm sure you'll get your opportunity to examine the fund's financial records.'

From the platform the Reverend indicated it was time to make a start.

Lance left Bob with Veronica, climbed the wooden steps and took his place at the centre table. To his left was the Reverend Eustace, then an empty seat where Jacob Snyder should have been, followed by Edna Sutton, from the Women's Institute, and Bert Beamish, the pub landlord. To his right sat Colonel Bagshott, then Amelia Procter, the postmistress, followed by Helena Fairfax, the school teacher, and Ned Cooper, the blacksmith.

After arranging the contents of the file he'd been carrying, Lance lifted the gavel and rapped loudly three times on the tabletop.

'Good evening, everyone. I'd like to bring this meeting to order,' Lance began, a frisson of anxiety coursing through his body. 'As most of you know, Lord Cedrick was the chairman of this committee and since he can no longer be with us, I've assumed his role.'

A hushed murmur ran around the hall.

Lance continued the meeting by progressing through the agenda item by item. From his position on the platform, he could see Veronica taking copious notes. Just as they reached item number three, the report from the treasurer, the door to the hall burst open and Mrs Snyder hurried down the aisle to the front.

'I'm sorry to be so late,' she cried, 'but my husband has asked that I come along and apologise for his non-attendance.'

The committee members were somewhat startled by Mrs Snyder's dramatic entrance and muttered to each other on the platform while the audience mumbled amongst themselves, causing a din to resound around the hall.

Lance rapped the gavel a number of times in an attempt to restore some sort of order. 'Am I to understand Jacob will *not* be attending?' he enquired sternly.

A rosy flush spread across Mrs Snyder's wrinkled cheeks and she shrank at Lance's show of authority.

'I'm afraid that's so, m'lord. Jacob is unwell,' she replied in a feeble tone.

Once more the hall buzzed with whispers.

Lance rapped the gavel again. 'I see,' he said gravely. 'And did he provide you with a copy of the treasurer's report to give to the committee?'

'I'm sorry, sir. I know nothing about any report. Jacob did give me this note to bring along.' She waved a crumpled piece of paper in the air.

Ned Cooper got up, retrieved the note from Mrs Snyder and gave it to Lance. After scanning its contents, Lance stood up and read it aloud:

June 13th 1919

To whom it may concern.

It has come to my attention that a number of malicious rumours have been circulating in the village regarding the competency of my skills relating to the handling of the Memorial Fund.

Although I have been an upstanding member of the Parish for over twenty years without, I may say, any blemish on my integrity, these rumours are nonetheless very upsetting.

I have therefore decided that in the best interests of the village I should relinquish my position as Treasurer of the Memorial Fund with immediate effect.

Unfortunately, due to pressure of work, I have not had the opportunity to formulate an up-to-date record of the fund. As this has happened during my tenure, I will endeavour to correct this matter over the coming months before handing over the documentation.

Your obedient servant,

Jacob Snyder.

Lance glanced up and down the trestle tables looking for a response from the committee members. None was forthcoming, although he detected that Edna Sutton was somewhat uncomfortable as she fidgeted in her seat. He was more than a little vexed. He suspected the man wasn't ill at all, and either couldn't or wouldn't explain himself publicly. But Snyder had to be held accountable to the good people of this parish.

'Thank you for coming along to inform the committee of your husband's absence, Mrs Snyder,' Lance said politely. 'We all wish him a speedy recovery,' he added with a hint of cynicism.

Sylvia bobbed a small curtsey and hurried away down the aisle.

When the door to the hall closed behind her, a commotion broke out, reverberating around the room. Lance banged his gavel.

'Unfortunately we won't have an opportunity to review the financial position of the Memorial Fund at this gathering as we'd planned,' he said, valiantly attempting to re-establish some sort of order.

Another wave of frenzied indignation resounded from the crowd. It was becoming obvious that Jacob Snyder was right about one thing: unhelpful gossip relating to the fund's finances had been doing the rounds of the village before the meeting.

Mrs Bird stood up from her seat in the audience. 'Excuse me, sir,' she said politely, 'I wanted to ask Mr Snyder about my recent donation to the fund.'

'Yes, this is an intolerable situation,' came a loud rasping voice from the crowd. 'What about our fundraising efforts at the village fete.'

'Aye, an' what about the WI and them other fundraising activities?' bellowed another voice. 'We'd all like to know how much has been raised so far an' we ain't waitin' months for the facts!'

Lance was startled by how strongly the villagers felt and feared he was losing control of the meeting. With some difficulty he restored a level of harmony to proceedings, but not without first giving a personal pledge to get to the bottom of the financial position of the fund. His reassurances begrudgingly accepted, a uneasy calm settled over the room as the committee swiftly moved through the rest of the agenda.

Bill Parks was asked to describe what he had discussed with Lord Cedrick. A vote was taken by the committee and unanimously agreed. The stonemason was asked to proceed with the granite monument forthwith.

As the meeting broke up Lance made his way back to Veronica.

'I've got a good piece for the paper this week,' she said excitedly as she packed her pencil and notepad away in her bag. 'But my word, that was a bit hairy!'

'I'll admit it was touch and go for a while,' Lance said, relieved to have got to the end relatively unscathed.

Just then the Reverend and Colonel Bagshott joined them.

'My, what a difficult time you had at your first meeting,' the rector exclaimed. 'But I knew you were up to the job. Quite masterful, I thought. Yes, quite masterful. Your father would've been proud.'

'Thanks,' Lance said, still trying to recover his composure. 'I don't mind telling you, the strength of feeling from the villagers took me quite by surprise.'

'Never allow yourself to be surprised, young man,' barked Colonel Bagshott. 'First rule of the jungle that. Got broken into at the hotel last year, don't you know. A couple of ne'er-do-wells thought they'd take a pop at me takings. Soon sorted that out with me elephant gun.'

'Quite so, Colonel. I'll certainly bear that advice in mind for the future,' Lance said, picturing himself with an elephant gun.

'What will you do now?' the Colonel asked.

'I suppose I'll have to go round to Snyder's premises and collect the paperwork so we can work out the true financial position for ourselves,' Lance replied with a sigh.

'It's not going to be easy,' Veronica said. 'According to his note he doesn't intend to hand over the paperwork anytime soon.'

'Yes, I think he'll make it as difficult as possible,' Lance said. 'I suppose he hopes to cover his tracks and make it tricky for us to discover any anomalies.'

As people drifted away from the hall, Lance glanced at the clock above the door; it was nine thirty. 'Did you travel here on your bicycle?' he asked Veronica.

'Yes, I've just got time to cycle back to the station before the last train leaves.'

'Look, don't go back to Exeter. Come and stay at Landacre tonight. We can review the evening's events over a nightcap.'

She paused for a moment. 'Okay, but I must be back at the *Chronicle* first thing in the morning.'

'Fine,' Lance said, attempting to conceal his elation. 'I'll fasten your bicycle to the two-seater and Bob can hop in the back,' he added, his heart leaping.

Back at Landacre, dinner was over by the time Lance and Veronica arrived. The family were settled in the drawing room availing themselves of an after-dinner drink, Treadwell informed them as he took Veronica's hat and coat in the hallway.

'We'd better make an appearance. Then we can slip quietly away to the study,' Lance said.

He opened the door to the drawing room. Lady Maud's booming voice could be heard above the sound of the jazz being played loudly on the gramophone.

'Hello, everyone,' he said brightly.

His mother, who was seated on the Chesterfield in deep conversation with Dame Lettice, looked up. 'Oh, hello, Lance. You're back.'

'Yes, Mother. I've asked Veronica to stay the night since she's missed her last train,' he said.

'Hello, big brother. Hello, Veronica,' Tabitha said, hugging a cushion as she pranced past them in time to the strains of the Dixieland Jazz Band.

Hugo and Clara were playing bridge with Ruth and Lady Maud. Hugo got up from the card table and greeted them. 'I'm dummy. I'm sitting this one out. Can I get you both a drink?'

'I think Lance needs one after this evening's goings-on,' Veronica replied.

'Why, whatever do you mean?' Lady Cynthia asked.

'It's all right, Mother. It's nothing I can't handle.'

'Do tell,' cried Tabitha as she came whirling around again.

Lance told them about the tempestuous meeting while his brother mixed their drinks.

'Sounds horrendous,' Hugo said as he handed Veronica a brandy on the rocks.

As soon they had their drinks Lance guided her away towards the study and shut the door. At last he had her to himself and no chance of David queering his pitch.

CHAPTER 17:
CONFIDENCES SHARED

VERONICA SAT DOWN IN one of the large easy chairs beside the fireplace, kicked off her shoes and tucked her feet up under her. 'That's better,' she said. 'What a night!'

Lance removed his jacket, loosened his tie and freed the top button of his shirt. A feeling of contentment descended as he made himself comfortable in the other easy chair from where he could appreciate her all the more.

'First, all those revelations from Peter Hopwood yesterday,' Veronica said, taking a sip of her brandy. 'Then Jacob Snyder practically admitting to skulduggery with the accounts by failing to turn up at the committee meeting this evening.'

'You shouldn't jump to conclusions over Snyder's failure to attend the meeting,' Lance said. 'There may be nothing in it, you know.' He gazed adoringly at Veronica, hoping she would notice.

'Pull the other one. You saw the villagers' reaction. They obviously think something dubious is going on.'

'Everyone's innocent until proven guilty. We've no proof that Snyder is guilty of anything … yet.'

'Hmm … well, I still think he's guilty by exception,' she mused absentmindedly as she looked into the empty fireplace.

Lance sat back in his chair and put his feet up on a stool in front of him. An aura of peace and serenity filled the room. He'd never felt more at ease in a woman's presence, especially a woman he felt such a desire for; he was usually so awkward with them. Engulfed by the utterly unfamiliar experience, he suddenly felt exhausted; his arms and legs felt heavy; all tension floated away. The setting sun cast the room in a soft amber glow and enhanced Lance's mellow mood. Now's my chance, he thought.

'I get the feeling you're rather enjoying this little escapade, Veronica. You're not like any woman I've ever known. Most women in my circle content themselves with charity events and attending bazaars or doing good works, but not you. You have a vigour about you that's not easy to explain. You're exciting to be with.'

'You must stop making fun of me, Lance,' she replied softly, focusing on her brandy glass.

'I'm not! I really admire your grit and determination. It can't be easy resisting the pressure to be pigeonholed.'

Veronica let out a long, deep sigh and languidly flicked a wisp of dark hair away from her eyes, a gesture Lance found incredibly seductive.

'It's not. There are times when I wonder why I'm doing it. Most women of my class are satisfied with their lot, but I want to be something other than a man's possession. I suppose that's what spurs me on to try and achieve something for myself on my own terms. I don't want to be reliant on a husband for my existence.'

That doesn't bode well, Lance thought before pressing on undaunted. 'Tell me about yourself,' he said, swilling the remnants of his whisky around in the glass.

'There's nothing much to tell. I was adopted by the Reverend and Mrs Barnes of Plymouth when I was about two years old. I had a happy conventional childhood with my adopted brother, William. I attended St Hilda's Boarding School for girls in Bath, and then Oxford University where I studied English. Since then I've been working at the *Chronicle* in Exeter.'

'You're adopted?' Lance said, unable to keep the surprise out of his voice.

'Yes. I never knew my biological mother and father. I was left on the steps of the convent just outside Plymouth. No one seems to know what happened to my birth parents or where they came from,' she added wistfully.

'Have you ever thought of trying to find them?'

'I have, yes, but somehow it's never been the right time. My adoptive parents might think I had been unhappy and take it as a slight when nothing could be further from the truth. They took me in when I needed a home. They chose *me* above all the other little girls and boys waiting for adoption. I couldn't hurt them like that.'

'I suppose not. What are they like, your adoptive parents?'

'They're thoroughly kind people. They have an utterly unconventional modern outlook for a vicar and his wife. They taught me that there's nothing a girl can't aspire to, that it just takes hard work and determination to achieve your goals in life. It's down to them that I was one of the few women accepted at Oxford. That's a very positive outlook indeed in a world where everyone is expected to know their place.'

'I should say so,' Lance said, impressed all over again by her bold, bright attitude. 'What about your adoptive brother William? Tell me about him.'

A shadow crossed her face as if the sun had suddenly been eclipsed by a passing cloud.

'That's just it. We don't know where he is or what's happened to him. He enlisted with the 4th Infantry at the start of the war. He was so happy to be part of it, proudly marching to the sound of military bands through the streets of Plymouth, the crowds cheering, flags waving. It seemed like such an adventure. There was no thought that he might not come home. Then in the summer of 1916, my parents received a telegram informing them that William was missing in action at the Battle of the Somme. We always hoped he'd been captured and taken prisoner of war, that he'd return home when the war ended. But he didn't.'

'Did you try to find him?'

'Oh yes, of course. My parents spent months and months making desperate efforts to discover his whereabouts. They contacted the War Office in London and the German authorities. They even tried his regiment and his old army pals fighting with him in France. As a last resort my father went over to Gommecourt in the Pas-de-Calais, all without success. We know as much now as we knew then. He's simply disappeared without trace.'

'I'm so very sorry,' Lance said, mortified. 'I didn't mean to dredge it all up.'

Veronica sighed. 'It's fine. I'm fine. It might have happened three years ago, but I'm not ready just yet to admit I've lost my brother.'

'Of course not,' he replied, silently scolding himself for making such a gaffe.

'What about you? Tell me about your life,' Veronica said with a little smile.

'There's nothing much to report,' he replied, suddenly feeling uncomfortable now the spotlight was on him.

'There must be. What about your childhood.'

Lance finished the last of his whisky. 'Well, it was all pretty normal really. I spent my early years here in Coombe End with my brother and sister.'

'Surely there must be more to it than that.'

'I had a very good chum,' he said. 'We were more like twins really. We did everything together – attended the same schools, joined the navy, we were even assigned the same ships.'

'What was his name?'

'Robert … Robert Sixsmith,' Lance said, fighting to keep his eyes from filling with tears.

'What happened to him?'

A deathly hush filled the room. After what seemed like an age Lance eventually whispered, 'He drowned at sea after our ship was torpedoed by a German U-boat in October last year.'

'Oh no! That must have been awful.'

'It was,' Lance said, his pent up emotions rising to the

surface. 'Especially as I was captain of the ship – HMS *Panther*.' He shuddered.

Veronica remained silent.

'Robert wasn't picked up, as I was, by the other destroyer in the area, although she circled for some time looking for survivors. I've spent countless hours wondering if I was to blame. Could I have done anything differently? Was I too reckless? All those dedicated servicemen dead.'

'I'm sure you did what you could,' Veronica replied, her tone sympathetic.

'My injuries weren't too bad – the ones you can see, that is,' Lance murmured, rubbing the top of his thigh. 'The mind – that's different. They sent me back to England to begin treatment at the Kensington neurological hospital, but it was no good. The medical profession didn't seem to know how to cope with *unseen* injuries. Soon afterwards I was discharged back to my flat in London, but nothing seemed to help with the emptiness and the shame. I could have … should have, done more.'

Veronica shook her head. 'I'm sure you did your best.'

'It was my doctors who suggested I acquire a pet, believing it would give me an interest outside of myself, something to interact with and draw me out of my torpor. That's when I found Bob.'

He looked down fondly at his beloved dog apparently dozing at his feet while alert to every movement and sound.

'So I took a trip to the local dogs' home where an abandoned black puppy instantly and inexplicably captured my heart. He was a bag of sorry bones, but something drew me to him. Perhaps it was his bleak future prospects, which mirrored my own. Whatever it was we instantly had a connection. And it felt good to think that I could at least save a scrawny dog from certain death.'

'Why did you call him Bob?'

Lance smiled weakly. 'That's what I used to call Robert. I hoped this young pup would fill the gaping hole left by my dearest pal in all the world, and that our budding new friendship would mark a fresh start for us both.'

'Neither of us have emerged from the war unscathed, have we?' observed Veronica, looking down at Bob happily curled up on the floor. 'I don't suppose many people have. Change is inevitable,' she added.

As if by magic, Lance suddenly felt much lighter. Exposing his intimate innermost thoughts seemed to have lifted the weight of his painful past, and it was all down to Veronica. Emboldened, he decided to take a leap into the unknown.

'Where do you see your future now?' he asked her.

Veronica brightened a little. 'Oh, I'm going to be the best, most effective correspondent in England,' she responded without hesitation. 'I'm going to report on all the social injustices and revolutionise women's role in society.'

'Is marriage in your plans?' he asked tentatively.

'Oh good Lord, no! Can you imagine it, the drudgery! I'm sure a husband would expect me to give up my career and have children. That's the way of it for women these days.'

'Not necessarily,' Lance said indignantly. 'Not if you met the right person. Not all men are so hidebound by tradition. Some are quite modern in their thinking. They'd let a wife have a career.'

'Well, I haven't met anyone yet who fits that description. In any event, why would I want to tie myself to some selfish brute of a man?'

Lance was crushed. It was clear that her vision for the future did not include matrimony. There was a rather long expectant pause before Veronica felt compelled to fill the void.

'What about you? I suppose your life's all mapped out, now you're the eighth Baron Westex.'

'Yes, I suppose it is,' he said, sighing. He felt utterly deflated by her forthright rejection of marriage.

The third malt whiskey he'd been enjoying hit his system and Lance found himself letting his guard down completely and disclosing a confidence.

'You know, since my late teens my father's had a sort of longstanding unwritten agreement with Viscount Montagu of Somerset that I should marry his daughter Lucinda.'

Veronica looked aghast.

'I don't talk about it much,' he went on. 'It's not something I care to think about. To my shame I must admit I've been trying to delay matters for some time. Now Father's no longer with us I hope I won't have to go through with it. She's not really my type. I don't think we have anything in common at all. My family think I must make a good marriage and Lucinda *is* the Viscount's only heir, so joining forces, so to speak, would make our families very powerful in the area.'

'Not to mention exceedingly rich,' Veronica added sharply.

Lance thought he detected a petulant tone in her voice. Was she jealous of Lucinda? Perhaps his revelation would help her see him in a fresh light. He found that he still harboured hopes of winning Veronica's affections and that they'd spend the rest of their lives together. He decided he wasn't about to let the girl of his dreams slip though his fingers without giving it another shot. Parking these thoughts, he returned to the present.

'What are you going to write in the *Chronicle* about the meeting this evening?' he asked.

'Oh, I think I'll just stick to the facts,' she replied. 'I won't make any comment at the moment. I don't think the villagers of Coombe End are entirely ready for my incisive, penetrating writing style just yet.' A wry smile played around her lips.

'So you're not about to enhance your prospects by making a big splash with a local scoop then?'

'You shouldn't mock me, Lance,' she chided him. 'Someday I'll make it to the big time, and when I do I'll make sure you're the first to know.'

They watched Bob as he lazily stretched out his legs before settling back to sleep.

'What did you make of Peter Hopwood's revelations? Now that would make a good scoop!' Veronica said, her face becoming animated.

Lance noted how sheer beauty and intelligence shone from her eyes whenever she talked about her career. He would certainly encourage her aspiration to become the best reporter in England, if only she'd give him the chance.

'You promised me you wouldn't write anything without passing it by me first,' he reminded her. 'We promised Hopwood that his conversation would remain entirely confidential. We can't betray his trust, Veronica. If we do, no one will ever confide in us again.'

'I don't intend to write about that for the time being. No, that'll keep until we've solved the riddle and I can reveal all to my readers.'

'I'm glad to hear it,' he said, staring into his empty glass.

They had been talking for hours. Lance caught a glimpse of the early morning sunlight creeping around the edges of the curtains.

'Good Lord, what time is it?' he exclaimed looking at his gold half-hunter. 'It's daybreak and I've kept you up nattering all night.'

Veronica stretched and yawned. 'Yes, we have been talking rather a long time. I suppose we ought to think about retiring.'

Just then they were interrupted by a light tap on the study door. Treadwell entered looking abnormally perturbed.

'Excuse me, m'lord, I thought I should inform you that I have sent Digweed into Exeter for the police.'

'Whatever for?' Lance asked, flabbergasted.

'It's Peter Hopwood, sir,' replied the butler, his usually even-toned voice wavering. 'I'm afraid his body's been found down by the lake. He appears to have drowned, sir.'

CHAPTER 18:
FISHY GOINGS-ON

Saturday June 14th 1919

LANCE AND VERONICA LOOKED at one another in horror. Had the gamekeeper been right to worry for his safety after all?

'Who discovered the body?' Lance asked.

'It was Evans, m'lord.'

'What the devil was he doing down by the lake *this* early in the morning?'

'I'm afraid I can't help you with that, sir.'

Lance thought for a moment. 'I'd better speak to Evans before the police arrive. Please instruct him to come to the study now, Treadwell,' Lance said, making up his mind to get to the bottom of things before Chief Superintendent Schilling appeared.

'Very good, m'lord.'

'Oh, and Treadwell, please ask the groundsmen to ensure that no one disturbs the scene at the lake.'

'I've already informed the estate manager, Mr Harrison. I believe he has it well in hand, sir,' the butler said reassuringly before leaving the room.

Veronica could contain herself no longer. 'Do you think he was killed because he told us about *Titanic*?'

'I don't think we should make that connection, not at the moment anyway. He only spoke to us recently. There wasn't time for anyone to learn what he said to us.'

'Suppose he was overheard,' she hissed, a note of panic rising in her voice.

'Whoever could have done that?'

'Someone standing outside the patio window or at the study door. Remember, that's how I listened in to your conversation with the police. Perhaps the people watching you were snooping around.'

'Steady on, old girl! Let's not get ahead of ourselves. He may just have had an accident and fallen into the lake. We don't know all the circumstances yet.'

Presently there was a soft rap at the study door.

'Come,' said Lance with authority.

Evans entered the room. He was a tall, gangly young man in his mid-twenties.

'You wanted to see me, sir?'

'Yes, thank you, Evans,' Lance said, smiling in order to lure the man into a false sense of security. 'I understand you found Hopwood's body down by the lake this morning. Can you tell me how you came to be there so early?'

The second footman pursed his lips. 'Well, sir, I was unable to sleep, so I thought an early morning stroll would clear my mind, ready for the day's assignments.'

'Do you often go for a walk down by the lake in the early morning?' Lance asked, trying to keep his scepticism at bay.

'Yes, sir,' Evans replied a little more confidently. 'When I can't sleep,' he added with a thin smile.

'Tell me how you came to find the body.'

'Well, as I said, I was walking down by the lake when I found myself by the small wooden jetty that runs part way out into the water. I was strolling to the end of the jetty when I noticed something floating in the reeds.'

'Go on,' urged Lance.

'Well, I raced back to the bank and found a good sturdy branch lying under one of the trees and returned to the jetty to snag the object with it.'

Veronica's eyes widened.

'As I thrust the spur into the water I caught the thing awkwardly and it rolled over.'

'Whatever did you do?' Veronica asked agog.

'With the shock of it all, Miss, I dropped the branch and fell over backwards, the body bobbing around in the water not six inches from my face!'

Veronica winced.

'When I recovered my fortitude I realised it was Mr Hopwood. I raced back to the house to inform Mr Treadwell. He sent Mr Digweed for the police.'

'I see,' mused Lance.

'Didn't you try to get Hopwood to the shore and endeavour to revive him?' interjected Veronica.

'No, Miss, I could see from the state of the body that he was dead. I thought he must have fallen in and died earlier.'

'Earlier than what?' Lance fired back.

'Earlier than the time I discovered him … sir,' the second footman replied, the trace of a smirk drifting across his face.

Lance narrowed his eyes and nodded, seemingly accepting Evans response without question.

'I understand you've been unaccountably missing from your post lately,' Lance said, moving effortlessly from one line of interrogation to another.

The sudden change in direction caught Evans off guard. 'I don't know what you mean, sir,' he replied, struggling to conceal his discomfort. 'If you mean that Mr Treadwell has it in for me ...'

'I mean nothing of the sort,' Lance replied abruptly. 'But it has been noticed that you've been absent without any valid explanation. Can you tell me where you've been on these occasions?'

'I'm sure I don't know what you mean, sir.'

'You haven't been absent from your duties then?'

The second footman shook his head slowly and shrugged. 'I really don't know what you mean, sir,' he said again, this time with more assurance.

This was going to get them nowhere, Lance thought, so he decided to move on. 'I also understand you've been rather disturbed by recent events affecting the household.'

Evans looked blankly at Lance. He made no comment, just shook his head imperceptibly.

Lance tried a different tack. 'Something about one of our guests has caused you some disquiet?'

Again the second footman parried the question, choosing instead to concentrate his gaze on the wall just over Lance's shoulder.

'You were assigned as temporary valet to Bruce Hamilton. Is that not correct, Evans?' Lance said impatiently. 'Was there something about that position you found troubling?'

'No, sir.'

'Come man,' Lance said in exasperation. 'It's all over the servants' quarters that you've been expressing doubts ...'

Lance left the sentence hanging in the air, a rather useful trick he'd learned during his tenure as captain of the *Panther*.

Evans seemed in no hurry to finish Lance's sentence. After a moment or two's hesitation he replied cautiously, 'There was somethin' about Mr Hamilton's effects that struck me as odd sir.'

'What was that?' Lance asked, relieved that the second footman appeared to be more forthcoming at last.

'It was his collars, sir.'

'What about them?'

'Four of them are a different size to the others, sir.'

Veronica involuntarily drew in a sharp breath.

'Indeed. What size are the irregular collars?' Lance asked.

'They're three sizes bigger than the others, sir.'

Veronica looked as if she were about to erupt. Lance shot her a desperate look, pleading with her to remain mute. 'Anything else about them strike you as unusual?' he went on.

'The laundry mark, sir. It was different to the others.'

Lance paused. 'I don't remember you mentioning this information to Superintendent Schilling when you were interviewed, Evans?'

'No, sir.'

'Why not?'

'He didn't ask me, sir.'

Vexed by the second footman's selective co-operation, Lance asked, 'Is there anything else you're holding back, something you haven't told us?'

Evans appeared uncomfortable.

'Come man, let's have it – if you wish to remain engaged at Landacre.'

'Very well, sir. I think you should ask your brother where he was on the afternoon of Lord Cedrick's death.'

Lance was poleaxed. 'Whatever do you mean? Do you have the audacity to stand there and cast doubt on my brother's whereabouts that Friday afternoon?'

The second footman licked his lips nervously. 'You did ask me to tell you everything, sir. I happen to know he wasn't out riding with Miss Tabitha at that time, as he says he was.'

'How do you know? Do you have evidence of some kind?'

'No, sir. I have no physical evidence – only what I saw with my own eyes.'

'What did you see, man?'

'Master Hugo walking down to the boathouse.'

'And you're sure it was the same Friday afternoon that Lord Cedrick had his accident?'

'Yes, sir, I'm positive.'

'What time was this, Evans?'

'Around two o'clock, sir.'

A wave of panic washed over Lance. 'Thank you, Evans. That will be all,' he said hurriedly.

The second footman nodded and left the room.

Lance and Veronica looked at one another, momentarily speechless as they tried to register the implications of Evans's testimony.

'I don't like that man,' Lance said, breaking the silence. 'There's something about him that just isn't right. Oh, he acts the role of the perfect footman, but that's just it – he's acting. He's too perfect.'

'Whatever d'you mean?'

'He's too clever, too sure of himself.'

'In what way?'

'Well, for a start he uses words like "assignments" and "fortitude" in his everyday language. That's not normal for a second footman. I would almost say he's been educated at one of England's more lofty educational establishments. And he's sharp, quick-witted, the sort that'll cut himself with his own perspicacity if he's not careful. Yet he seems happy to content himself in a lowly servant's position. The question is why.'

'Are you sure you're not judging him too harshly because of what he said about your brother?' Veronica asked.

'Oh, it's not that. I don't have any faith in his accusations against Hugo.'

'But you *must* ask your brother about it, surely Lance.'

'I will, if only to prove to you that Evans's assertions are completely without foundation.'

Veronica nodded. 'Did you notice how Evans addressed you?'

'What do you mean?'

'He called you "sir" all the time. He never referred to you as "m'lord".'

'Is that significant? Perhaps he can't get used to the fact I'm the new Baron Westex.'

'I'm not so sure … I think there might be more to it than that. You just said yourself how clever he seems. A man of his intellect should easily be able to get to grips with his employer's new status.'

'I think you're being a tad oversensitive,' Lance said dismissively.

'If you say so,' she replied. 'What did you make of this "collar" business? Why would there be four odd-size collars amongst Bruce Hamilton's belongings?'

'I don't know, but I'll wager it's a significant piece of the puzzle.'

There was a gentle knock at the study door and Treadwell came in. He coughed respectfully. 'Chief Superintendent Schilling and Inspector Quick have arrived, m'lord. I have shown them into the library.'

'Thank you, Treadwell, we'll be there directly.'

'Very good, sir.'

'We'll have to tell Superintendent Schilling about our discussion with Hopwood,' Lance said after Treadwell had gone.

'I know. Perhaps we should also tell him about Florence Seymour's letter and our trip to Southampton since there seems to be a connection between Hopwood and *Titanic*.'

'Yes, you're right. I think it's time we put our cards on the table with the Superintendent.'

'We should also tell him of Evans's revelation apropos the collars. I'm sure he'll want to know about that.'

'Yes, but let's leave Hugo out of this for the moment until I've had the chance to talk to him.'

Veronica cast Lance a worried glance. 'Okay,' she said with a note of reluctance.

'Let's go and face the music then,' Lance said, his tired smile an attempt to reassure her that *duty at all times* was his unswerving maxim.

* * *

Inspector Quick was seated at the library table and Chief Superintendent Schilling was pacing the room, his hands behind his back, when the pair entered the library.

'Good morning,' said Lance.

'Good morning, m'lord,' Superintendent Schilling replied, removing his hat and placing it on the library table. 'I gather there's been another unfortunate incident.'

'I'm afraid there has, yes,' Lance said, suddenly finding his energy flagging. Between them, Lance and Veronica told Superintendent Schilling what Treadwell had told them about Hopwood and explained how Evans had come to find the body. Inspector Quick took copious notes.

'I see,' said Schilling. 'And this Evans – you don't believe him when he says he was just taking an early morning walk?'

'No, I'm afraid I don't,' Lance replied forcefully. 'I'm sure there was another reason for him to be down by the lake. He's as cunning as a fox that one. To my mind his motive for being there is most likely one much more to his own advantage.'

Superintendent Schilling raised an eyebrow.

'There's something else you should know, Superintendent,' chimed in Veronica.

The Superintendent listened quietly while they told him of their discovery of the copy letter to Florence Seymour, the visit to Southampton, their subsequent discussion with Hopwood and Evans's revelation about Bruce Hamilton's collars.

Superintendent Schilling scratched his head thoughtfully. 'You getting all this down, Inspector Quick?' he asked.

The Inspector nodded.

'Might the two sets of collars suggest that the body in the mausoleum is not Bruce Hamilton after all?' Veronica said excitedly.

'No go there, I'm afraid, Miss,' Schilling replied. 'The dental records have arrived from America. It's him all right. The collars are probably just a mistake with his laundry.'

But Veronica was not to be discouraged. 'Then why was the face so disfigured when the body was found, Superintendent? Surely that *must* point to the fact someone doesn't want us to know the body isn't that of Bruce Hamilton?'

'In my experience, Miss, people do some mighty terrible things when provoked,' the Superintendent replied pragmatically. 'Whoever the murderer was could have been consumed with such hatred that they carried out an extreme attack to his head. Or it might be much simpler than that – they may have wanted to conceal the original cause of death beneath a lot of other injuries. In any event his wife has identified the body and we've received confirmation from America with the dental evidence. On that basis we don't have any doubt that the body found in the mausoleum is that of Bruce Hamilton, Miss.'

Veronica sighed and sat down in the nearest armchair.

'What will you do now, Superintendent?' Lance asked.

'Well, there will have to be an inquest, of course, but for the time being it's more than likely to be adjourned, the same as Lord Cedrick's and Bruce Hamilton's. We must have time to establish if there's any connection between these three deaths before we ask the coroner to rule on our findings.'

Lance nodded. 'Is there anything more you require of us, Superintendent?'

'Not at the moment, m'lord. Obviously we've a lot of work to carry out. Please keep yourselves available. We may wish to question you both further.'

When Chief Superintendent Schilling and Inspector Quick left, Lance flopped down in an armchair too.

'You look dead beat, Veronica,' he said.

'You don't look so hot yourself,' she snapped.

'You should get some rest. You're welcome to nap here.'

Veronica agreed to stay on at Landacre for a few hours' sleep before returning home and they made their way up to their rooms.

'I must get ready to greet Hugo's wedding guests,' Lance said as they climbed the stairs. 'We've got literally hundreds of people arriving today. Those that Landacre can't accommodate will be staying over at Colonel Bagshott's hotel.' Lance paused on the landing; the mention of the Exmoor Hunting Lodge Hotel had given him an idea. 'Do you ride, Veronica?' he asked.

'Yes, I do, but I haven't ridden for some years,' she replied, surprised by his question.

'Good, that's settled then. We've a hunt arranged for the wedding party on Monday. You can accompany me as my guest.'

Veronica, too tired to argue, made her way towards her room, leaving Lance standing at the top of the staircase feeling rather pleased with himself.

CHAPTER 19:
INDISCRETIONS

Sunday June 15th 1919

THE NEXT MORNING LANCE awoke at his usual hour feeling reinvigorated. After a refreshing cup of his favourite Earl Grey tea, he bathed, splashing on a subtle cologne before Bentley assisted him into a cream flannel suit and crisp cotton shirt. Limping down to breakfast with Bob, Lance could hear the distant chatter of the newly installed guests drifting up the staircase from the dining room. As he walked across the hallway he passed Tabby kitted out in her riding apparel.

'The house is so unbearably crowded this morning, Lance. I'm just off for a ride before church,' she said breezily, waving her crop in mid-air.

The dining room was certainly congested. Lady Maud was seated next to her husband, Lord Duncan Maltravers, and opposite them sat Dame Lettice and her husband, Lord Randolph, the explorer deep in conversation with Lord Duncan about his latest trip to the Congo.

Ruth and Clara were seated at the other end of the table next to Hugo and Monica Whytte, a younger cousin of

Clara's on her father's side and bridesmaid for the wedding. Also at that end of the table were Monica's parents, Zachary and Martha Whytte, and Monica's younger brother Nathan. All were in animated discussion about their trip from America and the tour they'd taken around England before arriving at Landacre.

As time allowed between serving tea and coffee, Rose, the parlourmaid, and Evans ran to and fro the kitchen endeavouring to keep the warming plates topped up with Mrs Hughes's renowned breakfast goodies, all of which were going down a storm.

A general din filled Lance's ears as he helped himself to bacon and scrambled egg on toast before he squeezed himself into a seat between Lady Maud and Zachary Whytte, Bob sitting full of hope beside his master and looking up with an adoring unblinking gaze.

'Morning all,' Lance said brightly.

He was greeted by a chorus of 'Good mornings'.

'I don't know what's got into your sister, Lance,' Lady Maud boomed as he sat down. 'She's been out riding every day since I arrived. It's not natural for a girl of her age. She should be doing good works and meeting eligible young men, not wasting her time on some horse! I shall speak to Cynthia about it.'

'Now, now, my dear,' Lord Duncan soothed. 'It's a healthy pursuit, is it not?'

Lance smiled. 'Tabby's always loved riding horses, Aunt Maud.'

'I can't think why,' she retorted. 'I tried it once. It was the worst two minutes of my life!'

Lance tried to shake off the image forming in his mind's eye of his stout, ungainly aunt on an unfortunate horse. In an effort to stifle a snigger he quickly looked away but only made things worse by catching Hugo grinning back at him.

'How are you and your family finding England, Mr Whytte?' Lance asked hurriedly.

Zachary Whytte, younger brother of Willard, Ruth's first husband, was a large portly man in his mid-fifties with a shock of thick white hair, a large handlebar moustache and bushy beard. His ruddy cheeks and twinkling grey eyes rather put Lance in mind of Father Christmas.

'Mighty fine, young man, mighty fine,' Zachary said, slapping him heartily on the back.

Lance almost choked on his scrambled egg. Resisting the urge to cough up a piece of toast, he croaked, 'I'm so glad, Mr Whytte. Please let me know if there's anything you or your family require during your stay.'

'Please, call me Zac,' the man said, pushing another forkful of bacon into his mouth as he spoke. 'Everyone calls me Zac. Isn't that right, Martha,' he mumbled while chewing his food.

Martha Whytte, a small woman with grey hair who seemed much more reserved than her rambunctious husband, was tackling her breakfast with a noticeable delicacy. 'That's right, Zac dear,' she replied, her mild Scottish-American lilt drifting across the table.

'No Lady Cynthia this morning?' Monica coyly enquired of Hugo. She was a strikingly beautiful girl in her twenties with auburn hair, a fair complexion and sparkling blue eyes.

'Oh, Mother always breakfasts in her room,' he replied, giving Monica a charming smile. 'She almost never comes down to breakfast.'

Clara cast Hugo a disapproving look.

'When you've finished, Monica, we should repair to our rooms and ready ourselves for church this morning,' Martha said, looking from Clara to her daughter.

Nathan, a young stripling recently into long trousers and bearing a strong resemblance to his mother, chipped in, 'Oh Mother, do we have to?'

'Yes, we do,' she responded firmly.

As breakfast finished, the guests drifted away one by one from the dining room to prepare themselves for the Sunday morning service. Later, the Hall's fleet of cars was brought around to the front entrance to ferry everyone to the village. Digweed stood beside the open door of the black Bullnose Morris, waiting patiently for his first passengers, his flat cap rolled tightly in his hands. The last to leave the Hall were Lady Cynthia and Tabitha who climbed into the returned vehicle with more than a hint of trepidation, knowing what to expect under Digweed's care in the 'new-fangled contraption'. Meanwhile Lance jumped into his two-seater with Bob and arrived at St Peter's just ahead of them.

Reverend Simon Eustace was standing at the south door welcoming his congregation, which this morning consisted not only of his usual flock from the village and the Hall but also the newly arrived visitors who would be attending Hugo and Clara's wedding in a few days' time.

Lance alighted from his car and, leaving Bob curled up on the passenger seat, he stood chatting to the Reverend outside the church as he waited for Digweed to arrive with Lady Cynthia and Tabitha.

At last the car lurched up to the church gate. Digweed ambled around to the passenger door and held it open respectfully while Lady Cynthia and Tabitha stumbled out, straightening their hats. Bert Beamish and his wife, Laura, had just arrived on foot, and all four made their way up the path together.

'Such a lovely day, Lady Cynthia, Miss Tabitha,' Laura said.

Bert looked at Tabitha, a wicked grin spreading across his face. 'Yes, a good morning for a ride out with Laurence Harrison, Miss Tabitha.'

Tabby blushed.

'Come to think on it, you've bin out ridin' with that young fella quiet a lot recently. Didn't I see you with him a couple of Fridays ago?' Bert asked.

His wife dug her elbow hard into Bert's ribs. 'It's no concern of yours, Bert Beamish, what Miss Tabitha does,' she hissed, practically pushing him into the church. 'I do apologise Lady Cynthia, Miss Tabitha,' she said, her face flushed.

Lady Cynthia smiled and, scooping Tabitha's arm in hers, marched her up to the family's pew at the front of the church.

Lance was about to follow his mother and sister inside when to his surprise he saw Chief Superintendent Schilling and Inspector Quick walking purposefully up the path.

'Good morning, Superintendent. I didn't know this was your local place of worship, Inspector,' Lance said.

'No, m'lord, it isn't. Mrs Quick and I generally frequent All Hallows in Exeter.'

'This is a very unofficial visit, sir,' interjected Superintendent Schilling quickly. 'We just happened to be in the area and thought we'd attend the service – a kind of spur of the moment decision if you like.'

'Happened to be in the area, my eye!' Lance said to the Reverend in a low voice after the two policemen had gone into the church. 'They've come to look over the suspects in their natural habitat more like.'

While the Reverend made his way up to the pulpit, Lance sat down next to his mother and sister in the family pew. Glancing around the church, he noticed Ruth sitting next to Hugo and Clara in the pew behind. She was wearing an orange ensemble with a large navy-blue straw hat. She looked rather like a small pumpkin today, he thought. He nodded to her and she gave him a brief smile.

The Reverend indicated to the organist, who was fumbling over some Bach, that he was about to start the service and the instrument fell silent.

After an hour and a half on the theme of New Beginnings, including two Bible readings, a sermon and the enthusiastic if somewhat discordant singing of hymns, the congregation found themselves spilling back out into the churchyard.

The Reverend stood at the entrance to the porch chatting to his parishioners as they exited.

'A very uplifting sermon, vicar,' Lady Maud boomed from under an impossibly fussy yellow hat. 'Especially in consideration of recent events. I shall certainly speak favourably to the Archbishop about it.'

'Yes, thank you, Simon. A very well-judged address,' Lady Cynthia said, blinking rapidly as she emerged with Tabitha from the darkness into the bright mid-day sun.

Lance was standing in the yard with Hugo, Zac, Dame Lettice and Lord Randolph.

'That organist plays as well as Digweed drives!' Hugo exclaimed with a whimsical smile. 'I do hope Mrs Pike will have practised the pieces for our wedding next Saturday.'

'Yes, I feel she was to some degree wrestling with the organ. It almost became a race to the finish with the choir!' drawled Zac before moving away to join the rest of his family.

Chief Superintendent Schilling and Inspector Quick emerged from the porch. 'A very fine service, Reverend,' the Superintendent said before making his way over to Lance and his party.

'Anything new on Hopwood's death, Superintendent?' Lance enquired casually.

'We're progressing with our enquiries, m'lord,' Superintendent Schilling said stiffly.

But Lance was not to be so easily deflected. 'Has any determination been reached on the cause of death?'

'The pathologist hasn't completed his written report yet, sir, but unofficially it looks as though he was hit with a blunt instrument from behind, something of a bad habit around these parts it seems.'

'Whatever do you mean, Superintendent,' Hugo asked.

'I'm afraid Mr Hamilton also seems to have died from a blunt trauma to the head, sir, the blow that killed him being concealed by the terrible injuries exacted after death.'

Hugo glanced towards Ruth and Clara talking animatedly with their American cousins a few feet away. 'I think we should be careful what we say in front of his wife, Superintendent,' he whispered. 'She's had more than enough distress to cope with these last few days. It's Clara's wish that we put these dreadful events behind us and concentrate on the wedding.'

'As you wish, sir.'

'Hopwood didn't fall in and drown by accident then?' Lance asked.

'It doesn't look that way, no, m'lord,' Schilling said. 'No water in the lungs you see. He was dead before he hit the water.'

The two policemen were about to make their way back down the church path when the Superintendent stopped suddenly.

'Oh by the way, m'lord,' Schilling said, retrieving two forensic bags from inside his spacious overcoat. 'Do you recognise these?'

Lance looked at each bag. One contained a brass button and the other held a black leather glove, the kind worn by a man of means.

'No, Superintendent, I'm afraid not. Is it important?'

'The button was found under the body of Bruce Hamilton, m'lord, and the glove was found down by the lake. What about you Master Hugo?'

Hugo glanced briefly at the bags, shook his head and shrugged. 'No, Superintendent.'

'No matter,' the Superintendent said. 'We've brought in Sir Bernard Spilsbury to assist. You may remember he was instrumental in proving the case against Dr Crippen in 1910, and gave evidence at the Brides in the Bath trial four years ago. Given his expertise I'm sure he'll be able to identify evidence that will prove useful. Well, good afternoon to you both.'

The Superintendent tipped his hat and the two policemen strolled off down the church path.

'You hear that, Lance,' hissed his brother. 'They've got Sir Bernard Spilsbury on the case.'

'That's good news,' Lance replied, bemused that Hugo seemed so awestruck by the famous forensics expert. 'That could very well bring this whole horrible affair to a close quickly. Which reminds me ...' Lance took his brother roughly by the arm and led him around the side of the church.

'What are you doing?' Hugo wailed.

'I want to talk to you, brother of mine, and I don't want to be overheard.'

'Can't it wait? I've got to accompany Clara and her mother back to Landacre.'

'No it can't. I want to know where you were on the afternoon Pa died.'

'You know where I was – I went riding with Tabby.'

'Don't talk rot. You weren't with her at all.'

A look of anguish flashed across Hugo's face. 'Why do you say that, Lance? What have you heard?'

'Someone noticed that you didn't go out riding with Tabby that afternoon. I want to know where you were and why you lied.'

'That's a bit much. I didn't lie exactly.'

'What would you call it then?'

Hugo tried to free himself from his brother's grasp. 'I've nothing else to say on the matter.'

'Look Hugo, if I can catch you out in a lie so can Superintendent Schilling. How d'you think it'll seem to him? He only has to ask the head groom if you took a horse out that afternoon and the game's up. You don't want to spend your wedding day in the clink. If you explain to me now, we'll have time to work out how to inform the authorities without casting suspicion on you.'

'You can't think I had anything to do with Pa's death!'

'Of course I don't, you idiot, but Schilling might if he finds out you've been keeping something from him.'

Hugo stared at Lance for a second or two. 'Well, if you must know I was helping Tabby out, that's all,' he blurted out.

'Tabby?'

'Yes, she didn't want Ma to know she was out riding with Laurence. You know what Ma's like – she wouldn't have approved if she'd known what Tabby was really doing.'

'Laurence?'

'Yes, Laurence Harrison, the estate manager. I got dressed up in my hacking togs and agreed to say she was out riding with me.'

'Did you take a horse out that afternoon at all?'

'No, there wasn't any need to. I just left the Hall in my riding gear and went for a walk.'

'You're a complete ass, Hugo. If that's all it was why not come clean and tell Schilling about it when you were interviewed. I'm sure he wouldn't go blabbing to Ma.'

'I thought it would look bad for me, Lance. The Superintendent might form the opinion that fabrication comes easily to me, that I've no compunction about deceiving people. He may not believe anything I say in the future.'

'It's going to look far worse now, you dolt. No matter. We must put it right straight away. How long were you out?'

'I thought I'd better give Tabby a decent length of time with Laurence so I left the Hall after lunch and returned around five o'clock.'

'And you didn't see anyone who could confirm your movements for the duration?'

'No, I didn't. Do you think it will come to that – me having to produce proof?'

'Let's hope not. Leave it to me. I'll have a word with Schilling.'

'Thanks. You're a good egg, Lance.'

The brothers made their way back round to the front of the church and rejoined the others who were keen to get back to the Hall for their Sunday lunch.

CHAPTER 20:
TALLY-HO

Monday June 16th 1919

BRIGHT AND EARLY THE next morning Lance sent Digweed to fetch Veronica from the station. After he had dressed in his red hunting jacket and buff riding breeches, he waited impatiently for her to arrive, keeping an eye out through the glass doors at the entrance of the Hall. As he stood there, Tabitha came through on her way to the stables dressed in her ladies hunting outfit: a blue jacket and faun jodhpurs.

'Oh hello, Lance. You waiting for someone?' she asked.

'Yes, Veronica's coming with us on the hunt today. I'm just waiting for Digweed to return from Exhampton with her.'

'You're pretty stuck on her, aren't you. I'm not sure what Ma will make of it. Aren't you supposed to be courting Lucinda Willoughby-Vane?'

Lance pulled a face. 'I know, I know,' he replied irritably. 'But damn it all, Tabby, I think I should be allowed to choose who I marry.'

'Fat chance of that. Ma went mad when we returned from church yesterday. Old Bert Beamish well and truly let the cat out of the bag when he mentioned that I'd been out riding with Laurence Harrison. She gave me hell when she found out.'

'Bad luck,' said Lance. 'I hope you're not getting too fond of Laurence, Tabby. You know Ma will never let it amount to anything. I wouldn't like to see you get hurt.'

'But why can't *I* marry for love? After all Hugo's marrying an *American*!'

Lance smiled fondly at his little sister. 'Sometimes life's very, very unfair, Tabby.'

'More like the Whyttes are *very, very* rich,' she responded spitefully.

'You shouldn't talk like that about your brother's marriage,' Lance said, a little shocked by his sister's uncharacteristic outburst. 'I'm sure Pa had his reasons for countenancing Hugo's betrothal to Clara.'

'Arghhhhh!' she said and walked out the front door waving her crop in the air.

Presently the Bullnose Morris came trundling up the drive, and Digweed brought the vehicle to a haphazard halt as Lance opened the main door to the Hall and waited on the stone steps for Veronica to emerge.

'Good trip?' he enquired when she stepped out of the car clothed in an old, worn tweed hunting jacket and heavy cavalry twill jodhpurs.

'Wonderful,' she replied, flashing a bright smile at Digweed who remained impassive. She gave herself a little shake and tugged down her jacket.

'You look lovely this morning,' Lance said wistfully, drinking her in.

'Oh these old things!' she said, blushing a little. 'I'm afraid they're a bit threadbare. I dug them out from a large trunk I keep in the attic. I can't remember the last time I went riding.'

'Well, I think they're delightful,' Lance replied, taking her by the arm and whisking her around to the stable yard where Seb Smithers, the head groom, was waiting to assist the family and guests with their mounts for the day.

'Morning, Smithers,' Lance said. 'I thought Veronica could ride Versailles today. That horse is very steady and reliable for someone who hasn't ridden for a while.'

"Right ho, sir,' replied the head groom, reverently touching his forelock hidden under a moth-eaten Harris Tweed cap.

He gave orders to one of his underlings to tack-up and lead the horse out.

Before long the sound of horseshoes on cobbles filled the yard as out of the stable door materialised a majestic mare of approximately sixteen hands, her coat the colour of snow, and with a long thick white mane and tail, dark eyes under long dark eyelashes and black polished hooves.

'She's absolutely gorgeous!' Veronica said breathlessly as she approached the graceful animal to say hello.

Lance found himself longing to hear Veronica speak about him in that tone of voice; she was clearly smitten.

Behind Versailles the head groom led out a jet-black stallion, his coat gleaming in the early morning sun.

'Your usual mount, m'lord.'

'Thank you, Smithers.'

Lance took the reins and in one swift movement propelled himself up into the saddle. The stallion danced about on the spot, a sign he was eager to get going.

'Whoa boy,' he said gently as he brought the steed under control. He was a good rider and sat deep in the saddle.

'What a beautiful horse,' Veronica said from her position high up on Versailles who was calmly waiting for the off, unimpressed by her stablemate's flamboyant antics. 'What's his name?'

'This is Sorcerer. He's a bit of a handful, but he's a wonderful animal – good breeding stock.'

Veronica grinned. 'He's a bit of a show-off – like all men,' she said before urging Versailles into a walk.

At the other end of the stable yard Tabitha was seated on her mount, a chestnut mare, waiting patiently for Laurence Harrison to get astride his ride for the day.

Lance and Veronica moved off through the stable arch on the opening leg of the journey to the Exmoor Hunting Lodge Hotel where members of the Exminster Deer Hounds were gathering.

'Wait for us,' yelled Tabby from the bottom of the stable yard.

The four hacked across the moor to the hotel, arriving just as the Master of the Hunt rounded one of the side entrances to the building with a number of his mounted lieutenants in attendance and a pack of deer hounds swirling around their feet.

As they waited outside the hotel's Georgian stone portico, Hugo rode up in the company of Zac and Monica who had also been loaned horses from the Hall, and a chorus of greetings rang out around the hotel courtyard.

The sound of clattering horse's hooves announced the arrival of Viscount Somerset and, riding side-saddle, his daughter, the Honourable Lucinda Willoughby-Vane. She was a slender girl in her late twenties, who exuded wealth and status even in her hunting garb. She wore a long navy riding skirt with a white blouse fastened at the neck by a gold and pearl brooch in the shape of the family crest, and she gripped a silver-topped riding cane in one of her gloved hands. A navy fur-felt dressage hat held her blonde hair in a stylish chignon and a net veil discreetly covered her face. Her mount for the day, furnished by the hotel, was Apollo, a magnificent half-Arabian, half-thoroughbred bay gelding with four white socks and a white blaze. Together they made a perfect picture of country elegance and privilege.

The Viscount and his daughter trotted across the courtyard to join the party.

'Morning, Lance,' barked Viscount Somerset. 'Lovely morning for the hunt, what?'

'Good morning, m'lord,' Lance responded graciously.

Lucinda urged her horse forward so she was directly beside Sorcerer.

'Aren't you going to say hello to *me*, Lance darling?' she enquired, her syrupy voice making Lance feel slightly nauseous.

'Of course, Lucinda. How are you?' he asked unenthusiastically. 'Let me introduce you to everyone.' He moved around the party making introductions. '... and I don't think you've met Veronica Barnes,' Lance concluded, smiling warmly as he looked at her. 'She's a journalist from the *Chronicle*. She's covering Hugo's wedding.'

Lucinda cocked her head a little and narrowed her eyes. After she had looked Veronica up and down, she said, 'Good morning, Miss Barnes. How nice of the stable lads to lend you some hunting apparel so you could join us today.' She smiled, arching one of her perfectly shaped eyebrows.

Lance glared at her, furious at her barbed comment. It hadn't gone unnoticed by some of the other riders, and Veronica, who had gone scarlet from ear to ear, ducked her head to stare at the ground. Lance felt torn. He couldn't bear to see Veronica humiliated in such a way, but now was not the time to make a scene.

Lucinda gave Lance a winsome smile and, yanking on Apollo's reins, moved off to engage with other members of the hunt.

Just then, the sound of thundering hooves approaching from behind heralded the arrival of Lord Duncan and Lord Randolph. Pleasantries were exchanged, which helped to dissipate the tension, and conversation resumed amongst their circle.

'You all right?' Lance quietly asked Veronica.

'I'm fine really. Please don't distress yourself. I wouldn't want to keep you from your responsibilities hosting the other guests.'

'Well, if you're sure,' Lance said and he moved off to circulate amongst others in the party.

There was quite a gathering milling around now with a number of the wedding guests on horses provided by the hotel. Those from Landacre who were not riding – Lady

Cynthia, Lady Maud, Dame Lettice, Ruth, Clara and Nathan Whytte – had arrived by car to watch the event. Participants and spectators alike mingled happily in the courtyard, everyone excitedly anticipating the sport.

Colonel George Bagshott descended the stone steps of his establishment carrying a large silver tray bearing small glasses of sherry and port which he began to offer up to the riders.

Lucinda, standing in close proximity to Veronica, leaned down for a glass of sherry when for some reason her horse took a sudden side step, barging into Versailles and causing Lucinda to spill her sherry over Veronica. Lucinda pulled hard on Apollo's reins.

'Oh, I'm so sorry, my dear, I'm still getting used to him. No harm done though,' she said with a cold smile. She looked down her nose at Veronica before guiding her horse away towards her father.

Veronica was wiping herself down when Hugo rode over. 'This your first time with the Exminster Hunt?' he asked kindly, handing her his handkerchief to help her dry off.

'Yes, does it show that much?' she replied.

'There're a good bunch really,' he said. 'They just take a bit of getting used to, that's all.'

Veronica smiled.

'Don't take any notice of that cow Lucinda,' he added. 'Just be yourself and you're bound to have them under your spell in no time.'

On hearing his kind words her eyes prickled with the sudden rare appearance of tears. She used his handkerchief to discreetly dab at her eyes.

'Thanks,' she said, handing the handkerchief back to Hugo.

Just then, the Master of the Hunt blew his horn and the pack of hounds yapped merrily as the riders followed them out onto the moor. Meanwhile, the spectators leisurely made their way into the hotel to seat themselves in the large bay windows, which had impressive panoramic views over the landscape.

The morning sun enhanced the natural beauty of the moor as the hunt made its way over the pink and purple heather, yellow gorse punctuating the open spaces with tall thorny fronds flowering profusely. Newly unfurled lime-green bracken rose up from the soft peaty ground amid the fine grass kept tightly cut by the hordes of rabbits.

Lance stayed close to Veronica as the riders spread out, the sound of the hunting horn drifting towards them on the warm summer breeze. He was delighted that she seemed to find Versailles easy to ride. They rode on across the crest of the moor, the hollow thud of cantering hooves muffled by the soft turf and their senses enveloped by the aroma of earthy mulch.

They'd been riding for about half an hour when Versailles suddenly threw her head back and let out a piercing neigh. The horse's pace quickened and she began to froth at the mouth.

Veronica sat down in her saddle, leaning back and desperately pulling hard on the reins, but it was useless. The horse had her head down now and was galloping at full speed across the moor, outpacing the other riders.

'Lance, I can't hold her,' Veronica shouted frantically.

Lance kicked Sorcerer into action and raced after her. 'Hold on, Veronica,' he yelled, 'I'm coming.'

Versailles thundered on, galloping as if her life depended on it, Veronica clinging on to her mane as well as the reins. Suddenly a large tree trunk loomed up through the undergrowth. With a great leap Versailles took off, sailing gracefully through the air, but seconds later, rider and horse parted company, Veronica falling to earth in an ungainly heap. As the horse disappeared into the distance Lance rode up on Sorcerer to find Veronica lying motionless amongst the heather. He jumped down and tenderly knelt over her; there was blood trickling from her head.

'Veronica! Veronica!' he cried desperately.

Just then, others from the hunt arrived.

'Quick, someone ride back to the hotel and get one of their cars,' Lance shouted. 'We've got to get her medical help.'

'I'll go,' Laurence Harrison said, pulling sharply on the reins of his horse. Turning Marquis on a sixpence, he galloped off at full pelt back across the moor towards the hotel.

'It's all my fault, it's all my fault,' Lance murmured, distraught as he kept watch over Veronica's lifeless body.

CHAPTER 21:
AN INVITATION

BACK AT THE HOTEL, Laurence sent for Doctor David Beauchamp, the GP from Coombe End, before racing back to the moor to collect Veronica in one of the small vans used by the hotel to transport luggage. Doctor Beauchamp, a tall, lean attractive man in his early thirties, arrived in his black Morris Cowley just as the van carrying Veronica pulled up at the portico entrance. Immediately taking charge of his patient, he arranged to examine her in one of the vacant downstairs rooms.

Lance and Tabitha galloped at breakneck speed to the hotel and arrived just in time to see a group of porters co-opted as stretcher-bearers making their way unsteadily up the steps and into the reception area. Dismounting at speed, Lance hared into the hotel behind the porters and attempted to follow the stretcher into the temporary examination room.

'No need for anyone else at the moment,' Dr Beauchamp said breezily, shutting the door politely but firmly on Lance.

Spectators who had witnessed the accident from the hotel's windows began to gather outside the examination room, anxiously waiting for news. Lance stood in the reception area utterly bewildered, staring vacantly into the distance where the remainder of the hunt was still coursing over the moor. Finding the wait intolerable, he began to pace frantically up and down.

'I shouldn't have pushed her into riding today,' he kept muttering over and over.

'Oh do sit down, Lance,' boomed Lady Maud who was seated in one of the bay windows with Lady Cynthia and Dame Lettice and sipping tea from a china tea service. 'I'm sure the doctor will inform us as soon as he's made his diagnosis.'

Lance fumed silently at his aunt's insensitivity and sat down on a large comfy sofa and fidgeted.

'It's been such a terrible experience for Lance,' Dame Lettice said. 'We should be supportive in these difficult times, Maud dear.'

'We're British!' retorted Lady Maud. 'We should be getting on with the hunt, not flailing about like pieces of limp celery! I'm sure the girl will be all right.'

Dame Lettice, exasperated, looked at Lady Cynthia and in unison they rolled their eyes.

Lady Cynthia rose from her seat in the window and went over to Lance. 'I'm sure she'll be perfectly fine, Lance dear,' she said reassuringly, putting a supportive arm through his and patting his hand. 'She's probably just winded, that's all. She's in the best hands. David Beauchamp is a wonderful doctor.'

But Lance was inconsolable. 'She's had a terrible fall, Mother. She's taken a very bad knock to her head.'

Presently the Colonel appeared. 'There's a gentleman at the rear entrance. He's asking to speak with you, m'lord. Says his name is Smithers.'

Lance looked up. 'What,' he mumbled, too stunned to take in what was happening around him.

'It's all right,' Laurence Harrison said. 'He's the Hall's head groom. I'll go and see what he wants.'

After what seemed to Lance to be hours later, but had in fact been barely twenty minutes, the door to the temporary examination room opened and Doctor Beauchamp emerged, marching briskly across the reception floor carrying his large black bag and a pork-pie hat.

'She's had a very nasty fall,' the doctor said without breaking his stride. 'However, there are no bones broken and the injury to her head is quite superficial. She'll need some rest, of course, but you can go in and see her for a few minutes if you like. Must push on now. Got a baby waiting over at Stapleford. Good morning, good morning,' and with that he put on his hat and was gone.

'Well really!' remarked Lady Maud. 'What an economical doctor he is. I shall certainly speak to Sir Giles Toddington on the General Medical Council about his complete lack of bedside manner.'

Lance rushed into the examination room to see Veronica sitting up on the edge of a chaise longue holding her head in her hands, her riding jacket torn and her jodhpurs covered in mud.

A wave of relief surged through him. 'You all right, Veronica?' he asked tenderly.

She looked up. 'Yes, I think so,' she replied. 'What happened? I don't remember—'

Just then, Laurence came charging into the room, a look of consternation clouding his face. 'Smithers just told me that Versailles returned to the Hall's stables.'

'Thank goodness,' Lance replied, a second wave of relief coursing through his body. Puzzled by Laurence's expression he said, 'That's a good thing isn't it?'

'In normal circumstances it would be, m'lord, except in this case Smithers has had to send for Mr Fitzgerald, the local vet from Exeter.'

'Why, whatever for?' Lance asked, his sense of unease rising again.

'He thinks Versailles been drugged with something. Apparently she came skittering into the yard at full gallop, swinging her head, frothing at the mouth and covered in sweat. According to Smithers it's not like Versailles at all. I don't mind telling you, sir, I'm worried. What's going on?'

Lance and Veronica glanced anxiously at each other. Had some mysterious villain arranged Veronica's accident, Lance wondered? Were they in danger by investigating the recent deaths?

'It's nothing to worry about, Laurence. It must be some kind of terrible mishap, that's all,' Lance replied.

Turning to Veronica, Laurence asked, 'How d'you feel? You took a nasty fall back there. For a minute things didn't look too good for you.'

'I'm okay, really, Laurence,' she replied, giving him a weak smile. 'I just need to rest. If someone could take me home I'd be very grateful.'

'Of course, I'll take you,' Lance said instantly. 'Laurence, you take Sorcerer back to the Hall and I'll take Veronica into Exeter.'

Laurence was about to leave when Tabby came bowling into the room. 'You all right?' she asked Veronica.

'Yes, I'm fine, Tabby, really. I just want to go home,' Veronica said.

'Come on, Tabby, let's get the horses back to Landacre,' Laurence said, smiling and holding the door open for her.

* * *

Lance's and Veronica's journey back to Exeter was mostly spent in quiet reflection. Veronica was having trouble remembering what had happened and although Lance recounted the sequence of events leading up to her accident, it was no good – the final few minutes remained a complete blank to her.

'My most vivid memory is of Lucinda being an absolute cow to me just before we left the hotel grounds,' Veronica said. She paused for a moment or two. 'My accident – it can't be connected with the three recent deaths, can it, Lance?'

'We'll have to see what the vet has to say. If Versailles *was* drugged, that would point to it being a premeditated act. Someone would have had to obtain the drug prior to the hunt and bring it along with them to the hotel this morning. That's very deliberate.'

'Hmm … but why me? Who knew I was invited?'

'I did warn you that asking questions about this business could result in some kind of danger.'

'Yes, I know you did, but it also means someone thinks we're getting too close to the truth and wants to get rid of us. But why try to bump me off without getting rid of you as well? You know as much as I do about this whole affair. It doesn't make any sense.'

'Well, I suppose you have the means to publish and make public what we *do* know. That could be dangerous to whoever's behind this business. And maybe that same person has forged a plan to get rid of me at some later date,' he added wryly.

Veronica grinned. 'The only person I know who would be malicious enough to do such a nasty thing would be Lucinda!'

'Steady on, old thing. I know Lucinda can be foul, but I don't think even she would go to those lengths. Why on earth would she?'

'She's jealous, you fool!' Veronica replied, laughing. 'She sees me as some kind of threat. She doesn't know we're just comrades.'

Is that all we are? thought Lance. Oh how he wished they were more than that.

* * *

Back at Deacon Heights Veronica made slow and painful progress up the stairs to her apartment. Standing at the door, she thanked Lance for bringing her home.

She was about to turn and go in when he said, 'We're having a big bash tomorrow evening. It's the pre-wedding ball for Hugo and Clara before the main event on Saturday. Everyone who's anyone will be attending, and I was wondering if you would accompany me as my partner for the evening?'

'And what will Lucinda make of that? Isn't she expecting to be your partner?' Veronica asked. 'I'm not sure I'm up for any more "accidents" befalling me just yet, not until I get over these bumps and bruises at any rate.'

'Oh, damn Lucinda! I don't care what she thinks. I want to go with you ... if you'll have me.'

Veronica thought about it for a moment. 'Okay, it's a date,' she said, smiling wickedly.

'And will you permit me one further impertinence?' Lance asked softly.

'That depends.'

'Will you allow me to ask Madame Cristobal's of Exeter to furnish you with your gown for the evening?' He took hold of the tattered and torn sleeve of her riding jacket. 'I want you to outshine everyone at the ball ... and I do mean everyone,' he added, giving her a meaningful look as if they were entering some sort of conspiracy together.

'Oh Lance, I couldn't. You know I like to be an independent woman. I can't let you do that.'

'But you must, Veronica. I want you to. I won't hear another word about it.'

She looked at him for a moment or two. 'Fine, if you insist ... but I'm only going along with it because I want to show Lucinda up for the stuck-up cow she is.'

Lance beamed from ear to ear. 'I'll send a dresser round from Madame Cristobal's at five tomorrow evening and Digweed will collect you around seven, all right?'

After calling at the dress shop to arrange for a dresser and stylist for Veronica, Lance made his way back to Landacre. Driving through Devon's twisting country lanes, he felt very pleased with himself, a smile playing about his lips at the thought of seeing Lucinda's startled reaction when she realised that Veronica was his partner for the ball.

With the remnants of these agreeable thoughts dissipating from his mind like the wisps of an early morning mist over Landacre's lake, Lance steered the Bullnose Morris between the stone pillars of the estate and up the long winding drive to the Hall.

* * *

'Good afternoon, m'lord,' Treadwell said as Lance alighted from the car. 'Mr John Fitzgerald, the veterinarian, is waiting to see you, sir. I have shown him into the library.'

'Thank you, Treadwell,' Lance replied as he made his way up the low, worn steps to the Hall's main door.

John Fitzgerald had gone to school with Lance and Robert Sixsmith and they were old chums. When Lance went into the library, John was standing at the French windows admiring the view.

'Afternoon, John,' Lance said affably. 'What's all this about Versailles? Smithers thinks she may have been drugged.'

'I'm afraid Smithers could well be right,' John replied, shaking Lance's hand.

'Good Lord! I've never heard of such a thing. What do you think it was? More importantly when could it have been given to her?'

'The "when" would probably be about thirty minutes or so before Versailles began to show any effects. The "what" will take a bit more investigation.'

'But that would mean she was given the drug when we were all waiting outside the hotel this morning. How d'you think it could have been administered without anyone noticing?'

'Well, there are a number of ways it could have been given — orally on a sugar lump or something of the kind, or dispensed through the skin. In any event the effect would be the same. As soon as the stimulant entered the bloodstream the horse would have gone loco. I've taken some blood samples and I'll get them off to the lab as soon as I get back to the surgery, but my best guess would be that it is an amphetamine of some kind.'

'Amphetamine? I don't think I've heard of that before.'

'You probably haven't. It's a class of drug discovered in Germany at the end of the last century. I've been reading up on its effect in animals since I became the on-call vet for the Devon and Exeter Racecourse over at Haldon Hill. You wouldn't believe the lengths some people will go to for the sake of winning a race. The doping of horses has reached almost epidemic proportions.'

'Where would someone get hold of such a substance?'

'I'm sure there are any number of illicit suppliers who'd be happy to sell it to someone, no questions asked. Anyway, I've given Versailles something to calm her down. She should be fine in a day or two, but these drugs do sometimes have a few nasty side effects, so don't let anyone ride her out until Smithers is entirely happy with her. I'll be back in a couple of days to see how she's progressing.'

After John left, Lance sat in his study with an early evening gin and tonic, wondering who could have doped Versailles.

'If the substance could be given to Versailles without anyone noticing, then it could have been anyone who was at the hotel this morning,' Lance said aloud to Bob. The dog gave a half-hearted wag of his tail. 'There were so many people milling around, both on and off horses. I certainly didn't see anyone behaving suspiciously.'

Exhausted, Lance leaned back in his chair and closed his eyes. He let the events of the day wash over him and lingered on thoughts of Veronica accompanying him to the ball the next day.

CHAPTER 22:
PREPARATIONS AND
PROTESTATIONS

Tuesday June 17th 1919

THE NEXT MORNING LANCE awoke feeling enthusiastic. In the evening was Hugo's and Clara's pre-wedding ball when the great and the good of Britain and America would be attending Landacre, resplendent in their finest couture.

As Lance washed and dressed for the day, attended fastidiously by Bentley, he found himself daydreaming about the moment when he and Veronica would make their entrance at the ball later. He could almost hear the impromptu gasps and see the admiring glances of the assembled guests. He felt an unbearable chasm of unoccupied time begin to open up ahead of the evening's affair and realised that for him it was going to be an achingly long day. How could he divert himself until the time of the ball?

He finished adjusting his cufflinks and reviewed his attire in front of the splendid full-length antique mirror.

'I shall be going into Coombe End this morning to see Jacob Snyder, Bentley,' Lance said.

'Very good, m'lord,' his valet responded, fussily brushing the back of Lance's jacket.

'And I think my naval mess uniform for this evening, don't you? I wouldn't want to let Hugo and Clara down on their special night.'

'Assuredly so, sir,' Bentley replied, giving his master an approving nod.

With Bob beside him, Lance went down for breakfast. At the bottom of the stairs he passed his brother approaching from the other direction.

'Morning, Hugo. Looking forward to your big shindig tonight?' he asked, smiling broadly.

'This wedding's been such a long time in the making I can barely believe we're almost there! I shall certainly be relieved when Clara and I actually get to the altar. It's been nothing short of challenging all the way. I hope nothing else befalls us to derail our plans.'

'Buck up, brother of mine,' Lance replied breezily over his shoulder. 'You're in the final furlong now. Not far to the finish line.'

Making his way towards the gentle hum of conversation emanating from the dining room, he passed a figure hidden behind the open broadsheet pages of *The Times* sitting in one of the alcoves. From the cut of his jib, Lance recognised his Uncle Randolph.

'Morning, Uncle,' Lance said, pulling the top of the newspaper down with his finger. 'What are you doing out here?'

His uncle looked up. 'Oh, it's you, Lance,' he spluttered. 'Just trying to avoid Maud, don't you know. To tell you the truth, she's a bit much for me first thing in the morning.' He gave Lance a conspiratorial wink.

Aunt Maud was a bit much at any time of the day, Lance thought sagely. 'Any news worth noting in the paper this morning?' he asked.

'Nothing much,' his uncle said. 'Alcock and Brown have won the *Daily Mail*'s prize for being the first to cross the Atlantic non-stop by air. Jolly good show for the British, what?'

'Yes indeed,' Lance replied and continued on his way to the dining room to tuck into a light breakfast.

Having spent a pleasant hour at the dining table enjoying his bacon and eggs and chatting happily with the numerous guests staying at Landacre, Lance and Bob jumped into the two-seater and motored the short distance down to Coombe End.

'I'm going to ask Snyder for the Memorial Fund accounts, Bob,' Lance said as he sped through the narrow country lanes. 'And I won't put up with any nonsense about them not being in a fit state for collection,' he added.

The dog offered no opinion one way or another and continued to look about him as the countryside flashed by, his ears flapping in the wind.

Parking the car a short distance up the street from the apothecary's, Lance hopped out and was just making his way up the wooden steps to the shop when, through the shop window, he caught sight of Jacob Snyder disappearing behind the heavy yellow curtain that hung across the opening to the dispensary.

Lance opened the door, the bell giving its distinctive tinkle as he and Bob entered the building. They stood for a few minutes waiting inside the empty shop. After a short while Lance called out, 'Mr Snyder, are you there?'

He could hear whispered conversation coming from the dispensary and then, abruptly, Mrs Snyder appeared from behind the curtain.

'I'm so sorry to have kept you waiting, m'lord. How may I be of assistance this morning?' she asked, her voice sounding strained.

'I wonder if I might have a quick word with Mr Snyder.'

Mrs Snyder looked like a rabbit caught in headlights, her huge eyes darting wildly from side to side. 'I'm afraid Mr Snyder isn't here at the moment, sir,' she said awkwardly.

'Indeed? That's odd. I thought I saw him walk through the curtains not a moment ago.'

'Yes,' she replied, her wrinkled cheeks suddenly blooming with colour. 'He was here, but he had an urgent call to make and had to go out immediately. You probably saw him leaving.'

'When do you expect him to return?' Lance asked, caught a tad off balance by Mrs Snyder's response.

'I'm afraid I don't expect him for some time.'

'Oh, I see.' Lance was just turning to leave when he had a thought. 'I say, aren't you and Mr Snyder attending the ball at Landacre this evening?'

'Yes, we are,' Mrs Snyder replied, her face brightening considerably. 'And we're both looking forward to it immensely. What an event it will be. The whole county is talking about it—'

'Would you give Mr Snyder a message for me?' broke in Lance. 'Will you ask him to bring the ledgers and all the

233

supporting paperwork for the Memorial Fund with him this evening? I should like to look them over.'

Mrs Snyder frowned. 'Is there a problem, m'lord?'

'I hope not, but if Mr Snyder will furnish me with the books and documents I *would* be very grateful.'

The colour drained from her face. 'I will certainly give him your message, sir.'

'Thank you Mrs Snyder. Then I'll bid you good morning.' And with that, Lance turned on his heels and left.

'He's a sly one, Bob,' Lance said as he leapt into the front seat of his car and zipped off back to Landacre. 'But by golly I *will* have those accounts,' he said through gritted teeth.

* * *

Back at the Hall the afternoon dragged on interminably. Landacre was bustling with noise and chaos as the staff prepared for the ball, and as the afternoon wore on the noise reached an almost unbearable crescendo.

Although Lance could not be more eager to introduce Veronica to his family and friends, the thought of making small talk with the two hundred and fifty people invited was quite daunting for him. In need of some peace and quiet to bolster his reserves, he decided to take Bob for a long leisurely walk around the grounds of the estate to soak up some of nature's tranquillity. When they returned, Lance found Rose, the parlourmaid, assisting Mrs Pierce to wind ornate flower decorations around the banister in the hallway. Remembering Bentley's suggestion that he should speak to her, Lance decided now would be as good a time as any.

'I wonder if I might have a word with Rose, Mrs Pierce?' Lance asked.

The housekeeper hesitated.

'It will only take a few minutes. I promise I won't keep her from her duties for long.'

'Of course, m'lord,' Mrs Pierce said.

Rose laid down the flower garland and followed Lance into the study.

Rose was a hardworking, plain, pleasant-natured girl not twenty years of age from a large family that eked out an existence in one of the neighbouring valleys.

'I just wanted to have a brief discussion, Rose,' Lance said kindly.

Rose stood in respectful silence, watching wide-eyed as Lance perched himself on the corner of the desk.

'It's been brought to my attention that you might have something on your mind to do with Lord Cedrick's death,' he began.

'No, m'lord,' she replied.

'Now, Rose, you know it's a crime to hold anything back from the police. "Perverting the course of justice" they call it and the penalties for doing so can be quite severe. It could even lead to a spell in prison.'

Rose took a deep breath and stood frozen to the spot.

'I'm sure you wouldn't want to be accused of *that*, Rose, so if you have anything to add you should tell me now and I'll ensure that the Superintendent doesn't take any action against you. I'm sure you'd like to help apprehend the person responsible.'

'Of course, m'lord, but I've already told Superintendent Schilling, I don't know anything,' she protested.

'Yes, I do remember you saying that, but I think there *is* something worrying you. Something you feel you should tell someone. Are you sure you wouldn't like to unburden yourself to me?'

Rose shook her head, her hands playing nervously with the hem of her apron.

'This is your last chance. If the Superintendent finds out later that you withheld information, I can't promise you won't end up behind bars. Think about it, Rose. What prospects would you have if you were dismissed from Landacre with no references and a prison record to boot.'

'Well ... I did hear Lord Cedrick having a terrible row on the morning of his death, m'lord,' Rose blurted out. 'But that can't be important, can it, sir?'

'Who was the argument with?' Lance asked gently, considerably interested in the new information.

The parlourmaid glanced about the room nervously. 'I saw Master Hugo leave the study a few minutes afterwards, sir.'

Good Lord! Hugo again, thought Lance. Why is it always Hugo?

'I know you wouldn't deliberately eavesdrop, but might the argument have been so loud that it was easy to overhear?'

'I only heard fragments, m'lord.'

'Tell me what you heard.'

'Lord Cedrick said "this is absolutely the last time I bail you out" and then Master Hugo replied "I should have thought it would be worth it to get me off your hands".'

'Did you hear anything more?'

'No, m'lord, not that I remember.'

'Thank you, Rose, you may go,' Lance said, quietly troubled that once again everything seemed to lead back to Hugo.

CHAPTER 23:
THE BALL

BACK IN HIS ROOMS that night, Lance, with Bentley's assistance, took considerable pains with his dress. What he saw when he looked in the mirror was a tall blond handsome man in a cropped black naval mess jacket adorned with brass buttons and gold brocade insignia on the sleeves, stiff black trousers, a crisp white shirt secured with black studs, a stiff wing collar, a black bow tie and a white waistcoat.

Taking his peaked cap from under his arm, he placed it firmly on his head before giving the traditional sharp salute.

'What do you think?' Lance asked, looking down at Bob. 'Will I pass muster?'

Bob wagged his tail.

At seven o'clock Lance descended the grand staircase to the vestibule. The Hall looked lovely this evening, full of fresh blooms from the gardens arranged elaborately in jardinières on stands positioned around the room. The subdued lighting created by the numerous floor-standing crystal candelabras created a wonderfully romantic effect.

Evans, along with a number of other footmen, was being kept busy welcoming guests from the Exmoor Hunting Lodge Hotel and the village, and taking their hats, coats and wraps to the cloakroom. Everyone was shown into the drawing room where serving staff circled with silver trays laden with assorted drinks and canapés.

On entering the room Lance saw his mother was already down, as were most of the family, mingling with the great and the good, all of whom looked resplendent in their finest costumes and glittering jewellery. Lady Cynthia smoothly detached herself from the throng and glided over to him.

'Oh, there you are, Lance,' she said, kissing him gently on the cheek. 'I do hope everything goes off well this evening. There are so many distinguished and worthy people here. I don't know why I feel so nervous. If only your father were here.' She blinked rapidly and sniffed.

'I'm sure you've arranged everything marvellously, Mother,' Lance said kind-heartedly. 'The ball will be remembered as *the* social event of the decade,' he added, snatching a drink from a passing tray. Steeling himself, he moved into the room to greet their guests.

At the appointed time Treadwell approached Lady Cynthia to indicate that formalities were about to start.

Lance took his gold half-hunter from his waistcoat pocket; it was seven forty-five. Veronica had yet to arrive. He patted his jacket pocket to reassure himself that the red leather embossed jewellery case he had retrieved from the safe was within.

Presently the doors to the ballroom were opened and the orchestra seated there began to play a selection of classical melodies, the guests gathering in the hallway as Hugo and Clara made their grand entrance down the stairway.

Hugo looked every inch an officer and a gentleman in his red and black regimental mess uniform. On his arm Clara looked magnificent in a midnight-blue velvet ensemble, her pale complexion and Titian hair enhanced by a newly acquired sapphire and diamond tiara from Tiffany's with matching necklace and earrings.

A gasp of appreciation for the attractive young couple filled the room.

Just then Lance felt someone touch his elbow lightly and heard a syrupy voice whisper warmly in his ear, 'Will we look that splendid when it's our turn, Lance?'

A stab of anxiety ran through him. He turned to see Lucinda smiling wickedly at him. She looked beautiful in a sea-green creation augmented by her family's priceless heirlooms – the infamous emerald and diamond 'Desdemona' tiara glittering in her hair and a Garrard's emerald-encrusted necklace sparkling around her neck.

Lance mumbled that he was needed urgently to welcome guests and, quickly extricating himself from Lucinda, he went to stand at the head of the line next to his mother. Lance took a step back and tapped his brother on the shoulder.

'I want to speak to you later, Hugo,' he hissed.

Hugo frowned. 'What about?'

'Father!'

'Can't we give that a rest for this evening, Lance. This *is* a celebration, you know,' Hugo whispered.

The master of ceremonies, standing at the door to the ballroom, banged his mace three times on the floor and then began the introductions, taking each invitation card and announcing the name at full volume.

'The American Ambassador John W. Davis and his wife Ellen.'

Lance stood shaking hands and uttering pleasantries as guest after guest was introduced and made their way down the line before walking through into the ballroom where a marvellous buffet had been laid out at the end of the room.

'The Earl and Countess of Bath and their son Viscount Beaumont,' rang out the master of ceremonies.

Lance was beginning to feel the muscles in his cheeks ache from the constant smile he felt obliged to maintain.

'Viscount Somerset and his daughter the Honourable Lucinda Willoughby-Vane.'

'I hope we shall have the opportunity to dance later, Lance,' Lucinda purred as she offered him her hand.

'I shall look forward to it,' Lance said stiffly.

'Evening, Lance,' barked Viscount Somerset gruffly, grasping Lance firmly by the hand. 'I *must* have a word with you later, young man.'

An overwhelming feeling of dread and panic gripped Lance; the Viscount was probably expecting him to name the day for his marriage to Lucinda.

Lance smiled back weakly. 'Of course, sir.'

The line of introductions seemed never-ending. Presently the master of ceremonies announced 'Councillor Jacob Snyder and Mrs Sylvia Snyder.'

'Good evening, Mrs Snyder,' Lance said before turning to Jacob and shaking his hand.

Jacob Snyder looked discomfited and smiled feebly. 'Good evening, m'lord,' he said and hurried along the line.

Lance resolved to catch up with him later.

'MISS VERONICA BARNES,' boomed the master of ceremonies.

A sudden rush of jumbled feelings swept over Lance as he looked up to see Veronica standing in the doorway wearing a gold satin gown over which hung a spider's web of white chiffon embroidered with sparkling crystal beads and sequins. Her jet-black hair had been styled into a vertical French pleat finished with numerous crystal stars twinkling throughout. Her complexion was like alabaster, and her full lips were painted a deep vermilion. The overall effect was breathtaking. Lance couldn't take his eyes off her.

Veronica held out her hand. 'Good evening, Lance,' she said, looking up coyly. 'Will this meet the occasion?'

Lance was stunned by her beauty and, at first, struggled to find words. 'You look absolutely enchanting, Veronica,' he eventually managed to whisper.

Enthralled, Lance completely forgot his responsibilities as host and broke away from his position to escort her along the remainder of the line. 'Mother, you remember Miss Barnes, the reporter from the *Chronicle*.'

Lady Cynthia, arrayed in an oyster-pink affair, stared at Veronica for a moment, clearly struggling to recall her. 'How lovely to see you again, Miss Barnes,' she said politely. 'I do hope you have a very pleasant evening.'

Hugo was next in line. 'Hello, Veronica,' he said, grinning. 'You clean up well.' Clara leaned across her fiancé and held out her hand to Veronica, giving Hugo a little nudge as she did so. 'You know Clara, don't you,' Hugo added quickly.

'Good evening, Veronica,' Clara said with her soft American twang. 'What a wonderful gown! You must give me the name of your couturier.'

Veronica smiled back. 'I'd be happy to.'

Lance gently directed Veronica further along the line towards Ruth and Zac.

'I think you know Ruth,' Lance said. 'And Zac, Clara's uncle.'

Ruth was wearing a fussy ensemble in a dark shade of amethyst, which instantly put Lance in mind of Tempranillo grapes. 'How nice to see you again, Miss Barnes,' she twittered inanely. 'I do hope you'll write something charming in your column about my daughter's forthcoming wedding.'

'I'm certainly looking forward to talking with you and Clara about it,' Veronica replied. 'Perhaps we can make an appointment some time very soon.'

Zac took Veronica's hand and shook it enthusiastically. 'Very nice to make your acquaintance again, young miss,' he said. 'We met briefly at the hunt the other day. Are you recovered from your accident?'

'Yes, I'm quite mended, thank you,' she replied.

The introductions over, Lance steered Veronica skilfully through the ballroom and out into the sweet evening air on the terrace.

'You look stunning,' he said.

'So you said. But what are we doing out here?' she asked. 'Has something happened in the case?'

'No, no, nothing like that.' Lance reached into his jacket pocket and pulled out the red leather embossed jewellery case he'd placed there earlier. 'I'd like you to wear this for the evening. It belonged to my grandmother.'

He opened the case to reveal the most exquisite diamond necklace, at the centre of which hung a diamond pendant as large as an egg.

'It's called the Moon of Exmoor,' Lance explained. 'Legend has it that the stone was discovered on the moor one moonlit night by the Second Baron Westex. It's been passed down through the family ever since.'

Veronica gasped and put a gloved hand to her mouth. 'I couldn't possibly—'

'Calm yourself,' Lance replied with a little laugh. 'It's just for this evening. I'll return it to the safe in the morning.'

'Accepting this, even just for this evening, goes against all my principles, Lance,' Veronica said. She fingered the necklace and sighed gently. 'But I'll go along with it tonight for your sake. Tomorrow I shall return to my feminist principles.'

Lance took the necklace from its case and, standing behind her, secured the clasp around her neck. 'There,' he said as she turned towards him. The Moon of Exmoor was almost as dazzling as Veronica's face. 'That's perfect.'

'I feel a bit like Cinderella,' Veronica said, giggling.

Lance heard the orchestra strike up the first dance and saw the ballroom floor begin to fill.

'Then you must dance with your prince,' he said, gently taking Veronica by hand and leading her inside to the dance floor amid gasps from the assembled guests. Lance placed his arm around her waist and together they glided lightly across the room in a waltz. Lance was oblivious to the other two hundred and fifty guests; he had eyes only for her. If only this dance could go on all night, he thought as they swirled gracefully around the room.

CHAPTER 24:
AN AWKWARD SITUATION

AFIZZ OF EXCITEMENT COURSED through Lance as he felt Veronica relax against him. He had never felt happier. Dance after dance he refused to release her from his grasp until the orchestra paused for an intermission. Even then he was reluctant to let go. He escorted her to the banqueting table for a refreshing glass of champagne and a few of Mrs Hughes's spectacular hors d'oeuvres.

'Are you enjoying yourself?' he asked.

Veronica gazed up at him. Her eyes were sparkling like stars. 'Oh Lance, it's been the best night of my life.'

All at once the magic was shattered by the sound of a familiar, and unwelcome, voice.

'Oh, there you are, Lance darling. I've been looking for you for ages. Where have you been, you naughty boy!'

Veronica jumped and took a few steps back.

'Oh, hello Lucinda,' Lance replied, his heart sinking to the pit of his stomach.

'You're such a tease, Lance. You promised to dance with *me* this evening,' she said, her eyes narrowing as she looked at Veronica.

The orchestra, returned from its break, struck up another waltz. Grabbing Lance by the hand, Lucinda led him back onto the dancefloor. 'I'm sure you don't mind, Veronica dear. There are plenty of other eligible bachelors here tonight who are much more your type,' she added spitefully, giving Veronica an insincere smile.

Left standing alone, Veronica turned back to the buffet table where Lance couldn't see her expression.

'What did you mean by your last remark?' Lance asked Lucinda crossly as they dipped and turned around the room.

'Why nothing, darling!' Lucinda exclaimed. 'Absolutely nothing at all. I just thought that Veronica would feel far more comfortable dancing with someone from her own social class, that's all.'

'You're a complete snob!' Lance snapped back.

'Really, Lance, you should know better than to fraternise with working-class women in your position,' she replied coolly. 'We must think about our families' reputations.'

'Damn our families' reputation!' exploded Lance, coming to an abrupt halt in the middle of the room. 'Things are changing, Lucinda, and to my mind it's all for the better. It's about time you and our precious families got used to it!' He turned on his heel and stormed off the dancefloor, the other guests staring after him.

Lance returned to the banqueting table but Veronica was nowhere to be seen. Distraught, he looked wildly around the ballroom trying to find her. Hugo and Clara were standing nearby deep in conversation with Ruth and Zac.

'Did you see where Veronica went?' Lance butted in.

'Sorry, old boy,' Hugo replied, a little taken aback by his brother's abruptness. 'I'm afraid I didn't.'

'You do look rather flushed, Lance,' chirruped Ruth. 'Have you been overdoing the champagne?' She giggled.

'Hush, Mother,' Clara replied, detecting that Lance was in no mood for frivolity.

'Sorry dear.' Ruth hiccupped, put a hand to her mouth and giggled again. 'Perhaps I'd better sit down,' she said and tottered off in search of some quiet comfortable seating led by Clara.

Lance was about to search another room when his mother approached. 'Viscount Somerset is looking for you, Lance,' she said. 'He looks awfully serious.'

Lance glared at his mother. 'Oh, curse Viscount Somerset and his foul daughter!'

'Lance dear! Whatever's the matter?'

Lance suddenly became conscious that he was making a spectacle of himself and fast becoming the focus of the guests' attention.

'It's nothing, Mother. Go back and enjoy what's left of the evening,' he muttered as he hurried out of the ballroom.

He frantically searched the crowd standing tightly packed in the vestibule. Having no luck, he dived into the drawing room where an unsteady Tabby was standing in the middle of a group of eligible young men, each with prospects of inheriting titles. Laurence Harrison stood a little to one side keeping an amused but protective eye on her.

'Hello, big brother,' Tabby said, slurring her words and giggling. 'I'm having an absolutely wonderful time. You having a good time with your Veronica?'

'Have you seen her, Tabby?'

His tone of desperate urgency failed to have any sobering influence on his little sister. 'You lost your darling Veronica!' she said, flinging her arms around and spilling champagne from her glass.

Laurence stepped forward. 'Is everything all right, m'lord?' he asked, sensing Lance's distress.

'I'm fine, Laurence, really. Veronica seems to have disappeared for the minute, that's all. If you bump into her, please tell her I'm looking for her.'

'Of course,' he replied, watching Tabby encircle one of the eligible youths in her outstretched arms.

Lance pushed through the crush of people who were milling around the room. Coming upon Lord Randolph, he asked, 'Have you seen Veronica, Uncle?'

'What's that my boy?' Lord Randolph asked, cupping a hand around one ear.

'Veronica, the girl I've been dancing with all evening – have you seen her?' Lance shouted.

His uncle frowned and shook his head. Then he turned to a stout elderly fellow to his right. 'Have you met Lord Swan, Lance?'

Lance was in no mood to engage in trivial pleasantries with someone he didn't know; he badly wanted to find Veronica. He nodded curtly at the man and turned to leave.

'I think you should have a chat with him, my boy,' his uncle persisted. 'He's just been telling me your father was on his way to see him the night he died.'

Lance stopped dead in his tracks. He felt torn. He longed to find Veronica, but he was also eager to learn what

Lord Swan had to say. He *must* take the time to talk with him now before he too was swallowed up by the crowd.

Lance closed his eyes for a long moment, turned to Lord Swan and, with a polite smile, asked, 'Can we go somewhere quiet and discuss the matter, sir?'

'Of course,' the gentleman replied.

Lance led the way to his study, passing the butler en route. He asked Treadwell to ensure they were undisturbed. 'Oh, and if you see Miss Barnes,' he added, 'could you instruct her to wait until I have concluded my discussion with Lord Swan?'

In the study Lord Swan made himself comfortable with a glass of malt whiskey and once the introductions and pleasantries were out of the way, Lance got straight to the point.

'You've heard, of course, of my father's accident.'

'Yes, I was sorry to learn about it. Damn shame. Sorry for your loss.'

'Were you aware that the police think some underhand force may have been involved?'

'No!' exclaimed Lord Swan. 'Really?'

'Yes, they think the brakes of his car had been tampered with.'

Lord Swan frowned but made no response.

'How exactly did you know my father?' Lance asked.

'I didn't really know him. We weren't close friends – more acquaintances really. We passed each other in the Lords, that sort of thing. No, it's the memsaab who knows your mother rather better.'

'And you say he was coming to see you on the afternoon of his death?'

'Yes, that's right. He wrote to me about two weeks beforehand asking for an appointment. I suggested he come down to Forde House.'

'Forde House?'

'Yes, our country seat at Cotleigh Marsh.'

Lance wished Veronica were present to hear this. 'Your Christian name doesn't happen to begin with a "J", does it?'

'As a matter of fact it does,' Lord Swan replied in astonishment. 'It's Jonathan. Why do you ask?'

'Oh it's nothing, just something Father wrote in his diary.' So that was the meaning of his father's rather cryptic notation for 6th June. *Jonathan Swan at Cotleigh Marsh*, not John Seymour at Combe Martyn.

'Did he say in his letter what he wanted to talk to you about?' Lance asked.

'Not really. I got the impression it had something to do with your brother's wedding.'

'Half a minute,' Lance said, rising from his chair. 'I've some things I'd like you to look at.' He put down his whisky and went to the study safe from where he retrieved two brown envelopes and brought them back to the fireplace.

'You don't happen to know who the people in this photograph are?' Lance enquired, handing the picture of the group of people to Lord Swan.

Lord Swan looked hard at the faces staring back at him. 'Where did you get this? It must have been taken years ago.'

'You know them then?'

'Yes. There's your father, of course, and me with some of the directors and their wives from the White Star Line.'

'Do you know when it was taken?'

'I think it must have been around 1910, 1911 – sometime around then. The photograph was taken just before I resigned from the board. Is that important?'

'I think it may have something to do with why Father wanted to see you. He was carrying a copy of this photograph when he died.'

'Oh! And you want to know if I can tell you something about the people in the picture.'

'If you can.'

'Well, let me see. I was a director with White Star from 1902 to 1911.'

'Go on,' Lance said encouragingly.

'Well, if I remember correctly these are some of the American directors of the shipping company. Not all the directors are in the picture though. It also had a good number of British directors too.'

'I see. Do you mind telling me why you stepped down as a director of White Star?'

'I didn't agree with some of their methods. The company was in a particularly aggressive trade war with a number of German shipping companies, as well as its arch rival Cunard. They were all engaged in becoming the world leader in luxury transatlantic crossings. White Star took the decision to instruct the Belfast company, Harland and Wolff, in the production of three very expensive ocean-going liners. They were to be the *Olympic*, *Titanic* and *Gigantic*, although the latter subsequently became known as *Britannic*. However, the company was highly leveraged at the time …'

'Leveraged?'

'Yes, you know, they'd borrowed a lot. They'd taken on too much debt and in their haste to bring these leviathans to the water some of the directors cut financial corners. I didn't agree with it, that's all, so I stepped down.'

'That's interesting. Did you have any reason to think that some of those cost-cutting measures might result in a serious fire aboard *Titanic*?'

'Well, I know from Lord Fleming, a close friend of mine who sits in the Lords, that the British Board of Trade, of which Lord Fleming is also a member, was concerned at the time about the quality of the steel being used in their construction. He asked me if I could bring some influence to bear on White Star to upgrade the steel, but since I was no longer a director there was nothing I could do.'

'That *is* interesting,' Lance said. 'What do you make of this.' He handed the copy of the SS *Californian*'s manifest to Lord Swan.

'It looks like a standard manifest to me.' He shrugged his shoulders. 'Should it mean anything?'

'Look at the name of the ship. Do you recognise the name?' Lance asked.

There was a pause while Lord Swan studied the paperwork. 'I'm pretty sure the SS *Californian* belongs to the same stable as *Titanic*. She's part of the fleet owned by the Leyland Line, which in turn is owned by White Star's parent company, International Mercantile Marine.'

'Is that so,' Lance said, trying to recall where he'd heard that name recently.

'I'm not sure if it's relevant but J. P. Morgan, the American financier, has a hand in both International Mercantile Marine and White Star,' Lord Swan added.

'Does he indeed.' Lance remembered that Peter Hopwood had mentioned J. P. Morgan and wondered if it was significant.

All at once his train of thought was shattered by the sound of an almighty commotion taking place immediately outside the study. Suddenly the door was flung open and Lucinda barged in looking wildly around the room, closely followed by an apologetic butler.

'I'm very sorry, m'lord,' exclaimed Treadwell a little out of breath. 'I've been trying to explain to Miss Willoughby-Vane that Miss Barnes left the premises some time ago while you were in private conference with Lord Swan.'

Lord Swan took one look at Lucinda's face, made his apologies and hurriedly vacated the room, leaving the photograph and manifest on the table. Lance was not pleased; he hadn't finished asking his questions.

After dismissing Treadwell, Lance braced himself for Lucinda.

'I won't be made a fool of, Lance,' she roared. 'Not with that working-class Jezebel!'

'Good Lord, Lucinda, what's all the fuss?'

'How *dare* you leave me standing alone on the dancefloor,' she screamed. 'Chasing off after that accursed woman and humiliating me in front of all our friends and families, making me a laughing stock.'

'I've had just about as much of your petty jealousies and outbursts as I can take, Lucinda,' Lance growled, barely keeping his temper. 'Your conduct at the hunt as well as this evening has been completely unacceptable.'

'*My* conduct, MY CONDUCT. I'll tell you what *is* unacceptable,' she screeched, her voice hoarse with rage, 'you cavorting with that woman and your stubborn refusal to name a date for our marriage, that's what's unacceptable! I'm going to speak to Daddy about it, you see if I don't,' she added, her eyes narrowing, and with that she swept out of the room, slamming the study door behind her.

A welcome stillness filled the room and Lance took a deep breath. A few moments later there was a discreet tap at the door.

'Enter,' Lance said, still feeling somewhat shaken from the stormy encounter.

'Begging your pardon, m'lord,' Treadwell said softly. 'I'm afraid Miss Barnes did not take kindly to being *instructed* to wait, m'lord. She wished you goodnight and asked me to return this to you.' He held out the Moon of Exmoor in his gloved hand.

CHAPTER 25:
ULTIMATUMS

AFTER TREADWELL LEFT THE room, Lance lit a cigar. He couldn't help feeling amused that Veronica had taken umbrage at being *instructed* to wait for him. He'd probably get a good scolding from her. He sat thoughtfully at the desk finishing off the dregs of his malt whiskey, his mind running through the earlier conversation with Lord Swan. He knew it was significant but he couldn't put his finger on why.

Picking up the photograph from the table where Lord Swan had left it, he wondered what was so important about it. Why had his father had it with him when he died? It was just a photograph of White Star's directors. Why would they be significant?

Presently, his mother entered the room. 'Oh, here you are, Lance,' she said. 'Why are you hiding yourself away in here?'

'I'm not *hiding* myself away, Mother. I'm just taking some time away from the festivities.'

'Well, it's not good enough, Lance,' she said crossly. 'We have guests, and as head of the family your presence is expected. Skulking around in here when you should be at your brother's pre-nuptial celebration, whatever next!'

'Very well, Mother,' Lance replied, reconciled to the thought of returning to the party without Veronica. 'Let me finish my cigar in peace. I'll be out shortly.'

'Make sure you are,' Lady Cynthia replied sharply.

When Lance emerged, guests at the ball were much less inhibited, having taken advantage of the free-flowing champagne. He squeezed his way through the throng of revellers and went back into the ballroom where the orchestra was still playing. Among the melee of waltzing couples he could see Hugo dancing with Clara, and Tabby in a vaguely rhythmic embrace with a pimply-faced young man. Then he spotted Jacob Snyder standing beside the banqueting table and made his way towards him.

'Good evening, Jacob,' Lance said, coming up behind him. 'I trust you and Mrs Snyder are having an enjoyable evening.'

Jacob, in the midst of stuffing his face with some of Mrs Hughes excellent hors d'oeuvres, almost choked.

'Oh, good evening, m'lord,' he said, turning round. 'Yes, we're having an absolutely marvellous time, aren't we, Sylvia?' He started to cough.

'Oh yes, indeed,' Mrs Snyder replied. 'What an absolutely wonderful occasion, m'lord. We're thrilled to have been invited. Everyone looks so splendid in their best—'

'Jacob, I was wondering if you'd brought the books and documentation for the Memorial Fund I requested earlier?' Lance asked, taking a step forward and effectively boxing Jacob into the corner of the room.

'I'm glad you mentioned that, sir,' Jacob replied, blinking rapidly. 'I've been hoping for an opportunity to talk with you this evening. You won't believe what has happened!'

What's going to be his excuse this time? Lance thought wearily.

'We've … we've … been broken into, m'lord, and the books and paperwork for the Memorial Fund have been stolen!' he blurted out in desperation.

Lance could barely believe his ears. 'You've been broken into?'

'Yes, that's right, isn't it, Sylvia my dear?' her husband said, eyeing her frantically.

Mrs Snyder nodded and her mouth fell open but she didn't make any sound.

'Have you informed the police?' Lance enquired.

'Not yet. We didn't have time,' Jacob replied, beads of perspiration appearing on his forehead. 'We only discovered the documentation was missing before coming here this evening. That's right, isn't it my dear?' He turned to his wife again.

Still Ms Snyder said nothing; she just stared at her husband boggle-eyed.

Lance found the whole thing ludicrous. 'I simply *must* have the paperwork, Jacob,' he snapped. The apothecary cast a look of panic at his wife. 'Mrs Bird has asked me to ensure that her donation has been safely received into the fund,' Lance went on. 'So you really *must* provide me with a copy of the documentation without further delay.'

Jacob reached into his trouser pocket and produced a handkerchief with which he mopped his brow.

Lance wasn't finished yet. 'Unless you deliver the documents to me immediately I'll have no alternative but to go to the Board of Charity Commissioners.' That ought to shake him up a bit, he thought.

'But that's just it, m'lord, the cash tin containing Mrs Bird's donation has also gone missing,' he cried.

Lance closed his eyes for a moment. The stupid man was only digging a deeper hole for himself. 'You must inform the police immediately, Jacob,' he said. 'Please do so at once.'

'Just what I was thinking. I'll do it now,' Jacob said, putting down his plate next to a half-empty glass of champagne and escorting his startled wife from the room.

Lance watched them hurry away. Of all the ridiculous, feeble excuses, he thought, peeved that once again the apothecary had managed to dodge the issue. But he would get to the bottom of this if it was the last thing he did.

In need of some invigorating fresh air, Lance grabbed a glass of brandy and walked out onto the terrace where he lit another cigar. Drawing heavily on the end of his stogie as he sucked in the flame from his lighter, he felt himself relax, the aroma from the thick cloud of smoke surrounding him before rising lazily into the warm night air.

'What-ho, Lance,' said an amiable voice out of the darkness.

Lance turned to see his Uncle Randolph and Aunt Lettice with another elderly couple sitting on wrought-iron garden chairs around a table illuminated by the flickering light of a candelabra.

'Come and sit over here with us,' his uncle beckoned, patting an empty seat.

Lance sat down, grateful to be taking the weight off his leg which was beginning to ache as a result of his recent exertions on the dance floor. 'Are you all having a spiffing time?' he asked genially.

'Landacre certainly knows how to throw a party, Lance,' his uncle said, guffawing. 'We're just taking a breather, what.'

'Do you know Lord Byron Agnew and his wife Lady Grace?' enquired Aunt Lettice, introducing the other couple. 'Lady Grace is an old school chum of your mother's, Lance. We all went to the same school together when we were gals.'

Oh, this is fortuitous, thought Lance, recalling that he wanted to speak to Lady Grace about her experience on board the *Titanic* and wondering how he could steer the conversation round to the subject.

'So kind of you to attend our little gathering,' he said, smiling at Lord and Lady Agnew. 'I do hope you're enjoying your evening. Mother has gone to so much effort.'

'It's been absolutely first class,' Lord Byron said, lifting his glass in the air in a mock toast. 'First class, my boy!'

'Yes, Cynthia has been nothing short of wonderful,' Lady Grace said, beaming. 'She's thought of everything and is so lucky to have such an accomplished cook – all this heavenly food.'

'Thank you. Mother will be pleased,' Lance said. 'But I expect you're no stranger to fine dining, Lady Grace. I imagine the food on the *Titanic* was sublime.'

Lady Grace sat up stiffly in her chair.

'Lady Grace doesn't like to remember her experience on the *Titanic*,' Lord Byron said in a low voice.

'My apologies,' Lance replied.

'Must've been quite a shocking affair,' interjected Uncle Randolph. He took a puff of his cigar. 'Must've given the poor woman nightmares for years after, what!'

'Randolph!' exclaimed Aunt Lettice. She smiled sympathetically in her friend's direction.

'Please don't worry, Lettice,' Lady Grace said. 'That awful episode no longer holds the horrors it once did for me.'

Lance decided to seize the opportunity. 'In that case, would you mind talking to me about it, Lady Grace? I'm terribly interested.'

'It's not something I've thought about for a while,' Lady Grace said. 'I haven't spoken about it since attending the official British Board of Trade inquiry in London. Time heals most wounds, so they say, but I find it never completely erases them,' she added wistfully. Turning to Lance she asked, 'What would you like to know?'

'It must have been unbelievably traumatic for you when you realised the ship had struck an iceberg and was sinking.'

'To tell you the truth, I didn't really know *Titanic* had struck anything at the time, much less an iceberg. I remember seeing a glass of water on my nightstand shuddering as I lay in my bed reading, but that was all.'

Lance nodded by way of encouragement.

'It wasn't until the purser knocked at my cabin door just after midnight and asked me to put on a lifebelt and go out on deck that I realised something rather serious had occurred. It certainly never entered my mind that *Titanic* was sinking. After all, she was the unsinkable ship.'

'But you must've been worried,' Lance said.

'Not at all. The officers on board were most reassuring. They kept telling us we weren't to worry, that we should get into the lifeboats – we wouldn't have long to wait for the *Californian* to steam alongside and rescue everyone.'

'The *Californian*?' Lance's mind went into overdrive at the mention of the ship named on the manifest sent to him anonymously. 'Are you sure that was the name?'

'Yes, I'm quite sure. You see, the purpose of my voyage was to visit a distant cousin who lives in California, so the name of the ship stuck in my mind. I distinctly remember *Titanic*'s first officer saying "Don't worry, there's no call for any anxiety. The *Californian* will pick everyone up".'

How could the officers have known the *Californian* was close by, wondered Lance. 'Had the *Californian* sent word it was on its way?' he asked.

'The first officer didn't say so, but he did seem very sure of his facts. He must have been to repeat them to all the first-class passengers, mustn't he.'

'In the end it was the *Carpathia* that rescued the survivors, wasn't it?' Lance said.

'Yes, that's right. I was one of the first to be lowered into a lifeboat along with my maid. We were rowed away from *Titanic* and waited patiently at a safe distance.'

Lance looked intently into Lady Grace's face, inviting her to continue.

'The water was very calm that night, like a mill pond. The screams and shouts echoing across the icy sea from people who'd either fallen in or jumped overboard were so piercing. It was dreadful. I shall never forget those shrieks as long as I live. Then *Titanic* slipped beneath the waves and all at once there was silence.' Lady Grace shivered as if she was back there.

An image of the *Panther* reared up in Lance's memory. An unwelcome rush of adrenalin coursed through his veins and his heart started to pound.

'Our lifeboat rowed back among the debris to pick up anyone clinging to the wreckage, but we found no one alive. About two hours later the *Carpathia* arrived and we were helped on board, wrapped in blankets and given hot drinks.'

'Weren't you surprised it was the *Carpathia*?' Lance asked, pushing down his own unsavoury memories.

'I was a bit, yes, and thinking back on it now I was also astonished at the length of time it took the ship to arrive. The officers were so sure we wouldn't have long to wait. But by that time we were just grateful to be rescued at all. We arrived in New York three days later, relieved to be on dry land but extremely mindful of the dreadful loss of life.'

Lance, lost momentarily in his own haunting thoughts, allowed the conversation to lapse. A deathly hush fell over the table.

'Good grief, Lance,' Lord Randolph said jovially. 'You certainly know how to dampen party spirits, old lad.'

Lance shook his head and smiled. 'Sorry Uncle, sorry everyone.'

Just then, Treadwell materialised and stood beside Lance waiting for an appropriate moment to intercede. He gave an apologetic cough. 'Begging your pardon, m'lord, Viscount Somerset has requested to speak with you. I have shown him into the study, sir.'

The breath caught in Lance's throat as if a noose were tightening around his neck. He was going to have to talk to the man about marrying his wretched daughter. There was no avoiding the subject. He'd just have to face him.

'Thank you, Treadwell. I'll cut along and see him now.'

Lance apologised again for raking up difficult memories and took his leave of the elderly party.

* * *

Lance braced himself and entered the study to find Viscount Somerset seated in one of the chairs beside the fireplace, sipping a glass of Lance's favourite malt whiskey in the dim glow of an oil lamp.

'I gather you wanted to speak to me, Lord Somerset,' he said, waiting for the inevitable onslaught.

The Viscount got to his feet, an unfriendly grimace on his face. 'Indeed I do, Lance,' he boomed. 'Lucinda has informed me of your abominable behaviour towards her this evening. I find it utterly intolerable, sir. A gentleman does not treat his intended in such a way. I expect you to honour my agreement with your father to the letter and name the day of your marriage without any further delay.'

Viscount Somerset in full flight was certainly intimidating; in certain circles he was well-known for being an overbearing bully.

Lance drew himself up, even though he could feel his legs turning to jelly. 'Are you sure you want me for your son-in-law, sir? I don't think I'll make Lucinda very happy,' he said.

'Happiness? Pah!' the Viscount spat out. 'People of our station care nothing for happiness, Lance. You should know that. It's breeding that counts, *breeding*!'

'I'm not sure I agree with you, sir,' Lance said. 'Happiness must come into the equation somewhere surely. Otherwise you'd be condemning your daughter to a life of misery.'

'Poppycock!' the Viscount exclaimed. 'Lucinda knows where her duty lies, and so should you, Lance. Name the day or be damned.'

Lance took a deep breath. 'I don't think I'm quite ready to do that, Lord Somerset.'

'Then you force my hand, sir.'

'There's nothing you can say that will change my mind, Lord Somerset,' Lance said, holding his head high.

'It's not what I'll *say* that counts, it's what I shall *DO*,' blustered the Viscount, his face turning purple and the veins on his forehead standing out.

Lance thought the Viscount was going to burst. 'I really don't know what you're driving at,' he said, alarmed.

'It's quite elementary, sir,' the Viscount roared. Suddenly his voice became unnervingly cold. 'An interesting woman that Ruth Hamilton-Whytte. She's a bit simple. If brains were dynamite she wouldn't have enough to blow off her hat, but she's quite talkative when the wine is flowing. She tells me her first husband's will settles a vast sum of money into Clara's trust fund one month and a day after her marriage.'

'I believe that is so, yes, but what's that got to do with your agreement with my father?' Lance asked, his eyes narrowing.

'It seems Clara will only inherit if her prospective husband *and his family* are free from any controversy at the time the marriage takes place,' the Viscount said with a smile. 'In the event of any scandal being attached to the in-laws, the trust fund will be dissolved and the funds incorporated back into the family business. She will inherit nothing.'

Lance felt as if he were a mouse being toyed with by a malign Maine Coon. Now he saw where this line of conversation was heading.

'Unless you name the day of your marriage to Lucinda before Hugo and Clara walk down the aisle,' the Viscount continued, 'I will instigate legal proceedings against you and your family for breach of promise. Every newspaper in the land will carry the outrage. I don't think Clara is the sort of girl to give up a fortune for a penniless sop like your brother, do you?'

Lance swallowed hard.

'If you disappoint my daughter, you'll be putting an end to your brother's marriage and consigning your family to a life of poverty. Think it over, Lance. Can you live with the knowledge that you, and you alone, are responsible for all their misery?' The Viscount leaned into Lance's face, his hot stale breath reeking of malt whiskey and cigar smoke.

He walked over to the study door. 'Think on it, Lance,' he said with a sneer. 'You have until the day of your brother's wedding to give me an answer.' He stormed out through the door, slamming it shut behind him.

Submerged in a torrent of despair, Lance slumped down into one of the fireside chairs and reached for the whisky.

CHAPTER 26:
A SIBLING PACT

Wednesday June 18th 1919

LOST IN HIS MELANCHOLY thoughts, Lance didn't notice the passage of time until he learned from his half-hunter that it was well past midnight. Just then, someone softly opened the study door and tiptoed into the room.

A shaft of light thrown onto the carpet cast the huge elongated shadow of a lithe figure haphazardly moving towards the fireplace where it plopped down into the vacant fireside chair.

'Oh, it's you, Tabby,' Lance said in a monotone. 'Is the party over?'

Tabitha gave a little jump at the sound of her brother's voice. 'Goodness, Lance! What are you doing in here in the dark?' she said, her words slurring somewhat. 'The party's still going, but a lot of the guests have gone.'

For a few moments they sat in dismal stillness.

'You look worse for wear,' Lance said, breaking the hushed atmosphere. 'Too much fizz I suppose. Can't hold your drink, little one.'

Growing up together at Landacre, a strong bond had developed between the three siblings and they always looked out for each other. It hadn't stopped Hugo and Lance from teasing Tabitha endlessly as she'd tried to keep up with them climbing trees, building dens and sailing boats on the lake and she'd soon learned to toughen up. But when push came to shove, the two boys had kept a protective eye on their little sister, and now they were adults that hadn't changed.

'Certainly not!' replied Tabby indignantly. 'I just need some peace and quiet for a while, that's all.' She grimaced and put a hand to her temple. 'Besides, what are you doing hiding away in here? Ma will be on the warpath if we're both found to be missing from the party.' She gave him a weak smile.

'I've had a bit of a shock, Tabby,' he replied, the solemnity of his words hanging in the air.

Tabby said nothing.

'... and I don't know how I'm going to face the future,' Lance wailed, suddenly overpowered by an irresistible need to confide in someone.

Tabby sank down on to the floor at her brother's feet. 'What is it, Lance?' she asked, tenderly hugging his legs. 'Tell me what's wrong. Perhaps I can help,' she whispered.

Lance stroked his sister's hair. 'It's no good, Tabby,' he said, his voice choked with tears. 'There's nothing you can do. There's nothing anyone can do!'

His voice brimming with emotion, Lance recounted how Viscount Somerset had confronted him and issued an ultimatum. 'So you see, Tabby dear, either I marry Lucinda and give up any hope of a happy life for myself or he'll drag our family through the courts, destroying Hugo's marriage and consigning us to a poverty-stricken future in the process.'

'He can't do that!'

'Oh yes he can,' Lance said, 'and he means to do it if I don't name the day before Hugo and Clara walk down the aisle on Saturday. Can you see Mother living an impoverished life? I'd probably have to sell Landacre just to pay them off,' he added despondently.

'You can't sell Landacre! You simply can't,' Tabby said. 'It's our home!'

'Don't worry, little sis, it hasn't come to that yet,' Lance said, wrestling heroically to regain his self-control.

'I *hate* Lucinda,' spat Tabby. 'Can't she see she's not right for you, that she could *never* make you happy? If she had any integrity she'd tell her father to go and jump!'

'It's not really Lucinda's fault,' Lance said gallantly. 'Our fathers made an agreement years ago when we were both young. She's can't be held responsible.'

'What are you going to do then?' Tabby asked. Then she gasped. 'You're not going to marry her are you?'

'I don't see what other choice I have. I couldn't live with myself if I ruined the lives of my family.'

'And if you do marry Lucinda? D'you think you could eventually find happiness with her?'

'Not the kind of happiness you mean, Tabby. I just don't think of her in that way and I never will.' Lance looked down fondly at his sister. 'It's a case of having to make the best of a bad situation for everyone's sake I suppose,' he added with an air of resignation.

'Well, I don't think you should marry someone you're not madly in love with, whatever the consequences,' Tabby said defiantly.

Lance could read her like a book. 'Laurence is a nice chap,' he said softly, 'but Ma will never allow you to marry him. He's not from our class. You'll be expected to marry a Viscount or a Baron or some such.'

Tabby pulled a face. 'And be unhappy for the rest of my life? I'd rather stay single than marry a spotty-faced, goofy prig. Pa would never have expected me to marry without feeling some affection for my husband.'

'Maybe not,' conceded Lance, 'but he'd have wanted you to marry well for the sake of your own happiness. Living the life you were brought up to, not having to worry about the next penny or where it was coming from.'

'I don't care about money, Lance. It means nothing to me.'

'That's because you've never been without it. It's quite a different matter when you haven't any.'

Tabby wrinkled her nose.

'Have you heard the old saying "when poverty knocks at the door, love flies out of the window"? Sadly, I think you'd experience something of that kind if you went against Ma's wishes and married Laurence. You just don't have the practical experience or knowledge to make ends meet. You'd be hopelessly out of your depth.'

Tabby smiled weakly. 'You're probably right … but I still don't think you should marry Lucinda,' she declared.

Lance smiled back fondly. 'I think I'll be pushing off to bed now.' He sighed, aching to be alone with his own thoughts again. 'Thanks for listening, little sis. Somehow talking to you seems to have helped. I feel a little less miserable about the situation now.'

Tabby gave her brother's legs a good squeeze.

Just before he got to his feet, Lance recalled the conversation with Rose when she'd revealed that Hugo had had an argument with their father on the day of his accident. He thought about telling Tabby, but decided against it. No, he would talk to Hugo first. Hopefully the argument hadn't been important and there'd be no need to inform anyone else about it.

Lance stood up. 'Before I go, I want you to promise me one thing, Tabby.'

'Anything, big brother. Just name it.'

'That you'll never mention this conversation to anyone. Do you promise?' Lance implored. 'I'll not rock the boat for Hugo nor condemn you and Mother to a life of poverty. If I have to marry Lucinda then so be it.'

'All right, Lance, I promise if I must,' Tabby said. 'It'll be our secret,' she added conspiratorially, tapping the side of her nose.

* * *

The next morning, Lance took an early breakfast and was driven into Exeter St David's station by Bentley to catch the 9.02 to London, Bob at his side.

Determined to put any unpleasant thoughts of marriage to Lucinda out of his mind, he had regained his composure and decided to concentrate on solving the riddle of his father's death. If Lady Grace Agnew had given evidence at the official inquiry into the sinking of the *Titanic*, the authorised record of proceedings would hold the answers to his questions, Lance reasoned. Since the inquiry had been held at the Scottish Drill Hall in London, he surmised the documents must be lodged somewhere in the city, a conjecture that was prompting his journey that morning. He had three free days in which to progress the investigation ahead of Hugo's wedding, after which he'd be forced to officially proclaim his engagement to Lucinda who would swiftly put an end to his detective work and forbid any further collaboration with Veronica.

Lance had just settled into one of the first-class carriages when he caught sight of two familiar-looking dark figures making their way to the next compartment.

'I see our shadows haven't deserted us, Bob,' he said with a wry smile. 'I'm not sure if I should feel threatened by their presence or if they're a force for good,' he muttered to himself.

As the train sped through the countryside he leaned back in his seat and spent the greater part of the journey with his eyes closed going over the events of the past two weeks, making mental notes of the points he wanted to clarify from the records:

Was his father and/or Bruce Hamilton mentioned in the official *Titanic* inquiry documents? If so, how were they connected? Could this be the catalyst for their murders?

Had the inquiry found that the fire in one of *Titanic*'s coal bunkers had had serious consequences? If so, was it possible that Peter Hopwood's first-hand knowledge of the situation could have driven someone to murder?

Had the SS *Californian* sent word that she was on her way in response to *Titanic*'s distress calls? If so, how far away had she been? Why did the *Carpathia* arrive before her?

Was the *Californian*'s manifest, dated five days before *Titanic* sailed and indicating that the ship's only cargo was three thousand woollen blankets and jumpers, pertinent?

What was *Titanic*'s full complement of passengers and crew? Did the number correspond to the quantity of blankets and jumpers *Californian* was carrying?

Having satisfied himself of the main points, Lance deduced that the best use of his limited time would be to corner Lord Fleming, since Lord Swan had confirmed that he was on the Board of Trade at the time *Titanic* was under construction. He would have a good working knowledge of the inquiry and in all probability would know where the official records were kept, or at least be able to point him in the right direction. Desperate not to squander his free time, Lance wanted to catch Lord Fleming before he disappeared into the Lord's for a lengthy afternoon sitting; otherwise he would be inaccessible until the next day.

The train arrived at Paddington just after eleven thirty from where Lance and Bob took a taxi to the Palace of Westminster and hurried up the steps to the entrance hall.

'I'm sorry, sir,' rang out a shrill voice, 'but dogs are not allowed in the Palace.'

Their way was blocked by a doorkeeper dressed in a black long-tailed coat, white bow tie and a silver-gilt waist badge of office. Underneath the badge hung a figure of Mercury, the messenger of the gods, emblematic of the man's role in conveying messages between Parliament and the King.

'I'm here to see Lord Fleming,' Lance said, trying to remain polite despite the urgency of the situation. 'Can you get a message to him for me please?'

The fellow narrowed his eyes. 'Their Lordships will shortly be going into lunch, sir. They don't like their lunches disturbed, sir.'

'It really is quite urgent,' Lance said, stressing the word 'urgent'. 'In fact, you could say it's a matter of life and death.'

'In that case, sir,' the man, replied. 'What message may I convey?'

'Please inform Lord Fleming that Baron Westex is here to see him. It's absolutely imperative I have an audience with him without delay.'

Unhurriedly the man opened a door to his right. 'If you'll wait in here, m'lord, I'll inform his Lordship of your presence.'

Lance and Bob entered the ante-chamber indicated by the doorkeeper. It was a small square room with a dearth of furniture – just a few upright gilt chairs with plush red seats pushed back against the inlaid cherry-wood walls. In the centre of the polished wooden floor was a lush red carpet with an ornate gold border. Everything about the Palace of Westminster reeked of history and protracted formality.

Lance sat down in one of the chairs and Bob settled at his feet. Lance found it impossible not to fidget; a clock on the wall ticked loudly, a constant reminder of the precious time that was being frittered away.

Abruptly the door to the room opened and in walked the doorkeeper. 'I've informed Lord Fleming of your attendance, m'lord. Unfortunately, he's currently engaged with important matters of state. Sadly he'll be unable to see you today, sir. He has suggested you make an appointment for some time next week.'

'Next week! That will be much too late,' Lance blurted out. 'I really must see Lord Fleming today.'

'I'm sorry, m'lord, but that will not be possible,' the doorkeeper said firmly, at the same time proficiently guiding him towards the exit.

A pall of gloom and despondency hung over Lance as he and Bob descended the steps of the Palace. What was he to do now? He couldn't let this self-important popinjay defeat his attempt to meet with Lord Fleming. He simply had to get in to see him somehow.

'Good Lord, if it isn't old Hawkeye,' called out a man walking past Lance in the opposite direction.

Lance hadn't heard his old school nickname, earned for his bowling prowess on the cricket pitch, since leaving Eton. He turned to see a tall goofy-looking fellow with rather unruly blond hair whom he didn't immediately recognise, but the man's voice gave him away. It was his old school chum 'Biffo' Bertie de Bretagne, the Earl of Albemarle, a fellow cricketer renowned for smashing sixes.

'Good grief – Biffo!' Lance said, momentarily distracted from his troubles. 'Why, I haven't seen you since school. What a coincidence seeing you here after all these years.'

They stood on the steps catching up on events since they'd left college. Eventually Bertie asked, 'But what are you doing here, Hawkeye?'

Lance could feel his anxiety rising again as he recounted the history of the past two weeks. 'So you see I simply must talk with Lord Fleming today. It's absolutely essential.'

'Nothing easier, old chap,' Bertie replied happily. 'I'll fix it for you right away.'

'But the doorkeeper,' objected Lance. 'What about him?'

'Oh, pay no heed to him,' Bertie said, patting Lance's arm reassuringly. Lance couldn't help but notice the ornate signet ring on his friend's middle finger. 'I know Lord Fleming personally. We sit on a number of committees together. He won't refuse a request from me.' He led Lance back up the steps and into the Palace again. 'Just wait here a minute,' he added, indicating the small ante-chamber Lance and Bob had just left.

'Thanks awfully, Biffo. I shan't forget this.'

'Think nothing of it, old man. Happy to help, happy to help.' And with that Bertie disappeared out through the ante-chamber door.

Lance sat in the room impatiently, his heart thumping in his chest, the palms of his hands sweating. Would Biffo be able to pull it off? Lance needed some luck; if anyone could do it Bertie could.

After what seemed an age the door opened again and in shuffled an elderly gentleman with long white hair and black horn-rimmed glasses wearing black tails, waistcoat and breeches. 'Lord Westex I presume,' the man said, walking with the aid of a cane towards him and holding out his hand.

Lance stood up, wiping his clammy hands down his trousers. 'Yes sir, you must be Lord Fleming,' he said, stepping forward and shaking the man's hand. 'Thank you for agreeing to see me at such short notice, sir.'

'Indeed, indeed,' Lord Fleming said, breathlessly waving his walking stick towards the seats.

The two men sat down.

'I understand from the Earl of Albemarle that you simply had to see me, sir. What's so urgent as to disturb my luncheon?' Lord Fleming asked, mopping his forehead with a white handkerchief.

Lord Fleming removed an ear-trumpet from the inside pocket of his tail-coat and, inserting it in his left ear, turned it towards Lance as he unleashed the long story of how his father had died, the additional two murders, his discussion with Lord Swan and Lady Grace Agnew and how he was following a trail which seemed to have something to do with the *Titanic* disaster.

'I see,' Lord Fleming said, nodding, when Lance finished.

'It occurred to me, when Lady Grace mentioned the Board of Trade inquiry, that there must be an official record of the proceedings. Given you're on the Board of Trade I was wondering if you could help me track down a copy.'

'Sadly, sir, I'm no longer a member,' muttered Lord Fleming. 'However, I shall be happy to help you.'

Lance flashed a beaming smile at the white-haired old man.

'The official records of the inquiry are housed here in the Palace of Westminster. There are two copies, one each kept at the libraries of the House of Commons and the House of Lords under recommendations from King George the Fifth himself,' Lord Fleming explained.

Lance was impressed. So the King of England had taken a hand in preserving the inquiry records. He wondered if the King's attention was usual in such cases.

'I shall instruct Arthur Butler, the House of Lords' chief librarian, to provide access to the volumes you require.'

'Thank you, sir,' replied Lance.

Lord Fleming stood up and put his ear-trumpet back into his coat pocket, a sign that their meeting had concluded.

'Before you leave, Lord Fleming, I wonder if I could ask one further question,' Lance asked in a loud voice.

Lord Fleming nodded.

'Can you shed any light on Lord Swan's comment that the Board of Trade was concerned about the quality of steel being used in the construction of *Titanic*?'

Lord Fleming lifted one eyebrow and peered more closely at Lance. 'There was some concern, yes,' he said eventually. 'The Board of Trade wrote to Harland and Wolff requesting clarification of the steel specification. Unfortunately, the reply the board received was somewhat terse. I suspect the company was less than thrilled at having its professional judgement questioned. In any event, their response was certainly opaque.'

'Didn't the Board of Trade follow the matter up?'

'Speak up, young man,' Lord Fleming said, frowning. Lance repeated his question more loudly. 'Not to my knowledge,' the gentleman replied abruptly. 'And now, Lord Westex, I must leave you. Pressing business in the chamber, you know. I'll have the doorkeeper show you to the library.'

Lance watched as Lord Fleming slowly made his way out of the ante-chamber.

A few moments later the doorkeeper appeared, informing them that Bob was to be given a special dispensation to accompany his master, and led them through a maze of corridors until they reached the great library doors of the Palace of Westminster.

Lance walked into the hushed room and sat down at one of the library desks where the records he sought had been placed for his perusal. Bob settled in for a snooze at his feet. Opening the first of an array of leather-bound volumes, Lance began to read.

CHAPTER 27:
BOB LENDS A HAND

IT WAS ABOUT FOUR thirty when one of the library assistants approached Lance and, standing discreetly by his side, coughed quietly. 'A gentleman wishes to see you, m'lord.'

Lance looked up, his vision blurred from speed-reading at close quarters the assorted volumes. 'To see me?' he asked, rubbing his eyes.

'Yes sir. I've been instructed to escort you to one of the staterooms.'

Puzzled, Lance sat back in his chair. Who could possibly want to see him? Only Lord Fleming, Bertie de Bretagne and the doorkeeper knew he was there.

'If you'll follow me, sir,' the librarian said insistently.

With Bob sticking resolutely to his side, Lance followed the assistant along a labyrinth of dark corridors until they came to a small ordinary-looking mahogany door.

The librarian knocked twice before opening the door and stood aside to allow Lance to enter. 'Lord Westex,' he announced in clipped tones.

Lance did not expect to find such an impressive room behind the rather insignificant door. It had a high stone ceiling supported by cornices carved into heraldic shields, and the walls were lined with tall wooden bookcases filled with ancient leather volumes. A single window, framed by full-length red velvet curtains, overlooked a small courtyard to the rear of the building, and shafts of late-afternoon sunlight streamed across the room, illuminating the dust particles that hovered in the musty air.

In the centre of the room, three sumptuous red velvet sofas were arranged around three sides of a low wooden table in front of a white marble fireplace, its empty grate filled by a leafy green plant. A salver placed on the table held two crystal spirit glasses and three decanters, their silver labels indicating their contents: Sherry, Whisky, Brandy.

'Good afternoon, Lord Westex. How nice to make your acquaintance,' said a diminutive well-dressed man in his late fifties.

Lance returned a discreet bow.

'Let me introduce myself. I'm the Duke of Cumberland. Please, come in and take a seat,' the man continued, his fleshy lips forming an oily smile.

Lance moved guardedly across the room and sat down.

'Drink?' enquired Lord Cumberland.

'Thank you, I'll have a whisky.'

The Duke poured them each a drink.

'May I call you Lance?' he asked genially as he handed Lance a glass. A signet ring on the man's middle finger glinted in the sun's rays. Without waiting for an answer, he continued: 'I understand you've spent the afternoon in our magnificent library, Lance, researching the British Board of Trade inquiry records concerning *Titanic*'s sinking.'

Lance felt the hairs on the back of his neck stiffen. Taking a slug from his glass, he replied, 'You are correct, sir.'

'Bad business that. Of course the inquiry completely exonerated White Star of any blame in the matter.'

Instantly Lance formed the impression that the Duke was attempting to sound out his opinion on the subject, which Lance didn't feel incline to share. 'Indeed,' was all he replied.

Lord Cumberland tried again. 'The inquiry's verdict was very clear. It was just an unfortunate accident, a terrible incident attributable solely to fate and a poor decision on the captain's part not to slow down when steaming through an ice-field. I'm sure an intelligent man such as yourself can see the wisdom of the inquiry's final ruling.'

Lance found it curious that the Duke was putting so much emphasis on the inquiry's decision. 'I've learned that there was a fire onboard *Titanic* when she set sail from Belfast,' he said. 'Could that have played a part in her sinking, Lord Cumberland?'

'Oh, the inquiry went over all that evidence very thoroughly,' replied the Duke dismissively.

Lance raised an eyebrow.

'No, there was never any question that so small a fire could have had such a catastrophic effect on a ship built to the exceptionally high standards and specifications of *Titanic*,' he added with a little laugh, suggesting that it was foolish even to suggest such a thing.

'My information is that it wasn't a small fire, Lord Cumberland, but something rather more serious.'

The Duke frowned.

'Indeed,' Lance went on, 'the fire was of such proportions that on arriving in Southampton a significant number of crew members deemed *Titanic* unsafe – so unsafe, in fact, that they refused to sign on with her for the remainder of the trip to New York, despite there being no alternative employment for them to go to. Their action speaks volumes, does it not, sir?'

The host had stopped smiling and his jaw had tensed. 'There may have been some men who for their own reasons didn't sign on for the full passage to America, but in the main those reasons had nothing to do with the fire. In any event, they were so few as to be immaterial.'

A vein in Lance's temple throbbed. Lord Cumberland's categorical denial of the fire's ferocity and its subsequent effect on *Titanic* completely contradicted Peter Hopwood's claims, claims which Lance believed almost certainly cost the man his life. But to what end? Did the Duke believe that by promulgating his own version of events Lance would be dissuaded from pursuing the matter? What was it Lord Cumberland didn't want him to discover?

'What's your interest in *Titanic*, sir?' Lance asked.

'Let's just say there are matters of state which go far beyond the loss of a single ship in what was a most regrettable affair,' Lord Cumberland replied, staring intensely at Lance. 'It'll do no good for anyone to rake up the past,' he added, his eyes narrowing.

'Are you suggesting the state has an interest in this matter, sir?'

'I'm just proposing you let sleeping dogs lie, that's all,' the Duke said menacingly. 'Your digging into things is not in anyone's best interests.'

Lance didn't care for the disturbing undertone in his host's message. He took a final sip of whisky, set the half-empty glass down on the low table and got to his feet. Bob jumped up, the hostile atmosphere in the room putting him on edge too.

'I'm sorry, Lord Cumberland, but I've my own reasons for wanting to investigate *Titanic*. I must go wherever the information leads me,' Lance said, halfway to the door.

'I'm truly sorry to hear that, sir,' the Duke said in a voice low. He rose from the sofa. 'I was so hoping you'd see it our way and avoid any unnecessary disagreeable repercussions.'

The pretence of a cosy chat having completely evaporated, Lance abruptly stopped and turned to face his host. The swift uncharacteristic movement signalled to Bob that something was definitely wrong and he spun round, standing defensively between Lance and Lord Cumberland.

'*Our way? Repercussions?*' Lance repeated. 'You mean you're not the only one involved in this crude attempt to intimidate me, Lord Cumberland?'

'I'd hesitate to call our little discussion intimidation, Lance,' the Duke said. 'I see it more as a word from the wise who have your best interests at heart.'

Lance cocked his head and frowned. Who were these professed 'wise' men who'd deemed it necessary to issue him with such a warning?

'However,' the Duke continued, 'you should know that if you persist with these investigations, you'll come to learn that no one is bigger than the state, sir, no one. It can only result in your fall from grace.'

'Are you threatening me, Lord Cumberland?'

'No, sir. I'm merely giving you some heartfelt counsel that you'd be well advised to consider, that's all,' the Duke replied, keeping a wary eye on Bob who was now emitting a low growl.

'Who do you represent, Lord Cumberland? Is it the government?'

'In a way, Lance, in a way. You could say I'm a member of a *very* select committee.'

'And what's the purpose of such a group?'

The Duke smiled cryptically. 'What I'm about to reveal is an official secret. If you divulge any part of our conversation to persons outside this room you'll be laying yourself open to charges of treason.'

Peter Hopwood had mentioned official secrets too. Lance was stunned. Had he unwittingly become caught in the tentacles of some far-reaching sinister group?

'I will, of course, deny this meeting ever took place if formal enquiries are ever made,' Lord Cumberland added darkly.

Bob growled again.

The Duke continued: 'Our committee has been formed to protect, on an unofficial basis, the best interests of this great nation of ours. We see it as our bounden duty to ensure that all that can be done for the good of the kingdom is done, by whatever means necessary.'

'A group acting on behalf of our nation carrying out *unofficial* duties?' Lance said, finding it hard to take in what he was hearing. 'Are you saying that the government, elected by the good people of this country, have no knowledge of your existence?'

Lord Cumberland said nothing.

'So how does this secret committee of yours operate?' Lance asked.

'That is too sensitive for your ears. You don't need to know that.'

'But who are the people on this so-called committee? What are their qualifications? Who elected them to their posts?'

'I'm not at liberty to discuss the membership,' the Duke said. 'Suffice to say they're all highly regarded members of society who have a vested interest in the sovereignty of our nation.'

'And the name of this committee of yours?'

'The name is immaterial,' said the Duke brusquely.

It suddenly occurred to Lance that the ghostly companions who had stuck to him so assiduously over the last few days had probably been unleashed by this shadowy organisation.

'Is your committee having me followed, sir?'

'I've no knowledge of any authorised surveillance,' his host replied.

Lance's mouth went dry. He had inadvertently put himself in danger by being there. After all, no one apart from Lord Cumberland and the library assistant knew he had entered the inner sanctum of the Palace. Lance was filled by an overwhelming urge to get as far away as possible.

'I'll be on my way now,' he announced, striding towards the door. 'Come on, Bob.'

Bob didn't need any encouragement and slipped through the door as soon as it was opened.

'Think about what I've said, Lance,' Lord Cumberland called after him. 'It would be *very* unwise to go meddling in affairs of state.'

It was a few minutes past five when Lance stood outside the Palace of Westminster, his heart thumping and his head spinning. He took a few deep breaths of the sticky, sweet late-afternoon air, relieved to be free of the Duke's clutches. 'You didn't like him, did you, young pup?' he said, stroking Bob's soft head reassuringly. 'My goodness, you're a good judge of character. Come along, let's you and I get back to the flat.'

On their short walk to Westminster Tube Station, Lance thought over the disturbing encounter. What was this secret committee all about? Who were the members? Had the group been set up to further some sinister plot? And who would believe him if he disclosed the conversation he'd just had with Lord Cumberland? With the threat of being charged with treason hanging over him, he'd have to tread very carefully from now on, he thought.

It was rush hour and multitudes of civil servants, and office and shop workers were flooding the streets around him. Lance steered the way through the ocean of people as they swept down into the underground station. On the west bound platform, weary commuters stood shoulder to shoulder, four deep, awaiting the arrival of the next train. Lance and Bob found themselves standing near the edge of the platform ready to climb aboard. A sudden rush of warm humid air and a rattling din announced that the next train was about to rush into the station.

Just then, Lance was abruptly snapped from his thoughts by someone shoving him hard on his left shoulder. The man was trying to thrust Lance into the path of the oncoming train!

Lance made a grab for the man and managed to grasp a gabardine sleeve, which he held onto for grim death as he swung precariously back and forth over the void of the track. Eventually he fell face down onto the relative safety of the platform and the train pulled into the station.

Meanwhile, Bob had reared up on his hind legs and clamped his jaws round the man's other arm, a deep angry growl emanating from his throat. The harder the man tried to shake Bob off, the tighter the dog gripped the arm. In an instant, a heavy black boot connected firmly with Bob's head and a piercing yelp rang out. Then a sudden hush descended as Bob dropped to the ground motionless.

Getting to his feet Lance watched bleary-eyed as the man, wearing a squashed homburg and dark raincoat, pushed his way through the crowd towards the exit. He looked back to where Bob lay and shrieked and ran to his side. His heart in his mouth, familiar feelings of desperation and powerlessness swamped him. He couldn't lose his beloved dog. Bob was as close to him as any member of the family, closer even, since he'd been the one Lance had turned to throughout the most difficult period of his life. Lance would rather lose a limb than be without the comfort and wise silent counsel of his cherished friend.

The skirmish had lasted only a few seconds but to Lance a lifetime had slipped by. The next train was at a standstill in the station but the crowd that had gathered around

BOB LENDS A HAND

them, caught up in the unexpected brouhaha, showed little interest in boarding the waiting carriages.

A young lad appeared. 'I followed 'im as far as I could, gov'nor, but 'e disappeared into the street above,' he said, panting and trying to catch his breath. Eyeing the lifeless dog lying on the platform, he asked, 'Will he be all right, mister?'

'I don't know,' Lance said, his voice hoarse with emotion.

He scooped Bob up in his arms, the warmth of the dog's limp body permeating his shirt, and buried his face deep in the thick black coat of his beloved pal. Bob had improved the quality of his life immeasurably. How could he cope without him? Well, now it was his turn to do something in return for his treasured companion. The dog's velvet-soft ears flapped listlessly as Lance raced along the platform.

'Please, stand back, I must get help,' he said, pushing his way frantically through the crowds.

He burst through the door of the station master's office and carefully set Bob's inanimate body on top of the man's desk.

'E're,' said the official, who'd been idly reviewing the latest timetables, 'what's all this then?'

'Quick, man, where's the nearest telephone,' Lance shouted. 'My dog needs urgent veterinary care.'

CHAPTER 28:
AN INSURANCE
CONUNDRUM

Thursday June 19th 1919

THE APARTMENT IN BELGRAVIA Mansions was unusually still the next morning. Lacking any motivation to undergo his customary morning ablutions, Lance sat unkempt in his bath robe pushing a breakfast sausage absentmindedly around his plate. Glancing down at his feet where Bob always sat, Lance's eyes welled up. How he longed to see the pup's trusting, eager face.

Presently Bentley came bustling in from the kitchen and looked disapprovingly at Lance's largely untouched breakfast. 'Do you wish me to clear away, m'lord?' he asked.

Lance sighed and dropped his fork noisily onto the plate. 'Thank you, Bentley,' he replied gloomily. He went to his desk, opened the lock of the Tantalus and poured himself a large whisky.

'Mr Watson is a very fine veterinarian, m'lord, the best in London I'm told,' Bentley said as he busied himself with the breakfast things. 'If anything can be done for Bob I'm sure he'll leave no stone unturned, sir.'

'Thank you, Bentley. He's such a good dog and was so brave. You should have seen him – he was fearless!'

'I know, sir. As fine an animal as you could ever wish to own, m'lord.'

'I got Mr Watson to him just as soon as I could,' continued Lance, feeling in desperate need of approval for his actions.

'I know, sir. You could have done no more,' his valet said reassuringly.

'You'll be certain to let me know as soon as Mr Watson makes contact, Bentley?' Lance said. 'No matter what I'm doing?'

'Assuredly so, sir,' Bentley said, gliding back into the kitchen and taking the breakfast accoutrements with him.

Lance found it difficult to settle. Waiting for news of Bob was excruciating. He realised that he'd come to rely on the young pup more than he thought. What would he do without him? Taking a large gulp of whisky, he gazed at a small pile of letters that had arrived in the early morning mail. *The Times* newspaper, laid out by his ever-efficient valet, remained untouched. Long fingers of depression, which Bob had been so good at dispelling, were creeping back and Lance could feel them taking hold once more. A sense of hopelessness flooded his body, the sudden freefall into melancholy terrifying him. He got up and looked down onto the London street below, grappling with the prospect of losing yet another best friend. People were going about their business in the usual way. But how could they? Didn't they know that his best, most noblest pal in the entire world was fighting for his life?

Vaguely aware that there were only two free days left before he'd be forced to announce his engagement to Lucinda, Lance discovered that without Bob he'd lost all enthusiasm to continue his investigations. For the time being the welfare of his beloved dog came first and he reconciled himself to putting the pursuit of his father's killer on hold until he could be sure of Bob's health.

Just then, the shrill ring of the apartment doorbell sounded, interrupting his train of thought. Lance jumped. Could this be Mr Watson?

In an instant Bentley was out of the kitchen and rushing to open the door. It was the fastest Lance had ever seen him move. A few moments later the valet returned carrying the silver salver upon which lay a small embossed calling card.

Lance eagerly took the card and read it: '*Algernon Greville-Bains — Underwriter and Loss Adjuster, Lloyds of London*'. 'Oh,' Lance said with disappointment, slumping back into his chair. 'I forgot Mr Greville-Bains was going to call this morning. Please show him in, Bentley.'

'Very good, sir.'

The previous evening, after Lance had left Bob with the vet, he'd gone to his club where he'd bumped into fellow member Algernon Greville-Bains. Grateful for any distraction, Lance had sat talking to Algee in the smoking room until well after midnight. Somehow the subject of *Titanic* had cropped up, and to Lance's surprise Algee revealed that he had been one of the underwriters involved in ship's insurance cover. Lance had explained his interest in *Titanic* and asked his chum if he could furnish him with further details of her insurance cover and settlement particulars. At first Algee had refused – it would be quite irregular to allow external access to such information – but after much persuasion he'd agreed to covertly copy the file as a special favour for his friend and bring it from his offices at The Royal Exchange early the next morning.

'Mr Greville-Bains, m'lord,' Bentley announced.

'Morning, Lance,' Algee said. 'Any news of Bob?'

'Nothing yet. I'm still waiting to hear from Mr Watson.'

'I'm sure he'll be fine, old chap. You'll have him back as good as new in no time.'

Lance nodded glumly. 'Listen, thanks for coming over. I really do appreciate your efforts. Would you like to stay for a coffee … or a whisky?' He raised his glass.

'No thanks. It's a bit early for that sort of thing, even for me. Anyway, I've got to get back to the office before I'm missed.' He produced a brown foolscap file from his briefcase. 'I've brought along the duplicate file you wanted,' Algee said in hushed tones, 'and although I don't think they were ever paid out, I've also put in some details about claims relating to the RMS *Olympic*, *Titanic*'s sister ship. I thought you might be interested to see that information as well since they were both commissioned by White Star.'

'Thanks awfully,' Lance replied flatly.

'I've taken a terrible risk in letting you have this. I won't be dragged into the affair, will I?'

'I'll see you're kept out of it, Algee.'

'Okay, I've got to be buzzing along … incidentally, did you know there are two men standing on the corner of the street watching your apartment?'

Lance nodded wearily. 'I'm afraid they seem to be somewhat of a fixture these days. Be seeing you, Algee. Thanks again for your help.'

After Bentley had shown Algee out, Lance sank further into his leather wingback chair, the paperwork resting on his knee while he poured himself another whisky. Eventually, he opened the folder and forced himself to read the script dancing before his eyes, but it didn't make much sense and he sank into a melancholy torpor as he awaited news of his dog.

It was mid-day when the doorbell to the apartment rang again. Lance looked up expectantly as Bentley attended the caller. This time it was the long-awaited Mr Watson and, joy of joys, who should be by his side but Bob, eager to see his master again.

'Oh, thank you, Mr Watson! Thank you for returning him to me in one piece,' said a relieved and somewhat overcome Lance as he raced across the room to give his friend a hug.

Bob's brown eyes looked devotedly into Lance's and his warm pink tongue sponged his face excitedly. Pushing his body into Lance's chest, the dog squirmed with delight, nearly pushing him to the floor. Suppressing an overwhelming urge to weep, Lance regained his composure and stood up.

'Is he completely recovered, Mr Watson. No side effects or anything?'

Mr Watson, a portly man with a reassuring smile, handed the dog's lead to Lance and, with a hint of a Welsh burr, gave his diagnosis. 'He's had rather a nasty knock to his head which gave him a concussion, m'lord. But he seems to have recovered well with no obvious after-effects.'

Lance bent down again to stroke Bob's head and soft velvet ears. 'You had me worried there, young pup,' he said as the dog leaned happily against his legs.

'He should be fine now,' Mr Watson said. 'Give him plenty of fluid and rest for the next week. Just watch for any unusual actions such as walking into things or losing his balance, m'lord.'

'Is he well enough to travel back to Landacre by train?' asked Lance who, on seeing Bob fully recovered, had instantly decided to return to Exmoor to resume his sleuthing.

'Certainly. Just make sure he doesn't take any more knocks to his head,' Mr Watson said. 'If he does exhibit any unusual behaviour, return him to your vet in Devon without delay.'

After Lance had thanked Mr Watson effusively, Bentley showed him out and disappeared into the kitchen. A few minutes later he emerged carrying two silver platters with dome-shaped lids.

'Your luncheon, m'lord,' Bentley said, placing the platters on the dining table.

'Oh good. I'm absolutely famished,' said Lance. He darted over to the table and flicked a linen napkin over his legs as Bob happily assumed his usual position at his feet.

Bentley lifted the lid to the first platter. 'Your salmon, sir,' he said.

Lance rubbed his hands together and was about to pick up his knife and fork when Bentley lifted the silver dome to the second platter.

'I hope you will approve, sir. I have taken the liberty of preparing a fine marrow bone for Bob.'

Lance beamed at him. Who'd have thought it, the old softy. 'Of course, Bentley. Please serve it to him now.'

After lunch Lance asked Bentley to telegraph Veronica at her newspaper office in Exeter, informing her that he would be on the afternoon train from London and instructing her to meet him at her apartment around five o'clock. Then, while Bentley drove down to Landacre in the two-seater, Lance settled in for the long journey back to Devon on the 14:15 from Paddington. He spent the journey with his nose deep in the folder left by Algee, this time with a new enthusiasm, while Bob rested contentedly on the adjoining seat, his head on his master's lap.

It was a little past five fifteen when Lance knocked on the door of Apartment 2b, Deacon Heights. A few minutes later the door opened and Veronica stood there barring his entrance.

'Oh, it's you. What do you want?' she asked coldly.

'Didn't you get my telegram?' Lance asked, crestfallen.

Veronica raised an eyebrow. 'You mean the one *instructing* me to meet you here? Yes, I did.' She made no attempt to stand aside.

Lance would have to be rather more careful with his missives in future. He seemed to have a habit of issuing orders, one that was proving difficult to break now he was no longer captain of the *Panther*. 'Please let me in, Veronica. I want to explain.'

'I'm not sure I want to let you in, Lance. I don't like being summoned like one of your crew. You can't just expect me to come running at the drop of a hat.'

'Please, I want to apologise properly for what happened the other night too and I don't want to do it here on the doorstep,' Lance said in a low voice.

'You really are the limit. You leave me standing all alone feeling quite superfluous at your brother's ball the other night and then expect me to jump to attention the moment you want to see me again.'

'I know. I'm sorry about that. It wasn't my idea to leave you unattended. I'd planned to be with you all evening. Unfortunately, events rather got in the way.'

'Well, it's not good enough,' Veronica said fiercely. 'I felt so humiliated, and Lucinda's catty remarks didn't help.'

'I know. I was annoyed about that too. Please let me in so we can talk about it without everyone in the building overhearing.'

'Does Lucinda know you're here? I don't think she'd approve, do you? She could well burst in to my apartment and fly around on her broomstick like the possessive witch she is if I *were* to allow you in.'

'Oh, forget Lucinda,' snapped Lance, exasperated by her continued petulance.

'If only I could.'

'Please let me in, Veronica. I thought we were working as a team on this. I've got so much to tell you. Don't you want to know what I've learned over the last few days while I've been away?'

Veronica cocked her head to one side and narrowed her eyes.

That's got her, thought Lance. She's a sucker for a good story.

'Okay, Lance,' Veronica said, standing back from the doorway. 'But remember, this – our partnership – is just a business arrangement, nothing more.'

Sitting comfortably in her drawing room, Lance watched as she started to pour two large gin and tonics.

'Nothing for me, Veronica. I've got a bit of a head,' he said, putting down the file he'd been holding while Bob settled comfortably on the floor.

Sitting in a chair on the other side of Bob, Veronica raised an eyebrow again.

'Well?' she said sharply, 'you were going to tell me what you've found out.'

Lance recounted the events of the previous two days – his trip to the Palace of Westminster and his subsequent meeting with the Duke of Cumberland.

'Jumping Journalists! You don't mean to tell me that HMG *is* involved in this matter after all?' she said.

'Well, I don't think it's as straightforward as that,' Lance replied. 'We know it was the Home Office who requisitioned John Seymour's last letter home. And we've assumed that those people following me work for HMG. But the Duke led me to believe that this unofficial committee of his may be operating without the knowledge of the government.'

'I must admit that makes more sense. I don't see what possible motive HMG could have for being mixed up with the sinking of *Titanic*.'

'The Duke said that his committee was dedicated to working for the best interests of our nation. I've no idea

298

what he meant by that, but I'm sure as hell going to find out!'

Veronica took a sip from her drink.

'Then there was the incident at Westminster Tube Station,' Lance added.

'What incident?' Veronica asked, wide-eyed. She listened intently as he related the drama and Bob's heroic actions.

'Poor Bob,' she said when he got to the bit about taking a heavy boot to the head. She stroked the dog's ears gently.

'Poor Bob!' exclaimed Lance, hurt she hadn't acknowledged the danger he was in. 'What about *me*? I could've been killed!'

'Yes, I suppose you could,' she said flatly.

Lance, disappointed by her lack of concern for him, pressed on by telling her about the meeting with his pal Algee and explaining how he came to have a copy of insurance documents for *Titanic* and her sister ship *Olympic*.

'Is there anything in the insurance angle?'

Lance scratched his head. 'Well, it certainly makes interesting reading,' he said, picking up the file again and flipping through the pages. 'If you take the figures at face value it appears that *Titanic* was underinsured. Lloyds of London paid out a figure to the tune of five million dollars for the ship, but the hull had previously been valued at around eight million.'

'That's curious. Why would White Star underinsure *Titanic*?'

'I don't know,' Lance replied. 'Then there's the material Algee slipped in about *Olympic*.'

'What about her?'

'It seems she had a serious accident in September 1911 when she was in collision with HMS *Hawke* in Southampton waters,' he said, reading from the documentation. 'The insurance report indicates the accident caused significant damage to *Olympic* – steel frames buckled, thousands of popped rivets, steel plating dislodged over four decks, distortion to the starboard propeller and crankshaft, a bent keel which produced a pronounced list to port.'

'Is that relevant to our enquiry?'

'I can't help thinking that it is somehow,' he replied. He paused for a few moments to process his thoughts. 'Would your office have a file on the *Olympic*, d'you think? I should like to know more about her accident.'

'I expect there will be a file in the archives somewhere.'

'Can we go over to the offices now and retrieve it?'

'The offices close at five. We'll have to wait until morning.'

'I'm afraid I haven't got time to waste, Veronica. For reasons I'd prefer not to go into for the moment, I need to see the file tonight. Let's go over and see if we can let ourselves in.'

'You're asking me to break into my employer's premises, Lance. I could lose my job!'

'Needs must when the devil drives. Where's your spirit of adventure, old girl? I thought you were up for this investigative lark,' he said with a twinkle in his eye.

'Be it on your head then. If we get caught I shall say you made me do it and blame the whole business on you,' she retorted.

That evening, as Exeter's historic clock tower chimed eight, Veronica allowed Lance to heave her unceremoniously over the wooden fence that enclosed the *Chronicle*'s offices, while Bob squeezed through a crack in the timber.

CHAPTER 29:
THUNDERSTRUCK

THE STICKY WARMTH OF an oppressive evening hung heavily in air. Lance looked up into the darkening sky where a blanket of graphite-coloured cumulonimbus cloud was settling over the city.

'Looks as if we're in for a storm,' he remarked idly.

They made their way stealthily across the courtyard, the faint rumble of distant thunder echoing across the city. Breathless with nervous exhilaration, their senses fizzing, Lance and Veronica reached the entrance to the *Chronicle*'s towering red brick offices. Lance discreetly broke the glass panel beside the door and put his hand through to find the lock on the other side of the door.

'Tut tut, you'll have to pay for that, Lance,' Veronica whispered loudly.

He unlocked the door and, kicking the broken glass to one side, allowed Veronica and Bob into the building. They crept into the murky interior of the office reception and Lance pushed through the rasping swing doors on the far side, fumbling his way into the main newspaper office.

'Where are the archives kept, Veronica?' he asked in a low voice.

'They're down in the cellar,' she replied, following him into the room. 'We'd better take a lamp with us. It's going to be difficult to see down there.'

Lance picked up an oil lamp from the nearest desk and lit the wick, then followed Veronica towards a narrow white wooden staircase that went down to the vaults.

The staircase creaked ominously as the three of them descended carefully, their shadows flickering against the whitewashed bricks of the stairwell. At the bottom they came to a small wooden door set into the wall; someone had thoughtfully left the key in the lock. Lance turned the key and pushed the door open. The light from the lamp flooded the cold, dank room and a malodorous smell rushed to greet them. They descended two more wooden steps to a damp stone floor.

Holding the lamp high Lance could just make out the walls of a small square windowless room. Materialising out of the gloom like ancient monuments to the past rose a matrix of rusting metal racks holding row upon row of bulging cardboard boxes in various stages of disintegration.

'Goodness! I didn't expect so many files,' Lance said.

Veronica pushed past him, confidently leading the way into the vault, and Lance and Bob followed, the odour of mouldy paper filling their nostrils. They passed a diminutive padlocked door.

'What's in there?' Lance whispered.

'Oh, that's the blue room.'

'The blue room?'

'Yes, it actually houses the boiler for the building, but Mr Bevans, our editor, insists that all risqué and scandalous articles are locked away in there "out of harm's way from the babes in the wood", as he quaintly puts it.' She giggled.

Lance found himself wondering if Veronica had seen these so-called risqué documents, in which case Mr Bevans's precautions had been entirely futile.

Veronica pressed on past numerous racks, then turned to her left in front of an iron grating that covered a coal chute high up on an external wall. The grating was the only source of natural light in the room.

'David and I have been working down here,' she said, moving to the end of the enclosure where stood an old pine table covered with discarded files.

A shiver ran up Lance's spine. 'I admire you and David for working in such an unpleasant place,' he said, placing the lamp on the table.

'A good investigative reporter doesn't shrink from objectionable environments in the pursuit of truth,' she proclaimed.

Lance peered at the labels on the files, which were methodically sequenced by year and month. It was all a bit overwhelming. 'Where on earth do we start?'

'David and I have been looking at 1912, but I expect the file on the *Olympic* will be under 1911 since I think you said that was the date of her accident with HMS *Hawke*.'

'Yes, that's right.'

Together they set about looking through the racks labelled 1911. Presently they came upon a brown cardboard box marked 'RMS *Olympic*'. Lance lifted it down, placed it on the table and untied the mildewed tape that kept the lid attached to the box. He lifted the lid and emptied the contents of the box onto the table.

A brilliant flash of lightning suddenly illuminated the vault through the narrow coal grate followed shortly by an explosive thunderclap, which seemed amplified in the building's vault. Bob growled.

'It's all right, young pup. Nothing to worry about,' Lance said, stroking the dog's head as he and Veronica continued to pore over the newspaper clippings under the weak light of the oil lamp.

'Look at this, Lance,' Veronica said, holding up a clipping. '*Olympic* appears to have been very accident prone. This newspaper report is of a stern collision on the 21st of June 1911 involving the vessel OL *Hallenbech* in New York. The *Hallenbech* nearly sank!'

'Let me see?' Lance took the tattered cutting from her and held it under the lamp's green shade. 'That's only seven days after her maiden voyage from Southampton and just three months before her major collision with the *Hawke*.'

The pair continued to sift through the mountain of clippings.

'This is interesting,' Lance said, taking hold of another cutting.

'What?'

'I've found a report on a Royal Naval investigation into the accident with the *Hawke*. It seems the final ruling of the subsequent inquiry blamed *Olympic* for the incident, alleging that her large displacement generated a suction that pulled *Hawke* into her side.'

Veronica whistled. 'So ... White Star was responsible for the restitution of the *Hawke* as well as the repairs to *Olympic*. Doubtless they passed the claim on to their insurers. I'll bet that came to a pretty penny.'

'Yes, but the story doesn't end there,' Lance said, pulling yet another article from the pile. 'It seems that in December 1911, White Star disputed the final ruling of the Royal Navy inquiry and brought a claim against them in the Admiralty Court to the amount of seven hundred and fifty thousand dollars for loss and damage to the *Olympic*.'

'What happened?' Veronica asked.

Lance read aloud from the piece:

This morning at the Admiralty Court in London a verdict was handed down in the case of The White Star Line (Claimant) v/s His Majesty's Royal Navy (Defendant).

Despite counsel for the claimant arguing that the Royal Naval inquiry was seriously flawed and their subsequent final verdict in error, the Court ruled the collision with the Hawke was entirely the fault of the Olympic.

In respect of the defendants counter-claim, the Court found counsel's argument to be without merit. Dismissing the claim, the Court ruled no damages were payable by the White Star Line for the reinstatement of the Hawke since the Olympic was under compulsory pilotage at the time.

'Goodness! So they got away without having to pay anything to the Royal Navy then.'

'Yes, but it costs a fortune to undertake a legal case in the High Court. I'd wager that the cost of the court fees alone would have added significantly to the financial burden already suffered by White Star.'

'What financial burden?'

'Well, think about it for a minute,' Lance said. 'It's not unreasonable to assume that as their flagship was out of service for months on end the company would have incurred a considerable shortfall of revenue. Then there's the cost of the repair and refurbishment to the hull. If *Olympic* were underinsured, the same as *Titanic* undoubtedly was, the company would have had to fund a significant part of the repair costs themselves – that's in addition to the financial commitment the company had already made to complete two further superliners. The loss of the case coming on top of all these factors must have made a sizeable dent in the company's profits for the year, perhaps even rocking their long-term financial stability.'

'Wow! Let's keep looking. There may be more.'

Another few minutes went by as the pair continued to look through the documents.

'Hang on a minute, what's this doing here?' Veronica said. 'It seems to be misfiled with a number of other items.'

'What is it?'

'It's a photograph from 1912.'

'Let me see,' Lance said, taking hold of the snap. It was a large black-and-white shot of two superliners berthed side by side. He turned it over; the words *Olympic and Titanic – Belfast March 1912* were printed on the back. 'They're identical,' he whispered.

'Yes, aren't they. Even their own crews probably had difficulty telling them apart, don't you think?'

Outside the storm had moved closer and was practically overhead now, the lightning flashing through the coal grate more frequently and the rumbling thunder barely ceasing.

Lance examined another newspaper report which indicated that *Olympic* had suffered further bad luck. 'Look at this Veronica,' he said and he began to read aloud again: '... *having been put back into service in November 1911, on a return trip from New York in February 1912 Olympic ran over a sunken wreck on the Grand Banks damaging her starboard propeller with the loss of a blade. The ship limped back to Southampton on one engine, arriving on 28 February 1912. A spokesman for the company said ...*'

Suddenly a bolt of lightning hit the coal grate and arced across the room to the metal racks where they were standing. Lance was thrown across the room and hit the back wall of the vault where he slid down the whitewashed bricks and landed in a heap on the damp stone floor. The pine table they had been working at was knocked over, and the oil lamp crashed to the floor adding fuel to a fire that had already begun to take hold. The blaze ate through the paper files quickly, and the room filled with thick black acrid smoke.

Dazed, Veronica rushed to the back of the room. 'Lance, Lance,' she cried, shaking him frantically and coughing. 'Oh do come on, Lance,' she called out again weakly before falling to the floor comatose.

* * *

His eyes flickered and opened. Bright sunlight was streaming in through an open window, birds were chirping, the smell of freshly mown grass hung in the air. Lance looked around. Gradually he realised he was in his own comfortable bed at Landacre, Dr Beauchamp standing over him holding his wrist and looking at his watch.

'Oh, you're back with us again, Lance,' the doctor said, smiling as he carefully laid his patient's hand back on top of the bedspread.

Lance coughed. He felt awful. 'What happened?' he asked, sitting up. He started to cough and the doctor handed him a glass of water that was sitting on the bedside table.

'Don't you remember?'

'I'm afraid not. The last thing I recall is being down in the vault at the *Chronicle*'s offices. After that it's a complete blank.'

'You and your friend were very lucky. There was a fire in the building. You were saved by some quick thinking on the part of some people who happened to be in the vicinity.'

The springs of his bed gave gently as Bob soundlessly jumped up, desperate to be beside his master. The dog set his head on the corner of a pillow and, letting out a long contented sigh, looked adoringly into Lance's face.

A wave of relief surged through Lance. Bob had evidently escaped the catastrophe largely unscathed, apart from what appeared to be superficial scorch marks to his once gleaming black coat. 'Oh Bob, you're all right,' he murmured.

'That dog of yours is remarkable,' the doctor said. 'He's been here all night. He hasn't moved once since I visited yesterday evening.'

Lance patted Bob's head. 'He's my true friend.'

'Which reminds me. There's someone outside waiting to see you if you're up to it.'

'I can't face the family, Doc,' he replied. The last thing he wanted was his mother and aunts fussing over him.

'Oh, it's no one from the family,' the doctor said as he put his equipment back into his bag. 'I believe it's your friend – the young lady you were with yesterday evening.'

'Oh, is she all right? Do please ask her to come in on your way out.'

Doctor Beauchamp nodded.

'Can I get up?' Lance asked, remembering he had an investigation to finish and that he was running out of time.

'If you feel well enough, but don't go overdoing it,' the doctor said from the open doorway. 'Your body's still recovering from the effects of the fire.' He pulled the door shut behind him.

Lance put his arm around Bob who nestled tightly to his side. A few moments later the door opened quietly and Veronica slipped in, her face pale and drawn.

'Couldn't stay away, eh?' Lance said, giving her a weak smile. 'I knew you wouldn't be able to resist my seductive charm.'

'Don't talk rubbish,' she snapped, vigorously plumping up the pillows that Bob wasn't resting on and placing them behind Lance's back.

'What happened? How did we get out of the vault?' Lance asked, enjoying the attention he was getting from her.

'There was a lightning strike. It would seem that two men saw what happened and called the local fire brigade before running into the building and, at considerable risk to themselves, pulling us from the burning ruins.'

'Two men? I'll bet they were the two men who've been following me these past two weeks.'

'Yes, I thought that myself. If so, I shall always be grateful to them for saving our lives.'

Lance nodded.

'It's odd though, because they disappeared before the police arrived,' Veronica added. 'I didn't have an opportunity to thank them. I only know what happened because a few people in the crowd told me after I came round on the pavement.'

'Was there much damage done?'

'Quite a lot actually. The vault was completely destroyed – all the archives are gone.'

'What, nothing left?'

'Nothing … apart from this.' Veronica grinned as she took the photograph of the two superliners from her bag. 'I concealed it under my blouse just as the fire took hold.'

'Oh, clever you!' he said and started to cough again. He reached for the glass of water. 'What about the offices upstairs?' he asked when he'd had a sip.

'They're badly smoked damaged, but the company should be able to restore them to their original splendour.'

'I don't suppose I'll have to pay for that broken glass now then.'

Veronica laughed. 'You really are incorrigible, Lance,' she said, shaking her head.

'Excuse me, m'lord,' said Bentley who'd just silently entered the room, 'Chief Superintendent Schilling has arrived. He wonders if you would be well enough to see him, sir. Mr Treadwell has asked him to wait in the library.'

CHAPTER 30:
COMPLICATIONS

Friday June 20th 1919

LANCE ASKED VERONICA TO wait for him downstairs in the study. He would bring her in to join him and Chief Superintendent Schilling in the library as she had made it abundantly clear that she wanted to hear of any new developments for herself, direct from the 'horse's mouth', as she put it.

Lance was about to get out of bed when his bedroom door was flung open and Hugo came in.

'Are you recovered, Lance?'

'I'm on the mend, Hugo. Well enough to be getting out of bed at any rate. Haven't you heard of knocking?'

'No time for that. We've all been so worried about you. Ma and the aunts are furious with you. I wouldn't want to be in your shoes when you see them later. What were you doing down in the cellar of the *Chronicle*'s offices anyway?'

'Oh, it's a long story – too complicated to go into at the moment,' Lance replied. 'Listen, old chap, I've got to get dressed. Chief Superintendent Schilling's downstairs waiting to see me.'

'Yes, I know. What the devil does he want? Can't he leave us alone?'

Bentley appeared and hovered around, helping Lance as he got dressed.

'While you're here, Hugo, I want a word with you,' Lance said.

Hugo scowled.

'That's all, thank you, Bentley,' Lance said, not wishing his valet to overhear what he was about to say.

'Very good, m'lord.'

As Bentley closed the door to the bedroom Lance shot his brother a stern glance. 'I've heard something very disturbing about you,' he said, 'something I think you should've told me from the outset.'

Hugo's face went very red and he swallowed hard. 'I don't know what you're talking about, Lance,' he said indignantly.

'I think you do, my dear brother,' Lance said and went on to recount his earlier conversation with Rose, the parlourmaid.

'So what were you and Pa arguing about that day and why in God's name didn't you tell me about it earlier?'

Hugo seemed extremely ill at ease and paced the room without speaking.

'Well!' Lance said sternly. 'Out with it, Hugo.'

'Oh very well, but please don't think badly of me,' Hugo said, slumping down onto the corner of the bed.

'How could I? You're my brother,' Lance said more kindly. 'What's it all about?'

'I don't quite know where to start,' Hugo mumbled.

'The beginning's a good place.'

'Well, you know I've been courting Clara for some time – nine years to be exact. It hasn't been easy, I can tell you. The loss of her father and brother affected her badly, and she's been so cold and remote towards everyone. What's a chap to do, I ask you?'

Lance smiled encouragingly. 'Tell me about it. I want to help.'

'Well, there was this young parlourmaid, Betty Sharples. Pa took her on about two years ago. She's a pretty young thing – always happy in her work, pleasant to be around. We got talking and before I knew it one thing led to another.'

Lance frowned. 'One thing led to another?'

'Egad, Lance don't you know anything! She told me she was going to have pups.'

Lance was even more confused 'Can't you speak the King's English, Hugo. What d'you mean "she was going to have pups"?

'She got pregnant!'

Lance gasped and took a step back. 'Are you saying you're the father?'

'Yes!' Hugo said.

'Good heavens! What did Pa say?'

'That's what the argument was about. In fact there were several over the last few weeks since Betty's parents came to the Hall demanding I do right by their daughter. That's how Pa found out, damn them!'

'What did you expect! Pa was bound to find out eventually. Of course he was going to be upset. What did he say to you?'

'He was furious. He kept saying I was putting my whole future in jeopardy for the sake of some "bloody simple-minded domestic drudge with no prospects" to use his words.'

Lance's head was spinning. 'What happened next?'

'Well … as I said Pa wasn't happy, but he did agree to pay off the Sharples family in return for their silence and their promise that Betty would get rid of the unborn child. If news of her pregnancy got out, my marriage to Clara could be threatened.'

'Not to mention the fact that you would have contravened the clause in her father's will, leaving you and Clara without a penny from her trust fund,' Lance added cynically. 'Hardly a propitious start to anyone's marriage.'

'Betty's family agreed that she would leave her employment at the Hall that day on the understanding that I met with her and her father to discuss the arrangements Pa was going to put in place for her future.' Hugo looked down at the carpet. 'On the afternoon Pa drove off for the last time, I met Betty and her father down at the boathouse to tell them what preparations were in progress. That's where I really was when I said I was out riding with Tabby. You see I couldn't very well tell everyone where I actually was or why.'

Lance nodded. 'No, indeed not!'

'I explained that Pa was arranging for an abortion to take place in Harley Street, that he had drawn up a legal document, and that he had put one hundred pounds in cash in the safe to be used for Betty's procedure and her future. I told them that we'd arrange a later meeting at the boathouse when I'd give them the clinic's address together with the date of Betty's appointment. They'd both be required to sign Pa's legal document after which I'd hand over the money in final settlement so to speak.'

'Why didn't you arrange to meet the family here at the Hall?'

'Don't be an ass, Lance! We couldn't risk anyone here finding out what was going on.'

'What happened next?' Lance asked, feeling more and more disillusioned.

'Well, last Friday afternoon I received a note demanding I come down to the boathouse that evening. It specifically stated "at eleven o'clock – if you know what's good for you". I went down at the appointed hour but no one was there. I waited and waited but no one came, so I walked back to the Hall.'

'Last Friday? That was the night Hopwood was murdered,' Lance whispered.

'Yes, I know. Why d'you think I've been going out of my mind this last week.'

'Was the note from Betty and her father?'

'At the time I thought it was. I had the idea that now Pa was dead they saw me as a soft touch and were trying to extort a bigger payoff from me. But thinking about it since, I've a notion it may have been from someone else, someone who wanted to make sure I didn't have an alibi for the night of Hopwood's murder. I remember it wasn't signed so I really couldn't be sure who it was from.'

'What happened to the note? Have you still got it?'

'No, I'm afraid I haven't.'

'What did you do with it then?'

'I burnt it. I didn't want anyone to find out what was going on. Can you imagine the ruckus if Clara had found it?'

'You oaf! Now we only have your word for it that there was any note at all.'

Hugo shrugged his shoulders.

'So you were at the scene of Hopwood's murder without anyone to corroborate your story,' Lance said.

'That's about the size of it.'

'Did you see anyone else down by the lake that night?'

'Not really.'

'What d'you mean "not really"? Either you did or you didn't.'

'I thought I saw someone on the jetty. The moon was pretty full and I thought I saw a figure clad in a long coat and one of those Fedora-type hats. In any event I didn't hang around – I had to get down to the boathouse before anyone saw me creeping about.'

'D'you think it was Hopwood?'

'I don't know, Lance, really I don't. I only saw the back of them.'

'Do try to remember, Hugo!' Lance exclaimed. 'Was it someone else, someone you may have recognised by the way they moved about?'

Hugo was silent for a few moments and closed his eyes. 'No sorry, Lance,' he said, opening his eyes again. 'I can't say I recognised anything about the figure at all. I was quite a long way off.'

Lance took a couple of paces across the room, turned and came back to stand in front of Hugo again. 'So ...

what happened to the money? It wasn't in the safe when we opened it.'

'Well, when Inspector Quick arrived on the first night saying Pa had died in a crash, I panicked. I knew the police would want to look inside Pa's safe so I thought it would be better to remove any trace of the cash before they got to it. I imagined they'd want to impound it, or whatever it is they do with evidence and I just had to have the wherewithal to pay off the Sharples. So I slipped down in the early hours of the morning and took it from the safe.'

'How did you do that without the key?' Lance asked in amazement.

'Oh Lance, you're such an innocent. I've always known where Pa kept the safe key, but I couldn't let on, could I?'

Lance was thrown for a second. Then he said, 'So did you give it to the Sharples? Where's the money now?'

'I haven't seen or heard from them yet. I couldn't put it back in the safe. You'd already looked inside the day after Pa's death, so I stashed it in my room.'

The pair sat in silence for a moment or two.

'There's nothing for it, Hugo, we're going to have to tell Superintendent Schilling all about it. The good thing about this mess is that I haven't had a chance to speak to him yet about you not riding out with Tabby. How would it look now if we had to explain this further complication? Schilling would never trust anything you said again. As it is he's bound to think you're the number one candidate for murdering Hopwood!'

'You don't think he'll believe I did it,' Hugo said, horrified.

'What would you think if you were Mr Plod? You admit you were at the scene of the crime and you've got one hundred pounds you took from Pa's safe hidden in your bedroom. It's quite likely Schilling will think you were being blackmailed by Hopwood and decided to get rid of him once and for all.'

'Oh God,' Hugo wailed. 'I know it looks bad, Lance, but I didn't do it, really I didn't.'

'Come on, old chap, let's see Schilling. You've got to tell the truth and shame the devil now.'

'But what if he doesn't accept what I say as true?'

'Then we'll just have to convince him it is the truth, won't we,' Lance replied.

Hugo and Lance went down to the library where Superintendent Schilling was waiting with Inspector Quick.

'Good morning, Superintendent. I gather you want to see me,' Lance said as he entered the room.

'Yes m'lord. Actually it's rather fortuitous that your brother is with you. I wonder if we might go over a few things with you both.'

The four men sat around one of the library tables, Inspector Quick with his notebook and pencil at the ready.

'I wonder, Master Hugo, if you'd mind explaining your movements again on the afternoon of your father's death. I believe you said you were out riding with your sister. Is that correct?'

Lance broke in: 'I think Hugo would like to impart something to you, Superintendent, that he may have inadvisably thought better to keep to himself when he was originally questioned by Inspector Quick.'

A muscle in the Superintendent's jaw twitched. 'Indeed, sir?'

'Yes, go on Hugo – tell the Superintendent what happened.'

Hugo began to mutter quietly.

'I'm sorry, sir, will you speak up so Inspector Quick can get all the information down.'

Hugo cleared his throat and took a deep breath, then launched into his story. He told of his predicament with the maid Betty, his argument with his father, the subsequent plan to hush the matter up, his actual whereabouts on the afternoon of Lord Cedrick's death and his receipt of the anonymous note which consequently led to a lonely wait at the boathouse on the night of Hopwood's murder.

Inspector Quick busily jotted down Hugo's statement.

'I see,' Schilling said gravely.

'I believe my brother is sincere when he says he had nothing to do with Hopwood's death, Superintendent. You won't have to discuss the matter of the parlourmaid's pregnancy with the rest of the family, will you? I don't think it'll move matters on significantly and will only cause untold distress and misery for everyone.'

Schilling made no reply. He leaned over the table, lifted a brown paper bag sitting innocuously beside Inspector Quick and took the enclosed article out, setting it carefully on top of the table.

'Do either of you recognise this?'

Lance and Hugo peered at a black leather glove, the fingers of which had been cut open along the seams.

'It looks like a man's glove, Superintendent,' Lance said cautiously.

'Indeed, sir, that's exactly what it is. Do either of you own such an item?'

Hugo heaved a huge sigh.

'Sir Bernard and his team have been able to remove a number of prints from inside the glove, m'lord. Would either of you have any objection to having your fingerprints taken?'

'There's no need, Superintendent,' Hugo cut in. 'It's my glove.'

Superintendent Schilling smiled in a satisfied way. 'Can you tell me why you didn't inform me it was your glove when I showed it to you at St Peter's last Sunday?'

Lance and Hugo remained silent.

'Are you missing a glove, sir?'

'Not that I know of, Superintendent,' Hugo replied. 'It is summer. No one wears winter gloves in summer, do they, so I'd have no cause to look for them.'

'I think it better we carry on this conversation at the station house, Master Hugo,' Schilling said, getting to his feet.

Hugo gulped. 'What for? I've told you all I know.'

'I think the time has come to pursue the matter on a more official basis, sir,' the Superintendent replied.

Hugo looked wildly around the room. 'But I've told you I had nothing to do with Hopwood's death.'

'I know, sir. Let's just go quietly down to the station and discuss the matter further.'

'Are you arresting me, Superintendent?'

'Not at the moment, sir. Let's just say you're assisting the police with their enquiries.'

'It's all right, Hugo I'll get hold of the family's solicitors in Exeter. You go along with the Superintendent, but don't say anything until you've spoken with Mr Drake,' Lance said.

'But I can't go, Lance. I'm getting married tomorrow,' cried Hugo.

'You'll be back soon enough,' Lance replied, trying to soothe his brother.

Superintendent Schilling stood up. 'Just one more thing, m'lord.'

'What's that, Superintendent?'

'We'd like to search Master Hugo's room, sir.'

'Whatever for?'

'Well, for one thing we'd like to find the money.'

'I can't think that's necessary, Superintendent. Hugo's told you all about it.'

'We think it's important, sir. We call it evidence,' Schilling replied brusquely. 'We have a warrant, m'lord,' he added, nodding to Inspector Quick who produced the document.

Lance glanced at the paperwork.

'There's no need to worry,' the Superintendent said. 'Anything taken away will be returned to you once the matter has been resolved, m'lord. Quick here will give you a receipt for any items removed from the premises.'

The four men went to Hugo's bedroom where he showed the Superintendent the money he'd hidden in a case under his bed. Meanwhile, Inspector Quick began a thorough search, pulling out drawers and generally having a good rummage around the room. Opening a cupboard door he found a large travelling trunk partially covered by clean bedding. He uncovered it and opened the lid.

'That's interesting,' mused the Inspector gazing inside. At the bottom lay a black leather glove and a tweed riding jacket that covered a number of ingrained brown stains on the bottom of the chest. 'Is this your trunk, Master Hugo?'

'I've never seen it before in my life,' he wailed, looking desperately at Lance.

'It seems we've found the twin of the glove we already have in evidence,' remarked Quick. 'Is this your riding jacket, Master Hugo?'

Hugo stared open-mouthed.

'We'll have to take the trunk and its contents as well, m'lord,' Schilling said briskly.

With that, the two policemen guided Hugo down the grand staircase towards the main exit where a police car was waiting for them.

CHAPTER 31:
AN UNEXPECTED
CONFESSION

L ANCE STOOD AT THE main door to Landacre watching
Hugo being escorted to the waiting police car where
a constable firmly assisted him into the rear seat.
Just then another dark saloon car came speeding up the
long drive to the Hall, a pall of dry dusty earth roiling in its
wake. The sound of crushed gravel filled the air as it slewed
to a halt. Then the front passenger seat door was flung open
and Sergeant Bolt raced over to Superintendent Schilling.

'What's all the hullabaloo, Sergeant?'

'Sorry, sir,' replied the breathless police officer as he stood
pinching together two corners of his handkerchief, 'but I
thought you should see this as a matter of urgency.' He held
the opened handkerchief out towards the Superintendent.

Schilling looked mildly surprised. 'What is it?'

Sergeant Bolt cast a guarded look at Lance standing on
the steps. Schilling immediately understood that what Bolt
had to say was not for general consumption and moved out
towards the open parkland, his sergeant following. There
followed an animated conversation as Schilling carefully

inspected whatever it was that Bolt was holding. Nodding several times before issuing further orders, Schilling took hold of the handkerchief.

The sergeant strode purposefully back to the recently vacated car and, opening the rear door, stood waiting patiently for the Superintendent.

Schilling walked over to Lance.

'It seems Jacob Snyder's body has been discovered at Exworthy Reservoir just a mile from here, m'lord. Initial indications seem to suggest the cause of death is suicide.'

Lance gasped.

'I wonder if you'd care to take a look at this,' Schilling said, thrusting the opened handkerchief under his gaze.

Lance looked down at a handwritten note:

I can't go on any longer.

The constant threat of being unmasked for fraud has become intolerable.

I know that nothing I do now will restore the life of the honorable man I have dispatched in order to cover my abhorrent actions, but my conscience would not permit me to go to my grave without first clearing my wife of any involvement in the murder of Lord Cedrick and his chauffeur.

She had no knowledge of the terrible deeds I have been forced to carry out, and I can only hope she will find it in her heart to forgive me.

'Good grief! He's confessing to the murder of my father!' Lance said, not sure what to be more shocked by – the news of Snyder's untimely death or his confession.

'Hmm, I'm not sure that all is as it seems,' the Superintendent said. 'Had Snyder spent any time in America?

'Not that I know of,' Lance replied. 'Why do you ask?'

'Look at the spelling of "honourable",' Schilling said. 'Of course Snyder may just have been poor at spelling,' he added. 'In any event it may account for the death of Lord Cedrick. I understand there is a serious question mark hanging over the Coombe End Memorial Fund's accounts.'

'Where did you hear that, Superintendent?'

'Oh we have our sources, m'lord. Word's all around the village about Snyder's shenanigans – his repeated failure to explain the accounts, the latest being at the recent village hall meeting.'

'Oh that.'

'Yes, m'lord, *that*. I'm somewhat surprised you didn't feel it necessary to confide all these facts to the police, sir.'

Lance shuffled uncomfortably. 'I wasn't sure it was relevant, Superintendent.'

'Everything's relevant in a murder enquiry, sir,' Schilling said.

'Point taken.'

'Perhaps Lord Cedrick had obtained proof positive of Snyder's embezzlement and Snyder, not wishing to be exposed, took matters into his own hands before your father was able to publicly reveal his findings.'

'You think Snyder tampered with Father's brakes, Superintendent?'

'It's one working theory, sir.'

'Do you have any others?'

'None that I wish to discuss at the moment, m'lord,' Schilling replied brusquely. Tipping his hat, he made his way over to the car where Bolt was waiting.

The car carrying Hugo, Inspector Quick and the items removed from the Hall set off on its way to the police station in Exeter. Getting into the back of the second police car, Schilling nodded to his sergeant and they headed down the drive to Exworthy Reservoir.

Lance turned and went back into the vestibule where he sent for Bentley.

'You wished to see me, m'lord?'

'Yes, I want you to take a telegram down to the post office in Coombe End. It's rather urgent so I'd like you to go immediately. You can take the two-seater.'

Lance swiftly dictated his missive asking Mr Drake of Froggatt, Cubitt and Drake to attend Hugo at Exeter Police Station without delay. Bentley left straightaway to attend to the task at hand.

'Good Lord, I've forgotten Veronica,' Lance muttered to himself, suddenly remembering that he had asked her to wait for him in the study. He hurried down the passageway hoping she wouldn't be too annoyed at having been left for so long.

'Oh there you are! You take an age to get dressed, don't you?' Veronica said sharply as he entered the room.

'I'm so sorry, Veronica. I've was unavoidably delayed by Superintendent Schilling who's just seen fit to take Hugo back to the police station.'

'Good gracious, whatever's happened?' she asked.

Lance explained the events of that morning – the glove found at the scene of Hopwood's demise, his brother's admission that it was his, the search of his room and the removal of a trunk containing the other glove and Hugo's tweed hunting jacket. He conveniently left out his brother's earlier confession regarding Betty Sharples, thinking it desirable to keep the salacious details of Hugo's recent antics from everyone for as long as he could. Lance also wasn't sure whether Veronica, on hearing the particulars, could be relied upon to keep them to herself. In his view such a sensational story concerning a local aristocratic family would certainly be a juicy story for an up-and-coming young journalist. If it were to be put into print the cat would undoubtedly be out of the bag in more ways than one. What a terrible disaster that would be for the Donaldson-Gilks family.

'Do the police think your brother's involved in these murders then?' Veronica asked.

'Schilling believes he has strong reasons to tie Hugo to Hopwood's murder. He was down by the lake that night. Schilling probably thinks Hopwood was meeting Hugo and things got a bit rough.'

'But what could Hopwood be meeting Hugo about?'

'I haven't the foggiest,' Lance said, hoping they could get off the subject soon.

'What about the brown stains in the trunk? Schilling's bound to ask his forensics men to check them out. What if they turn out to be blood?'

Lance shook his head. 'I don't know. All I do know is that we've got to get to the bottom of this business and pretty sharpish too, otherwise Schilling will have Hugo trussed up like a Christmas turkey before very much longer.'

'So what's our next move?'

'I think it's time we had a good look around Hopwood's lodgings. We might find something the police have missed, which could help Hugo prove he had nothing to do with his death.'

Lance and Veronica walked the short distance from the Hall to a small wooden shack hidden from view in Bluebell Wood, a dense sprawling forest to the west of the great house.

'Here we are. Welcome to The Bothy,' Lance said as they approached a dilapidated-looking wooden house with a moss-covered roof and a pile of recently hewn logs stacked up against one end.

Tentatively they opened the door to Hopwood's abode, its hinges creaking as they entered the dark interior. Shafts of bright sunlight cut through the filthy glass of the small windows, throwing vivid spotlights onto the wooden floor, and a damp, earthy woodland smell filled the cabin. A gentle breeze took hold of the front door, snapping it shut behind them and making them both jump.

As their eyes acclimatised to the dim environs, Hopwood's scant belongings slowly materialised, strewn chaotically about the place as a result of a recent police search.

'This looks pretty basic,' whispered Veronica.

'You have a look in here, Veronica, and I'll look in the bedroom,' Lance said.

Methodically they went about their business, picking up the discarded items, looking for something that might assist Hugo.

'Anything yet?' he shouted from the bedroom.

'Nothing,' she replied, continuing her search.

Lance came back into the living area. 'Nothing in there either.'

They turned their attention to the cooking area and Lance opened a number of tins and jars sitting on a large heavy dresser. They contained nothing unusual or of interest.

'The oven's empty,' Veronica said, closing the door of a small greasy appliance, pulling a face at her dirty fingers. 'Your gamekeeper wasn't the most hygienic of people,' she added wiping her hand on a grimy towel left on the table. 'How can men live in such a state?'

'How many men do you know who attend to their living accommodation with the same fastidious high standards as a woman?' Lance replied, amused by her obvious distaste. 'He was on his own – no wife, don't forget.'

'I suppose you think that's all women of his class are good for – cooking and cleaning, looking after their men,' Veronica said caustically.

Oh no, thought Lance wearily, not another sermon on the suppression of womankind. 'If you were Hopwood where would you hide something you wanted to keep safe?' he asked, hoping to deflect her from the thorny subject of subjugated females.

Veronica looked around. 'There's not much here to hide anything in,' she remarked. 'He must have been a man with few interests. There're no books to speak of, nothing personal like photos, pictures, letters or anything. Just the basic day-to-day things he needed to live and carry out his duties on the estate. Did he have any other pastimes besides his work?'

'I didn't know him really,' Lance replied. 'I'm not sure what he got up to when he wasn't working. He probably spent most of his free time down at the Blue Boar.'

'Well, if I were him, I wouldn't hide anything *inside* the house. That's the first place anyone would look.'

'Good point. If he had anything worth hiding he would have stashed it outside,' Lance said, going to the door.

'Yes, but where.'

They stood on the wooden veranda surveying the area around the shack. A small wooden shed a few yards from the house seemed the most plausible option. They went over and let themselves in. The interior was dingy and had only a small window that allowed a tiny shaft of dim light to fall onto a workbench located beneath. A faint odour of dead animals wafted around the hut. Out of the gloom emerged three decaying rabbit carcasses hanging on a hook next to a number of skinning knives.

'Yikes,' Veronica said, stepping back abruptly.

'It's all right, they're quite dead,' Lance said, amused by her squeamishness. She wasn't as tough as she tried to make out, he thought.

Traps of all kinds were littered about the floor along with hessian sacking, twine and a number of spades and nets. Diligently they searched through it all.

'Nothing,' Lance said with a sigh.

'What happened to his gun? I didn't see one in his shack. He must have had one to shoot vermin and such.'

'It's been taken back up to the Hall. It would be very unwise to leave firearms lying around unattended – you never know who might be about.'

'Did he have a dog? Most gamekeepers I've ever known had a dog of some kind.'

'Patch, his Jack Russell, is being looked after by Digweed for now,' Lanced explained.

'Let's get back outside,' Veronica said, shivering. 'Investigative journalism is one thing, being in the company of dead animals is quite another.'

Lance followed her back out into the fresh air and sunlight.

'Did Patch have a kennel?' she asked.

'I don't know.' Lance looked around the clearing. 'I think he was a dog lover, so he probably had Patch inside with him.'

Lance's leg had started to throb and he decided to take the weight off it for a bit. He sat down on the corner step of the veranda and set both his feet on a protruding log from the pile to make himself as comfortable as possible.

'What are you doing, Lance! We haven't got time to laze about.'

'I'm not lazing. I'm giving my leg a bit of a rest, that's all.'

Just then the pressure of his feet on the logs caused the pile to tumble and they clattered to the ground, rolling away.

'Tsk, now look what you've done,' Veronica scolded.

But Lance was too busy studying something that had caught his eye. 'Look at this,' he said getting up awkwardly from the veranda. One of the displaced logs had been hollowed out and, as a result of the tumble, had split in two. A small black tin box lay unopened on the ground. He bent down and picked it up.

'What have you got there?' Veronica asked, coming to his side.

Lance showed her the box. 'It was hidden inside one of the logs,' he said, trying to pry it open. The tin remained stubbornly locked.

Lance went back to the shed and found an old rusty screwdriver lying on the workbench. After several attempts to prise the tin open, the lid finally flew off revealing a small packet wrapped in dirty brown hessian sacking.

'What is it?' Veronica asked breathlessly.

Lance unwrapped the hessian and exposed a roll of pristine white five pound notes. He gasped. 'There must be at least fifty pounds here!' he said.

'Where would Hopwood get all that money?'

'I don't know. It certainly can't be from his wages. He's only on ten bob a week. It would take him a month of Sundays to save that much. He must have obtained it by some other nefarious means.'

'Surely this will make it look even blacker for Hugo,' Veronica remarked. 'You said Superintendent Schilling is already of the mind that Hopwood was meeting your brother down by the lake. Perhaps Hugo had been giving him cash in return for his silence about something. Finding this money only supports Schilling's theory. It suggests that Hopwood's activities were less than honourable and his demands frequent.'

'You're right. Oh dear! Let's get back to the Hall,' Lance said, hurriedly putting the money back into the tin and pocketing it. 'We can work out what to do next over a cup of tea.'

Back at Landacre the pair were greeted in the vestibule by Treadwell. 'Your mother and her sisters have expressed a desire for your attendance in the conservatory as soon as you return, m'lord.'

Lance had no intention of breaking off from his investigations just to be rebuked for his earlier adventure at the *Chronicle*'s office. 'Thank you, Treadwell,' he said, ' but I'd be grateful if you would keep the news of my return to yourself for the time being. I've important business in the study. Oh, and Treadwell, please arrange for tea to be brought in.'

'Very good, m'lord,' the butler replied and he retreated to the kitchen.

Lance and Veronica scurried down the passageway, quietly shutting the door to the study behind them.

Lance laid the five pound notes out on the desk in two neat stacks and, letting out a sigh, sat back in his chair viewing the booty. Presently there was a quiet tap on the door.

'That'll be Treadwell with the tea,' Lance said and quickly threw the dirty sacking over the money to keep it from view.

To his surprise it was Bentley who entered, carrying a silver salver. 'Whilst I was at the post office, m'lord, a telegram arrived for you. To save their boy a trip I offered to bring it back to Landacre, sir.' He proffered the tray upon which lay the unopened communiqué.

CHAPTER 32:
THE WEDDING

Saturday June 21st 1919

THE DAY OF HUGO'S wedding dawned bright and clear. That morning, an exhilarated Hugo entered the dining room thankful that at long last it had finally arrived.

His immediate fear of being detained by the police and missing his own wedding had faded quickly when Mr Drake arranged for him to be released under the family's cognizance, subject to further investigation. It had been made abundantly clear that on no account was he to leave the country, a condition he'd readily accepted.

His familiar bonhomie temporarily restored, Hugo had returned to the Hall the day before just in time for a brief tender reunion with Clara before she, her mother and cousin Monica left Landacre for Exmoor Hunting Lodge Hotel where they spent the night. The last thing anyone wanted at this late stage was the bride and groom to meet before the ceremony, breaking an age-old custom and bringing any additional bad luck.

With a plate of bacon and eggs in his hand, Hugo sat down at the breakfast table. As usual the din rising from the guests filled the room, creating an air of excited anticipation as they chattered noisily about the day's upcoming celebrations.

'Morning, me boy,' Lord Randolph said, slapping Hugo heartily on his back. 'All ready for the off?'

Hugo smiled nervously.

'Lance not down yet?' Dame Lettice asked.

'No one knows where he is,' Tabby said, digging enthusiastically into a healthy portion of devilled kidneys. 'According to Treadwell, he left the Hall yesterday morning and hasn't been seen since.'

A look of panic flashed across Hugo's face. 'What! He's got to be back this morning. I'm getting married at two o'clock and he's the best man.'

'Lance would never let you down, Hugo,' Tabby said. 'He'll be here, I'm sure.'

'Blistering Barnacles',' blustered Lord Randolph. 'Whatever is the lad thinking of, running off like that before Hugo's big day.'

'Well, I shall certainly have something to say to that young man when I see him,' boomed Lady Maud. 'Putting his family though all this anguish – hasn't his poor mother suffered enough.'

Breakfast over, the family and their guests retired to their rooms to dress for the wedding. At the same time, under Treadwell's accomplished guidance, the household staff bustled about carrying tables, chairs, china, linen, silver and flowers out to the pavilion on the front lawn that had been erected the previous afternoon by Landacre's grounds staff.

Just back from decorating the church, Mrs Pierce and Rose were busy arranging exquisite garlands and table arrangements of delphiniums, hypericums and white roses from the Hall's glasshouses. A four-piece string quartet had also begun setting up on a wooden plinth, the discordant noise of instruments being tuned filling the marquee and adding to the general hubbub.

In the kitchens, Mrs Hughes, ably assisted by an army of helpers, was feverishly completing days of preparation for the wedding breakfast. A chaotic cacophony rose to the rafters as they put the final touches to hor d'oeuvres, Salmon Froid, slow-roasted ribs of beef and peach Melba, all to be plated up in time for the happy couple's return later that afternoon.

At one o'clock precisely the Hall's fleet of vehicles drove around to the front door, each decked out with white ribbon. Emerging from the Bullnose Morris, Digweed stood beside the open door in his best suit waiting patiently for his first passengers, his white carnation buttonhole drooping in the bright sunshine.

Presently a handful of guests appeared through the Hall's main doors decked out in their finery and climbed into the car that was to whisk them to St Peter's in the village. As Digweed fitfully pulled away from the house, the next vehicle moved into the vacated position to collect more guests.

At one thirty Hugo stood in the vestibule wearing his full dress uniform. Tabby came skipping down the grand staircase clothed in a flowing violet chiffon creation.

'My, you look wonderfully handsome, Hugo. Clara's a lucky girl,' Tabby said, rushing up to her brother and embracing him in a bear-hug.

But Hugo was far from relaxed. Shaking himself free of his sister, he scowled at her. 'Any news of Lance?' he growled.

'Not yet.'

'Good grief, what is it with him? I thought at least I could rely on my elder brother for the most important day of my life. I suppose I'll just have to get married without him then.' Hugo tugged nervously at his coat cuffs, ensuring they came down over the top of his white gloves.

'I'm sure Lance will be at the wedding,' she replied. 'He wouldn't miss it.'

'I can't take that chance, Tabby. I'll have to make other arrangements. Will you be my best man?'

For once in her life Tabby was speechless, but not for long.

'I'll come and stand with you in church, Hugo, but only until Lance arrives. He definitely won't let you down, I just know it.'

The pair got into the next vehicle that pulled up at the entrance. It was Digweed in the Bullnose Morris.

'Afternoon, Master Hugo, Miss Tabitha. Lovely day for the weddin',' Digweed said cheerily as he began another erratic trip into the village. 'The church is a fillin' up nicely now.'

Alighting at the lychgate somewhat shaken about, Hugo and Tabby heard the strains of Pachelbel's Canon in D Major being played with some enthusiasm by Mrs Pike, the organ's wheezing notes gently drifting along on the breeze and pleasantly intermingling with the soft call of a thrush. Outside the church doors were Veronica and David, attending in their official capacity as representatives of the local press, taking the names and pictures of everyone as they arrived for the next edition of the *Chronicle*.

Hugo and Tabby made their way up the path to the door, Reverend Eustace stepping forward to greet them both.

'No need to ask *your* names,' Veronica said, smiling.

David, in a black tailed suit, his long dark hair sticking out at odd angles from under his top hat, appeared from behind his tripod and camera.

'Hold it,' he said as the flash went off.

'Where's Lance,' Hugo whispered to Veronica.

'I've absolutely no idea,' she replied, a distinct edge to her voice. 'He received a mysterious telegram yesterday morning, then abruptly made his apologies, leaving me in the lurch without a word of explanation. I had to rely on Digweed to take me back to Exeter, and not for the first time, I may say.'

Hugo and Tabitha exchanges glances and continued into the church.

Then Viscount Somerset and his daughter arrived, Lucinda beautifully attired in a jade green ensemble.

Reverend Eustace welcomed them both.

'May I have your names,' Veronica asked with an officious zeal.

'I think you know who we are,' Lucinda replied, haughtily waving her to one side as if she were swatting a fly.

Hot on their heels came Lady Cynthia dressed in pale yellow with an enormous hat affixed to her head by a giant floral hatpin. She was accompanied by Lady Maud and Lord Duncan.

'Good afternoon, Simon,' Lady Cynthia said, inclining her head to the assembled gathering.

'Good afternoon, Lady Cynthia,' barked Viscount Somerset, without giving the vicar time to reply. 'Have you seen Lance this morning? I must have a word with him before the day is out.'

'No, Viscount. I haven't seen him since yesterday,' she replied stiffly and walked off into the church.

Lady Cynthia joined Dame Lettice and Lord Randolph in the family pew and let out a long sigh. She smiled nervously at Hugo and Tabby who were sitting on two chairs specially placed beside the altar. In the aisle seat of the adjacent pew sat Ruth wearing a garish crimson outfit and a green felt hat; to her left were Martha Whytte and Nathan.

'That Ruth woman is simply priceless, Cynthia,' remarked Lady Maud, setting her ample derrière down next to her sister. 'What kind of family is Hugo marring into? She has absolutely no dress sense at all. She looks for all the world like a summer strawberry!'

Dame Lettice glanced surreptitiously at Ruth and then back to Hugo, a look of compassion for her nephew sweeping across her face. Suddenly she became alarmed. 'What's Tabby doing with Hugo?' she asked.

'I think he's asked her to be his best man if Lance doesn't show up,' Lady Cynthia said.

'Well! If that doesn't take the biscuit,' retorted Lady Maud.

Sighting four white horses drawing an open landau up to the lychgate, the Reverend swiftly made his way around the church to the north transept door and appeared in front of the altar just in time to give the groom a reassuring glance while David finished taking pictures of the bridal group outside.

Suddenly the organ rang out with the first bright notes of Mendelssohn's Wedding March, a sign the ceremony was about to begin. Clara, her uncle Zachary, who was giving her away, and cousin Monica stood silhouetted under the open arch. Monica, as bridesmaid, fussed with Clara's immense train as the sound of the great oak doors being closed echoed high in the vaulted ceiling.

The congregation was by now standing, everyone's gaze directed at Hugo's beautiful bride who advanced regally towards her intended, robed in a magnificent white lace and satin dress with a pearl-encrusted veil over a diamond tiara. In her right hand she carried a bouquet of white roses and gypsophila; her other hand sat lightly on her uncle's arm. A shaft of bright sunlight streamed through the magnificent stain-glass window lighting her path along the aisle and making her look as though she were glowing. An almost imperceptible gasp rose from the congregation as her glittering beauty eclipsed even the exquisite floral decorations.

The organist reached the final few bars of music as the procession drew level with Hugo and Tabby and then all at once there was silence. A few hollow coughs reverberated around the church and the congregation sat down again.

'Dearly beloved, we are gathered here today in the sight of God to join this man and this woman in holy matrimony ...,' began Reverend Eustace as the wedding service got underway.

Tabby was anxious and felt wholly inadequate as a stand-in for her elder brother. Clutching the gold wedding bands in her hot hand, she continually glanced over her shoulder towards the door, hoping against hope that Lance would arrive at any minute.

The Reverend droned on: 'If anyone knows of an impediment to this marriage let them speak now or forever hold their peace.'

Suddenly the south door flew open. The Reverend stopped mid-sentence, his mouth hanging open, while the congregation turned in unison to see what had caused the interruption. To everyone's utter amazement racing down the aisle was a tired-looking Lance followed by Chief Superintendent Schilling, Inspector Quick and none other than Lord Cedrick Donaldson-Gilks.

Tabby squealed and ran towards her father. 'Pa, Pa, you're alive,' she cried, flinging herself at him.

Lady Cynthia, overcome by the knowledge that her husband was apparently alive and well let out a stifled moan and slumped down in her seat while her two sisters looked on in astonishment.

'Clara Whytte,' said Chief Superintendent Schilling, his voice echoing clearly around the church. 'I'm arresting you for the murders of Bruce Hamilton, Peter Hopwood and Jacob Snyder and for the attempted murders of Lord Cedrick Donaldson-Gilks and Edwin Speed.'

Inspector Quick grabbed her firmly by the arm.

Hugo, his face as white as a sheet, reached for the nearest pew as his legs buckling beneath him.

All of a sudden Ruth stood up and, opening her small red clutch bag, removed a tiny silver revolver. She pointed it at Lord Cedrick.

'Move away from your father, Tabitha dear,' she demanded in a cold clear voice.

Lord Cedrick pushed his daughter out of the way.

'Don't do anything silly, Ruth,' Lance said calmly. 'It's over now.'

'Not quite, Lance,' sneered Ruth. 'You've absolutely no idea what an evil figure your father is. He's responsible for all those deaths on *Titanic*. He knew she was going to sink and he did nothing to stop us boarding her in Southampton.'

A shot rang out. As one, the congregation ducked down in their pews. Lord Cedrick groaned. Clutching his chest, he collapsed slowly onto the flagstone floor.

Tabby leapt to his aid and kneeled down at her father's side. She pulled a white handkerchief from a pocket in her dress and pressed it against the wound which was spurting blood. 'Pa! Pa!' she shrieked desperately.

Chief Superintendent Schilling and Lance sprang forward and wrenched the gun from Ruth's hand while the churchgoers watched from behind the pews. After a brief skirmish, Inspector Quick and two newly arrived constables marched Clara and Ruth along the nave to a waiting police car, the two women protesting vehemently with a torrent of vile abuse.

Lance was shocked by the sudden change in Clara's character. Once seemingly so fragile and delicate, she now exuded a bitter hatred. Her mother, too, had transformed from a twittering, dim-witted woman into a scheming, wailing banshee.

A hushed murmur filled the church as the congregation began to get to their feet. Lance hurriedly turned his attention to his father. Crouching down beside Tabby he peered at the wound. It was bad.

With a throaty gasp Lord Cedrick whispered, 'You're in charge now, Lance. Make sure you look after them all.'

CHAPTER 33:
REVELATIONS AND
EXPLANATIONS

ACK AT LANDACRE THE wedding guests were asked to make their way into the pavilion where they sat at the redundant reception tables in silent bewilderment, waiting to be interviewed by the constabulary.

Lance, his immediate family and the remaining members of the Whytte clan together with Veronica, David and Reverend Eustace withdrew to the Hall's drawing room where they sat mute under a heavy cloud of shock and disbelief.

Hugo sat on the Chesterfield in a complete daze. Tabby settled down next to him, putting a comforting arm around his shoulder. On another sofa Lady Cynthia was being supported by Reverend Eustace while Lady Maud and Dame Lettice huddled together on the chaise longue. As they waited, Lord Duncan helped himself to a stiff whisky from the drinks cabinet. Zachary and Martha Whytte, on an adjacent couch with Monica and Nathan, silently clutched each other's hands. Meanwhile, Veronica and David stood by the French doors feeling like imposters as they watched the families process their shock.

Before long, Lance entered the drawing room, rapidly followed by Chief Superintendent Schilling.

'Look here, Lance, what's all this tommyrot about *Titanic*? What has her sinking seven years ago got to do with all this death and disaster?' Lord Randolph asked, puffing away on a cigar.

'Any news of Pa?' Tabby said, her eyes filled with tears.

Lance slowly shook his head.

Tabby squeezed Hugo all the more tightly, hot tears escaping down her cheeks.

Exhausted, Lance stood in front of the stone fireplace beside Chief Superintendent Schilling. He helped himself to a glass of brandy from the tray that Treadwell was silently carrying around the room.

'I think you need to tell us all what's going on, Lance,' Lord Duncan barked, taking a slug from his whisky glass. 'How the hell are Clara and Ruth involved?'

'Well, I suppose it does all revolve around the *Titanic*,' Lance said.

Everyone in the room fell silent.

'The day before his car accident, Father sent me a mysterious telegram. In it he requested my urgent attendance at Landacre and stressed that the situation was "very grave". He said he'd tell me everything upon my arrival.'

'What situation?' demanded Lady Maud.

'I'm getting to that, Aunt,' Lance said patiently. 'Sadly Father wasn't home when I arrived – apparently he had an

appointment that required the services of his chauffeur –
and the news of his death meant that I wasn't able to discover
what had prompted him to summon me so urgently.'

'Yes, what of his chauffeur?' interrupted Lord Randolph.
'What happened to him?'

'I spoke to Mr Speed by telephone yesterday,' Lance
replied.

'He's not dead then,' whispered Tabby.

'No. It seems that on the morning of Father's visit to
Lord Swan, Speed noticed a problem with the brakes of the
Rolls before they set off. A puddle of brake fluid under the
car alerted him to a cut brake pipe, which he duly reported
to Lord Cedrick. Father decided that the best way to flush
out the culprit would be to stage the intended accident,
to let the perpetrator think they'd been successful, lulling
him or her into a false sense of security and leading them
to lower their guard.'

'Where's Mr Speed now then?' asked Tabby.

'He's in Liverpool with his niece Elsie, Mother's maid.
Pa thought it best to get them both out of the way until
he'd cleared things up. After all, his chauffeur was supposed
to be dead. It wouldn't do to have him spotted about the
estate or for Elsie to let slip her uncle was still alive.'

'By Jove,' muttered Lord Randolph.

'Anyway, the same day that I received the telegram Pa
also sent me – anonymously – a package containing the
photograph of *Titanic* and the SS *Californian*'s manifest. He
calculated that this information, coupled with news of his
death, would ensure I'd want to learn the truth. So Veronica
and I began some investigations of our own.'

'But how on earth are the *Titanic*, Father's accident and Clara and Ruth connected? It just doesn't make sense,' wailed Tabby.

'Well ... it's quite a long story,' Lance said. 'It seems that Father has long been a member of a secret group sworn to uphold the sovereignty of the land, a group so secret, in fact, that members can only be identified by a signet ring bearing the insignia of the Knights Templar which they all wear. Meeting at the Palace of Westminster under the guise of a Select Committee, their brief was to act covertly behind the scenes in whatever capacity was required to bring about a favourable state of affairs in the national interest.'

'What kind of affairs?' Lady Maud demanded.

'In this case, additional ships to bolster the British naval fleet in the event of an outbreak of war,' Lance replied. 'As an impending conflict with Germany looked ever more likely, Father was asked to negotiate between the government and White Star's owners, International Mercantile Marine, for the use of their ships. He met several times with their British and American directors in London in 1910.'

'Yes, but how are Clara and Ruth involved?' Veronica butted in.

'As I said, it's a long story,' Lance said with a little smile. 'White Star was prepared to offer their ships to the British government in exchange for certain advantageous commercial considerations, and in December 1910, at a clandestine meeting in London, an agreement between the two parties was drawn up and signed.

'The government was content that it had successfully negotiated a contingency plan to bolster the naval fleet should hostilities break out in future. In return, White Star was given profitable business opportunities at a time when competition for transatlantic passengers was stiff. Both parties were extremely happy with the secret arrangement. Unfortunately, what no one foresaw was an accident in September 1911 when *Olympic* was critically damaged in a collision with HMS *Hawke* in Southampton waters.'

'Yes, but what has that got to do with *Titanic*?' Lord Duncan asked in exasperation.

'Bear with me, Uncle. *Olympic* was repaired temporarily, well enough for her to limp back to Harland and Wolff for more permanent repairs. However, on closer inspection in Belfast, White Star's directors realised it would take at least six months to get *Olympic* properly seaworthy again. The cost of the renovation would effectively wipe out the company's operating profit for the year and a third of the income of International Mercantile Marine. There would also be further huge losses from having no superliners at sea for at least six months.'

'But surely she was insured, Lance,' interjected Lord Randolph.

'Yes, she was, but with the help of a friend at Lloyds and a little digging in the archives at the *Chronicle*'s office, Veronica and I discovered that White Star's insurers rejected the claim on the basis of the Royal Navy inquiry into the accident between *Hawke* and *Olympic*, which ruled that *Olympic* was entirely to blame for the accident. That meant that the repairs would have had to be paid for by White

Star, which was already committed to sixteen million dollars-worth of work to complete *Titanic* and the half-built *Britannic.*'

'Ahhh, so that's where the insurance information fits in,' Veronica said.

'The company was staring financial ruin in the face,' Lance said, 'and decided that the best course of action would be to patch up *Olympic* for the time being, just enough to get her back into service without delay, albeit with a list to port. In order to recover their significant losses and enable them to proceed with the complete overhaul *Olympic* needed, White Star issued legal proceedings against the Royal Navy. But the court case went badly, and in December 1911 White Star lost its claim for compensation, leaving them with a dilemma. Without full repairs *Olympic* would never pass her annual Board of Trade inspection and wouldn't be able to put back to sea. Yet the company didn't have the finances to carry out full repairs.

'The final nail in *Olympic*'s watery coffin came three months later, in March 1912, when she was docked at Harland and Wolff for yet more expensive repairs after running over a shipwreck on the Grand Banks. A fire was discovered in a coal bunker causing the steel bulkheads to glow red and buckle. With *Olympic* soon due for re-inspection by the Board of Trade and no funds to pay for yet another expensive repair, White Star's only hope was the British government. Somehow they had to be persuaded to step in and help.

'Making contact with a government representative, White Star's directors stressed that without urgent assistance the company would be forced into bankruptcy and its fleet sold off. Under those circumstances there would certainly be no prospect of White Star loaning its superb ships to the government in the event of a war.

'On hearing of White Star's predicament, the secret committee's chairman – let's call him "Lord X" – informed White Star that it would be impossible for the British government to intercede directly because it would create a dangerous precedent if other businesses got into financial difficulty in the future. However, Lord X suggested an alternative plan, one that the other committee members knew nothing about. White Star would switch the identity of *Olympic* with the almost complete *Titanic*, a situation that wouldn't require much effort since both ships were practically identical and berthed side by side at Harland and Wolff.'

'Great Thundering Typhoons!' exclaimed Lord Randolph.

'White Star identified the small changes required to complete the swap – the nameplates at bow and stern, the twenty lifeboats, the forty-eight lifebelts, the ship's bells, and stationery items such as menus and letterheads. The directors believed this work could be done over one weekend by a small band of loyal employees who could be trusted to keep quiet. The plan was simple – send the crippled *Olympic* out as the newly constructed *Titanic* on her maiden voyage and scuttle her at a previously agreed rendezvous point deep on the ocean floor, conveniently out of reach from marine salvage, making discovery of the scheme impossible.

'Icebergs litter the Atlantic off the Newfoundland coast in April, so the thinking was that it wouldn't be difficult to fake a collision, forcing the passengers and crew to evacuate *Titanic*. Once they were off, the officers would remain on board and open the seacocks and hatches, resulting in thousands of tonnes of ice-cold water filling her hull in a controlled flood. In the meantime another ship from International Mercantile Marine's stable, the SS *Californian*, was to set sail from Liverpool on 5th April, five days prior to *Titanic*'s departure from Southampton, and wait for her distress call at the agreed destination point.

'We know from the Board of Trade inquiry that the SS *Californian* wasn't carrying any passengers – the manifest indicated her cargo was three thousand woollen blankets and jumpers. She'd only be a few miles over the horizon and could easily steam at full speed to *Titanic* in time to safely disembark all two thousand, two hundred and forty passengers and crew.'

'Good grief! What happened next?' asked Dame Lettice.

'The strategy for the company was simple – claim on *Titanic*'s insurance for what was in reality the *Olympic*, at a stroke disposing of a badly damaged ship and restoring the company's finances. It was to be the most daring insurance fraud of our times.'

'But what about the Board of Trade inquiry?' David asked. 'Surely they'd have discovered the fraud through the myriad of testimonies.'

'That was the beauty of it,' Lance replied. 'Lord X persuaded the government to appoint Lord Mersey to head the inquiry. Essentially, it was a review conducted by the Board of Trade into the actions of the Board of Trade, overseen by a sympathetic government man. Therefore it would be easy to gloss over details and obfuscate the facts.'

'Wait a minute, young man, how do you know all this?' asked Zachary Whytte.

'Father explained everything to me, sir. You see Lord X revealed the plan to the other members of the secret committee at some point after *Titanic* sailed from Queenstown in the south of Ireland. Father was resolutely against it, believing the idea was lunacy. However, he was reassured that no one would be injured and the action was in the national interest. Indeed, to underline just how safe the scheme was, Lord X told them that both J. Bruce Ismay, chairman and managing director of White Star, and Thomas Andrews, the ship's architect, were themselves travelling on *Titanic* to oversee the execution of the plan.

'Unhappily, as we all now know, the plan went tragically wrong. *Titanic* – or rather *Olympic* – actually hit a real iceberg long before she reached the designated rendezvous point, sinking with the unintended loss of over fifteen hundred passengers and crew.'

A heavy silence descended on the room for a few moments.

'But didn't we learn that *Titanic* was significantly underinsured?' Veronica asked. 'Why on earth would they send her double out to sea in the full knowledge that the insurance was deficient?'

'Because the plan had been hatched at the last minute,' Lance explained. 'They couldn't very well increase her cover just before she sailed. Someone at Lloyds was bound to smell a rat. At the very least it would have given them an opportunity to delay the claim while they investigated the circumstances, a situation that White Star would have found impossible to ride out financially. The company needed the money to continue in business and as the insurance documents clearly showed, the claim for the loss of *Titanic* was paid out in record time – within one week of her sinking.'

David let out a long whistle.

'However, I'm pretty sure that, conscious of the deficient insurance, White Star's directors had a quiet word with some of their more affluent passengers. Peter Hopwood told us that his pal in the hold was told to offload J. P. Morgan's bronze statues that had only just come aboard. The most plausible explanation is that J. P. Morgan had been warned of the plan and, knowing he'd be unable to claim the full value of his treasures on the insurance, decided to remove them altogether.'

'Gosh!' Veronica exclaimed.

'Then there's John Seymour's last letter to his sister Florence, the one he sent when *Titanic* docked in Southampton after her initial voyage from Belfast. He wrote "and I still don't like this ship". He had sailed on *Olympic* many times before and had a strong feeling he'd sailed on that particular vessel before. But as Florence pointed out, that couldn't be so if she were the newly built *Titanic* on her maiden voyage.

'Didn't he also tell Hopwood that all the floor coverings had been changed,' Veronica said.

'Indeed. *Olympic*'s floors would have been scuffed and worn, something a newly built ship's floors couldn't possibly have been. But they were unable to match *Titanic*'s carpet design at such short notice, so the directors instructed that a completely different pattern, one destined for one of their other ships, was put down.'

'That must be why the Home Office requisitioned John's letter then,' Veronica exclaimed, 'to keep the conspiracy covered up.'

'Yes, I'm coming on to that,' Lance said.

'But we still don't know how Clara and Ruth are involved?' Dame Lettice said, peevishly.

'Well, don't forget, Ruth had lost her first husband and her son, Clara her father and brother, on *Titanic*. I think it's probable that some time after Bruce and Ruth were married in 1916, Clara discovered Bruce's involvement in the insurance fraud,' Lance said. 'And that led her to learn of Father's connection with the committee. You see Bruce was one of the American directors of International Mercantile Marine. He was also a signatory on the secret 1910 agreement, and he probably kept copies of all the paperwork relating to the agreement, as well as a duplicate of the photograph found at the scene of Father's accident.'

'Good Lord,' said Lord Randolph. 'It must have come as quite a shock to see her prospective father-in-law in the picture and to realise that Cedrick had met Bruce long before *Titanic* sank.'

'I'm sure Bruce went to considerable lengths to ensure that neither Ruth nor her daughter realised his involvement in the scheme,' Lance said. 'Ruth had been left a very rich woman after her husband's death. I suspect Bruce's fortunes were not as robust as they had once been

– International Mercantile Marine fell into receivership in 1915 and that would have greatly depreciated Bruce's investments. He probably relied on Ruth's money to continue his affluent lifestyle and wouldn't have wanted Ruth to divorce him, which she would have done had she found out about his involvement with the *Titanic* tragedy. Unfortunately for Bruce, divorce was not what Clara had in mind when she uncovered the truth and sought retribution.

'It's my guess that Clara concluded wrongly that Father also had prior knowledge of the scheme, revealed all to her mother and enlisted her help in making Bruce and Father pay.'

'How terrible to be consumed by such hatred,' muttered Dame Lettice. 'Mere anarchy loosed upon the world.'

'It seems that their scheme was to murder Bruce and Pa and implicate Hugo, who'd doubtless be hanged for murders he didn't commit. In one blow they'd have exacted their retribution, subjecting our family to the same pain and despair they'd suffered after losing a father and son.'

'How diabolical,' said Lady Maud.

'But how did they do it, Lance?' Veronica asked.

'With the help of an accomplice,' Lance replied smoothly.

'What accomplice?' Tabby said, sitting bolt upright.

'He was arrested late last night after his fingerprints were found on the trunk taken from Hugo's room. He's been at Exeter Police Station since the early hours filling in the missing pieces in the hope of avoiding the rope. He was pretending to be Bruce all along,' Lance said.

Superintendent Schilling nodded.

'You mean the man who has been staying here isn't the real Bruce Hamilton?' Tabby said quietly.

'Yes, I'm afraid so. It seems that Ruth, Clara and the real Bruce Hamilton sailed over to England rather earlier than anyone suspected and made their way to the Exmoor Hunting Lodge Hotel where some time later, the real Bruce was murdered and his body stuffed into a travelling trunk.'

'Oh how gruesome!' whispered Veronica.

'With the help of a false beard, their accomplice assumed Bruce's identity and in the company of Clara and Ruth proceeded to Landacre Hall, the trunk containing the body being transported with their belongings.'

'Blistering Barnacles',' exclaimed Lord Randolph.

'No one was any the wiser until Pa, who'd met the real Bruce during his negotiations with White Star nine years ago, began to wonder if something fishy was going on. He couldn't quite put his finger on anything specific. It was just an accumulation of little things. But when the after-dinner conversation got around to White Star one evening, the Bruce sitting at the table didn't seem to know any of the directors of White Star, nor recognised Lord Swan's name when it came up. Lord Swan had also been a signatory on the secret agreement, the same agreement signed by, and in the presence of, Bruce.'

'Now I call that damn peculiar,' Lord Randolph said with a snort.

'I must say I had my reservations about Bruce as well, Lance,' the Reverend piped up. 'You remember that first evening after dinner when we were discussing America?

Bruce didn't seem to have any real knowledge of New York, yet he was supposed to have lived there all his life.'

'Whatever next,' Lady Maud said rather more quietly than usual.

'After discovering the brakes on the Rolls had been cut, Father contacted Lord X about his doubts over Bruce's identity. Worried that someone outside the committee knew of the group's involvement in *Titanic*'s sinking, Lord X helped Father to stage the accident on Queen Dart Hill and agreed to his plan to disappear in the hope of smoking out the culprit.'

'So where did Pa go?' Tabby asked.

'Oh not far, just over to the Exmoor Hunting Lodge Hotel.'

Tabby looked stunned.

'The thing is, Pa didn't trust Lord X either. Father felt he'd greatly exceeded his authority in suggesting the plan to scuttle *Titanic* in the first place. It was Pa's view that he'd go to any lengths to keep the committee's existence and its involvement in her sinking a secret. Pa was also uneasy about his own safety and thought it wiser to make his own independent enquires. That's why he involved me and made his own private arrangements for disappearing.'

'What arrangements?' Lord Duncan asked.

'Well, he noticed that Evans, the second footman, seemed to be a man of above average intelligence and since he was a new member of staff and hadn't had time to cultivate any special allegiance to the household staff, Father decided to take him into his confidence. Sworn to secrecy about the staged accident, Evans's brief was to keep Pa informed of progress and if necessary provide quiet assistance. On the morning Evans discovered Hopwood's body, he was on his way down to the boathouse to give Pa his report.

'What Father didn't know was that Evans was a double agent, an ex-military bod placed in the household by Lord X who had reservations about Pa's allegiance to the secret committee.'

'Gracious,' murmured Dame Lettice.

'Clara and Ruth realised pretty quickly that Bruce the imposter had somehow given the game away. So they grasped an early opportunity to get rid of him before Father could make any further enquiries. Clara visited the garages in the dead of night and cut the brake pipes on the Rolls. Then later the next evening the police arrived and advised the family of Pa's death.'

'So it was the phoney Bruce at dinner that first evening,' Tabby said.

'Yes, that's right,' Lance said. 'I thought there was something funny about him. His mannerisms and accent seemed overdone to me. Then later we learned about the odd-sized collars.'

'Odd-sized collars?' boomed Lady Maud.

'Yes, Evans told us that when packing Bruce's effects for shipment to America after his death he'd noticed four of his shirt collars were much larger than the others. It seems that, aside from Bruce the imposter having to employ a false beard, he and the real Bruce were identical in every aspect except one – the size of their collars. I find it fittingly elegant that their switch of identity was much like the switch between *Olympic* and *Titanic*,' Lance added. 'Indeed, Clara and her mother may have thought it poetic justice.'

A deathly hush filled the room.

'In the wee small hours of Saturday morning, Clara, Ruth and the imposter disposed of the real Bruce's body down at the mausoleum, leaving one of Hugo's buttons at the scene to implicate him. Then before anyone else was up that morning, the imposter left Landacre on foot, walking to Exhampton railway station where he made sure he was observed boarding a train for Exeter.'

'But why was the head so disfigured if the dead body was that of the genuine Bruce?' asked Veronica.

'Because no matter how good the likeness, his impersonator wasn't *completely* identical. It was crucial to their plot that no one should twig there'd been two Bruce's. Unfortunately, the plan started to go wrong. While out walking in the grounds looking for poachers Hopwood saw Bruce's body being disposed of in the mausoleum. Putting two and two together, he sent Clara a note demanding one hundred pounds in cash to keep quiet.'

'Ahh, so that's where that cash at Hopwood's cabin came from,' Veronica said. 'But we only found fifty pounds. What happened to the rest of it?'

'It was merely a down payment from Clara. She told Hopwood she needed to visit the bank in Exeter and would bring the balance down to the lake later in the week. In the meantime, the murderers hurriedly amended their original plan for a second time, on this occasion to rid themselves of a pesky blackmailer. Clara arranged to meet Hopwood on the pier at *eleven thirty* and sent Hugo an anonymous note instructing him to be at the boathouse at *eleven o'clock* the same night. By leaving Hugo's glove at the scene of

Hopwood's murder, Clara cold-bloodedly implicated Hugo in an additional crime.' Lance turned to Hugo. 'On your way down to the boathouse you saw a silhouetted figure furtively moving around on the jetty, isn't that right, Hugo?'

Hugo nodded, too shocked to speak.

'It was Clara dressed up in a long dark coat and Fedora waiting for Hopwood. She had guessed that the only person likely to see her would be Hugo and he couldn't very well tell the police he was at the scene of a murder. Anyway, later – on the night of the ball – Clara and Ruth surreptitiously left the party to put the empty blood-stained travelling trunk into Hugo's room along with his other glove and the riding jacket with the missing button where the police discovered them.'

'Oh my poor boy,' murmured Lady Cynthia.

'But who was this mysterious accomplice, Lance?' Lord Randolph asked.

'Oh, didn't I say? It was George Bagshott, owner of the Exmoor Hunting Lodge Hotel, long lost brother of Ruth, and Jacob Snyder's killer.'

A loud gasp went round the room.

'But I thought Jacob Snyder's death was suicide,' Veronica said. 'Everyone in the village is talking about it.'

'That's what we were meant to think. You see, Jacob had a problem with betting on horses. He was frequently to be seen over at the Devon and Exeter Racecourse where he owed vast sums of money to the bookies. Being an apothecary, getting his hands on amphetamine was quite easy and over the months he had used it to dope horses and fix a number of races to his advantage.

'George found out what Jacob was up to and when he also discovered that Jacob had been cooking the books of the Memorial Fund, he used this knowledge to blackmail Jacob into supplying him with amphetamine.'

'How awful,' murmured Monica.

'But Jacob was becoming unreliable,' Lance continued, 'and George knew it was only a matter of time before I unmasked Jacob's dishonesty regarding the fund. George couldn't risk Jacob blurting out the details of his little drug deal to me, so Ruth, Clara and George decided he had to go. George asked Jacob over to the hotel where he put a sedative into his coffee. After Jacob passed out George moved his unconscious body to the Exminster Reservoir and strung him up from a tree, leaving the suicide note written by Clara. But Clara inadvertently gave herself away when composing the note, spelling the word '*honourable*' the American way, without the "u".'

'So it was George Bagshott who doped Versailles at the hunt?' Veronica asked in amazement.

'Yes, although it was a mistake. He'd meant to dope Sorcerer, the idea being that I'd be thrown off and killed in what would look like a hunting accident. But he got his sugar lumps mixed up and unintentionally gave the doped one to Versailles. When their first scheme to kill me off me didn't work, George followed me to London and attempted to push me off the platform in front of a train, but he didn't reckon on Bob.' Lance looked down fondly at his faithful companion sprawled out on the drawing-room carpet. 'When the police arrested George he had a very nasty injury on his left arm where Bob had bitten him.'

'But how did the police identify George Bagshott's fingerprints on the trunk found in Hugo's room?' Veronica asked.

'Because last year the Exmoor Hunting Lodge Hotel had been burgled and the police took everyone's fingerprints in order to eliminate them. So they still had his prints on file and were able to match them to the prints on the trunk.'

'What I want to know,' boomed Lady Maud, 'is who this Lord X is you keep referring to?'

'Ahhh, I've been sworn to secrecy about that one, Aunt. It's an official state secret,' Lance replied.

'You mean we're never going to know who is he?' Lord Duncan asked.

'That's about the size of it,' Lance said, looking at Chief Superintendent Schilling.

'I never could take to that Clara and her mother – not quite up to snuff,' harrumphed Lady Maud. 'As I've said before the vulgarity of new money is certainly no substitute for good character. That was quite a close shave for Hugo. He should be thankful Lance found out about her before they were married. Just think, we could have had a murderer in the family!'

Lance cast a concerned look toward his brother. 'I think Hugo will need all the support we can give him, Aunt, to help him cope with the realisation that the girl of his dreams intended to murder his father and consign him to the gallows.'

Superintendent Schilling stepped forward. 'Now, ladies and gentlemen, my officers will take your statements. I should be grateful if you would remain here until you're called to the library to provide your testimony.'

CHAPTER 34:
ABSOLUTE PROOF

Sunday June 22nd 1919

AFTER BREAKFAST THE NEXT morning Lance sat in the morning room peacefully reading his newspaper, Bob curled up at his feet. Landacre was very much quieter now that most of the guests had returned home after giving their statements.

Treadwell entered the room, a light cough indicating his presence. 'Miss Veronica Barnes is here to see you, m'lord—'

Without waiting to be fully announced Veronica pushed passed the butler. 'Oh there you are,' she exclaimed. 'I've come to give you an opportunity to look over my piece for the *Chronicle* before it's published, just as I promised,' Veronica continued in a business-like fashion.

Lance winced. He had hoped she would decide not to write the story. He really didn't want his family's dirty linen splashed all over the press for the gossipmongers to feed on.

'I sat up all night writing it,' she added excitedly. 'I'm sure this will get me noticed by *The Times*.' She thrust a sheaf of papers under his nose.

Lance reluctantly took the pages and slowly read through the piece without making any comment. He was glad to see that she'd at least had the good grace to keep his family's involvement to a bare minimum. As he turned over the last page he said, 'I don't think you'll be able to publish this, Veronica.'

'Why ever not!' she replied tartly.

'Because we've no absolute proof that *Olympic* and *Titanic* switched identities.'

Veronica was crestfallen, but recovered quickly. 'Then I'll jolly well get some,' she said, a defiant note to her voice.

'How do you expect to do that with the weight of the government squarely behind a cover-up?'

'There must be a way,' she said, slumping down in a nearby chair.

Lance suddenly recalled Hugo's story about his proposal to Clara on board *Olympic*. 'Indeed, there might be a way,' he said, 'but we'd need to see it for ourselves.'

He turned to the back pages of *The Times* where they published all the shipping information.

'What are you looking for?'

'The sailing dates and times for *Olympic*.' He ran his finger down the page. Suddenly he stopped. 'We're in luck. *Olympic* arrives in Southampton this very afternoon for onward passage to New York. Let's motor down and look her over ourselves.'

'What, right now?'

'Yes, now. You want to get your piece published don't you? Then let's get the concrete proof you need once and for all.'

On the way down to Southampton, Lance told Veronica the story of Hugo's proposal to Clara.

'Golly,' Veronica said after he'd finished. 'You mean the real *Olympic* will have a carving of their initials in Suite B41?'

'Yes, that right. If there's no carving on the panel, then she's the *Titanic*. Ergo it must have been the *Olympic* that sank!'

They drove on in silence before Veronica asked, 'Who was that telegram from, you know the one you received the other day before disappearing without so much as a by your leave?'

'It was from Father. He'd heard that Hugo had been taken to Exeter Police Station for questioning and asked me to meet him alone at Hopwood's cottage. That's why I couldn't tell you anything about it. He wanted to know what was going on before presenting himself to Superintendent Schilling to help clear Hugo. By the time we'd got to Schilling the police forensics team had identified George Bagshott's fingerprints on the trunk. We waited all night at the police station while Bagshott was interviewed and that's how we learned of Clara's and Ruth's involvement.'

'Oh,' said Veronica. 'And did your father reveal the purpose of his visit to Florence Seymour?'

'Is it important?'

'Yes, I want to get all the facts right for my piece in the *Chronicle*.'

'Oh I see,' replied Lance rather flatly. 'Well, if it's that vital. Father remembered he'd met John Seymour at an award ceremony held at White Star's offices in Southampton some years earlier.'

'That's right. Miss Seymour pointed the award out to us when we visited her. She seemed jolly proud of it.'

'Well, it was presented to John by one of the directors of White Star's parent company. That director was Bruce Hamilton.'

'What a happy coincidence!'

'Yes, wasn't it! Father hoped to see John with a view to discussing Bruce. He hadn't realised that John had since perished on *Titanic*.'

'Of course,' replied Veronica nodding gently. 'But what about the letter? Why was your father so bothered by it?'

'When Florence showed him the letter, Pa was worried that John had written about his suspicions regarding the ship's identity. Sensing that it might prove useful to him later as a sort of insurance against Lord X, Father took a copy. Then he dutifully informed Lord X, knowing the committee would send someone to destroy the original evidence. Father then left a copy of the letter in his diary for me to find later, hoping it would point me in the right direction.'

Lance and Veronica continued chatting away happily as they motored down to Southampton, and soon they arrived at the quay where Lance drove onto the bustling White Star dock.

Olympic was already tied up, her gleaming black-and-white livery sparkling in the afternoon sun and an army of dock workers was busy loading her cargo, provisions and luggage as passengers boarded, excitedly looking forward to their trip.

Lance helped Veronica from the car as a stiff cool breeze blew in off the Solent, the smell of the sea air invigorating them both, and they went over to the ship. *Olympic* towered high above them, making the buildings nearby her seem minuscule.

'My goodness, she's enormous,' Veronica said, completely awestruck.

'Come on,' Lance said, taking her by the hand and almost pulling her up the gangplank.

At the top they were greeted by two officers who were ticking names off on their passenger list.

'We've just come aboard to wish farewell and bon voyage to my aunt in Suite B41,' Lance said to the purser.

'Would that be Lady Caroline, sir?' the purser asked.

'Yes, that's right,' Lance replied and, without waiting to engage in any further conversation, he dragged Veronica onto the deck and raced along to the first-class quarters.

The purser called after them to come back, but Lance paid no heed. Finding Suite B41, Lance knocked quietly on the cabin door. There was no answer.

'Good, they're probably out on deck waving goodbye,' he whispered to Veronica.

Interrupting a passing steward from his housekeeping duties, Lance asked if he could open the door for them as they'd lost their key. The steward naively obliged. They went into the cabin and closed the door quietly behind them.

The room was indeed sumptuous, with elegant furniture of the Georgian period dotted about the lavish accommodation. Lance wasted no time; he went over to the chaise longue and moved the baroque clock from the adjacent side table, then examined the mahogany panelling.

'Can you see anything?' Veronica asked.

'No, nothing!'

'Are you sure?'

'Yes, there's absolutely *nothing*. Look! The panelling is as smooth as a baby's bottom.'

'Then this must be *Titanic*!' Veronica said, excitedly clapping her hands and jumping up and down.

Just then the door to suite B41 opened and in walked Bertie de Bretagne, Earl of Albemarle, together with two coves in long coats and Fedoras. The three men filled the doorway, barring any exit.

'It's a pity you've ignored Lord Cumberland's wise counsel, Lance,' remarked Lord Albemarle gravely. 'We all hoped you would heed his excellent advice.'

'Who's this?' Veronica asked, scowling.

'Veronica, I'd like to introduce you to my schoolboy chum, Bertie de Bretagne, Earl of Albemarle ... also known as Lord X,' Lance said coolly.

Veronica stared wide-eyed at the tall assured figure in the centre of the group, his boyish goofy looks betraying nothing of the mendacity and ruthlessness of Lord X.

'I'm afraid I'll have to ask you both to accompany me back to London,' the Earl said with authority.

'I can't possibly go with you, Lord Albemarle,' retorted Veronica, 'I've got a deadline to meet at the *Chronicle*.'

'I'm afraid there'll be no deadline, Miss Barnes, nor any scoop about this business. Your little fantasy will never see the light of day.'

'Fantasy, Lord Albemarle? Surely not,' Veronica replied boldly. 'We've just established evidence of the most profound fraud imaginable.'

'What evidence?' Lord Albemarle sneered.

'Look here,' Veronica said loudly, pointing to the mahogany wall panel. 'We're standing on it. This ship is the RMS *Titanic*!'

'I think not, Miss Barnes. Now you really must come with me,' the Earl said again, this time more firmly.

'You can't go around abducting people against their will,' Veronica said with dismay. 'This is England. We'll see what Superintendent Schilling has to say about this.'

'You haven't told her then, Lance,' the Earl said.

'Haven't told me what?' exclaimed Veronica.

'It would do no good to contact Superintendent Schilling, Veronica,' Lance said softly. 'He's one of Bertie's men, assigned to the case early on by the Home Office. His primary aim is to ensure that this matter doesn't get out of hand and become an embarrassment for the government.'

'So he's in on the conspiracy as well?' Veronica asked, sitting down heavily on a nearby chair.

'Let's not bandy words like *conspiracy* about, Miss Barnes. Let's just say that it's all for the best,' the Earl said.

'But the best for whom, Lord Albemarle?' Veronica said defiantly. 'It certainly wasn't best for the people who drowned. What's been done in the name of the state is nothing short of murder!'

With that, Lord Albemarle's gladiators took Veronica firmly by the elbows and led her from the room, Lance following close behind.

* * *

Later that day, Lance and Veronica left an innocuous-looking building in London to begin the long drive back to Devon. Neither of them felt like talking.

'What did they say to you in there?' Lance asked some time into the journey.

'Oh nothing much. They just made me sign the Official Secrets Act, which bars me from writing anything about this matter, thus ruining my life as a crack reporter, that's all. Now I'll never be noticed by *The Times*.'

'Don't talk rot, Veronica. There'll be other stories.'

'Not like this one.'

After a short pause Lance asked, 'What will you do now?'

'I suppose I'll have to go back to reporting weddings and fêtes.' She sighed heavily.

'Will you be working with David?' Lance asked, a pang of jealousy stabbing at his heart.

'David?'

'Yes, I saw how close you were with him the other day. Are you two walking out together?'

Veronica laughed. '*There are none so blind as those that will not see,*' she said, smiling.

'I don't know what you mean,' Lance said, hurt by her response.

Veronica pursed her lips and stared silently out at the landscape flashing by. Eventually she said, 'David isn't of that persuasion, Lance. He prefers men.'

Lance was certainly surprised by what she'd told him, but that feeling was completely eclipsed by the sheer relief he felt that David wasn't interested in Veronica in that way.

His heart began to leap with joy; she was available after all! He vowed at that moment to pursue her until she became his. A fig for the consequences with Lucinda and her father.

'What about you, Lance, what will you do now?' Veronica asked.

'I suppose I'll have to knuckle down to the duties and responsibilities of Landacre,' he said with a sigh.

'Oh, I see,' Veronica said flatly.

'After I'd signed the Official Secrets Act Bertie asked me to join their band of merry men.'

'You mean he asked you to become a member of his secret committee?'

'More or less.'

'I hope you told him to take a running jump!'

'I told him I'd think about it. You see, Bertie explained to me that the future well-being of this great country of ours lies in espionage. Apparently the government is setting up a more formal operation in Whitehall and he says they're looking for intelligent chaps like me to join.'

'If it means perverting the course of justice you should give it a wide berth,' Veronica pronounced.

Lance smiled. Veronica was delightful when she was bossing him around. As his thoughts turned to Landacre and his new responsibilities as the eighth Baron Westex, he put his foot on the accelerator. A comfortable peace settled over him as he drove home to his beloved Bob with the girl of his dreams by his side.

EPILOGUE

WILLIAM MCNAIR STOOD IN the carpenters shop at the great Thompson Dry Dock in Belfast, his hand to his chin. A skilled master-craftsman, he was pondering the best use of mahogany in creating a seamless patch to a section of damaged panelling.

'What's going on?' asked Tommy, his apprentice.

'Oh, its *Olympic*,' William said. 'She's back from her maiden voyage for some repairs after her first shakedown.'

'Repairs to the interior, not the exterior?' Tommy said.

'Aye, some rich idiot with more money than sense thought it would be a good idea to carve their initials into a wall panel in one of the first-class suites. I ask you, who'd do such a thing to a masterpiece like *Olympic*? The gaffer's hopping mad. We've to replace the panelling before she sets sail on her next crossing.'

'What do you want me to do?' Tommy asked.

'Hand me that sheet of mahogany from the stack, will you,' William said, pointing to a piece of fine patinaed timber and pulling his pencil from behind his ear.

REFLECTIONS
FROM THE AUTHOR

AFTER MORE THAN ONE hundred years, how enigmatic the story of *Titanic* remains. That was the first thought that struck me when I discovered a little-known conspiracy theory involving a switch of identities between *Titanic* and *Olympic*.

I was struck by the sheer number of purported facts that seemed to support the theory:

- The Board of Trade's concern over the quality of steel being used in the leviathans' construction at Harland and Wolff.
- *Olympic*'s ill-fated accident with HMS *Hawke* in September 1911.
- White Star's disastrous court case against the Royal Navy in December 1911.
- Whispers of a serious fire in one of the ship's coal bunkers.
- How few were the number of items that needed to be changed in order to effect a switch of identities.

- The fateful words of *Titanic*'s Chief Officer in his letter home – '*I still don't like this ship*'.
- J.P. Morgan's cancellation of his passage and removal of statues at short notice.
- SS *Californian* had heaved to a few miles from the scene of disaster with a cargo of three thousand woollen blankets and jumpers – more than enough to warm the 2,240 people aboard the doomed liner.
- The seemingly deficient insurance cover and the speed at which it was paid out.

Over the years a number of conjectures have been made as to who was involved in a possible conspiracy and how far up the establishment ladder the plot went. These claims, if ever proved true, could be the smoking gun for one of the greatest insurance frauds in history.

I decided to make these strands the basis for the plot of *Fathom*. I have borrowed the theory and wrapped it around a fictitious aristocratic family living on Exmoor in 1919. The romance of the age coupled with the mystique of the doomed liner felt like a good fit and in so doing I hope my novel reflects the deepest respect and sympathy I feel for all those who were connected to the disaster. I hope you enjoyed reading it as much as I enjoyed writing it.

If you enjoyed FATHOM, please consider leaving a review on Amazon. Reviews help authors more than you might think and it would be greatly appreciated.

Review on Amazon UK
Review on Amazon US

You can connect with Jacqui Black on:
www.jacquiblack.uk
Facebook @JacquiBlackAuthor

Sign up to Jacqui's email list and be among the first to receive information about new books in the series.

Admin@jacquiblack.uk

LIST OF CHARACTERS

Aggie .... Neighbour to Florence Seymour - Southampton

Agnew, Byron (Lord) .... Husband to Lady Grace Agnew

Agnew, Grace (Lady)................... Survivor - Titanic disaster

Bagshott, GeorgeOwner - Exmoor Hunting Lodge Hotel

Barnes, VeronicaJournalist - The Exminster Chronicle - Exeter

Bath, Countess .... Wedding Guest

Bath, Earl of .... Wedding Guest

Beamish, Bert.............. Landlord Blue Boar - Coombe End

Beamish, Laura .... Wife to Bert Beamish

Beauchamp. David .... Doctor - Coombe End

Beaumont, Viscount .... Wedding Guest

Bentley, Richard....................................... Valet to Lance

Bevans, Cyril................. Editor - The Exminster Chronicle

Bird, Winifred ..... Memorial Fund Benefactor - Coombe End

Bob ....Black Labrador Puppy newly acquired by Lance

Bolt, Ian.............. Detective Sergeant - Exeter Police Station

Broome, Elsie ....Lady Cynthia's personal maid - Landacre Hall

Brown, Rose .... Housemaid - Landacre Hall

Cooper, Ned .... Blacksmith - Coombe End

Cumberland, Duke of......... Member of the House of Lords

Dacres, George............ Bank Manager - Exminster National Bank - Exeter

de Bretagne, Bertie .... Old school chum of Lance

Digweed, Herbert .... Head Gardener - Landacre Hall

Disney, Miss .....Secretary - Exminster National Bank - Exeter

Donaldson-Gilks, Cedrick (Lord) .... 7th Baron Westex of Exmoor

Donaldson-Gilks, Cynthia (Lady) .... Wife to Lord Cedrick

Donaldson-Gilks, Hugo .... Younger brother to Lance

Donaldson-Gilks, Lance .... Eldest Son of Baron Westex

Donaldson-Gilks, Tabitha........................... Sister to Lance

Drake, Edward . Family Solicitor - Froggatt, Cubitt and Drake

Eustace, Simon ....Vicar - Coombe End

Evans, Reece............................. Footman - Landacre Hall

Fairfax, Helena.... Primary School Teacher - Coombe End

Featherstone-Haugh, Julian .....Master of the Exminster Deer Hounds

Fitzgerald, John................................. Vet - Coombe End

Fleming, Lord .... Member of the House of Lords

Greville-Bains, Algernon .. Insurance Underwriter - Lloyds of London

Hamilton, Bruce ...Second Husband to Ruth Hamilton-Whytte

Hamilton-Whytte, Ruth............Married to Bruce Hamilton

Harrison, Laurence............. Estate Manager - Landacre Hall

Hopwood, Peter .... Gamekeeper - Landacre Hall

Hubbard, Mr ... Chief Clerk - Exminster National Bank - Exeter

Hughes, Mrs ....Cook - Landacre Hall

Lock, Matthew . Photographer - The Southampton Messenger

Maltravers, Duncan (Lord) .... Married to Lady Maud

Maltravers, Maud (Lady) .... Older Sister to Lady Cynthia

Mayflower, Robert ....Manager - White Star Line Offices
- Southampton

McNair, William .... Master Carpenter - Harland and
Wolff - Belfast

Parks, Bill .... Stonemason - Stapleford Village

Pierce, Mrs .... Housekeeper - Landacre Hall

Pike, Mrs .... Organist - St Peter's Church - Coombe End

Price, David .... Photographer - The Exminster Chronicle

Procter, Amelia .... Post Mistress - Coombe End

Quick, Desmond . Detective Inspector - Exeter Police Station

Rolf-Sylvester, Lettice........... Younger sister to Lady Cynthia

Rolf-Sylvester, Randolph (Lord) ... Husband to Dame Lettice
- African Explorer

Schilling, Edmond ....Detective Chief Superintendent - Scotland
Yard

Seymour, Florence.......................... Sister of John Seymour

Seymour, John .... Third Officer - Titanic

Sharples, Betty.................. Ex Parlour maid - Landacre Hall

Smithers, Seb .... Head Groom - Landacre Hall

Snyder, Jacob .... Apothecary and Member of Parish
Council

Snyder, Sylvia .... Wife to Jacob Snyder

Somerset, Viscount .... Father to The Honourable Lucinda
Willoughby-Vane

Sorcerer............ Black Stallion - Lance's mount for the Hunt

Speed, Edwin .... Chauffeur - Landacre Hall

Sutton, Edna .... Chairwoman of WI - Coombe End

Swan, Jonathon (Lord) ...ex Director Harland and Wolff - Belfast

Toddington, Giles (Sir) .... Member of the General Medical
Council

Tommy… Apprentice Carpenter - Harland and Wolff - Belfast
Treadwell, Bernard ....Butler - Landacre Hall
Versailles .... White Mare - Veronica's mount for the Hunt
Watson, Lionel .... Vet - London
Whytte, Clara ....Daughter of Ruth Hamilton-Whytte
Whytte, Henry .... Late son of Ruth Hamilton-Whytte
Whytte, Martha ....American Aunt to Clara
Whytte, Monica........................American Cousin to Clara
Whytte, Nathan ....American Cousin to Clara
Whytte, Willard .... Late husband of Ruth Hamilton-Whytte
Whytte, Zachary........................ American Uncle to Clara
Willoughby-Vane, Lucinda (The Honourable) ....Daughter of
Viscount Somerset